CAROLINE'S DREAM

Caroline nodded toward Andrew's empty plate. "Would you like another piece of pie?"

"Nay." He patted his trim stomach. "I'm sure I could not hold another bite."

"More *kaffi*?"

"I'll get it." Andrew stood and retrieved the coffeepot from the stove. He poured them both a fresh cup, then returned to his seat across from her.

Being that close to him, having him carry Emma to bed, then partnering in the kitchen to slice the pie and pour coffee. The word *family* popped into her head, clear as day. This had to be what it was like to be married, to have a husband and helpmate.

Suddenly, she wanted that more than she had ever wanted anything in her life . . .

CAROLINE'S SECRET

AMY LILLARD

ZEBRA BOOKS
KENSINGTON PUBLISHING CORP.
http://www.kensingtonbooks.com

ZEBRA BOOKS are published by

Kensington Publishing Corp.
119 West 40th Street
New York, NY 10018

All Kensington titles, imprints, and distributed lines are available at special quantity discounts for bulk purchases for sales promotion, premiums, fund-raising, educational, or institutional use.

Special book excerpts or customized printings can also be created to fit specific needs. For details, write or phone the office of the Kensington Special Sales Manager: Attn.: Special Sales Department. Kensington Publishing Corp., 119 West 40th Street, New York, NY 10018. Phone: 1-800-221-2647.

Zebra and the Z logo Reg. U.S. Pat. & TM Off.

First Mass-Market Paperback Printing: August 2014
ISBN-13: 978-1-4201-3453-7
ISBN-10: 1-4201-3453-1

First Electronic Edition: August 2014
eISBN-13: 978-1-4201-3454-4
eISBN-10: 1-4201-3454-X

10 9 8 7 6

Printed in the United States of America

To my grandmother,
Bernice Wallis Davis,
for sharing so much with me over the years—
romance novels, Remington Steele, and butterbeans.
You always meant the world to me.
Wish you were here to see this.
Love you like a pig!

ACKNOWLEDGMENTS

Writers may write alone, but a book is never a solo venture. I have my characters to keep me company, but also a host of Facebook friends to get me through my "workday." Among these special friends are my groups: the Wells Landing Reader's Group and my fabulous Street Team who helps me spread the word about upcoming releases and other good news. Everyone in both groups is special to me. I'm so glad to have them on my side.

A special thanks goes out to all the people who help me make my books the best they can be. First to my editor John and the team at Kensington. Thanks for believing in Caroline and Andrew. To my agent, Mary Sue Seymour, and everyone at the Seymour Agency. And to my faithless friends who read everything I send to them regardless of everything they have on their own plates. You know who you are, but I'm naming names. Amy Clipston, Sarah Grimm, Laura Marie Altom, and Stacey Barbalace. You ladies rock!

And thanks to all the readers out there who read my books. You make it all worthwhile. I'd love to see each and every one of you in the Wells Landing Reader's Group. Thanks for letting me share my stories with you.

Blessings,
Amy

Dear Mamm,

Words cannot tell you how sorry I am for the shame I have brought upon our family. I never meant any harm, and yet I fell into the temptations that the elders have warned about time and time again. I listened to my foolish heart instead of the teachings of the church. A valuable lesson learned, but too late, for sure. You will never know how much I regret my decisions.

I am writing to let you know that I am safe. I had thought I'd make it all the way to Colorado and the new settlements there that I've been reading about, but I got sick after only half the journey. I guess the rocking of the bus and traveling so fast was more than my poor stomach could take. I got off in Oklahoma, fully intending to continue on when I felt stronger, but now that I am here, I think I might stay for a while. I have met a really nice woman. She's Plain like us, but different. She is Beachy Amish, but different than I expected. It's hard to explain, and I will try to do so in my next letter. But for now I must close. It's late and I have to get up early to help Esther in the bakery.

I hope that one day, Dat can forgive me for what I have done. In the meantime, please tell him that I am sorry and that I love him. I never meant to hurt either of you.

Love,
Caroline

Chapter One

"Who is that?"

Caroline Hostetler shifted Emma in her lap so she could peer around the sleeping toddler's head. A young man was unloading a headboard from a wagon trailer hitched to a bright green tractor. "That's Abe Fitch's tractor."

The strings of Emily Ebersol's prayer *kapp* danced with her nod. "*Jah*. It is."

"I bet that's Abe's nephew come down from Missouri." Lorie Kauffman moved to get a better look.

If there was one thing Caroline could say about Wells Landing, Oklahoma, it was that not much happened. Such was the way of small Amish communities, even Beachy ones. Life was slow, but it was a *gut* slow. Not much changed, like the stores and shops on Main Street and the three friends who ate their lunch in the park each afternoon.

Emily nudged Caroline in the ribs. "Did Esther say anything about buying new furniture?"

Caroline leaned to the left and squinted in the warm April sun, trying to get a better look.

"*Dat* said his name was Andy or . . . Andrew. *Jah*,

Andrew." Lorie waved a hand in front of Caroline's face. "Hello? Caroline?"

Caroline shook herself out of her stupor, only then aware that she had been staring at the young man unloading the rails for the bed. He was the most handsome man she had ever seen. Even from across the street she could tell. Broad shoulders, dark wavy hair, there was just something about him that made her want to sit and watch him all day long.

"Esther and I talked about buying a new bed, but we decided against it." Caroline shifted her sleeping fifteen-month-old again.

Abe's nephew had parked the tractor between the only two shops in the building directly across from the small city park where they sat. He could only be delivering the beautiful handmade piece to Esther's Bakery, where Caroline worked, or to the Kauffman Family Restaurant, where Lorie helped her father and stepmother feed tourists daily.

Emily flicked her hand toward the building across the street. "Where else would he be taking it?"

"The restaurant." For sure and for certain. She had told Esther that she did not need a new bed. They could not afford one, not with the new oven they had just bought for the bakery. There had barely been enough money for that.

"*Nay*, we did not order it. You did say Esther wanted you to have a new bed." As Lorie said the words, the handsome young man picked up the headboard and started for the bakery.

"Oh, *nay*. She did not." Caroline stood, carefully adjusting Emma so she wouldn't wake her, and started toward the bakery.

She had to wait as a car passed, followed by a horse-drawn buggy. The minister, Dan Troyer, gave a quick wave as he passed. Caroline, arms full of Emma, could only nod in return. Then she continued across Main Street.

"What are you doing?" She stopped just short of running into the young delivery man, fueled by disbelief and anger.

He propped the headboard against his legs and pushed his straw hat back on his head. *"Goedemiddag."*

His eyes were the purest blue she had ever seen, crystal clear and the color of the ocean in the pictures over at the travel agency.

"Goedemiddag." She backtracked. "What are you doing?"

"Delivering this bed." He picked up the headboard, then started around her.

She moved in front of him, effectively blocking his path. "Why?"

He set the headboard down again and scratched his head just under his hat. Two of the deepest dimples she had ever seen slashed down his cheeks as he smiled. "It's what I do."

Huh? What was the question?

He picked up the headboard once again, moved easily around her, and continued toward the bakery. She mentally chastised herself for allowing him to distract her as she followed behind.

"But why?"

He stopped, and she nearly crashed into him. Emma stirred as Caroline ground to a quick halt.

"It's my job."

She shook her head and lifted Emma a little higher. When had her baby gotten so heavy?

"No, it's not my job?"

She adjusted Emma again. Her arms were going to sleep under the limp weight of the toddler. "I don't want the bed."

"That's fine, then, because I'm not giving it to you."

"You are taking it to Esther."

"That is what my *onkle* told me to do."

"But Esther bought it for me. After I told her not to. So you can take it back where it came from." She could feel Emma sliding down once again. Why was he being so stubborn? Why wouldn't he take the bed back to his uncle's shop and stop arguing with her before she dropped Emma completely?

"Sorry." He didn't look sorry as he gently nudged past her and into the bakery. Caroline had no choice but to follow him inside.

Esther came around the high bakery counter just as Caroline pushed through the doors. "It's here." The woman who had been both savior and mentor to her in the past two years smiled with pleasure.

"Esther Lapp." She and the handsome nephew of Abe Fitch said her name at the same time.

"Jah?" She looked at each of them in turn.

"I'm here with the bed you ordered," the nephew said.

Caroline admonished, "You weren't supposed to do this."

The ever-cheerful, sweetly plump widow turned her attention to the dark-haired delivery man. It was better by far for Caroline to think of him in those terms rather than as the most attractive man she had seen in a long time. Or ever. Those were the thoughts of a carefree teenager, and she was neither a teenager nor carefree any longer.

"Gut, gut." Esther smiled as she took the invoice from him and penned her name at the bottom. "Will you take it around back to our apartment and set it up?"

"Jah," he said with another of those heart-stopping smiles. "I left it unlocked for you."

"Nay. Nay. Nay." Caroline stepped forward. She had to do something. She could not accept the bed. Just as she could not allow him to come into her rooms.

"Is she always this . . . negative?"

Caroline rubbed Emma's back as the child stirred. "I am not negative. I told Esther last week that she could not order me a bed, and she did anyway. So you can just take it back to your *onkle*. I apologize for any inconvenience."

"I told you last week that you work too hard by far for me to not offer you a bonus. If you won't take money, then I will gift you with a bed," Esther said.

"I told you it was not necessary," Caroline countered.

"I told you it was."

"But—" Caroline turned as the nephew started out the door.

"When you ladies are finished, I'll be around setting up the bed."

As quick as that, she lost the argument.

Emma stirred in her arms, waking now that all the excitement was over.

Esther reached for the child, and she went straightway into her arms. Caroline rubbed her hands together, trying to get the feeling back into them.

"You've done so much for me and Emma, I—"

"Shush," Esther said, planting a kiss on the top of Emma's dark curls. "I wanted to, and I did."

Caroline shook her head and gave the woman a one-armed hug. How could she explain that she appreciated all of the things that Esther did, but the more she did, the less capable it made Caroline feel?

"You are like a daughter to me," Esther said, leaning into the hug even though she had her arms full of toddler. Emma rubbed her fists into her sleepy eyes and gave a yawn.

Caroline was overcome with love. Only two short years ago when she had come here to Wells Landing she had thought her life to be over, but now . . . now she had more than she had ever dreamed.

She blinked back her tears of gratitude and happiness. "*Danki*, Esther."

"*Gern gschehne.*" Esther handed Emma back, then moved behind the counter as a customer came into the bakery. "You'd better make sure that handsome young man puts your bed where you want it. Then come on back. We have a cake to bake for tomorrow."

"*Jah*," Caroline said, then rushed out the door to see to the delivery.

Andrew Fitch unloaded the last of the rails and the footboard for the bed he'd been asked to deliver and carried them around the back of the building to the living quarters Esther Lapp had indicated. At least now he was able to do his job without that blond-haired *narrisch* woman with the sleeping *boppli* in her arms.

Okay, so she wasn't really crazy, more like . . . determined. Either way, he'd never forget the flash of defiance in her hazel eyes as she stood in front of him blocking the way.

For a minute, though, he thought perhaps his uncle had let his preoccupation get the better of him. Thankfully Esther had confirmed, and Andrew had breathed a sigh of relief.

He propped the pieces against the wall and smiled to himself.

"What is it that you find so pleasing?"

He jerked his head up, meeting that unforgettable hazel gaze. "*Nix,*" he replied with a hidden smile.

She gave a curt nod, and Andrew wondered if she was always this . . . guarded. He wasn't sure where the word came from, but there it was. Guarded. She watched him as if he were about to commit some heinous crime. Or discover all her secrets.

"I came to deliver the bed, to set it for use. That is all."

She watched him, the dark-haired baby on her hip. "I'm sorry. I wasn't expecting you." She deposited the baby in the playpen and started picking up the toys scattered all over the floor. The apartment wasn't messy, just lived in.

The baby started fussin' at being put down, pulling herself up and dancing around, seeking the woman's attention. She handed the child a blanket as a peace offering.

He'd like to ask if the child was indeed hers or if she was merely watching her for the mother. But it was too familiar a question to ask of this guarded angel. They were just so different was all. She had golden blond hair and hazel eyes, whereas the baby had dark hair and the most unusual gray-colored eyes, the likes of which he had never seen.

"My bedroom is the one on the left." As the woman said the words, a pink flush on her cheeks hinted to the intimacy of the statement.

"Esther asked that the old bed be taken away and the new one put in its place, *jah*?"

More pink. "That is fine."

"I think we started off wrong." Andrew straightened and tipped his hat to the woman. "Pleased to meet you. I'm Andrew Fitch. I just moved here from Missouri to help my *onkle* with his furniture business."

A hesitant smile flickered across her lips. "*Gut* to meet you, Andrew. I'm Caroline Hostetler. And this is Emma."

He allowed himself one last look, one last smile, then he went back to work.

Caroline lingered on the fringes, always watching but never in his way. He wasn't sure how he felt about her hovering. Was she interested or spying? Curious or distrustful? He'd probably never know.

What did it matter anyway? He shook away the thought and focused on the job at hand.

In no time at all he had the new bed set up and the old one loaded into the wagon.

"Hope to see you around, Caroline and Emma." He nodded toward the pair, and with no more reason to stay, he let himself out.

Andrew stepped into his uncle's furniture store, breathing in the earthy scent of wood mixed with furniture wax. It was a far cry from the smells of farming, but Andrew kept telling himself that he would get used to it.

He sighed. There was a lot in his world that he was trying to get used to, come to terms with, and all those other sayings that were clever disguises for "learn to keep living."

"Andrew? Is that you?"

"Jah, Onkle."

Abe Fitch shuffled out of the back, wiping his stained hands on an equally soiled rag. Years of turning wood had left him stooped-shouldered. Though he had never married, Abe still wore the traditional beard of Amish men after they wed, a sure sign that he had passed his fortieth birthday. The hair on his chin was dark, streaked with gray, and almost as curly as the fuzzy hair on his head. "Did you get the bed all set up for Esther Lapp?"

"Jah," Andrew said.

"Gut, gut."

He ran his thumbs underneath the galluses attached to his barn-door pants and rocked back on his heels. "It was really for Caroline Hostetler."

Abe pushed his wire-rimmed glasses farther up on the bridge of his nose and squinted back at him. *"Jah.* Caroline. It seems Esther did mention something about that."

"What do you know about her?"

"Well, now, I've known Esther all my life. She married John Lapp, right after she joined the church. Let me see, that would have been about—"

"I was asking about Caroline."

"Oh. *Oh*. She just showed up one day. Nigh on two years now. Widowed, pregnant."

"She's a widow?" He shouldn't be so pleased that she wasn't married.

Why did he even care? It wasn't like he was ready to start courtin' again. Or if he'd ever be. Maybe it was the simple fact that they had something in common: They both had lost someone dear to them. She had lost her husband, and he had lost—

"She's a *gut* girl, that Caroline. She'd make a fine *fraa*."

"Nay." Andrew shook his head, nearly flinging his hat to the floor. "That is not why I am asking. I just, uh . . . Well, I'm just trying to get to know the people in the district . . . if I am going to live here and . . . uh, live here."

His words in no way reflected the truth, but Abe was too involved in his own world to seem to notice. Thankfully he didn't see the red flush creeping up Andrew's neck. But that was his uncle, a little brilliant, a little absentminded, and one of the best furniture makers in Oklahoma.

Abe shrugged. "You unload the old bed?"

"Jah, I did."

"Gut, gut. After I finish this table, we'll head on back. Esther invited us to supper tonight."

"You what?"

"I invited Abe and his young nephew to supper tonight." Caroline resisted the urge to prop her hands on her hips.

A defiant pose would only look suspicious. "Now why would you go and do a thing like that?"

"Seeing the two of you together this afternoon made me realize how much you work and how you are never around people your age."

"I'm around people my age all the time. Emily is twenty-one, as is Lorie. I'm just two years older."

Esther shrugged. "I thought it would be fun to have company."

"Fun? For who?" She stopped and eyed the woman who had taken her in when she had no one. "It is you, *jah*? Maybe you are the one who needs company?"

Esther had the good grace to blush. She turned back to the bubbling pot on the stove. "Don't be *gegisch*."

"*Nay*, of course not." Caroline smiled to herself as she used a wet rag to wipe the peas from between Emma's fingers. "I'm not being silly a'tall."

So Esther liked Abe. What an unlikely pair: the plump baker and the absentminded furniture maker. Still, it would be a *gut* match. Abe needed someone to take care of him, and Esther liked to nurture. Otherwise she would have never taken Caroline in on that rainy September night.

"You should change your apron," Esther said, pointing at the smear of flour across Caroline's middle. Two years and she still hadn't mastered the art of baking without wearing as much flour as she needed for each recipe. "You wouldn't want to give the wrong impression to young Andrew."

Caroline pulled Emma from the high chair and planted a kiss on her newly cleaned cheek. "I will change my apron, but not for the reasons you are thinking."

"What would that be, *liebschdi*?"

"I will change my apron because the one I have on is soiled and not because we have company."

Esther poured some water into the pot and stirred it once again. "It is no matter why you do it, but that it is done."

Caroline left the room smiling just the same.

"Andrew, would you like another biscuit? Caroline, give Andrew another biscuit. It's her own recipe," Esther added. "One of the best things I got when she came to live here."

"Oh, *jah*?" Andrew shot her a quick smile filled with those incredible dimples. For once Caroline was glad that Esther was so chatty.

Nay, that wasn't right. She didn't care what Andrew thought about her biscuits. Nor did she care about his smile. Tonight was for Esther, even if the woman kept insisting that Andrew praise Caroline for every little thing, from how the butter set in its dish to the texture of her blackberry jelly.

"Esther exaggerates the truth. I would have nothing if not for her, including a fine new bed."

At the mention of furniture, Abe lifted his head. "What was that?"

"That was a fine bed you made for Caroline." Esther leaned in a little closer to Abe as she spoke. The talented furniture maker seemed not to notice, but Caroline did. As did Andrew.

She looked at him and smiled. The moment hung, suspended between them.

Caroline dropped her gaze first, glancing over to check on Emma even though she had looked at the child only moments before.

Out of the corner of her eye, she saw Andrew flash another quick smile of his own and stare down at his plate.

"How about some dessert?" Caroline pushed back from the table, standing and running her hands down the front of her black *fer gut* apron.

"That'd be *gut*." Abe rubbed his hands together in anticipation.

"Andrew, why don't you help Caroline get the pie, hmmm?"

"*Jah*, of course."

There was the scrape of the chair as Andrew stood and followed her from the dining area around the side and into the kitchen. She heard his sure footsteps and somehow knew when he stopped directly behind her.

"I'm not sure which is worse, Esther's attempt at matchmaking or her crush on *Onkle*."

Caroline spun around as he chuckled. "I'm glad you find this funny, Andrew Fitch."

He shrugged. "I see no reason not to find pleasure in a sweet woman who cares about others."

"There are many who might disagree." She started slicing the thick wedges of pie.

"I suppose. Is there *kaffi*?"

Caroline indicated the pot on the stove. "Right there."

"And the cups?"

"You don't really have to help."

"Oh, I'm not helping you."

"No?"

He shook his dark head, and Caroline tried not to notice how the soft-looking strands brushed against the collar of his blue shirt. "I figure with as preoccupied as my *onkle* is from day to day, Esther needs all the help she can get."

Caroline couldn't stop the smile from her lips or the small laugh that escaped them. "Third cabinet on the right."

She continued to dish up the pie as Andrew got down cups and filled them with the warm, rich coffee. Together they loaded up the tray. Caroline had to push away the thoughts of how good it felt to have him beside her, doing and helping. It was something she had never had before.

Something she would never have in the future. *Don't get used to it*. But for the time being, she could enjoy it.

"I'll carry that." Andrew hoisted the tray and waited for Caroline to lead the way.

Everything looked pretty much the same when they reentered the dining room. Esther was gazing at Abe, who was examining the wood grain in her table.

Andrew shot Caroline a look that clearly said, "I told you."

She smiled at their private joke and got down to the business of serving pie.

Abe and Andrew lingered over their dessert, having a second cup of coffee and telling stories until the sun went down.

Emma lost interest in staying awake and crawled into Caroline's lap. She fell asleep with one of the strings of Caroline's prayer *kapp* wrapped around her finger.

Caroline looked down into the sweet face of her child and planted a kiss on one pink cheek. "I think it's time to put the little one down for the night." She stood and carried Emma to the bedroom and the new bed Esther had bought for her that very day.

It was an extravagant gift, too expensive for her to accept, yet what choice did she have? Esther was one of the most stubborn women she knew. She was a survivor, opening her own business after her husband died and making something for herself in the small Oklahoma town. When Esther put her mind to something, it was set, and there was no going back.

Caroline tucked Emma into the big bed they would now share and went back to the living room to where the others had gathered.

"Andrew, can I have a word, please?"

He stood and took his hat from the peg board on the wall.

Caroline ignored the satisfied smile on Esther's face as Andrew opened the door for her and followed her outside.

It was a beautiful Oklahoma *nacht*. The stars sparkled despite the lights of the small town. Not much was open this time of day, and Caroline was glad. The darkness would allow her a little camouflage for what she needed to say. She took a deep breath and dove right in.

"I don't want you to get the wrong idea, Andrew."

He took her elbow as they walked across the street and into the park. "I am pretty sure there is no chance of that."

She folded her arms over her middle. "I thought you were going to let me have my say, Andrew Fitch."

He gave a nod. "*Jah*, then. Go on."

They made it as far as the swing set. Caroline eased down into one of the seats, using her feet to gently push her into motion. The street lamp next to them cast both light and shadow.

"Esther has been like a mother to me," she started. "Ever since I came to Wells Landing. Like any *gut mudder*, she would like to see her children—me—married and happy."

"You don't want to be happy?"

"I don't want to be married."

The laughter dimmed but didn't leave his eyes. "I'm not looking for a *fraa*." What was he hiding behind that dazzling smile?

"*Gut*." She nodded in return. "As long as we are agreed."

"We are, but that doesn't mean we cannot be *freinden, jah*?"

"You want to be my friend?"

"*Jah*, sure. Why wouldn't I?"

"I was not exactly kind to you this afternoon."

He shook his head. "*Nay*, not kind. And very *foahvitzich*."

Her mouth fell open. "I was most certainly not bossy."

"I have six sisters." He gave a sage nod. "I know *foahvitzich* when I hear it."

"You have six sisters?"

"You are changing the topic, Caroline Hostetler."

"*Nay*. Maybe. *Jah*." She rocked back and forth for a minute more, listening to the birds and the soft sounds of the night.

"So, *freinden*?" Andrew asked.

Caroline's smile crept back to her lips. "*Jah*," she said finally. "Friends would be *gut*."

Dear Mamm and Dat,

I hope this letter finds you well. I can't believe it's been almost two years since I came to Oklahoma. Sometimes it seems like yesterday and others like forever. Emma is growing so big. It seems like she sprouts up overnight. I have included a picture of her for you. I know that it is against the Ordnung, but I can't stand the thought of her growing so much while you have never seen her. I pray about it every night. It's not gut to be proud, but it is so hard not to look at Emma and not feel the twinges of delight at having made a child so perfect and beautiful.

I wish you could meet Esther as well. She has been so good to me. And I know she would like to meet you. Maybe one day . . .

Please, write when you can. I love getting your letters. I read them to Emma so that she might know you as she grows. I love you both and miss you terribly.

Love,
Caroline

Chapter Two

"And we could all get together for supper one night," Danny Fitch added.

Andrew picked up one end of the table as his cousin did the same.

"You know," Danny continued. "So you can meet her and get to know her better."

"Jah," Andrew said, absently.

Two days had passed since Andrew had made the delivery to the back room at Esther's bakery. Two days of working, eating, breathing, the continual learning to live again that had consumed him since Beth died.

And *she* had managed to take over his thoughts, Caroline Hostetler. Just when he least expected it, her face would pop into his head. But he wasn't ready to admit that to anyone, not even himself.

It was just a fluke. One of those strange coincidences. And no wonder. Caroline was the only person who didn't stare at him with pity in her eyes. Probably because there was no room there because of her own pain.

"What do you know about her?"

"I've known Sarah half my life. She's nice to look at, I suppose, and she bakes a tasty apple pie."

Andrew shook his head. "Not Sarah, Caroline."

"Hostetler?" Danny wobbled his shoulders in a pseudo shrug as they backed the table from the workroom to the showroom. "Not a lot. Why?"

Andrew shook his head. "No reason."

"So what do you say? Are you up for supper tomorrow night?"

"What?"

Danny dropped his end of the oak, forcing Andrew to do the same. "You've not heard a word I've said, have you?"

"Of course I have." Andrew waited for Danny to lift the table once again. "Who do you want me to have dinner with?"

"Sarah Yoder, Julie's cousin."

A setup. Maybe that was why he had blocked out the particulars. Andrew shook his head. "I don't know, Dan. I don't think I'm ready to court again."

"Who said anything about courtin'? I'm talking dinner."

Andrew turned to the side, pushing the table toward the large showroom window with his legs. "You and I both know how girls view dinners like the one you're talking about."

Danny shook his head and critically eyed the table's position. "Do you think it should go up a little more?"

"We still have to put the chairs around it."

"What chairs?"

"The chairs in the—" Andrew walked back to the storeroom. No chairs. "*Onkle* Abe strikes again."

Danny laughed. "Left them at home, did he?"

What could Andrew do but join in?

"What's so funny?"

Andrew whirled around to find Caroline Hostetler standing just inside the shop, a pink bakery box in her hands.

Danny wiped the tears of mirth from his eyes and squelched his chuckles. "Our *onkle*."

Caroline's entire face lit up when she smiled, a feat Andrew found amazing and charming all at the same time. "What did Abe do now?"

"He forgot to bring the chairs that go with the table."

"It's beautiful."

"It'd be even better with chairs." Andrew sighed. "I guess we'll have to go back to the farm and get them."

"Speak for yourself." Danny shook his head. "I've got to leave early, remember?"

Doctor's appointments, dentist's appointments, it seemed like Danny was constantly taking his younger siblings to one thing or another.

"Oh, *jah*. It looks like it's just me then."

"Before you leave," Caroline said, holding the opened bakery box toward his cousin, "Esther asked me to bring you some cookies to taste. It's a new recipe and she wanted someone to try them."

"New recipe, huh?" Danny was the first with his hand in the box pulling out two of the fresh-baked goodies.

Andrew followed suit and grabbed a couple of his own. "They're delicious," he said around a mouthful of oats and chocolate chips.

"They're called cowboy cookies. It's an *Englisch* recipe."

"Those cowboys sure know their cookies." Danny reached for another one and stuffed it into his mouth like a *kinner*. "Off to the eye doctor." He plopped his hat onto his head and started for the door, backtracking one last time to snatch up another cookie. Then with a grin and a wave, Danny sauntered out of the shop.

"I don't know . . . do you think he liked them?"

Andrew turned toward Caroline, only the twinkling in her hazel eyes giving away her jest.

He shrugged, playing along. "Hard to say for sure."

"At least there are a couple left for your uncle."

"I wouldn't count on it." Andrew snatched another cookie and smiled at Caroline.

She laughed. "I guess I need to make more."

"Consider it a compliment."

"I will." She set the box and the few remaining cookies on the desk and wiped her hands down her apron. For some reason she seemed almost nervous. "I suppose I should go so you can get on your way."

"What? Oh, yeah. Say, Caroline, do you want to run out to the farm with me?"

She hesitated for only a fraction of a second. "*Jah*, that would be *gut*. Let me make sure it's okay with Esther."

They walked to the bakery together, the silence easy between them.

Caroline opened the door and stuck her head inside. "Esther," she called to the woman behind the counter. "Is it *allrecht* if I go with Andrew to pick up some chairs?"

Esther glanced at the wall clock, then to the large oven timer. "It should be fine."

"Emma will be up in about an hour. I should be back long before that." She looked at Andrew for confirmation.

He nodded.

Esther smiled. "Go on. Have fun." The timer dinged, and she grabbed a pot holder to pull the tray of goodies from the oven.

"Those aren't cowboy cookies, are they?"

Esther laughed. "You'll have to get Caroline to make you more of those. That's her secret recipe."

Andrew returned the chuckle and cut his gaze toward Caroline.

She blushed and pushed him out the door, no doubt eager to be away from Esther and her meddling matchmaking.

* * *

"I don't think I've ever traveled by tractor before." Caroline lifted her face to the wind, enjoying the sensation of the breeze on her skin. The strings of her prayer *kapp* floated behind her, and she felt as if she were flying.

"Ever?" Andrew asked, only briefly taking his gaze from the road to study her.

Caroline shook her head and smiled. "Never ever."

"They didn't have tractors in your district?"

"Nay," she said, a little uncomfortable that the subject had come up. Normally she shied away from talking about her past. It was just easier that way.

Andrew shook his head. "No tractors . . . must have been very conservative."

"Jah." What else could she say? "Conservative" was not quite the best word to describe the Swartzentruber district where she had grown up. But if she told Andrew that, more questions would come. Questions that she wasn't prepared to answer. Not yet, anyway.

Andrew nudged her with his elbow and pointed toward the pasture on their left. "See that?"

A beautiful black mare nuzzled the neck of a shiny colt of the same color.

The breath caught in Caroline's throat. What a wondrous sight, that magnificent horse and her offspring.

The tractor spat and jerked as Andrew downshifted and slowed the vehicle. He turned the big green machine into the long dirt drive to the other side of the pasture.

"She's yours? The horse?"

He shook his head as he completed the turn and chugged the tractor up the winding drive. *"Nay. Onkle* leases the land to several owners and breeders."

"Really? So you have horses here all the time?"

"Jah."

Caroline sighed. She loved horses. Other than her family, she missed them the most. She and Esther had no need for a horse and buggy living in town like they did. They simply rode their bikes wherever they needed to go. If their destination was farther than that, they hired a driver or rode with friends. Caroline missed the rocking of the buggy and the slow clop of horse hooves.

It was her one regret; that Emma would never have that experience. She stopped that negative thought before it could grow any bigger. No one knew what the future held for any of them. Only God. And though her faith had been sorely tested in the months since Emma's birth, she'd do well to remember that.

"You are welcome to come out anytime and visit the horses."

Was her face that easy to read? "I'd like that, but I don't have a way here."

"Just say the word, and I'll bring you here. Emma too. I love the horses. It's one of the things I miss the most about farming." He pulled the tractor to a stop in front of a long building with a green tin roof and turned off the engine.

He hopped down from the driver's seat and reached up to help Caroline do the same.

She ignored the little zing she felt when Andrew placed his hands on her waist and swung her to the ground. Evidently she was the only one who felt it, for he released her without a word and reached into his pocket for the shop keys.

She just wasn't used to such touches was all. Her community back in Tennessee was one of the most conservative among the Amish. She hadn't had many suitors, and her relationship with Emma's father was shatteringly brief. She couldn't be expected to be accustomed to such familiarity.

She couldn't allow that weird tingle to stand in the way of their friendship. She and Andrew had agreed to be friends and friends only. She'd do well to remember that.

"I won't be but a few minutes." Andrew pointed toward the fenced-in pasture behind the building. "The horses tend to come up to the gate when we pull in. You can go see them while I load the chairs."

"I'd love that."

True to his word, a beautiful dapple gray with a thick black mane and a chestnut with a white blaze down his nose stood, waiting patiently for a human to come around the side of the building. As soon as they spotted her, they shifted their weight and gave a small nicker and a flick of their tails.

"Look at the *schpass* horses," Caroline crooned. She approached quietly as to not startle them, though they looked to be gentle and eager for attention.

She ran a hand down the dapple's silky nose, then laughed as the horse nudged her neck as if looking for a treat. If she had known, she would have brought a lump of sugar or a carrot for these wonderful creatures.

She lavished attention on the other horse, then sighed as they backed away from the gate, no doubt because there were no treats to be found. Caroline gazed out over the lush green field dotted in yellow and pink of the occasional wildflower.

How peaceful it was here, a lot like home but not the same either. The serenity was similar, the hushed air and tangible presence of God, but the general condition of the farm was different. Whereas her home community didn't believe in adding so much to the land except for a garden to support the family dinner table, the people of Wells Landing planted extra flowers around their outbuildings and across the front of their houses. It was beautiful and unnecessary and brought tears to her eyes. What was wrong with beauty for the sake of beauty anyway? Did the denial bring a person closer to God? She didn't think so.

She bowed her head and said a quick prayer of forgiveness. She shouldn't be having those negative thoughts. In fact, it was thoughts like those that had her running from home in the first place. Everyone was allowed religious freedom in this great country. That was the main reason her people had come here so long ago. And they were still able to follow God as they saw fit, a right that should not be taken lightly.

"All done."

Caroline lifted her head as Andrew came around the building.

"Are you *allrecht*?"

"*Jah*. It's just so beautiful here."

A knowing light gleamed in Andrew's blue eyes. "That it is."

Caroline gazed longingly across the lush fields. Seeing the open fields, the green grass bumping against the blue sky, made her homesick unlike anything she had felt since leaving Tennessee. But she was here now, part of this community. She had left Ethridge and everything it stood for behind her. And that was just the way it was.

"I've been thinking," Andrew said over the hum of the tractor engine.

"*Jah?*"

"About Esther and Abe."

They were halfway back to town before Caroline had

completely swallowed the lump in her throat. Coming out to the farm with Andrew had brought back more memories than she cared to admit. She hadn't gotten a letter back from her *mamm* after the last one she sent with the picture of Emma tucked inside. After all the pieces of the *Ordnung* that she had gone against, photographs seemed trivial at best. But it seemed her mother had different ideas. Perhaps Caroline should write her again and apologize . . .

"What about Esther and Abe?" she asked, pushing thoughts of her Tennessee home to the back of her mind.

"Well, it seems to me that if they are ever going to get to be a couple, they are going to need some encouragement."

"You mean like matchmaking?"

"Isn't that what Esther is trying to do with us?"

Caroline shrugged. "I guess."

"But she's really interested in *Onkle*, right?"

"Right."

Andrew pulled the tractor onto Main Street and chugged toward the bakery. "He's a bit . . . distracted, so the only way she's going to gain his attention is with outside help."

He had a point. Esther had married her husband young and had been widowed early in their marriage. She never remarried and, as far as Caroline knew, had never even courted again. Going after a man was not in her traditional Amish makeup even if she knew what to do to garner Abe's attention. Caroline wanted nothing more than Esther's happiness. And Abe . . . well, Abe was about as distracted as they came.

Andrew pulled into the parking lot in front of the bakery and left the engine running as he swung down from the cab.

"What do you suppose we can do about it?"

Andrew smiled as he clasped Caroline around the waist and hoisted her to the ground. This time she had to ignore the charm of his crooked grin as well as the little tingles his touch produced. "Esther seems intent on pushing us together, right?"

"*Jah.*"

"So we just include them in whatever activities that Esther concocts for us."

"You really want to do this?"

Andrew nodded, the wind stirring the strands of his dark, dark hair where it stuck out from under his plain straw hat. "My *onkle* could use a little more happiness in his life. What about Esther?"

Esther had done so much for her in the nearly two years Caroline had been in Wells Landing. What way was more perfect to pay her back than by helping her grab the attention of her new true love?

"*Jah* . . . okay, then. I'll help you." After all, it was the least she could do.

Dear Mamm and Dat,

I'm sorry if you are upset about the photograph of Emma. I know it is a sin to be proud, but I can't help, but feel something even greater than love whenever I look at her. This tiny creature that God helped me bring into the world.

There is so much that can be said about God's will. Was it God's will that I had Emma or the devil's handiwork? I can't help but look into her sweet face and see the hand of our Lord and maker.

And it is surely God's will that I got off the bus here in Wells Landing. I have made so many gut friends since I have been here. Not only Esther, but Lorie and Emily as well. You remember them, I hope. They are such gut freinden. I met another friend this week. His name is Andrew and his onkle makes furniture. Beautiful pieces that grossdaadi would love. Anyway, Andrew and I went out to his uncle's farm where he stables horses for others. Oh, the smell of the earth and the green grass! It reminded me so much of home that it brought tears to my eyes. As much as I have enjoyed getting to know these new people here in Oklahoma, I still miss all that is familiar to me in Ethridge.

I love you both and think of you often. I just wanted you to know.

Love,
Caroline

Chapter Three

The bell over the bakery door rang, signifying that another customer had come into the shop.

Caroline wiped her hands on a towel and pushed the little tendrils of escaped hair off her forehead with the back of her wrist. And turned around to greet . . .

"Andrew."

"Hi, Caroline."

Caroline gazed down at herself in dismay. The front of her apron was covered with flour.

"Did you have a problem?"

She brushed herself off and tried to smile. *"Nay."*

"So you are always this messy?"

"Andrew, what a thing to say."

He smiled sheepishly. "Sorry, I just . . ." He trailed off with a shrug.

"Is that what you came here for? To critique my baking process?"

"Actually, no." He leaned in a little closer to her and whispered, "Can we go for a walk? I have something I want to talk to you about."

Just then Esther came out of the back room carrying a

stack of newly washed baking pans. Caroline could well imagine what it looked like to the other woman, Andrew bent low to whisper in her ear. Close, intimate.

"Esther, is it okay if I take a quick break?"

The older woman set the pans on the counter, then looked from Caroline to Andrew and back again. Her eyes lit with prospects. "Of course, *liebschdi*. Take all the time you need."

Caroline resisted the urge to roll her eyes. They had several loaves of bread on order today as well as a birthday cake for the Baptist pastor's upcoming celebration. She didn't have time to loiter with Andrew, but it seemed that Esther felt some things were more important.

If Andrew noticed, he didn't say anything, just waited patiently with a small smile on his face as Caroline removed her apron and did the best she could to smooth down her hair without the aid of a mirror. Why she even attempted was a matter for discussion. Once she walked out into the Oklahoma wind, she'd be lucky if the pins held her prayer *kapp* in place, much less the wayward strands of her unruly hair.

Andrew held the door open for her and out they walked into the warm summer sunshine.

"So, what did you need to talk about?" Caroline asked as they started down Main Street.

"I have an idea."

"Oh?"

"About how to get Esther and *Onkle* together."

"I'm listening."

"After church on Sunday, I'll invite you and Esther out to the house. You know she'll come so that she can get the two of us together. After we eat, you and I can head down and look at the horses, and that'll give them plenty of time together . . . alone. Surely Esther can get him to pay attention to her if we leave them alone."

"Don't be so sure." Caroline laughed, and Andrew joined in. "We can always hope."

"What about Emma?"

A small frown creased his brow. "Of course she's invited too."

Caroline shook her head with a smile. "I would hope so. I meant, what will we do with her when we go to see the horses?"

"Take her with us. I mean, if that's all right. She's not afraid of horses, is she?"

"Nay," she said, though she wasn't sure if Emma was afraid of the great beasts or not. The toddler had never been around horses for more than a minute or two, passing on the street or in the parking lot at the store. But oh, how Caroline wanted her to have some experience with the beautiful creatures. "That would be wonderful."

"Jah?"

"Jah." They reached the end of the shopping center and turned back toward the bakery.

Her friend Lorie stood just inside the Kauffman Family Restaurant and waved, a wondering look on her pretty face. Lunch in the park today would be full of questions, for sure and for certain.

Caroline waved back to Lorie and kept walking beside Andrew.

"So we're set, then?" Andrew asked as they neared the bakery's big glass door.

"All set." Caroline smiled.

"I'll see you Sunday, then." Andrew tipped his hat and headed across the street and back to the furniture store.

"So what's going on with you and Andrew Fitch?" Lorie had no more than set the Styrofoam container holding her lunch on the picnic table before the question flew out of her mouth.

Caroline opened her brown paper sack, setting Emma's finger foods in front of her before extracting her own sandwich. "Nothing. But you're not going to believe me."

"It didn't look like 'nothing' to me."

Emily popped the top on her soda and looked at each of them in turn. "What did I miss?"

"Caroline and Andrew Fitch walking down the street arm in arm this morning."

"We were not arm in arm," Caroline emphatically corrected.

"But you were walking down the street together?" Emily looked from Caroline to Lorie for confirmation.

Lorie nodded.

"It's not like that," Caroline protested.

Emily studied her with her knowing eyes. "Then what's it like?"

Caroline expelled an exasperated sigh. "Why does everyone want to get me married off?"

"Because you're the nicest person I know," Lorie started. "And I want to see you happy."

"Why does everyone think I'm unhappy?"

Emily shook her head. "It's not that we think you're unhappy, we just don't think you are happy."

"Is there a difference?"

"Jah," Lorie said. "Not unhappy is floating along and not really going anywhere."

"Existing," Emily added. "Just getting by."

"But happy . . ." Lorie's entire face lit up like the streetlights every evening. "Happy is floating on air, each step lighter than the next."

Caroline shook her head, a small smile on her lips.

"You've been reading those *Englisch* romance novels again, haven't you?"

"Is it wrong to want true love?" Lorie asked.

"No." Emily's answer was emphatic.

"I appreciate your concern," Caroline said. "But I'm fine with 'not unhappy.' I have Emma to think about."

"That's it." Emily snapped her fingers. "You do have Emma to think about. And she's the very reason you should get married again."

Caroline swung her gaze to her lap to keep the shame from shining in her eyes. Married again would be impossible, seeing as how she had never married the first time. Even as close as she had become with Lorie and Emily, she had never told them the truth about her relationship with Emma's father.

"Marriage is a fine thing." Emily patted the back of her prayer *kapp*.

"*Jah*, but why does it have to involve Andrew Fitch?" Caroline asked.

"I didn't bring up Andrew," Emily said slyly. "You did."

"You need someone like you," Lorie explained. "Just look at me and Jonah."

"I thought you were having doubts," Emily said.

"Well, only a few. But doubts don't equal unhappy."

Caroline breathed a sigh of relief that the conversation had shifted away from her. She was not in the market for another relationship. She had her hands full with Emma, Esther, and the bakery. But if she were to want to date again . . .

Well, Andrew would make some lucky woman a fine wife. Once he got over whatever caused the pain haunting his so-blue eyes.

Caroline had enough of her own heartache. It wouldn't do at all to take on someone else's.

* * *

An hour later, Caroline carried her sleeping angel into the back rooms at the bakery and turned on the monitor. She had fought long and hard with the elders concerning the use of the *Englisch* device. Well, Esther had. Caroline had asked, been denied, and started making other plans. But ever her champion, Esther had not relented until the bishop saw and agreed to Caroline's need for the monitor.

She clipped the speaker to the band of her apron and made her way back into the bakery kitchen.

In Tennessee, she would have never challenged her church leaders in such a manner, especially in her conservative district. But Esther was feisty, a fighter in her own right, having survived the tragic death of her husband and starting her own business instead of bowing to the traditions and getting married again.

Caroline wasn't used to such forward thinking. A widowed woman—any woman—wanting to start her own business would have been denied the right by her bishop and that would have been that. And baby monitors? Definitely not allowed. They didn't even have indoor plumbing!

"Emma asleep?" Esther asked as she washed her hands and prepared to start the preacher's cake.

"Like a baby," Caroline replied with a soft smile.

Esther returned it with a smile of her own. "They don't stay babies long."

"Nay." Already Emma was growing up, each day able to accomplish a little more than the day before.

She only wished her parents could see their only grandchild. And that Emma's father could see the miracle that they had created.

It had been a long time since Trey had filled her thoughts. Almost as long since she wished things could have been different. But if they had been different, then she would not have come here, met Esther, Lorie, and Emily, Andrew and Abe. How different her life would have been if things had not turned out the way they had.

"Esther, do you believe that my coming here was God's will?"

"Of course I do," Esther answered without hesitation. "What else could have brought you to Wells Landing?"

Caroline shrugged and started measuring flour into a large mixing bowl. She stretched up on her tiptoes to get the baking powder, and succeeded in once again smearing the front of her apron with flour.

From the front of the shop, the doorbell tinkled out its alert.

Esther wiped her hands on a dish towel and covered the loaf of bread she had been shaping with a clean, dry towel. "I'll get it."

Caroline pushed all thoughts of Trey from her mind and got down to the business of baking.

Dear Mamm and Dat,

Oklahoma is as beautiful as I remembered. Wells Landing hasn't grown very much in the last few years. Esther Lapp still owns the bakery on the corner at Main Street and Sycamore. Cephas Ebersol is still the bishop. It's strange to me how one man can be open-minded and conservative at the same time, but Cephas is well practiced at listening to his members and balancing their needs against what the Bible tells us is right.

You were right about Onkle Abe, he is absentminded for sure. I'm not sure why he never married, if only to have someone look after him. I miss being there with you. Jah, I miss the food most of all. But Kauffman's is still as gut as it always was. Though I am thankful that Lizzie made me learn how to cook. She was worried about me taking care of Beth. Funny how things change.

Danny is wanting me to date. I keep telling him it is too early for me. I may not ever be ready again. I know this isn't true, but right now I can't even imagine loving another the way I loved Beth. I know Danny means well. He just wants to see me happy and settled down. I think he and Julie will announce their intentions soon. I am happy for him, of course, and I wish him all of the best.

*Give my love to Becky and the rest of my
shveshtah. Believe it or not, I miss them all.
Miss you too.*

*All my love,
Andrew*

Chapter Four

"So what about it?"

Andrew hung his hat on the peg just inside the door and blinked a couple of times until his eyes adjusted to the artificial light in the furniture store. "What about what?" he asked Danny.

"Sarah." Danny's voice was ripe with impatience. "What about going to dinner with Sarah?"

"I don't know. I wouldn't want to give her the wrong idea."

"And what idea would that be?"

"That there's a chance of more."

"More than dinner?" Danny scoffed. "Girls aren't like that around here."

"Girls are like that everywhere," Andrew countered. "Aren't they, *Onkle*?"

"Eh?" Abe looked from one of them to the other, then shrugged and started staining the bench once again.

"I'm telling you, it's just a dinner with friends."

"And I'm telling you that I'm not ready."

Danny frowned at him. "What about Caroline?"

"What about her?"

"Would you go if it was with Caroline instead of Sarah?"

"Caroline is just my friend."

"I thought all girls were the same."

"Caroline is different," Andrew said, already tired of the argument. Maybe he should give in just so he didn't have to listen to Danny talk about it all day long. "If I agree to go to dinner with Sarah, will you let it rest?"

Danny grinned and slapped him on the shoulder. "Welcome back to the land of the living."

Andrew still wasn't sure how or why he let Danny talk him into this.

He pulled on his suspenders and combed his dark hair. And wondered what Sarah Yoder felt about being set up on a date.

A small pang of guilt rang through him. Wasn't this the very thing he and Caroline had vowed to do for Abe and Esther?

He shook the feeling away. That was different.

How many times had he said that over the course of the last couple of days?

"*Onkle*, I'm leaving now."

A rumbling grunt was his only response. Abe Fitch's nose was buried in a catalog of wood samples. How was a guy supposed to get his attention?

With a shake of his head, Andrew let himself out of the house and made his way over to the tractor. He'd have taken the horse and buggy if he hadn't waited until the last minute to get dressed and out the door. As it was now, he'd still be a little late even with the faster mode of transportation.

He swung himself into the cab and started the engine.

He remembered the way Caroline had thrown her hand back to keep her prayer *kapp* from flying off in the wind and the look of sheer joy on her face as they motored down the country roads.

Her district seemed even more conservative than his home in Missouri if she had never even ridden in a tractor. Then again, maybe it was just something that he was used to. He'd spent a couple of summers here a few years back, helping his uncles with their trade. His uncle Joe, Abe's brother and Danny's father, had a big farm just south of town. That was where he was headed tonight. Dinner with the Fitch clan. Well, at least with Danny. And Julie. And Sarah.

Andrew sighed as he steered the tractor up the drive leading to his *onkle* Joe's big, rambling house. He didn't know for certain how many times it had been added on to, but from the jutting legs of newly painted additions, he'd say four or five.

Joe Fitch lived there with his own father, Jacob, his three sons, two daughters and several *grosskinner*. It was a big, typical Amish household. Andrew just wished he wasn't dreading the evening so much.

He pulled the tractor to the side of the barn. He should have never agreed to this dinner.

"*Ach*, there you are." Danny rushed out of the house and over to where Andrew was climbing out of the tractor cab.

"Did you think I'd be somewhere else?" Like any of the thousands of places he'd rather be.

Suddenly Caroline's sweet face popped into his head. Dinner with her, that was something he could look forward to. That and their plans for getting Esther and Abe to be a couple.

What was it that made Caroline so different?

She doesn't want anything from you, the voice inside whispered.

And that meant that she didn't want anything that he wasn't able to give. Unlike others around him.

"Cousin." Danny all but snapped his fingers under Andrew's nose. "Are you listening to me?"

Andrew shook himself into focus. "*Jah*. Are you certain this is a *gut* idea?" Surely it wouldn't be all that bad. *Jah*, he was having supper with Sarah, but it wasn't so much like a date. There would be other people there: his *onkle* and his other cousins, his *aenti* and Danny's intended, Julie. As long as there was a big group of people, how could Sarah misinterpret his intentions?

"Of course it is." Danny steered him toward the back of the house. A large oak tree stood tall and proud, its mighty limbs shadowing a wooden picnic table.

Andrew's steps faltered, but luckily he caught himself before he fell headlong into the grass. "Is this where we're eating?"

It wasn't the smartest question. The table had been covered with a vinyl tablecloth and set for four. Julie sat on one side of the table while Sarah sat on the other.

"Nice, huh?"

"Danny." Andrew's voice was full of warning, but Danny either didn't hear or was ignoring him completely. Andrew figured it was a case of sheer disregard.

"Hi, Andrew." Julie half stood in greeting, but Sarah only dropped her gaze as if too shy to fully look at him.

"Hi, Julie. Sarah." He climbed stiffly over the bench seat and settled in. Best get this over with.

Danny remained standing. "How about a game of horseshoes before we get started?"

He barely got the words out of his mouth before Andrew shook his head.

"I'm really hungry," he lied and immediately felt bad. His cousin's matchmaking efforts had him going against his raisin'. He'd been taught never to lie, but how was he supposed to remain a gentleman and not break the girl's heart without telling a fib or two?

Andrew glared at his cousin as the girls went into the house to fetch their dinner.

"What?" Danny asked innocently.

Andrew just shook his head. It was too late now.

Sarah and Julie came back out with plates of meat loaf and bread stacked on top of plastic containers filled with potato salad, coleslaw, and fresh-cut vegetables from the garden.

Andrew had to admit that it was a fine meal, but every time he moved he seemed to bump into Sarah.

"Excuse me," he murmured for what had to be the hundredth time.

"Would you like some meat loaf?" Sarah passed him the platter.

"I'm full. *Danki*." Lie number two. But he took the platter from her and placed it in the center of the table.

He could eat another plate full for sure and for certain, but the longer he took to eat, the harder it would be to get out of there without hurting Sarah's feelings.

"Too full for dessert?" Julie asked the question, and it took everything Andrew had not to turn his stare on Danny. His cousin knew better than anyone that his sweet tooth was as big as a house.

"Sarah made strawberry pie." Julie stood and started gathering up their dinner plates.

What could he do but accept? He leaned back in his seat, thankful to have a little room as Sarah stood and started helping Julie. Andrew patted his stomach. "I think I can find room for one slice."

* * *

It was after dark when he returned back to the farm. He pulled the tractor into the barn and closed the big double doors behind him.

The night sky was full of stars, and he found his steps slowing as he neared the house.

Suddenly he wished that he lived closer to town, or that he could make a feasible excuse to "drop in" and see Caroline.

He shook his head at his own foolishness. Caroline most probably had to get up before the sun tomorrow, maybe even before most of the farmers in the area. If she wasn't asleep, she was most assuredly in for the night.

Tomorrow. He could always find an excuse to wander down to the bakery tomorrow and see how she was doing.

Probably the lamest thought he had ever had, but he just wanted to see her. Look into those hazel eyes of his new friend.

There was nothing wrong with that, *jah*? He and Caroline had made their pact. They knew what to expect from the other. But maybe he should tell her about Sarah just in case. Not that there was anything going on between the two of them—him and Sarah or Caroline and him. But it wouldn't hurt to be up front about Danny's matchmaking efforts. He surely wouldn't want Caroline to find out that he had been seeing Sarah and jump to the wrong conclusions.

It was settled. Tomorrow he would walk down to the bakery and explain his relationship with Sarah to Caroline.

A small smile on his face at the thought of seeing Caroline the following day, Andrew loped up the porch stairs and let himself into the house.

As soon as he finished staining this table, he was heading down to the bakery to see Caroline. Andrew had told himself that the trip would serve a dual purpose. He could tell her about Sarah and get a quick snack at the same time—but he was just kidding himself. He wanted to see her. She had become important to him in some strange way. Most probably because she was so easy to talk to. Yet he felt she had secrets to keep.

He took a step back and examined the table top. It was the beautiful amber and rose color of cedar, a fine contrast. He had only wanted to bring out the natural grain and had decided to clear-coat it for shine and protection. A body would think that clear would be easier to apply than color, but this particular piece was giving him fits. Or maybe it was the two women on his mind.

"I think Sarah really had a *gut* time last night."

Andrew sighed and tried not to shake his head at it all. "Danny, I don't think your dinner last night gave Sarah the right notions about me."

Danny only smiled and patted him on the back. "Cousin, it's time that you started dating again."

But Andrew shook his head. He might not be ready for a while. The Amish believed that everything happened within God's will. When it was time for him to date again, it would happen, and without Danny's interference.

But that was just Danny, a little wrapped up in his own world, unable to see beyond today. He had no idea how hard it was for Andrew to stand by Beth's parents as they laid her to rest. Knowing that she was ill and wouldn't live to be more than thirty years old did not ease the pain of her loss any. He would date again . . . only when he was ready.

Telling Danny that would be like talking to the table top he'd just polished.

There were a couple of bubbles that popped up on one edge. They would need to be sanded out and refilled. But that could wait until after he saw Caroline.

"I'm going to get a snack." Andrew wiped his hands on

a nearby rag, then tossed it onto the untidy workbench. He'd clean up the mess when he got back. Until then, he needed a break from Danny's scheming and his own swirling thoughts.

He had just settled his hat on his head when the bell over the door rang.

Danny went to check on their visitor, his voice making its way clearly into the back room where Andrew stood. "Why, Sarah. How nice to see you today."

Andrew exhaled. This day was not turning out at all like he had intended.

He unclenched his jaw and made his way to the front of the shop. Sarah was waiting there, looking uncomfortable. He had a feeling that she was unaccustomed to being this forward with a man. She seemed the shy type, which was most probably how she reached the age of twenty without a suitor or two.

"Sarah, *goedemiddag*," Andrew said, offering her a stiff smile.

"Hi," she said, her blush deepening. She was a pretty girl, pale brown hair and clear blue eyes. And he was certain she would make a man a fine Amish bride. Just not him.

"What brings you by today?"

"Oh." She started as if just remembering why she was there. "I brought you something to eat." She held up a brown paper sack. Then her expression fell. "You haven't eaten yet, have you?"

Andrew was fairly certain he'd used up all his white lies at last night's supper. *"Nay,"* he said as Danny smiled.

His cousin meant well, Andrew knew, but if Danny kept interfering, Sarah might just end up with a broken heart.

"Danki," he said, motioning toward the door of the shop. "Would you join me?"

Sarah turned the color of his mother's winter roses, a deep pink. "That would be *gut. Danki*."

"Take your time," Danny called as Andrew followed Sarah out into the warm Oklahoma sunshine.

The park was the natural place to go share the contents of the paper sack. It was a little early for lunch, too late for breakfast. With any luck there wouldn't be many more people milling around than necessary. He didn't know why he felt the need to keep this meeting a secret, but the fewer people who knew meant the fewer people to ask questions.

For all their talk about the sins of gossip, Amish people loved to go on and on about community happenings. Call them rumors or caring talk, the fact still remained: News of Andrew sitting with Sarah in the park would make the rounds between frolics, sister's days, and the idle chitchat at the market.

He found a picnic table and slid into one side. Unlike last night, he sat across from her.

"Sarah, I—"

She stopped pulling food out of the bag and instead turned her attention to him. *"Jah?"*

Some of his courage drained. Truth was, he didn't have a lot of experience with girls. He had never courted another, only Beth. They had known from the start that they were destined to be together; there were never any awkward moments lingering between them, just a gentle understanding.

"I don't want you to get the wrong impression about me."

She nodded, and he felt encouraged to continue. "I don't know what Danny has been telling you, but I'm not here to court anybody."

She crumpled up the empty bag and folded her hands in her lap. "You have a broken heart," she said simply.

He blinked, a bit stunned by her words. "Did Danny say something?"

She shook her head. "I can see it in your eyes." The wind stirred the strings on her prayer *kapp* as her lips formed a sweet smile.

In that instant he wished it could be different. He wished he could fall in love with the woman seated across from him. But she deserved a man who loved her first, foremost, and forever.

"She died," he whispered into the breeze. Every time he said the words, it got a little more real, yet every time he said her name he missed her all the more.

"I'm so sorry." From the corner of his eye he saw her shift in her seat, though he wasn't looking at her directly.

Across the park Caroline and her friends, Lorie Kauffman and Emily Ebersol, had settled down for their *middawk*. "Has it been very long ago?"

He quickly looked away as Lorie looked up, her blue gaze meeting his. "Six months," he whispered.

"Danny just cares about you. And of course he can spend more time with Julie if he can get me to come along."

Andrew laughed, though in the back of his mind he wondered if Lorie had said anything to Caroline and if she was wondering why he told her that they could only be friends, then headed off for a lunch date with another.

He and Caroline had an agreement, but he wouldn't want her to get the wrong impression.

"You're a *gut* man, Andrew Fitch." His attention swiveled back to Sarah. "For sure and for certain you will find your way again. When you do, I hope you'll consider me."

He didn't know when that might be. "I'd be honored."

Sarah gathered the remains of their lunch and tossed it into the trash. The Oklahoma wind stirred the leaves in the trees above them.

"I guess I'll—" She made a motion with her hand.

"I'll see you at church?"

Sarah smiled. "I'd like that." She turned and made her way down the street, turning back only once to see if he was watching. Once she turned the corner on the other side of the hardware store, he headed across the grass that separated the two picnic areas.

Caroline.

Lorie saw him first, catching sight of him walking toward them and touching Caroline's hand to alert her.

Caroline herself turned in her seat to watch him. *"Goedemiddag,"* she greeted him as she shielded her eyes with one hand.

"Goedemiddag," Andrew returned. "Lorie, Emily." He nodded to each of them, then turned his attention back to Caroline. "Where's Emma?"

"She took an early nap."

"She's feeling all right, I hope."

"Oh, *jah*," Caroline said. "Just growing, I s'pose."

"Can I have a word, please?"

Lorie and Emily exchanged a look, but Caroline ignored them. *"Jah,"* she said, pushing back from the table to fall in beside him.

They walked across the sunlit grass, Andrew wanting to get far away from any inquisitive ears before speaking his mind.

Once they were under the shade of one of the mighty oaks in the park, he turned to Caroline.

"I didn't want you to think anything about . . . well, what I mean is . . . I didn't know Sarah was coming by today with lunch."

"Okay," Caroline said slowly.

Andrew took a deep breath. He was making a mess of this. "Danny talked me into having dinner with her last night. I'm afraid she got the wrong impression. So I came out here to talk to her about it, and now I'm afraid that I've made you think that I'm a liar."

Caroline stopped and laid her hand on his arm. "Andrew, what is all this about?"

He shrugged. "I told you that I wasn't ready to date anyone. I didn't want you to think that I had started seeing Sarah."

She shook her head with a smile. "You are *gegisch*, Andrew Fitch."

"I'm silly?"

Caroline dipped her chin. "We agreed to be *freinden, jah*?"

"Jah," he echoed.

"And we are."

He released his breath, not realizing until that moment that he had been holding it. Caroline's friendship had come to mean a lot to him in such a short period of time. He wouldn't do anything to jeopardize it. "So we're still on for Sunday?"

"Jah," she said with a smile. She patted his arm and turned back toward her friends and their watchful eyes.

Andrew was certain the sun shone a bit brighter.

Dear Mamm and Dat,

Church here is so very different than back home. We still meet in our homes and the women sit on one side of the room and the men on the other, but the service is in English. We even have English Bibles. The bishop allows us to meet before the service and talk about any Bible verse that we have read during the week and want to discuss. The Englisch call this Sunday School. We don't call it anything but a good reason to get together and talk about God's word. I enjoy being able to read the Bible on my own and talk about it without fear that the bishop might think me boastful or questioning of God. It's very calming to me to be able to discuss passages with others and to learn from what they have read and not just what the preacher feels moved to teach.

But I do miss my Sundays at home with you and Dat and all my cousins. Even after all of this time I miss the smell of the roasted chicken you used to make for the after service. Do you still take it as your food offering for the meal? I have tried to make it many times since I have been gone, but I've never managed to get the spices correct. It will always be one of my favorite memories of Tennessee.

I must close for now, for I hear Emma stirring from her nap, and it is almost time for the postman to come. Please write when you are able. And give Dat my love.

                                        Love,
                                        Caroline

Chapter Five

"Esther, are you ready to go?" Caroline stepped from her bedroom as she called for her friend. "If we don't hurry, we'll be late for church."

"I'm coming."

Esther hurried into the hallway between their rooms, the strings from her prayer *kapp* trailing behind her. "Almost ready. Just got to get my Bible and—"

"Is that what you're wearing?" The words burst from Caroline before she had time to check them.

Esther looked down at herself in confusion, then back up to meet Caroline's gaze. *"Jah."*

"I mean, why don't you wear the green dress I made for you? It makes your eyes stand out."

Esther allowed her one more cautious stare, then grabbed her purse from the back of the kitchen chair and her Bible from the sideboard. "This dress is fine for church."

"Jah, I mean . . ."

"Is there something bothering you, Caroline?"

She shook her head and hoisted Emma into her arms. The girl was getting heavier by the day. *"Nay*. It's just that . . ."

"What?" Esther helped her slide the strap of her own bag across her shoulder, then turned out the kitchen light. Together they made their way to the door of their backroom apartment.

"We should strive to look our best every day, *jah*?" Caroline asked.

"Vanity is a sin," Esther answered.

"Not vanity," Caroline countered. "But . . . but . . ."

"But what?"

Caroline shook her head. "Never mind," she said. She had already messed up any plans she could have made concerning Esther and Abe. Even if Esther wore a sparkly *Englisch* evening gown to church, Caroline doubted that Abe would notice. Now, if she wore a lovely shade of mahogany . . .

An errant chuckle escaped her as she unchained her bike and deposited Emma in her little plastic seat on the back.

"What's so funny?" Esther asked.

But Caroline just shook her head.

Once they were all loaded up and ready to go, they pedaled down Main Street, past the Kauffman Family Restaurant, Abe's furniture store, and the grocery store on the right.

The wind and sun on her face felt *gut*, and Caroline had to resist the urge to close her eyes and just enjoy the sensation of a Sunday morning on the way to church.

Their bishop in Tennessee would have never allowed his members to ride bicycles of any sort. According to him, they could take a Plain person too far away from all the things they needed to remain close to.

Caroline couldn't figure out exactly what that meant. She wouldn't think about riding the bike outside of the Wells Landing city limits. The highway was too dangerous by far. But since she and Esther lived in town, they had no place to keep a horse and buggy and only one way to get around.

Several other three-wheelers were parked to the side of

the Yoders' house when Esther and Caroline pulled in. On the other side of the barn, the buggies had been left, the horses released into the pasture for the long church service. There were even a few tractors parked in between.

Caroline unstrapped Emma and grabbed her bag before heading toward the milling crowd.

She scanned the faces looking for Andrew as she made her way to where the women had gathered before the service. Soon they would go in and take their places on either side of the cool interior of the barn. But she wanted to see him. Just once before the service started.

Her heart gave a thump in her chest as her eyes met his sea-blue ones across the milling people. She smiled, happy to know that he was there. After the service they would put their plan together to help Esther and Abe fall in love.

Surely that wasn't a bad thing, to help two people along on the road to happiness. She just hoped that what she was doing didn't interfere with God's will, just spurred it along a little. Whenever absentminded Abe was involved, Caroline thought perhaps God could use all the help He could get. But just in case, she would add it to her prayer list.

Caroline bounced Emma on her hip and halfheartedly listened to the women talk about quilts and canning as she waited for the bishop to call for church to start. Lorie was over talking to Jonah Miller while Elam Riehl seemed to have cornered Emily once again.

Soon the bishop motioned everyone into the barn. Caroline chose a seat in the back just in case Emma got fussy. Ever the friend, Esther settled down next to her and waited for God's message.

Caroline set her purse on the floor and glanced to her right, only to find Andrew seated just the width of the aisle away. She smiled at him, and he shrugged with a sheepish grin.

She had to bite her lip to keep from laughing.

Abe sat on the opposite side of Andrew and seemed to be more interested in the nick out of the bench in front of him than anything else going on.

A hush fell over the congregation as the bishop stood and called for prayer.

Andrew was ashamed of himself. Well, almost. But Danny was at it again, trying to push him and Sarah together. *Jah*, he had agreed to have dinner with her, but that didn't mean he wanted to sit close to her in church. A meal was one thing, but he didn't want to give the girl the wrong impression. So he found a seat in the back and refused to budge from it.

How ironic—or maybe it was blessed—that he was seated so close to Caroline. He couldn't have planned that better even if he had tried.

With a happy smile, he opened his hymn book and prepared to sing.

Somewhere toward the middle of the service, Emma grew fussy. She was such a sweet baby that she didn't create too much ruckus, though Andrew could tell Caroline was concerned that her daughter was making it hard on the others around them to hear the preacher.

She gathered Emma in her arms and quietly stood, taking her to the back of the barn.

In all honesty, Andrew didn't think Emma was that noisy. In fact, if he hadn't been seated directly across from her, he wouldn't have even heard the child's whimpering cries.

But Caroline's concern for those around her was just part of her makeup. She was conscious of others. Andrew smiled to himself as he remembered her slamming her hands on her hips and demanding that he take the bed his uncle had made for her back to the shop. She hadn't wanted it, not because it wasn't beautiful enough or wasn't made correctly, like some of the *Englisch* complaints might be. *Nay*, she hadn't wanted to keep it because it cost too much money and she didn't want Esther to spend it on her.

But Andrew peeked into the bakery every time he passed these days. Caroline worked hard for Esther. He couldn't think of anyone more deserving of the beautiful cherry-wood furniture.

He resisted the urge to turn and see if Caroline was in the back of the barn or if she had taken Emma outside for a breath of fresh air. Instead, he tried to focus his attention on the service. A few seats in front of him, Johnny Yoder stood and accepted his infant son from his wife Mary.

Caroline didn't have anyone to help with Emma. Well, no one except Esther. And Andrew couldn't help but wonder why she had never remarried. Most women would have already found another. That was just how the Amish life worked. Accepting God's will and getting on with living.

Caroline was hardworking, caring, and gentle, beautiful even. And he was surprised that none of the Amish men surrounding him had tried to take her hand and start a life together.

Caroline returned to her seat a few moments later, a flushed and sleeping Emma in her arms.

She looked to him and smiled, and Andrew felt his heart expand with the simple serenity of it all, sweet mother, sweet child. It was a beautiful sight.

He turned his gaze back to the front and tried his best not to be so aware of every little move she made. But he couldn't help his bubbling excitement at the afternoon they had planned. His uncle was another so deserving of love, yet not finding it. *Jah*, it was going to be a *gut* afternoon, for sure.

As they stood for the final prayer before dismissal, Andrew fully realized why it was customary for the men and women to sit on opposite sides during church. Being so close to Caroline was more than distracting. He just hoped no one wanted to discuss the sermon later. He couldn't remember a word.

Dear Caroline,

Words cannot express the joy I feel when I see your name in the mailbox. I have taken to running to meet the postman as soon as I hear him coming down the road.

I have to hide your letters from your father. He still cannot speak your name, nor will he allow anyone else to do so in his presence. I hope you understand that his anger stems from love and one day he will be accepting (though I don't think he will ever be happy about it). That is my nightly prayer, that his acceptance come soon. Then you will be able to return and join us here once again.

Along with your letters I have hidden the picture of Emma. I only allow myself to take it out once a week when your father goes into town. Even then, it has started to show creases and wear. Of course the bishop knows nothing about it. He is such a gut man that I hate to have secrets, but this one is best kept between you and me.

Emma. What a wonderful and beautiful child God has given you! How I wish I could be there with the two of you. My arms long to hold her and rock her to sleep as I did you when you were but a tiny boppli. Even now I would give anything I have

*to be able to touch your face and look into your eyes
once again.*

*I miss you, liebschdi, and pray every morning
and night that one day you'll be able to return to us.*

*With love always,
Mamm*

Chapter Six

Everyone milled about after the service, talking about the weather and planning their afternoon. Caroline heard rumors of a volleyball game brewing at the Detweilers' and a Bible reading at the Fishers'. But she had already made her plans.

"Are you ready to leave now?" Esther gazed at her with concern and questions shining in her deep brown eyes.

Where is Andrew? "Just a minute more." Caroline smiled though she wanted to grimace. Emma was a heavy weight in her arms, her warm body pressed so close, creating trickling beads of sweat.

She rocked from side to side in a gesture that appeared like she was soothing her sleeping child when it also enabled her to scan more of the crowd for her matchmaking partner.

"Here he comes." She managed not to sigh with relief.

"Who?" Esther turned one way and then the other, a small frown on her brow.

"I told Andrew I would meet him after the service."

"Oh." Then *"Oh"* as the notion dawned on her. "Well, that's *gut* then, *jah*?"

"Esther, I know that look, and it's not what you think. We're just friends."

"Jah, freinden." Esther smiled in a way that let Caroline know that she did not believe her. What could she do but let the matter drop as Andrew stopped before them.

"Good afternoon." He nodded at each of them in turn.

"Good afternoon," they both echoed.

"Onkle and I were hoping that you ladies would join us for a meal."

Caroline almost laughed at the light sparkling in Esther's eyes. She didn't know which had the older woman more excited, the idea of spending time with Abe or an afternoon of matchmaking between Caroline and Andrew. She hoped it was the first one.

"We'd love to," Caroline said with a smile.

"You can't ride your bikes all the way to the farm. Would you like to ride in the buggy with us?"

"Jah." Caroline hated how stiff her voice sounded. She had better start acting natural or one of them would see through their ruse. "That would be *gut.*"

Andrew nodded and started walking backward. "I'll just go get *Onkle.*" He bumped into someone, then turned and made his way through the milling congregation.

"If you wanted to go to dinner with Andrew, you didn't have to drag me along," Esther said.

"You don't want to have dinner with Abe?" Caroline asked.

"I-I did not say that, it's just . . ."

"Just what?" Caroline returned.

Esther pressed her lips together, then sighed. *"Danki,* Caroline."

Caroline gave her friend a small smile. "You're welcome, Esther." It was the least she could do.

* * *

Abe's buggy was big enough that they could all five fit comfortably inside.

As Abe helped Esther into the front seat, Andrew took the sleeping Emma from Caroline so she could swing herself into the back.

She reached her arms out for her baby, but Andrew managed to hop into the back, the child still cradled to his chest, and settle down without disturbing her.

"I can take her now."

"It's all right," he said. "I'm sure your arms are tired."

She didn't like to complain. She had made her choices, after all.

Caroline resisted the urge to rub the feeling back into her arms and instead enjoyed the sway of the horses. Clop, clop, clop, the hooves sounded against the pavement as they trotted toward the farm.

How long had it been since she had ridden in a buggy? The thought brought tears to her eyes. As much as she loved Esther and her new life in Wells Landing, if she could go back she wouldn't. Because that would mean a life without Emma. Caroline was homesick. It was as plain as that. She missed her family, her parents and their conservative ways. She missed her cousins, the closest thing she had to siblings of her own. She missed the services in German, the potluck after, and her mother's roasted chicken.

Andrew nudged her with his elbow, gently bringing her back to the present. "Are you all right?"

She nodded, unable to speak around the lump in her throat. Reminiscing and wondering were not ways to accept her newfound life. She could never go back to Ethridge, never go back to the life she had there.

"You don't look fine. You look like you're about to cry. What has you so sad, Caroline Hostetler?"

"I was just thinking about my parents."

Andrew's crystal eyes clouded over with regret. "I am sorry I mentioned it. Have they been gone long?"

It took a moment for his question to register, then Caroline shook her head. "They're not dead. Just in Tennessee."

"That's where you moved here from, Tennessee?"

"Jah."

"I miss my parents too, but after . . . Well, I thought it best to get away for a while."

"Does that mean that you're only visiting Wells Landing?"

He gave a small shrug. "That depends on *Onkle*. I came down to help, and when he decides he doesn't need my help anymore, I'll go back to Missouri."

"What's it like there?"

"Missouri? A lot like here, I guess. Except we don't use tractors. But everything else is pretty much the same. Our church services are in German. But that's all. And I farm instead of make furniture."

"Do you like one more than the other?"

But Andrew didn't have time to answer as they pulled to a stop. Abe hopped down from the front and opened the gate while Esther clicked the reins and directed the horses inside.

Once the gate was closed behind them, Abe climbed back into the buggy, shooting Esther a quick smile.

Andrew leaned close. "That was promising."

Caroline nodded, ignoring the soft scent of his detergent mixed with the sweet smell of the shampoo she used to wash Emma's hair. The combination gave her heart a squeeze.

What was wrong with her lately? She had gotten teary

eyed over her parents and near angry that Andrew had been gentlemanly enough to help her with Emma. Maybe she needed a trip to the doctor for a checkup.

She pushed the thought away as Abe reined in the horses and the buggy stopped.

"You ladies go on inside, and we'll be in directly." Abe pointed toward the front door of the little white house.

"I'll help you with the horses after I lay her down." Andrew gestured toward the sleeping child in his arms. Caroline did her best not to sigh wistfully at the sight they made together, her friend and her baby.

"I can help," Caroline added. It had been a long time since she had tended horses, but skills like that weren't easily forgotten.

Esther looked to the big roan beast that pulled Abe's buggy with distrust in her eyes. "It seems like you have plenty of help with horses. But I can stay if'n you want." Caroline wasn't sure if anyone else saw it or not, but Esther's eyes begged him to say no.

Abe shook his head. "You could go on into the house and make us something to eat."

"Why, Abe Fitch, is that the only reason you invited us out to sup? So we'd prepare food?" The teasing light in Esther's eyes took the sting out of the question and replaced the fear Caroline had seen there earlier.

Abe flushed red to the roots of his hair.

Caroline laughed.

"If that was the case, Esther Lapp, I would have invited you years ago."

"I think it's working," Andrew bent low and whispered in Caroline's ear.

Emma was sleeping soundly, snuggled on Abe's bed and surrounded by mounds of pillows to protect her from falling off.

Esther and Abe stood at the stove stirring soup and flipping grilled cheese sandwiches on the griddle.

"I think so too."

They shared a smile as Andrew pulled out the chair opposite Caroline and took a seat.

"*Onkle,*" Andrew said without taking his eyes from Caroline, "after we eat, why don't you take Esther down and show her that new horse the breeder brought in yesterday?"

Abe looked at Esther as if startled that she had followed him home from church.

Caroline hid her smile. She and Andrew might need divine help in order to get those two together.

"You want to see the horses?"

Esther beamed. "I'd like that, *jah.*"

"Then that is what we will do."

Bowls of soup were poured, sandwiches served, then they all sat down to eat.

Caroline bowed her head and said a prayer of thanks for the beautiful day, the good company, and the food they were about to eat.

"*Aemen,*" Abe uttered.

Caroline had no more than raised the spoon to her lips when Emma cried out.

She tried not to sigh as she pushed back from the table. But she was hungry. Beachy services were as lengthy as Old Order ones, and breakfast had been a long time ago. Yet duty called.

"I'll get her." Esther started to stand.

Caroline smiled politely but firmly, stilling Esther half in and half out of her seat. "I've got it."

Emma was kneeling on the bed rubbing her eyes and still surrounded by pillows when Caroline walked in.

Once Emma spied her, she raised her pudgy arms to be picked up. *"Mamm."*

Caroline's heart melted all over again.

She scooped Emma into her arms, loving the warm weight of her form. She planted a kiss on the dark curls of her hair. "Are you hungry, wee one?"

After a quick diaper change and hand washing, Caroline made it back to the table just in time for everyone to finish their meal.

"I'll reheat your soup," Esther offered, but Caroline shook her head.

"Tomato is good cold as well." There was no sense in dirtying another pan.

"Want me to hold her while you eat?"

"I thought you were going down to the pasture to see the new horse."

"I haven't seen the old horses yet. They will be there after a while."

Caroline settled Emma into the crook of her arm. "I can handle this. You go on ahead and see the horses."

Esther frowned but let the subject drop as Caroline tore off a piece of her now-cold grilled cheese and gave it to Emma to gnaw.

The screen door slammed shut with a springy bang as Esther and Abe made their way outside.

Andrew stood at the sink, looking out the window as his uncle and Esther made their way to the horse pasture. "I think it's working," he said once again, turning back to Caroline. "Want me to hold her while you eat?"

Caroline scooped up a spoonful of soup and held it toward her toddler's mouth. "I can manage."

"I didn't ask if you could manage. I merely offered my help." He sat down opposite her, but Caroline avoided his searching gaze, instead focusing on feeding Emma.

"Why do you do that?" he asked.

"Do what?" she hedged.

"Get all defensive when someone offers to help you with Emma?"

"I don't," she started, but he shot her a look that clearly stated he didn't believe her. "She is my responsibility."

"That doesn't mean you can't accept help with her."

He was right, of course, but Caroline had a difficult time accepting help. She had made her choices, brought a baby into this world. And now she would care for her . . . alone.

"If I need help, I ask." She scooped another bite of soup for the toddler and avoided looking at him directly. Somehow when she looked into his eyes, she wished for things to be different.

Her heart squeezed in her chest and she directed all of her attention on getting the soup into Emma's mouth. It was better by far than obsessing over the man seated across from her.

"After you're done, do you want to take her to the corral to see the horses?"

Caroline managed not to sigh with relief at the change of subject. "That would be *gut, jah*."

She tried not to be self-conscious of his lingering gaze as she finished up feeding them both. She rinsed the bowl in the sink and sat Emma on the counter. Quick as a wink, Andrew was there holding out a clean rag for her to use to wash Emma's face and hands.

Is this what it's like to have a father, a husband, a life mate to help with all the little parts of living? It was nice to know there was someone she could depend on.

She shook away the thought lest it become too comfortable and decide to stay. Emma was her responsibility and hers alone. It'd do neither any good a'tall to become accustomed to others doing for them.

"Are you ready?" Andrew plucked his hat from the peg on the wall and held open the door for them.

Caroline hid her sad thoughts behind her smile and swung Emma to her hip. "Lead the way," she said and stepped out into the warm Oklahoma afternoon.

Esther walked alongside Abe, enjoying being out in the fresh farm air and sunshine. She just wished that he would talk to her.

It had been a long time since she had been interested in someone, romantically speaking, but she couldn't nail down what there was about Abe that drew her in. He was a little *strubbly*; his shirt stayed partially untucked and one of the straps on his suspenders was turned wrong. And he was adorable.

His hands were strong and long-fingered, even if they were perpetually stained. He was an artist. It fascinated Esther that he could take something as simple as wood and make useful, beautiful furniture.

Abe walked up to the wooden fence and propped one foot on the bottom rung. "What do you think?"

She opened her mouth to respond, closing it again as she realized that he was talking about the horses. "Th-they're beautiful."

He hooked one arm toward her. "How can you tell from way over there?"

Esther hesitantly approached. Well, she inched forward a couple of feet.

Abe turned those blue eyes so like his nephew's on her, a frown of confusion wrinkling his brow. "I thought you wanted to see the horses?"

"*Jah*. Of course I do."

"*Ach*, then get over here and do it."

She heaved a big breath. "I'm a little afraid of horses." There, she said it.

Abe looked at her as if she had said she was turning English. "How can this be?"

She shrugged. "They're just so . . . big."

He continued to study her. "Earlier you drove the team through the gates."

"That's different."

"*Jah?*" Abe asked, but she could tell he was still confused.

She tried again. "They were . . . contained."

"With bridles and such?"

Esther nodded.

"Here they are behind a fence."

"But they are still all over the place." And could knock her to the ground in a heartbeat. "My brother . . . A horse killed my brother."

Abe cocked his head to one side in that thoughtful manner she found so charming. "I remember that. Well, that was nigh on fifty years ago."

It was, but when she saw horses like these, running around in a pasture, those memories appeared as clear as if they had happened the day before.

Abe stroked his beard. "What did you do when you and John had your place?"

"He took care of the horses for me, and as long as they were contained . . ." She shrugged.

"This will never do, never do." He reached his hand out to her.

Esther stared at it a moment, then placed her hand inside his.

His palm was rough from all the years of working with wood, but his grasp was gentle as he drew her closer to him, closer to the fence that separated her from the large beasts.

She took a shuddering breath. It had been a long time since she had trusted a man. A very long time. She allowed him to pull her closer to him, closer to the shiny rusty-colored horse.

The animal had an earthy smell that mixed with the faint scent of leather and the woody blend of the man beside her.

He continued to hold her hand in his as he reached out and ran her fingers down the horse's nose. The muzzle was as soft as satin, the horse's breath warm and moist on her palm as he blew out. She moved back, but Abe was behind her, holding her in place even though he only touched her hand.

"He won't hurt you," Abe crooned.

And just like that Abe the wood crafter became a different man, and Esther felt herself fall a little more in love with him.

She tried not to relax into him when she wanted nothing more than to melt into his embrace. She fought the urge to snuggle close to him and tell him exactly how much he meant to her. But that was the pinnacle of impropriety.

Besides that, he had never once indicated that they would ever be anything more than friends.

She stiffened. He dropped her hand and stepped away, giving the horse one last pat on his neck before gesturing back toward the house. "Are you ready to call it done?"

What else could she do but nod? With a dip of her chin she led the way up the path to the house.

* * *

Once outside, Caroline lowered Emma onto the grass, keeping a tight hold on her tiny hand. "Lead the way," she said and the trio started off down the thin path of dirt that led toward the stables.

Caroline tried her best not to notice how Andrew slowed his long stride to accommodate Emma's chubby little legs, or how he showed her a bunny nervously nibbling on a patch of clover just this side of the fence. Tried not to notice how nice he was.

How nice it was being with him.

"Look, Emma." He swung the toddler into his arms and pointed toward the approaching horse.

The black gelding advanced slowly, sorting out a greeting with a shake of his mighty head. He was easily the biggest horse Caroline had ever seen, but Emma was not afraid.

She clapped her hands together and squealed when the horse shook his mane and snorted again.

"Here." Andrew took one of her tiny hands into his much larger one and stretched it out until it was almost touching the velvet nose of the beast.

Caroline held her breath. She wasn't afraid of horses, but this one was just so huge.

The gelding snorted again, then nuzzled Emma's hand like a cat.

"He wants a treat." Andrew let go of Emma's hand to reach into his pocket. Out came a sugar cube, which he allowed the horse to eat off his palm.

Emma was enthralled, clapping her hands and bouncing in Andrew's arms.

Caroline exhaled, not realizing until that very moment that she had been holding her breath. It wasn't that she didn't trust Andrew; she was just so accustomed to doing things herself, taking care of Emma and not having to share her with others. It was more than strange to hand Emma over to Andrew and allow him to teach her and guide her in any matter.

"Does the horse bother you?"

Caroline turned toward Andrew, an answer not readily forming in her mind. "I guess I had forgotten how big they are."

Andrew smiled, a grin Caroline was sure could melt butter in January. "Or how small she is?"

"*Jah*, that too."

"Follow me." He gave a small gesture with his head. With Emma still cradled high in his strong arms, he led Caroline into the dim interior of the barn. She heard them before she saw them, their whines and grunts unmistakable.

"They were born sometime last night." He opened the door to the stall just off to the side of the tack room.

There nestled in the clean fresh hay was a black-and-white border collie nursing a litter of pups. At first count there were six, but a seventh, smaller one pushed its way from the bottom of the pile back to the top in order to get a better spot.

Andrew set Emma on her feet, supporting her until she was steady.

"They are so sweet." Caroline dropped to her knees on the hay, stretching out her hand for the mother to sniff. Once she had passed the test, Caroline stroked the dog's silky head.

Emma squealed and started forward, only to be caught by Andrew before she could reach her goal.

"Oh, no, wee one. They are much too small for even your little hands."

Caroline pushed back to her feet. "What did you call her?"

"Wee one." A frown of concern puckered his brow. "Is that a problem?"

She swallowed back the longing clogging her throat. "*Nay*, it's just that I call her that too." How ironic that they had both chosen the same endearment for her daughter. It was a connection that she didn't want to examine.

"Does that bother you? I can call her something else. Just Emma. Wee one seems to fit her."

"It is fine, Andrew Fitch. Of course you may call her wee one."

Andrew smiled and Caroline tried not to notice the brilliance in it all. He bounced Emma in his arms until she squealed. "Wee one, it's time to head back to the house. If I know my *onkle*, he's started ice cream and it should be just about ready."

Caroline felt a little strange trailing behind Andrew as he carried Emma back to the house. She wasn't used to seeing Emma in the arms of a man. Watching the two of them together made her realize the need to fortify her heart. She and Andrew had agreed to be friends. It was only to be expected that they would be around Emma together, and he was such a helpful and kind person that it stood to reason that he would help Caroline with the toddler. But having his help was one thing she would have to be careful not to get too accustomed to. Who knew how long before some *schee* Amish girl took Andrew's heart away.

"Uh-oh." Andrew motioned toward the porch as they neared the house. "Do you think something happened?"

Just as he had predicted, Abe had started the ice-cream maker and was cranking the handle on the side. What looked to be a cinder block wrapped in a towel set on top of the ice-cream bucket. Abe sat on the stairs and cranked while Esther pushed herself in the swing.

"I don't know," Caroline quietly replied. "But it doesn't look *gut*."

Maybe their matchmaking days were over. And that would mean not seeing Andrew as much, just church and the afternoons that he might stop by the bakery for a snack.

The idea didn't set well with Caroline. But that was ridiculous. They were friends. They had committed to the relationship of *freinden* and helping Esther and Abe find love. Surely that had to mean something. It wasn't like they couldn't see each other if the romance fell through between Abe and Esther, but it was a good excuse.

"You get Esther," Andrew said. "I'll see what I can find out from *Onkle*."

Caroline dipped her chin in agreement and made her way past Abe and onto the porch to sit in the swing next to Esther. Andrew stopped in front of his uncle and placed Emma on top of the towel-wrapped cement block. "Emma, sit here and help, *jah*?"

The toddler gave a small nod, but squirmed all the same as Abe continued to crank the handle on the old ice-cream churn.

Caroline leaned in closer to Esther to make sure her words were only heard by the other woman. Not that Abe would be paying attention to them. He seemed completely engrossed in the art of ice-cream making. "What happened?" she whispered.

Esther shrugged. *"Nix."*

"If nothing happened, why do you look like you just lost your best friend?"

Esther's mouth twisted into a grimace and she shook her head. "I've been widowed for nigh on thirty years. I just realized today that if Abe Fitch had feelings for me that are stronger than friendship, he's had a very long time to act on them."

Caroline frowned. "So you think because he hasn't asked you on a date in the last thirty years that he doesn't want to be more than friends with you?"

"It makes sense, *jah?*"

"No." Caroline shook her head. "Abe is . . ." She looked over to Andrew's *onkle*. He had allowed himself a rest and let Andrew take over the cranking while he sat nearby and sanded on what looked to be a small wooden horse. "Abe is Abe." She didn't know how else to say it. She had never met anyone like him before. He was smart and talented but as distracted as they came. "I think if you're going to capture his heart, the first thing you'll need to do is let him want it."

Esther shook her head. "I can't do that. That would be most improper."

Caroline glanced back to where Abe and Andrew sat. "Improper or not, it may just be the only way."

Half an hour later, Abe scooped up the semi-soft ice cream into bowls and passed them around.

"Yum . . . banana," Caroline said, taking her first bite after their silent prayer's ending *aemen*. "My favorite."

"I like strawberry the best," Andrew said, settling down next to her.

Esther accepted a small bowl from Abe and took it over to where Emma was playing quietly in the grass with the horse Abe had just finished.

Caroline was astounded by his talent and generosity, but he insisted that Emma take it home with her.

"You know if you give her that to eat by herself, she'll have it all over the place in no time," Caroline warned.

"*Jah*, but she'll wash up." Esther handed the bowl to the toddler, then plopped down on the grass next to her.

"You know what would be *gut* with this?" Andrew asked.

Caroline spooned a bite into her mouth and nearly sighed as the yummy concoction melted on her tongue. "What?" she asked, scooping up another bite.

"Cowboy cookies."

Caroline laughed. "You think everything needs cowboy cookies."

"*Jah*. Everything does." Then he lowered his voice. "What happened between the two of them?"

"I have no idea," Caroline whispered in return. She looked from Esther, sitting in the yard next to Emma, back to Abe.

When they had arrived at the house after church, everything had seemed fine. Between then and now, something had Abe acting like Abe, and Esther acting like he was invisible.

Normally Esther would be staring at the furniture maker with lovesick puppy eyes. Now she wouldn't even look at him.

The upside was Esther managed to get more of the ice cream in Emma than on her dress. At least the toddler wouldn't be too sticky for the ride home. And that was a *gut* thing. The slow ride back to town would be uncomfortable enough with the chasm that had cracked between Esther and Abe.

The rift that had formed between Esther and Abe seemed to grow by the yard all the way back to town.

Andrew rode back to the bakery with them, and Caroline was glad. Emma was tired from the afternoon's activities. She sat quietly in Caroline's lap all the way home, one thumb tucked in her mouth and the other hand fisted in Caroline's *kapp* strings.

Andrew kept casting question-filled glances in Caroline's direction, but she had no more idea what had happened than he did. Finally she mouthed that she would find out what was wrong as soon as she could and left the matter at that.

Finally, they arrived back on Main Street. Abe pulled the buggy to a stop and set the brake. Without waiting for any help, Esther slid the door open and hopped to the ground. "*Danki* for a lovely afternoon." She gave a quick nod to Abe, then turned on her heel and made her way around the side of the building. Caroline was just stepping down with Andrew's help when Esther disappeared around the back.

"Thanks for having us," Caroline said, including Abe in her sentiment. She shifted to bring the exhausted Emma into a more secure hold.

Abe gave her a nod but otherwise looked as distant as he usually did. Caroline wasn't sure if he really didn't notice that Esther was upset or if he was choosing to pretend like he didn't know. With a man like Abe Fitch, it was hard to say.

"Do you want me to take her around for you?" Andrew asked.

"*Nay.*" Caroline shook her head. "I'm sure you have a lot to do at the farm."

Andrew opened his mouth, then closed it again. "*Jah,*" he said. "Then I'll see you later."

"*Jah.*"

Andrew swung himself into the buggy next to his uncle. With a smile and a wave, they were gone.

Caroline let herself into the apartment and sat Emma in the playpen. It was too early to put her straight to bed. She needed a bath and some supper, but first Caroline needed to talk to Esther and find out what had happened this afternoon.

She went into the kitchen, where the older woman was slamming cabinets and banging pans.

"You want to talk about it?"

Esther shook her head, then retrieved the flour from the cabinet above her head. "I guess it's not right to ask for God's help."

Caroline hid her smile at the outburst and pulled out one of the dining chairs. She sat and waited for Esther to continue.

"I mean, there are so many more important issues that we should take to the Lord in prayer. Matters of the heart seem"—she shrugged—"trivial."

"Maybe," Caroline agreed. "But if it is important enough to you that you talk to God about it, then it's important enough to Him that He'll listen."

"I don't know." Esther started measuring out flour, counting to herself as she spooned it into a large mixing bowl.

When Esther got upset, she baked. Looked like there would be a new bakery item on sale tomorrow. Last year, she'd had a problem with the bank and baked straight through the spring. Four new items were added to the menu, and Caroline had gained six pounds.

"Are you going to tell me what happened?"

"Nothing happened," Esther said, but she didn't meet Caroline's steady gaze.

"Then why do I get the feeling that you're not telling me the truth?"

Esther stopped counting scoops of sugar and sighed. "Abe Fitch has had over thirty years to fall in love with me. It's a fool's dream to think that he will at this time in our lives."

Caroline slammed her hands onto her hips. "So you're just giving up."

"*Jah,*" Esther answered, though Caroline's words were more of a statement than a question.

"That's the most ridiculous thing I have ever heard."

Esther shrugged one shoulder and started creaming together the brown sugar and butter.

"Take it back or I'll go down to the furniture store tomorrow to tell him that you love him."

Esther gasped. "You wouldn't."

Caroline raised one brow.

"You would." Esther shook her head. "Fine," she conceded. "I won't give up. But I'm certainly not going to invite him to *nachtess* every night."

"You just leave that to me."

"How did you get to be so stubborn?" Esther asked.

Caroline smiled. "I learned from the best."

Dear Mamm,

I hope this letter finds you well. I am sitting in the park waiting on my freinden to join me for middawk. Emma is playing in the dirt, digging with a plastic shovel. I hope the town does not get upset that she tore up the grass in that spot. I don't think it will ever be the same. Seeing that big patch of missing grass reminded me of the time that the pigs got out of the pen and into the front yard. They tore out a big spot in the grass and you came out of the house waving a broom and a dishrag. I laughed so hard I barely made it to the outhouse. The grass never did grow back.

I guess that is just another reason why pride is a sin. We should not become dependent on the physical things around us for our happiness, but should rely on God. The same thing can be said for grass as well as automobiles.

It is so strange that the bishop here allows the church members to have tractors. And with rubber wheels, no less. It is nothing to see an Englisch car, a horse and buggy, then a tractor chugging along behind it. But they tell me the soil here is too filled with sandstone rocks for them to farm it any other way. Other than that, Oklahoma is not so different than Tennessee. Yet that doesn't make me miss you any less.

I do not know if I will ever be able to return home. It is something that I pray about every day as well. I am confident that God will reveal His plan to us in His own time. I just wish that He would do it soon.
Give my love to Dat.

Love,
Caroline

Chapter Seven

Caroline penned her name to the bottom of the letter and willed herself not to cry. She had made choices, and she would stand by them. It was the only way.

"Goedemiddag."

She looked up, shading her eyes from the sun as Andrew dropped down opposite her at the wooden picnic table.

"Hi, Andrew." She folded the letter so it would fit in the envelope, then glanced over for a quick check on Emma before she sealed it.

"Where are the rest?"

"Lorie and Emily?" She shrugged. "Most times they are here before me. They must have gotten busy doing something else."

"You looked pretty busy yourself."

She shook her head. "Just writing a letter to my folks back home."

"If you want to get it into the mail today, you'd better hurry. Fred Conrad was running early."

"I would like to get it out as soon as possible, but . . ." She trailed off as she glanced toward her daughter.

"Go ahead," Andrew said. "I'll keep an eye on her."

She bit her lip. "I don't know . . ." It wasn't so important that she should inconvenience Andrew. It could go out tomorrow.

"It's just around the corner. You'll be back before she even knows you're gone."

His words of the Sunday before came back to her. Why didn't she trust anyone else with Emma? Maybe it was time she started. "Okay," she said, pushing up from the narrow bench seat. "I'll be right back."

Of course, everyone else had the same thought as she, to hustle to the post office to get their letters and packages out before the truck left for Tulsa.

Caroline shifted impatiently from one foot to the other, glancing every few seconds at the large industrial clock on the wall.

It was only minutes before she had her turn, buying a stamp and sending her letter on its way.

In no time at all, she was down the street and back to the park.

But Andrew and Emma were nowhere to be found.

She sucked in a deep breath as her heart began to pound. They couldn't have gone far. The restaurant . . . the bakery . . .

Caroline dashed across the street, ignoring the car horn that followed after her.

If something had happened to Emma . . .

She burst through the bakery doors, the bell above the door tinkling furiously with her entrance. It was lunchtime, and the place was empty, just a couple of *Englisch* patrons looking for cakes and such for their special occasions.

She sucked in another breath, trying to calm her erratic fears as she spotted them. Emma was sitting on the table top, her thumb in her mouth and tears on her cheeks. Andrew was seated before her, his head bent over his task.

"Why are you here?" Her voice sounded shrill even to her own ears. She sucked in more air and tried to calm her nerves.

Andrew turned calmly toward her, and that was when she saw the blood.

She uttered a quick prayer as she rushed toward her baby.

"She fell," Andrew said as he continued to dab at the wound with a disinfectant. He blew on it as Emma started to whimper from the sting.

"Were you not watching her?"

He jerked as if she had slapped him. "I was. I watched her stand, start to run, then trip and fall."

Caroline scooped Emma up and away from Andrew. "And you did nothing to stop it?"

"There wasn't anything I could do. She fell that fast." He snapped his fingers.

Once she had seen her mother, Emma's bravery fled, and she dissolved into tears once again.

"Here," he said, reaching out to Emma. "Let me."

Caroline, heart still pounding, adrenaline pumping, turned away from him. "I think you've done enough for one day."

Andrew watched helplessly as Caroline walked away, cradling the crying Emma to her.

He hadn't done anything wrong. It was an accident. Caroline was completely overreacting.

"She's very protective where the *boppli* is concerned."

He could only agree with the truth in Esther Lapp's words. Caroline was more than protective; she was sheltering and obsessing.

"Now, I shouldn't say anything, but I can tell you this. As far as I know, that baby is the only person she has left in this world."

He shook his head. "She told me her parents are still alive in Tennessee."

"That may be, but I have yet to meet them. She hasn't gone any farther than Tulsa since she got off that bus two years ago."

"What are you saying, Esther?"

"Just give her some time, Andrew Fitch. She'll come around."

Caroline had finally stopped shaking by the time Esther locked the doors on the bakery and they headed toward their backroom apartment.

Emma's knee was bruised and cut, but she seemed not to notice the wound as she ran ahead of Caroline.

"She seems no worse for wear," Esther said casually. A little too casually. Caroline hadn't lived with her friend for the past two years and not come to know that when Esther used that tone, she had something on her mind. Caroline would know what it was soon enough.

"Kids are resilient," she replied.

"Fifteen-month-old babies are always falling."

Caroline closed the door behind them as Esther headed for the kitchen. "And that means what?"

Esther shrugged, and she started the soup for their supper. "Just what I said; fifteen-month-old babies fall a lot."

She eyed her friend. "Best get whatever it is off your mind, Esther."

"Yelling at Andrew was not the way to handle the situation. He was trying to help the child."

"But—I mean . . ." Caroline realized she wasn't angry with Andrew, but with herself. She had left them alone. She should have been there for her daughter. Yes, accidents would happen. "I overreacted today."

Esther unwrapped the loaf of crusty sourdough bread they would have with their dinner. "That you did."

She had hollered at Andrew, made it seem like the accident was all his fault. He was her friend and she should have never treated him so poorly.

And most of all, she owed Andrew a big, big apology.

"Andrew, there's someone here for you."

He looked up from the project he was sanding to find his cousin standing in the doorway of the shop. His eyes felt gritty and sleep deprived. He hadn't rested more than a couple of hours during the night, tossing and turning as he recalled the anger in Caroline's eyes.

He pulled off the safety glasses and resisted the urge to wipe his face on his sleeve. There was enough sawdust on his clothes to fill his eyes with grit for real.

"I'll be right there."

"You might want to, uh . . ." Danny took a step toward him, dusting his clothes. Then he shook his head as if it were a hopeless endeavor. "Take a bath," he finished.

"No time." Andrew pushed past his cousin and stepped into the main showroom of the furniture store. He had to finish this project for the First Methodist Church. They had said for them to take their time, then called back to put a rush on the order. Evidently the new pastor was to arrive in Wells Landing two weeks early.

But once he saw her, he wished that he had taken the time to clean up a bit more, at least get the wood shavings out of his hair. But it was too late; she had already seen him.

Caroline.

She shifted from one foot to the other, chewing on her

lip as she waited for him to come near. "I came to apologize for yesterday."

"Good afternoon to you too," he said, doing his best to keep his grin at bay. After yesterday, he was afraid she would never talk to him again.

A smile wavered on her lips, and he loved the rosy pink color that rose into her cheeks.

"Why is it that I seem to be constantly messing up where you are concerned?"

Andrew shrugged. "Just luck, I guess."

"I guess," she echoed. "I brought you a pie."

He glanced down to the perfectly browned pastry she held in her hands.

"It looks good."

"It's cherry."

"I love cherry pie."

A strange little heartbeat stretched between them. An awkward moment in which Andrew wasn't sure what to say . . . what to do. He shifted, suddenly uncomfortable in his own shoes.

"I'm not one to turn down dessert, but you didn't have to do this."

"*Jah*, I did. I overreacted yesterday. I know you wouldn't let anything happen to Emma on purpose."

He gave a nod, then realized Danny was staring at them, not even bothering to pretend that he wasn't hanging on their every word.

"I'll only accept on one condition."

"*Jah?*"

"That you share it with me."

Caroline smiled, revealing the sweet dimple in her right cheek. "I would love to."

"I'll be back in a few," he told Danny.

"But what about the Methodists' table?"

"I'll stay late tonight." Right now, he had amends to make.

They walked down Main Street, stopping in the bakery for a couple of spoons before taking the pie across the street and into the park.

"Where's Emma?" he asked as they settled down at one of the picnic tables and prepared to cut the pie.

"Napping."

Andrew turned the pie this way and that, searching for the best spot to cut.

"We should have brought some plates," Caroline said.

"And a knife?"

She smiled. "Definitely."

Andrew chuckled. "I'm not going to let that stop me." He buried his spoon in the center of the pie and managed to carve a jagged line to the outside crust. Spooning up a big bite, he shoveled it in, not realizing until that moment that he had postponed lunch in order to work on the table, and now he was more than hungry.

He scooped up another bite, his stomach rumbling with appreciation. "You know what this needs?"

Caroline licked the remains of her last bite from the spoon. "What?"

"Some of *Onkle*'s homemade vanilla ice cream."

"Yum," she agreed.

Andrew felt the tension drain out of his shoulders as they sat there in the park, the warm sun shining on his face and a *gut freind* across from him. The pie was just an added plus.

Her friendship had come to mean so much to him over the last couple of weeks. And he was so relieved that Caroline was no longer upset about the accident with Emma.

He scraped another bite together before asking, "How's Emma's knee?"

"It's fine." She stopped. "Andrew, I'm truly sorry about yesterday."

"Forget it."

She reached across the table and laid her hand on top of his. "I shouldn't have talked to you that way."

He patted her hand, resisted the instinct to turn it over and trace the lines on her palm. One thing was certain: He didn't want to let her go.

"I've already forgotten."

"You're a *gut freind*, Andrew Fitch."

"As are you, Caroline Hostetler. As are you."

"So . . ." She pulled her hand away as yet another awkward moment stretched between them. Did she feel it too? Maybe it was just him trying to work through all the feelings he'd held for Beth. "Are we back on for dinner tomorrow night?"

He'd been so upset over the fact that Caroline was angry that he had completely forgotten about their plans to get Abe and Esther to fall in love. *"Jah, jah,"* he said as he chewed the last bite of pie. "Your *haus* or mine?"

A small frown puckered her brow.

"I heard it in a movie once."

"A movie?"

"A motion picture show."

"I know what one is," Caroline answered, "I just didn't know any districts that allowed them."

Andrew chuckled. "It's not like that. I only saw one on my *rumspringa*. Best thing ever."

"Really?"

"It's the only thing about the *Englisch* world I could really get used to."

"Why is that?"

"I don't know really. It was just amazing. You walk into

this big room and the lights are dim and the picture is so big. It's like being in a completely different world."

"Now I can see why they are banned."

Andrew shrugged. "It would definitely take a body's attention away from God. What was your favorite part of *rumspringa*?"

She shifted uncomfortably in her seat. "I'd better get this pie plate back to the bakery before it's a stuck-on mess."

He reached out to stop her from walking away. "You don't want to talk about your *rumspringa*?"

She shook her head, her eyes on the empty pie plate she held. "My district doesn't condone a run-around time for the youth."

"Really? I mean, I have heard of that, just never met someone who was in such a district." He resisted the crazy urge to clasp her hands in his once more and rub his thumb across the smooth skin.

"They really exist."

"But how do you know if you want to join the church?"

"The bishop feels you either do or you don't. No amount of tasting the pleasures of the world is going to settle down a heart that wants what is on the outside."

"Is that how you ended up here?"

Caroline shook her head. "That's a long story."

For sure and for certain, she didn't want to talk about it. He could tell.

Andrew gestured toward the plate in her hands. "I suppose that's becoming a stuck-on mess."

"It is at that."

"Some other time then?"

"Jah."

Andrew watched her go, wondering what she was trying to hide.

* * *

Why, oh why was she always sticking her foot into a mess where Andrew was concerned? Caroline jerked open the door to the bakery, the bell above the door jangling frantically.

Esther came bustling in from the back, her cheeks pink from the heat of the ovens and the extra exertion.

"Caroline." She pressed a hand to her chest as if to slow her heart. "You scared me. *Was iss letz?*"

What is wrong?

Andrew is too nice by far? I want to tell him how much he's come to mean to me and answer all his many questions, but if I do will he forever look at me differently?

"Nothing," she mumbled.

"It doesn't seem like nothing the way you came flying in here."

"Just pulled the door too hard, that is all."

Maybe she was too sensitive, maybe she was guilt ridden. But when he had asked her about her run-around time, she had panicked and fled. Now she owed him another explanation.

"Now who is the one not telling the truth?"

Caroline shook her head. She had kept her secret for nigh on two years. There was no sense in sharing it now. It would only breed distrust and more problems for everyone involved.

Nay, her secret was one best not shared.

Amy Lillard

You can't go back on your word, so you have to think
about your future. A kompromatch is not a choice I
dream of for you. Are you ... but wedding? Father, ...
just as he died out.

Dear Mamm,

As we head further into the growing season, the differences between Wells Landing and Ethridge become more and more noticeable. The soil here is very rocky, and the men use tractors to farm their fields. The bishop also allows the men to drive the tractors into town and sometimes even to church!

The hardest change for me to get used to is living in town. It's convenient to be so close to everything, the stores and such, but I miss the chirp of the insects at night, eating green apples in the spring, and the horses.

I have a new friend here that lives on a farm. He invited me and Emma out after church, and we got to see the horses and puppies he has on his farm. That is one thing I wish for Emma. It saddens me that she won't grow up in the country, walking barefoot through the grass, milking goats and tending the tomatoes like I did.

We have a gut life here, gut friends, and a fine business. But there are times when I can't help but wish things had turned out a bit different. That's when I pray and work even harder to understand what God has in store for me and Emma.

I miss you and Dat so very much. I understand that he is still upset with me and has declared that

you may not mention my name to him. But I ask that at night when he is asleep, please whisper in his ear and tell him that I love him. And I always will.
   Ich liebe dich too.

                                        Love,
                                        Caroline

Chapter Eight

Caroline looked up from the pan of cookies she had just slid into the oven to see Andrew enter the bakery.

"Hi, Caroline." He whipped his hat from his head, and she was struck immediately with the urge to fluff the dark, silky strands.

"Hello." She twisted her hands in the fabric of her flour-streaked apron to still their absurd impulse. She had never been so bold. Not with anyone but Trey, and look how that turned out. *"Wie geht?"*

"I wanted to make sure that we are still planning on dinner tonight."

"Jah." Caroline threw a look over her shoulder toward Esther. Then she dropped her voice. "Have him here at seven. We'll eat and play a board game, then you and I can go out to the park. That'll give them plenty of time together."

Andrew chuckled. "It might be better if we stayed. *Onkle* isn't good at picking up on subtleties."

Caroline returned his laugh. "You may be onto something." She had debated on telling Andrew about Esther's declaration to give up on Abe, but since Esther had changed her mind, Caroline kept that information to herself.

How many secrets was she going to keep from him? She pushed the thought away and concentrated on what he was saying.

"We could send them out to . . . to . . . walk." Andrew shook his head. "I'm not sure that will make a difference. Maybe we should stick to our original plan."

"I think you may be right."

"*Goedemiddag*, Andrew."

Caroline jumped as Esther spoke behind her. "*Gut himmel.* You scared me."

Esther smiled as Caroline's heart continued to pound in her chest. More than anything Caroline wanted Esther and Abe to fall in love, but she didn't want her dearest friend to know that she and Andrew had any sort of hand in the matter.

"So tonight?" Andrew asked.

"Tonight what?" Esther asked, reaching into the display counter and pulling out a pastry. "Whoopie pie?" she asked, offering it to Andrew.

"*Danki.*" He accepted it with a grateful smile, then took a huge bite, leaving Caroline to answer.

"Andrew and I were talking about getting together tonight for supper."

Esther clapped her hands together. "What a *gut* idea. The two of you can go down to the restaurant, and I'll keep Emma."

Caroline shook her head. "*Nay!* I mean, Andrew and I were talking about sharing a meal. All four of us. Me, you, him, and Abe Fitch."

But Esther was already planning her own evening. "Perfect. He and I can keep Emma while you two go out."

"But I—"

Thankfully, Andrew picked that moment to swallow and

jump into the conversation. "Why don't we all go to the restaurant for dinner?"

"That's a fine idea, Andrew. A fine idea indeed."

He smiled, satisfied with his save.

Caroline breathed a small sigh of relief. "Seven o'clock?"

Andrew finished off the sweet treat then licked the filling from his fingers. "Seven o'clock."

"Onkle," Andrew started as the clock ticked steadily toward the hour of seven. "I thought you might want to change your shirt before we leave."

"Eh?" His uncle looked up from his work with the hand plane and pushed his glasses a little farther up the bridge of his nose.

Andrew tempered his sigh so it was not quite as discouraged as he felt. "You should change your shirt before we go to dinner."

Abe looked down at himself, then back up to Andrew. "This shirt is *allrecht*."

He shook his head. "It's covered with sawdust."

Abe glanced down again, brushing the fine particles from his shirt front. "We're just going to Kauffman's."

Andrew shook his head. "But we're going with Esther and Caroline."

"You want to go courtin', so I have to change my shirt."

"What if I told you that I think Esther likes you?"

But Andrew had no more started the sentence before Abe was once again bent over his latest project, smoothing out a rough spot his loving hands had found.

"Onkle?"

"Eh?"

"Are you going to change your shirt?"

Abe looked down at himself. *"Jah?"*

Andrew laughed. *"Jah, Onkle."*

Abe ran his hand over the spot again, then with a satisfied nod, went to the back room to fetch the extra shirt he kept there.

He returned moments later, pulling his galluses over his shoulders as he walked. Thankfully he had washed his hands, and the strands of hair surrounding his face were dark and shiny with water. It was more than Andrew could have hoped for.

"Ready?" he asked as Abe started past his workbench and slowed. He ran his hand across the top of the bureau he was crafting, an unsatisfied frown wrinkling his brow.

"Just let me—"

Andrew rolled his eyes affectionately and grasped Abe by the elbow. "Come now, *Onkle*. We have women waiting."

Kauffman's was busy for a Thursday night. Caroline crowded in with the rest of the group, rubbing elbows with tourists waiting on their own tables.

Millie Fisher ran by, a pitcher of tea in one hand and a pitcher of water in the other. "I am so sorry," she called to the group at large. "I will have you a table as soon as I can." Then she hurried away to fill drinks.

Abe stroked his beard. "Looks like a bus must have come in."

Caroline absently rubbed Emma's back as she looked around. "Maybe two." Every table was crowded with *Englischers* wearing shorts and T-shirts. Most of the shirts were the same, telling her without a doubt a tour bus had come into Wells Landing.

Esther tsked. "The chamber of commerce usually tells us so we can be prepared."

"But it's good for the town, right?" Andrew asked.

"Jah," Abe said.

Millie picked that moment to return and join in the conversation. "But it's also *gut* to have enough staff on hand to care for them."

"I think we should make other plans for supper tonight," Abe said, glancing around the room once again.

Caroline barely saw the crestfallen look on Esther's face before the other woman hid it behind her usual smile. "I suppose it would be best."

"I don't know about you, but I'm *hungerich*." Andrew patted his belly.

"If we eat here, it's going to be a while," Caroline said, adjusting Emma into a more comfortable spot on her hip.

"Why don't you put in an order to go?" Millie suggested.

Caroline looked at the milling people. Some were sitting, but most stood as all the chairs in the entry had been taken. "I guess we could wait at the bakery."

"I have a better idea." Andrew's so-blue eyes sparkled with something akin to mischief. "We can go play a board game."

"I could give you a call when it's ready," Millie suggested.

"That would be *gut*." Andrew's dimples slashed, and Caroline knew that he was quite pleased with the idea. Strange, though; a small part of her felt a little sad that he was only happy because it gave them the perfect excuse to get Esther and Abe together. There was another little part of her that wished he would be just as happy to spend the time with her.

They placed their orders and nudged their way out the door and to the sidewalk.

"It's going to be busy tomorrow," Esther said as they started toward the bakery.

"Jah," Abe agreed.

Andrew shot Caroline a look.

Tomorrow would be a busy day with two busloads of *Englischers* milling about, buying goods and taking pictures of everything from the *kinner* to their laundry lines. But hopefully the increased foot traffic would keep down the questions Caroline would have to face at lunch tomorrow. Really, she loved her *freinden*, but they seemed determined to marry her off to the first Amish man to come along.

Yet as determined as Lorie and Emily were, Caroline knew it would only delay the inevitable. It was no wonder they thought they saw a relationship brewing between her and Andrew. It was what they *wanted* to see. But would it be so bad?

She pushed the thoughts away as Esther unlocked the doors to their backroom apartment and lit the propane lamps. Caroline had had her chance at that kind of happiness, and it had slipped through her fingers.

"She looks heavy. Do you want me to take her?" Andrew sidled up beside her as they walked into the *schtupp*.

The family room.

Family. That was what they looked like standing there. Mother, father, baby.

"I'm fine," she managed to say through the knot of emotions.

But even as she said the words, Emma leaned toward Andrew, begging him to hold her. Caroline had no choice but to let her go.

Andrew's smile beamed. "I think she likes me."

What's not to like? "*Jah*, I think she does."

Esther chose that moment to return to the room, Scrabble and Upwords in her arms. "That's because you sneak her cookies when Caroline isn't looking."

"Andrew." Caroline turned toward him.

The faint pink of a blush stained his face from forehead to chin and even reached down to his neck.

"I just wanted her to like me."

She couldn't really be mad at him. "Now that you have accomplished your goal, will you please switch to apples or carrots?"

Andrew made a face and bounced Emma on his hip. "I suppose."

But he whispered something to the toddler, and Caroline was certain it was a promise for cookies to be mixed in with the healthier foods.

Caroline shook her head with a smile and sat down at the table.

Andrew sat down across from her, Emma still in his arms.

"You can't play Scrabble and hold her."

He raised one dark brow in a look so mischievous, it made her almost laugh. "Are you afraid I'll have an unfair advantage?"

"I just—" *I'm just not used to having people to help. To hold Emma, to share her with.* "She's getting too big to carry around all the time."

Andrew smoothed a hand down Emma's dark curls. "When she gets too heavy I'll let you know."

Out of reasonable protests, Caroline let the matter drop.

Esther set up the board while Abe passed out the letter stands. They each chose their tiles and the game began.

"English or *Deutsch*?"

"Deutsch," Andrew said on top of Caroline's request of "English."

Abe looked from one of them to the other, then back to Esther.

She shrugged. "English," Esther said. "How often do you get to work on English spelling?"

"That's a *gut* idea," Abe said. "The four of us hail from three different districts, which means three different *Deutsch* spellings."

Esther blushed at the compliment and smoothed the pleats of her apron.

"*Jah*, you're right," Andrew agreed. "It would be harder to play in *Deutsch* since the language was never formally written down."

"English it is," Abe said.

"I'll get the dictionary." Caroline pushed to her feet and went to fetch it.

"No looking for words," Esther said emphatically. "That's cheating. You have to have a word in mind to use the dictionary. Agreed?"

"Agreed," they echoed.

"One more thing," Andrew added as Caroline set the book on the side of the table. "Can we have a snack while we play? I'm hungry."

"Dinner will be ready in just a little bit," Caroline said, but Esther was already on her feet.

She returned moments later with a plate stacked high with tiny slices of bread covered in a creamy white cheese.

"This is something we've been working on at the bakery."

"What is it?" Abe eyed the offering with a look akin to distrust.

Andrew apparently had a more adventuresome outlook and snagged three of them before Esther could make room on the table.

"It's a bruschetta. A toasted bread with goat cheese. We thought the *Englischers* might like it."

"I know I do." Andrew reached for another piece and gave it to Emma before grabbing another for himself.

"You're going to be too full for supper," Caroline chastised with a smile and a shake of her head to take the sting from her words.

"Don't be so sure," Esther said. "My John could out-eat men twice his size."

"Jah," Andrew agreed. "I would eat even more if I farmed."

"I don't know where you put it all." Caroline shook her head just as the phone rang.

"That must be the restaurant."

Esther deposited the plate on the table and rushed to the front of the bakery where the business phone was located.

While she was gone, Caroline took Emma from Andrew and sat her in the high chair. The toddler slapped her hands against the tray as if demanding food.

Andrew chuckled. "Someone else is still hungry too, I see."

"Jah, but the *boppli* is still growing."

Andrew pulled a hurt face. "I am too."

Everyone laughed.

"Come on." Andrew motioned to Caroline to follow him to the door. "Let's go get the food. There's no sense in everyone walking down there."

He was absolutely right. But what a perfect plan for them to go and leave Esther and Abe with a little time alone. *Ach,* alone with a fifteen-month-old. But at least they'd have to make some sort of conversation with each other.

"I think this night is a big success," Andrew said as they started down the sidewalk back toward the Kauffman Family Restaurant.

"Jah." Caroline nodded, the strings of her prayer *kapp* dancing around her shoulders. "I was worried when I saw that the restaurant was so full."

"But this is better, *jah*? We can eat and talk and not have to worry about gawking *Englischers*."

"They mean well, don't you think?"

Andrew shrugged.

"I heard there were places in Pennsylvania where they let the *Englischers* take pictures as long as the Plain folk don't pose for them."

"That's the craziest thing I've ever heard," Andrew replied. "A picture is a picture. I don't know how one could be better than another."

A wave of shame washed over Caroline. There were three pictures that she treasured. One of Emma, one of Trey, and one of herself and Trey together. It was all she had left of him. Once her father had found out what she had done, he had gone into her room and searched until he found her secret box filled with mementoes of her time with Trey—a dried flower, a paperback copy of *Romeo and Juliet*, and the plastic ring he had given her at the carnival.

Then her father had destroyed all her reminders, all except the one she carried inside.

"Caroline?"

"Jah?" At the sound of Andrew's voice, she turned her attention back to the present. She had sworn not to live in the past. What was done was done. There was no going back. No future in the past.

"You were a million miles away."

Not quite so many. "I'm sorry." She realized that he was standing with the door open, waiting on her to go into the restaurant. *"Ach*, sorry," she said again and set her feet into motion.

Millie brought their food to the front of the restaurant and handed it to them with a tired smile. The number of diners had dropped off, giving the staff a little bit of a break.

"Caroline?"

She should have known this would happen. Caroline turned to face her friend. "Hi, Lorie. What are you doing here at night?"

Lorie's smile stretched far and wide. "They called me in since they were so busy. The question here is, what are you doing here?"

"Andrew and I came down to pick up some food for his uncle and Esther."

Lorie nodded in a manner that clearly said she didn't believe a word of it.

Caroline would have a lot of explaining to do to get out of this one. Tomorrow's lunch would be filled with a hundred questions about why she was seen at the diner with Andrew Fitch. Even though there was nothing to it. Why did girls see things where nothing existed? Caroline shook her head.

"Danki," Andrew said, accepting the large, handled to-go sack from Millie.

"Gern gschehne," Millie said with a smile of her own.

"Ready, Caroline?"

"Jah," she said, then turned back to Lorie. "It's a sin to gossip," Caroline reminded her.

Lorie's smile got a little bit wider. "But I only speak the truth, *mein freind.*"

"What was that all about?" Andrew asked once they were back on the sidewalk in front of the restaurant.

"Nix."

"If it was nothing, then why are you frowning and running like the devil is on your heels?"

Caroline slowed her steps. "I—" Truth was she didn't know why she was so angry. But she did not want everyone to get the wrong impression. "I don't want people to think there's more to our friendship than . . . well, friendship."

"Seems to me what matters most is what's in our hearts."

Caroline expelled the breath she had been holding. *"Ach,* you're right."

Andrew smiled that dazzling smile that warmed her from the inside out. "Of course I am."

He opened the door and Caroline stepped into the apartment just ahead of him. "Be careful, you don't want to bang that swelled head of yours on the door frame."

Andrew laughed. "Are you saying I've got a big head?"

"I'm saying vanity is frowned upon."

"I'll try to remember that," he said with a chuckle. Then he nodded to the table where Abe and Esther sat, heads close together as they looked through a book that lay open in front of them.

Seems like our plan is working after all. The thought warmed her almost as much as Andrew's smile.

"Supper's here."

"Ach, gut," Abe said, looking up from the Bible he and Esther had been reading. "I'm ready to eat."

"And then afterward we'll start our Scrabble game," Esther added. "Biblical words only."

"That's a fine idea," Caroline said. Then she smiled to herself and said a small prayer of thanks that the Lord had blessed her with such good friends.

Emma fell asleep just after supper. Caroline was amazed that the child could rest so well with all of the noise the adults were making as they played their word games. Yet the toddler had always been in the middle of things, baking times and party preparations, so it was no wonder she could sleep through the boisterous game raging in the dining area of the tiny apartment.

Once the last tile had been played, Caroline wiped the tears of laughter on the tail end of her apron and gave a sigh. She hadn't had this much fun in . . . well, she never remembered having this much fun ever in her life.

The thought was sobering.

She glanced from Abe and Esther as they gathered up the tiles, still playfully arguing over the use of proper names within their biblical-words-only game.

Esther reached for the corner of the board as Abe did the same. Their hands collided somewhere in the middle.

They stopped dead still that way, Abe staring at their touching hands, Esther staring at Abe.

Maybe Abe wasn't immune to Esther's charms after all.

Andrew cleared his throat behind her. "Would you like to take a quick walk?"

Caroline hid her smile as he shifted from one foot to the other. She wasn't sure if it was the budding romance before them that made him so uncomfortable or the part he was playing in their little charade.

She patted her stomach, joining in as best she could. "*Jah*, I could use a walk to burn off some of that chocolate pie we ate."

Caroline turned back to Esther, but the other woman only had eyes for Abe Fitch.

"Esther?"

"Jah?" Esther tore her gaze from Abe and finally turned her attention to Caroline.

"Andrew and I are going for a walk. Will you and Abe be all right? I mean, can you listen for Emma for me?"

Esther nodded as Abe folded the game board and handed it to her.

"I could use another cup of coffee," Abe hinted.

Esther's smile deepened. "I'll go start a fresh pot."

"We won't be gone long." Andrew took Caroline's elbow and led her toward the door.

Abe waved a hand toward them as he stared toward the kitchen door where Esther had recently disappeared. "Take your time," he said, still watching the door. "Take your time."

Caroline managed to hold her laughter until they were a fair distance across the street. She wouldn't do anything to hurt Abe or Esther, but this budding romance between the two of them was as sweet as sugar. How could she not find joy in the simple affection they were discovering together?

"Sometimes I wonder if Esther really thinks we are becoming more than friends or if she has finally realized we're working on getting her and Abe together." Caroline collapsed into one of the swings, clutching her sides from holding back her mirth.

"I think she figured it out tonight."

She shook her head as Andrew took the seat next to her. "It may not be so easy to get them to fall in love."

"Don't be so surprised if it's not. I do believe my *onkle* Abe is smitten."

Caroline laughed. "Smitten? I've seen him look at blocks of wood with more affection."

"I said smitten, not full-out love."

Caroline dissolved into giggles and used her feet to push her swing into motion. How long had it been since she had enjoyed the simple pleasure of swinging, the wind on her face, the strings of her prayer *kapp* trailing behind her?

Too long.

She came to the park nigh on every day to eat lunch and allow Emma to play. But it had been a very long time since she had come for the simple pleasure of being there herself.

She pumped her legs and took her swing even higher, reaching out her toes like she had when she was a young girl. Back then she was sure that she could touch the sky. But those were silly, foolish dreams. Just like the ones she had about her and Trey. Silly. Foolish. Destined to fail from the very beginning.

All of a sudden a dark cloud surrounded her mood. Why was it these days that every time she felt overabundance of joy, thoughts of Trey, of what might have been, of her family and all the mistakes that she had made crashed her back to reality?

"You better slow down."

Caroline pumped harder, only then realizing that Andrew had abandoned his swing and stood far in front of her, watching with worried eyes as she tried to touch the stars.

But there were no stars to touch, just faraway lights that twinkled and mocked and beckoned a reckless heart like her own.

Reckless.

That was the exact word her father used to describe her behavior. Reckless.

Caroline let go of the swing, flying through the air for mere seconds, an eternity, before crashing down, stumbling. Then Andrew's arms were around her, steadying her. Preventing her from falling.

She drew in a sharp breath. Her body tingled where he held her, scorched where it collided with his. But all that was just a trick of the night.

Her bishop back home had said to beware of the night. A body never knew what was lurking in the darkness. Friend or foe, the Lord or Lucifer. A person couldn't tell until it was too late.

Breathless, she turned her face up to Andrew's, needing to see his eyes, the face of a friend, and know that she was safe.

But when her eyes met his, something changed, something

shifted, and no longer did the night seem like it harbored danger. It was just her and Andrew and the shadows.

Then as if a shutter had been drawn, the keen light in his eyes was gone and nothing was in its place.

Using his hold on her arms, the grasp that had so recently saved her from falling, Andrew set her away from him.

Caroline swayed and almost lost her balance before she regained her footing.

Had she done something wrong? "Andrew?"

He turned away, shook his head, and stared toward the dark thatch of trees in the center of the town square.

It was too soon for him. Way too soon to be thinking about courtin' another, and yet there it was. The zing of her touch, the sizzle whenever she was near, and all the other signs that the *Englisch* wrote about in their romance books. He should know; he'd seen his share of them growing up. Oh, never out in the open, but tucked under quilts and hidden in treasure boxes under the bed. He'd even found one buried in the hayloft. With six sisters, it was no wonder.

That was how he recognized the signs, but this was not something he wanted. He had only lost Beth a few short months ago. He wasn't ready for love, he wasn't ready to forget the girl he'd known he wanted to marry since he was big enough to form thoughts into words.

He didn't want to love Caroline. Didn't want to respond to her. Best to keep his distance and let whatever it was he felt when she was near die a natural death. It seemed the only way he'd be able to fight it now. And fight it he must.

He turned away from her, not missing the flash of hurt in those pretty hazel eyes before she was out of his line of vision.

Hurt or not, it was better this way.

"Tell my *onkle* I'll wait for him at the shop."

* * *

Caroline tossed and turned long into the night. She was confused, and she prayed, but she wanted those answers in that moment. She had no patience to see what God had in store for her. Aside from Esther, Lorie, and Emily, Andrew was the best friend she had. And she didn't want to lose him. As a friend . . . or even more.

But something had happened between them tonight. If she were being honest with herself, it had happened a long time ago, the first time she saw him crossing the street cradling the rails of the very bed she lay in. The first time she had fallen headfirst into the sea blue of his crystalline eyes.

There was just something special about Andrew Fitch. And rather than saddle him with her problems, she opted to be his friend. She had jumped at the chance when he had offered it to her.

But now . . .

Well, now things were different.

She wouldn't be able to fool herself in to believing that she just wanted to be his *freind*, that his touch didn't make her heart skip a beat or his laugh bring a joy to her day.

Caroline rolled toward the inside of the bed, quietly pushing the dark curls off Emma's forehead. She couldn't think only of herself.

Emma was her world. The reason she got up each day, the reason she worked hard and continued on. She had given up everything for Emma, her life in Tennessee, her girlish hopes and dreams. And once she lost Trey . . . Emma had become her everything.

Caroline raised onto one arm in order to kiss her sleeping baby. Precious.

She might be reckless but Emma was precious, by far the

best of her and Trey combined. She was a gift from the Lord, and Caroline silently vowed to always treat her as such.

Regardless of anything she felt for Andrew Fitch now and in the future.

She closed her eyes and willed her heart to obey her words.

Dear Mamm,

It's amazing to me how two districts can call themselves Amish and be so different. Here in Wells Landing, so many of us make our living selling our wares to the English.

They come by the busload to stay at the Yoder Bed and Breakfast. They buy cases of jelly, stacks of quilts, and platters of baked goods. Anything and everything that has to do with Plain people.

Which reminds me, danki for making the doll for Emma. Seeing your tiny, even stitches brought tears to my eyes. Holding her first doll in my hands made me realize how quickly she is growing up. Did you feel the same as I grew and started to school?

It certainly gives me a new perspective on the Ordnung. Now I see that the rules aren't there to keep us from being individuals, but to protect us from a world that would pull us down into temptation. How strange that looking back at that summer I can see my mistakes so clearly, but at the time, I really thought I had my best interests in mind.

I know this won't change how Dat feels about me, or the troubles I have brought to my family, but it makes me understand how the two of you just wanted to keep me safe. Just as I strive every day to keep my dochder safe. It all makes sense now, even if it is too late.

Every morning and every night I pray that Dat will be able to forgive me soon. I know I will never be able to return to live in Tennessee, but I would like to know that I am forgiven by him as I do the best I can with the situation I am in.

I love you and miss you. Dat too.

Love,
Caroline

Chapter Nine

As Esther predicted, Friday was busy with the bus tourists crawling all over the town, doing everything in their power to experience all that they could of the Amish lifestyle in a short period of time.

The increased customer load as well as the normal orders and walk-ins had Esther and Caroline working straight through lunch to get the necessary items baked.

She was certain that Lorie and the other employees at the Kauffman restaurant were hard at work as well. Only Emily, who taught school to the scholars in their district, would not be affected by the number of tourists.

But her reprieve from the hundreds of questions her *freinden* would ask was only postponed until another day. Most probably Monday, when they would all meet back at the park for lunch.

With any luck, by then Emily and Lorie would see that she and Andrew were no more than friends.

Less than, if the look on his face the night before was any indication.

For a moment there in his arms she had felt something, a kinship, a rightness that she had never felt before. But then his expression changed, his eyes closed off, and she felt as if she were looking at a stranger.

She had no idea what she had done wrong.

Or maybe it wasn't a matter of something she did. Perhaps she had only thought there was something more in Andrew's eyes and she was mistaken.

"Are you okay?" Esther came up beside her, wiping her pink cheeks on the tail of her apron.

"*Jah*, why?"

"That's the thirteenth time you've looked out the window and sighed."

Caroline shook her head. "That's impossible."

"I may have missed a couple of times." Esther smiled in her kindly way and Caroline found herself wishing she could relive the night before. Maybe change the outcome between her and Andrew. But since that wasn't possible, she would just have to figure out a way to get her friend back. Or learn to live without him.

"It's strange, isn't it?"

"Huh?" Caroline turned to face Esther, only then realizing she had been lost in her own thoughts once again.

"I said it's strange."

"What's strange?"

"How you meet a person and in a very little time they become so very important to you."

"*Jah.*" All Caroline could do was agree.

"Take you and Andrew, for example."

Caroline shook her head. "There is nothing between me and Andrew Fitch."

"Are you saying that you haven't been staring out the window waiting for him to come in like he's done every day this week?"

"I didn't say that, but—"

Esther patted her hand. "It's okay, dear. It was the same

way with me and my John. I saw him one day. I mean really looked at him and knew that sometime in the future he'd be the most important person in my life."

"That's not how it is—"

"I know you say he's just your friend, but they are important too, *jah*?"

So very important. Esther was right. Somehow in the course of just a couple of weeks Andrew had grown important to her. Whatever happened between them last night needed to be cleared up.

"No time like right now."

Caroline glanced around the bakery. Everyone seemed to be doing okay. Customers sat at tables and enjoyed a snack and a fresh-brewed cup of *kaffi*. Some milled round, gazing into the large glass pastry cases as they tried to decide on their afternoon treat. The line of waiting patrons no longer snaked out the door and down the sidewalk in front of the bakery.

"I've got Jodie here to help if I get busy. Why don't you go on down and talk to him."

"Emma—" Caroline started, knowing it was nothing more than an excuse.

"She's fine right where she is."

It was the truth. Caroline could hear her babbling play floating in from the back room of the bakery.

She reached behind her to untie her cooking apron. As usual, she was covered in flour.

With a shy smile, their afternoon helper, fifteen-year-old Jodie Miller, handed Caroline a fresh apron.

Esther used a damp cloth to wipe clean the flour she had somehow managed to get on her back as Caroline smoothed down the sides of her hair and tucked any wayward strands back under her prayer *kapp*. She repinned the sides and took a deep breath. "How do I look?"

Esther reached up and pinched Caroline's cheeks. "Now that you have a little color? Perfect."

Caroline smiled, running her hands down her front. "I'll be back as soon as I can."

"Take all the time you need."

The old cowbell over the door clanked out its warning.

Danny had gone back out to the farm to get a few more of the wooden toys that Abe kept on hand for the tourists. They seemed to love all things Amish, and the simplistic games were no exception. But it was too soon for Danny's return.

His uncle had just gone out the back way, heading down to the hardware store for the new saw blade the manager there had ordered. But Andrew wouldn't put it past him to have forgotten something and come in the front to fetch it.

But most probably it was an *Englischer* looking for one last memento before loading back onto the bus that brought them to Wells Landing.

With a tired sigh, he set aside the sandpaper and wiped his hands on a rag before heading into the showroom.

But it wasn't a tourist, Danny, or his uncle standing nervously by the door.

"Caroline." He stopped short, his feet refusing to take him farther into the room.

"Andrew." She seemed to be as anxious as he felt. "I was hoping we might talk for a minute."

"I'm here alone right now. Meet you in the park in fifteen minutes?"

"It's hot out today. How about the diner?"

"I'll be there."

Fifteen minutes later, Andrew pushed his way into the

Kauffman Family Restaurant. As it was too late for the lunch crowd and too early for supper, only a few stragglers were still seated.

It was easy to spot Caroline, sitting in the front at a small table, cup of coffee steaming in front of her.

She looked up as he sat down, tipping his hat a little farther back on his head to better see her face.

"Would you like a cup of *kaffi*?"

He shook his head, unsure of where the conversation was headed. But he had an idea.

He'd seen that vulnerable look in her eyes last night, searching, expecting, wanting.

But what she had in mind was more than he was willing to give. He'd do best to start this before she said something both of them would regret.

"It's not that you aren't a fine woman, Caroline." He coughed. "I mean, any Amish man worth his salt would be more than *froh* to have you as his wife. But—"

"You don't have to say anything else."

"Jah, but I do. If we're going to continue to be friends, the people around us are going to assume there is more than that between us. The least I can do is tell you the truth."

He took her hand into his own, squeezed it once, then let it go. He enjoyed the solid feel of her hand in his. Caroline was strong, sure, and true. He didn't feel like he might break her if he tightened his grip. Nor could he become accustomed to the softness of her skin.

He took a deep, shuddering breath. He hadn't spoken about this since the day they buried her. To bring it up again would be like pouring salt in a fresh wound. Yet he cared enough about Caroline to do just that.

"I had promised to marry someone. Her name was Beth." He stopped. Sometimes it hurt to say her name out loud, but this time the pain didn't come. "She was as sweet as honey, such a good *maedel* was my Beth."

He paused, lining up his thoughts in order to speak them aloud. "She lived in the next house over from mine. My father's pasture and her father's pasture butted up against each other. I don't ever remember a time when I did not know her. All my life she lived right next door, and all my life I knew that one day she would be my *fraa*. God had other plans, is all."

The words didn't shred his insides when he said them, a true indicator that time could take away hurts. Time and prayer. He prayed every night for understanding. He'd always known that it was in God's plan for Beth to be taken earlier than most. But he had at least wanted the chance to show her how much he loved her, to make her his wife and live, if only for a little while, as married couples do.

"Tell me what she looked like."

"Her hair was dark, like the cocoa powder my *mamm* used in her chocolate pies, and her eyes were the same. She was small and frail."

He hadn't realized until that moment that he had taken Caroline's hand into his own again. He squeezed it gently, fully intending to let her go once the action was complete. But he couldn't make himself complete the task. He kept on holding her hand, and Caroline kept on letting him.

"Was she *grank*?"

"*Jah*. She had been born with a bad heart. We always knew that she would not live with us long."

"But you loved her anyway." The words did not accuse, merely let him know she understood.

"You don't get to pick and choose who you love." He turned to look at her then, his heart breaking at the sight of the glittering tears in her hazel eyes.

"I'm so sorry, Andrew. That must have been terribly difficult for you."

He nodded, swallowing down his own sorrow.

"And that's why you decided to come to Wells Landing?"

"I thought it would be *gut* to have a different view for a while."

She dipped her chin, then picked up her cup and took a sip. The action seemed uncomfortable.

"You know what it's like, losing someone who you've loved."

She jerked her gaze back to his. *"Jah,"* she said quietly. "I do."

A heartbeat thumped between them, and the feeling of well-being passed over Andrew. She hadn't gotten up and walked away. She hadn't gotten angry or accused him with those big hazel eyes of hers.

The person who had come to mean the most to him since Beth died had understood. It was more than he could have prayed for.

Caroline took a deep breath. "Andrew?"

"Jah?"

She shook her head. *"Nix."* She placed some coins on the table and stood. "I've get to get back to work."

He grasped her hand before she could leave. "See you Sunday?"

"It's not a church Sunday."

"Jonah Miller is trying to get together a volleyball game. I thought we might could go."

Her gaze centered somewhere around his left ear. "That would be *gut.*"

Caroline couldn't have asked for a *purtier* day. Sunday dawned with clear blue skies and not a cloud in sight.

"Why don't you go with us?" Caroline asked Esther over breakfast.

Esther shook her head. "You young people go on and have a *gut* time."

"It's not like that," Caroline protested, handing Emma a hunk of banana to go with her toast.

She should be ashamed of herself, but Caroline enjoyed the off Sunday from church. Monday through Saturday she worked at the bakery, only taking time to have lunch and put Emma down for a nap before working until the sun went down. Sunday's three-hour church service didn't leave a lot of time for much else other than traveling to the meeting, eating, and traveling back. It was good to have one day where she didn't have to rush around, get Emma fed and out the door.

"I've seen how you look at that boy."

Caroline's shoulders stiffened involuntarily. "What do you mean by that?"

Esther's tone turned serious as she reached across the table and clasped Caroline's fingers in her own plump grasp. "It's been two years since Emma's *dat* . . . Well, I think you deserve to find love again."

Caroline shook her head, hoping to dislodge the lump in her throat. "Esther, I—"

"I know it's painful to talk about, and you don't have to tell me anything that brings back those *baremlich* memories. I loved my John as long as the day. But I saved my love and my life for him after he was gone until I may have waited too late to find love again. I don't want to see that happen to you."

Love hurt entirely too much, but Caroline wasn't about to tell Esther that. Just thinking the words was sad enough. "Andrew is here to heal a grieving heart," she said instead.

"Sounds like someone else I know." Esther rose from the table as a knock sounded on their door. "That must be him."

Caroline eyed her daughter with a sigh. Banana was smeared in her dark wispy curls, and it looked as if she got more toast up her nose than in her mouth. Now Andrew was at the door and ready to go.

That was what she got for lollygagging around.

"You get the door, I'll get Emma," Esther said, but Caroline shook her head.

"I'll get Emma." Esther did way too much for them already. It wouldn't do for Caroline to take advantage of another's generosity.

Esther gave her a strange look before shaking her head and opening the door.

"*Guder mariye.*" Andrew took off his hat as he stepped into their tiny apartment. He smiled at them both, looking almost as nervous as Caroline felt.

She turned her attention back to wiping the banana out of her *boppli*'s hair. When had she gotten so nervous that her stomach was jumping rope like a scholar at recess? Or maybe the question was why?

"I guess I should be leaving for the Bible reading." Esther tied her black bonnet under her chin. "Unless you need some help."

Caroline shook her head. "I'm fine. You go on and have a *gut* time."

Esther frowned, but nodded. "I'll see you at supper."

"We'll only be a few more minutes," Caroline called after Esther had gone.

She groaned with dismay as she looked down at her dress. While she had been so busy trying to clean Emma's face and hair, the child had grabbed her dress with both messy hands. Now Caroline had almost as much breakfast on her as Emma did.

"Can I help?"

Caroline jumped as Andrew's voice sounded right behind her. She shook her head. "I can manage."

"I know you can manage, but can I help?" He smiled. "I feel like we've had this conversation before."

Emma reached her now-clean hands toward him, leaning against Caroline's hold.

"Come here, wee one," he said, planting a kiss on the baby's sweet cheek.

Caroline could only stare. It was strange to see a man kiss her daughter. There were no *onkles* or *grossdaadis* to shower affection onto the child. The action was a first for Caroline. But she was more than shocked. She was perhaps a little bit jealous. She and Andrew had had a moment of sorts that night in the park. He had pulled away from her then, yet he could sprinkle kisses in Emma's hair as if that was his purpose for being born.

She pushed away the silly thoughts. "If—if you can hold her for a minute, I'll go change."

"*Gut* plan."

Caroline hesitated only a moment more before making her way to her room to change. As she dressed, she tried to ignore the baby giggles floating in from the family room.

Emma adored Andrew, and it seemed as if the feeling was mutual.

"You sure have a way with *boppli*," Caroline said as she came back into the room. Andrew was sitting on the floor stacking blocks with Emma. As soon as he got four on top of each other, she toppled them down, then laughed and clapped at the faces he made.

"I told you, I have six sisters. All older than me." He

pushed to his feet, then lifted Emma into his arms with a natural grace.

"Then they have completely prepared you to be a *gut* husband." She stopped. "Oh, Andrew. I'm sorry. I did not mean—"

He shook his head. "There is nothing to be sorry about, Caroline. One day I hope to be a husband and a father." *Just not right now* went unsaid. "Are you ready to go?"

Thankfully the bib had taken the brunt of Emma's breakfast mess and she wouldn't need a change of clothes before they left.

"*Jah*." Caroline gathered her insulated bag for the trip for the Millers'.

"What's in the cooler?" Andrew asked as they made their way around to the street side of the bakery.

"Pineapple cake."

"Yum," he said with a halfhearted smile.

"You don't like pineapple cake?"

He laughed. "I was hoping for cowboy cookies."

Caroline returned his chuckle. "Next time, for sure."

They rounded the corner, and she stopped in her tracks. The beautiful roan horse that had pulled their buggy to church on Sunday was tied to the hitching post in front of the bakery.

Andrew grasped her elbow and led her to the shiny black buggy.

"We're only going to the Millers', *jah*?"

"*Jah*," he replied, taking the bag from her and depositing it in the small backseat. He sat Emma in the middle of the front and helped Caroline climb on board. "I thought you liked traveling by horse and buggy." He looked almost disappointed.

"I do, I do." Caroline settled down onto the cushioned

seat and straightened her skirts around her. "I just thought we'd take the tractor."

"*Nay*, the bishop likes for us to take our carriages as much as possible." He climbed up next to her and leaned close enough that her heart gave a little jump as she inhaled the sweet scent of his Sunday clothes. "I really did it for you, though."

Caroline smiled as he set the horses into motion.

Dear Lizzie,

I hope this letter finds you well and good. I am enjoying myself here in Oklahoma, though I never thought I'd be able to say that. However, life is not without its trials. But I guess you know that more than most. That is why I am writing you, *shveshtah*.

Although it's been less than a year, I can hardly remember Beth's face. Just writing that brings tears to my eyes. And please don't tell her elders or Mamm and Dat that I said as much. I wouldn't want to hurt them in any way. Yet the fact that her features have become blurry in my mind's eye bothers me more than I can say. At this rate I won't be able to recall her face by this time next year. Perhaps this is God's way of preparing me to go on.

Cousin Danny is determined to see me happily married, even though I tell him daily that I am not ready for a relationship. His girlfriend, Julie, has a friend named Sarah. Though she is sweet as pie and not hard to look at, I find myself counting the minutes until I can excuse myself from her.

On the bright side, I have met a *gut* friend. Her name is Caroline. She's a young widow with a small *boppli*. If I had to guess I'd say wee Emma is just over a year old. She's the cutest thing, with dark curls and eyes the color of the sky before it rains.

I must close for now and remind Onkle that it is time for our nightly devotional. Give everyone my love and write me soon.

Your bruder,
Andrew

Chapter Ten

Pulling into the drive at Jonah Miller's *haus* was like stepping back in time to the carefree days of courtin'. Even though Andrew had been to his share of youth gatherings since coming to Oklahoma, something about today felt different. Maybe it was the fact Caroline was at his side. Or rather next to him, with Emma in between.

He pulled the buggy alongside the rest of the line and un-hitched the horses as Caroline gathered Emma and their things.

In a flash, Andrew imagined that they were a family, ar-riving at a gathering, picnic, or barn raising. Just the three of them. It was what he had dreamed of as he had watched Beth waste away.

But as much as he tried, Caroline's was the only face that would materialize.

"Andrew? Are you *allrecht*?"

Caroline.

"Of course," he said, shaking away the image. "Do you want me to take Emma?"

She shook her head.

They had no sooner reached the empty side pasture

where the volleyball net had been set up than Danny hurried over. "Andrew! *Goedemiddag.*" Danny smacked him on the back in that jovial way of his. "*Mach schnell, mach schnell.* They are picking teams."

As much as Andrew wanted to rush off after his cousin, he had invited Caroline to come with him.

"Danny, do you know Caroline Hostetler?"

"We've met once before. *Wie geht*, Caroline?"

"Gut, danki," she said with a small nod. "Go ahead, Andrew."

He hesitated for a fraction of a second. "I'll see you after the game?"

"Of course."

Danny hooked an arm across his shoulders and steered him toward the playing field. "*Ach*, what are you doing?"

"I don't know what you mean." Andrew adjusted his stride to match his cousin's faster pace.

"You told Sarah that you weren't ready to start courtin', then you bring Caroline."

Andrew shook his head. "We're not dating."

"It sure looks like that to me."

He supposed it did. Even he had thought how it seemed like they were a family.

"What a mess." Danny sighed. "You should apologize to Sarah and explain after the game."

"I don't owe Sarah an explanation. You were the one to get her hopes up that there could be more between us." Saying the words felt mean-spirited, but they were true. He had never given Sarah any reason to believe that they were or could ever be anything more than *freinden*. That was all on Danny.

Sides were chosen and the game began. Andrew found it difficult to not glance at the sidelines to check on Caroline and Emma.

Once the game was over, he jogged to where they were waiting. Caroline had a tall glass of lemonade poured and ready for him.

He gratefully tipped it back, enjoying the sweet-tart taste and the refreshing coolness of it. Once half the drink was gone, he lowered the glass and wiped his mouth.

"I have to go talk to Sarah Yoder," he said. "Danny has seen fit to try to get us together and—"

"You don't have to explain to me." Caroline shaded her eyes as she looked up at him from the blanket where she and Emma sat.

He nodded. At least Caroline understood. "I won't be but a minute." Hopefully.

Caroline refilled his glass and handed it back to him. "I'll see you then."

Andrew walked away, wondering how his life had taken such a turn for the complicated. The whole reason for coming to Wells Landing had been to get away from the painful memories that lingered all around in his home district. He'd thought he'd at least get a reprieve from talking about Beth, reliving those last days. Yet he had talked about Beth more since he had been in Oklahoma than he ever had back home.

He found Sarah standing near the large tree near the garden. She was talking to Julie. Or rather Julie was talking, and Sarah was listening politely and occasionally looking far off toward the horses in the pasture.

"*Goedemiddag,*" he said, coming to a stop beside the pair.

They both turned and smiled, returning his greeting.

"Can I talk to you for a bit, Sarah?"

Julie beamed him a smile. "I think I'll go find Danny."

She backed away a couple of steps as Sarah shook her head. Then Julie turned and almost ran to find her intended.

"I'm sorry," Sarah said after Julie was out of hearing.

Andrew frowned. "For what?"

"You know . . . them."

"Me too."

"So you and Caroline?"

"What? No."

"But I saw you with Caroline Hostetler."

Andrew opened his mouth to tell her that he and Caroline were just friends, but the statement alone might possibly bring her hope. "I meant what I said the other night. About courtin'. Caroline and I are *freinden*. I didn't want you to think I was not telling you the truth."

Sarah shook her head.

"What?"

"It seems like the two of you are a bit more than that." Her words were softly spoken but held a punch.

Andrew shook his head as Sarah continued. "It's obvious in the way you look at her and she you. Even her baby adores you. It's a *gut* match for certain."

"I . . ." Andrew didn't know how to finish. Was that really how it looked to the people around them? "I didn't want to hurt your feelings." It wasn't exactly what he wanted to say. He'd planned to emphatically tell Sarah that he most certainly was not a match for Caroline, but the longer the words knocked around in his head, the more impossible they became to say.

Sarah gave him a weak smile. "It's *allrecht*, Andrew Fitch. I understand. I know that I am not outgoing like Julie or beautiful like Caroline, but I have my place in God's plan."

"Of course you are beautiful," he said, truly meaning his

words. Sarah Yoder was beautiful, both inside and out. "Any man would be honored to have you at his side." *Just not me.*

"I've put in to be the new teacher in Bishop Treger's district. I'll be happy the rest of my days if I'm allowed to work with the *kinner*."

"They would be blessed to have you." She was sweet and understanding, quiet and brave in her own way.

She gave him a shy smile. "*Danki*, Andrew Fitch."

He jerked a thumb toward the volleyball game. "I guess I should be getting back now."

Andrew took a couple of steps backward, then he turned on his heel and made his way back to the others.

Sarah Yoder was a fine young woman. A small part of him wished he could be what Danny wanted him to be for her, but he couldn't. Still, Andrew was certain the Lord had plans for such a kind heart.

Caroline tried not to follow the brim of Andrew's hat as he made his way toward Sarah Yoder. She was not jealous that he was talking to the other woman. Jealousy would mean that she had feelings other than friendship for Andrew and that just wasn't the case.

Instead she broke off pieces of one of the sandwiches she had brought and fed them and orange sections to Emma while she pretended she hadn't shifted her position to better see them as they talked. She was being ridiculous, so she shifted again as the teams were starting to form on the field in front of her.

"Hey." Andrew dropped down beside her on the quilt, and she did her best to temper her smile.

"Hey. Did you enjoy your chat?" Now, why did she say that?

If she came across as nosy or jealous, Andrew didn't

show it. "It seems that others might think that you and I have something going on."

Caroline laughed, then hated how forced it sounded. "Seriously?"

"*Jah*, I know. But what with the other young people keeping their intentions for each other a secret, what can we do?" He grinned at her, and Caroline was sure he didn't smile enough. He should smile like that all the time.

"Looks like another game is starting," he said.

"You'd better hurry if you want a spot."

"Would you like to play?"

"Me?" She hadn't played in years. Almost three of them. She surely hadn't played since she'd found out she carried a baby, and that summer with Trey . . . well, she'd been more interested in spending time with him than in sporting games.

"Why not? You like volleyball, don't you?"

"Jah." Who didn't?

"Then go get on a team before they find all their players."

She shook her head. "I don't know. I've got Emma and—"

"I'll watch the wee one for you."

She hesitated.

"You don't trust me with her." Andrew frowned, the simple motion of his mouth turning down at the corners transforming his face from sunshine to clouds.

Caroline bit her lip as she shook her head. "It's not that."

"Then what is it?"

"I'm not used to having help like this. People to care for her so I can go out and—"

"Have a little fun?"

"Jah."

"You need to get used to it," he said emphatically. "As long as you are my *freind*, I'll be here to help." He gave a shrill whistle through his teeth and wildly waved his arms over his head. "Jonah! I've got your last player right here." He pointed down at Caroline, and she was certain her temperature raised one hundred degrees.

Jonah Miller, host of the day's festivities and on-again-off-again boyfriend of Lorie Kauffman, motioned her to come over.

Everyone was watching. What else could she do?

That was only an excuse. She wanted to play. Wanted it almost more than anything she had ever wanted in her life. She stood and brushed off her dress.

"Are you sure about this?" she asked.

"Go show them how it's done."

Caroline jogged out onto the grassy field and took her position. Her heart was pounding, not from the exertion, but from excitement.

How long had it been since she felt like this?

Since before Emma. Since Trey and their stolen kisses and midnight meetings.

She pushed the thoughts away as the first serve was made. She had been handed a *wunderbaar* opportunity, and she was going to make the most of it.

Esther reached up a hand to knock on the door, her heart beating triple time. She had gone over and over in her head on the way out here what she would say to Abe once he opened the door, but as her mouth went dry and her pulse stuttered, everything she had worked on fled.

She knocked again. There were no stirrings inside the house. No movement to answer her summons.

She should have used the bakery phone to call the one Abe had in his barn. But what were the chances that someone would be there to answer it when it rang? Especially since she knew for a fact that Andrew was at Jonah Miller's. She would have left a message and been in the same situation that she was in right now.

She looked around, trying to decide what to do next. Her legs felt like rubber from the miles she had pedaled on her three-wheeler to get out to the farm, but she supposed that she had no choice but to return home without seeing Abe.

"You're a silly old woman, Esther Lapp," she told herself as she sank into the porch swing. She'd rest for a little bit, then head back to the bakery.

The day was turning out warm even by Oklahoma standards. They were in for a scorching summer if this kept up. But Abe's porch faced south and the shade was welcome. The breeze blew around her and cooled her as she gently pushed the swing into motion.

The farm was quiet, like church service during prayer, and there was a peacefulness about the place that she couldn't find in the city.

Esther had never regretted the choices she made after her John died, but she did miss country living. It was easier to hear the birds, the wind in the trees, and . . . the buzz of a saw?

She pushed to her feet. At least it sounded like a saw.

Esther stepped off the porch and started toward the side of the yard opposite the barn and the pastures that Abe leased to the horse breeders.

Whatever it was, the noise was coming from the outbuildings squatting there.

The racket grew louder as she neared the first building and even louder as she passed that door and continued on. At the third door in the row, she stopped. *Jah*, it was definitely a saw.

She pushed the door open to find Abe hard at work cutting wood for something or another.

"Abraham Fitch, whatever are you doing?"

He jumped and the noise from the saw stopped.

"*Ach*, Esther Lapp, you almost made me cut myself." He studied the injured digit, then satisfied that it wasn't gone, reached for the next piece on the pile of wood next to him.

"You are working."

"*Jah.*" He marked the wood with a pencil and lined up the cut.

"It's the Sabbath."

He stopped and tilted his head to one side in that way she found so utterly charming. Except this time she was a little too shocked to register the attraction she felt for him. "I s'pose it is."

Esther plopped one hand on her hip. "The bishop would have the deacon out here in a heartbeat if he knew that." She waved him toward her. "Come on. Let's go in and have a snack, and I'll forget everything I've seen here."

Abe squinted at her through the thick lenses of his wire-rimmed glasses. "What kind of snack?"

"I've got day-old bagels and honey goat cheese from the bishop's farm."

Abe gave a quick nod. "Just let me finish this cut."

Esther knew it was forward, but someone had to save Abe from himself and a possible shunning. She grasped his elbow and half directed, half dragged him from the workshop. "The cuts can wait until tomorrow."

Abe put aside the board and followed Esther out of the workshop.

"Why are you here?"

She wondered when he'd get around to asking that. "I

thought you might could use some company what with Andrew and Caroline off at the Millers'.""

He gave a quick nod, then said, "Or perhaps your apartment was a little too quiet without Caroline and Emma there."

"Jah," she agreed, but that was only part of the reason. She couldn't help but wonder at how quiet her house would be if her suspicions were correct. If Andrew and Caroline one day were to marry, and she moved out to start a family with him . . .

Esther pushed the thought away. Caroline and Emma had come to mean so much to her in the past couple of years. She wanted nothing more than for Caroline to be *froh.*

But if the good Lord was with her, Esther would somehow make Abe Fitch notice her long before that happened.

Dear Caroline,

I miss you so much. I hadn't intended to start my letter to you in such a sad way, but it's the truth. Since you've been gone I feel like my heart's been cut out. I know that your leaving was part of God's plan for you (I have to believe that lest the pain of it drive me out of my head), but that doesn't make me miss you any less. Every day and every night I pray that it be God's will for you to eventually return to Tennessee and the family who loves you.

I am glad that you have made such gut freinden. After God and family, they are most important.

I'm sad to say that your father still cannot bear to speak your name, though I caught him sitting in your room when he thought I was out hanging clothes on the line. I have left everything there just the way it was when you were here. I see no reason to change it. I too like to go in there and sit for a while. I pray there for your safety and good health, for Emma, and for God to bring you back to us.

Grossdaadi fell again last week. He says he is fine, but I have my doubts. He's even more stubborn and set in his ways than the other Swartzentruber and refuses to go to the doctor to find out about the dizzy spells. I worry that he will fall and hit his head, and no one will be there to help him. He still

*won't even talk about moving in here with us. He
told me he was born in that house, and he is going
to die there as well. At least he's only a hundred
yards from our back door. He doesn't know it, but I
sneak over often and peek in the windows to make
sure he's faring all right.*

*It's getting close to suppertime and your father
will be in from the fields soon. I must close for now.
Please give Emma a kiss from me and tell her that I
love her and I hope to one day get to hold her in my
arms just as I did you when you were a boppli.*

*With love always,
Mamm*

Chapter Eleven

Caroline dropped down on the quilt next to Andrew, all the while avoiding the sleeping Emma. She was breathless and laughing.

"Did you have fun?" Andrew asked with a smile.

"Jah." Caroline fanned herself, accepting a glass of lemonade from his hand. *"Danki."*

"For the lemonade?"

"For everything. Letting me play. Watching Emma. Putting the umbrella up for her to have shade."

Andrew shrugged, but she could tell that he was pleased with her words. *"Gern gschehne.* And *danki* to you as well."

Caroline took a big gulp of the lemonade. "For what?"

"Giving me a second chance to watch Emma."

She was surprised. It was perhaps the last thing she expected him to say. She had long since gotten over her trust issues where Andrew was concerned. It just wasn't easy to give over the care of Emma to someone else. Her reluctance wasn't typically Amish. She remembered some of the larger families in her district would use every hand they could get for help with the children. But she supposed she could no longer be called typically Amish either.

"It means that much to you?" she asked.

"It does, *jah*."

Caroline couldn't stop her smile, nor did she want to. "I'm glad, Andrew Fitch. So glad." She waved a hand toward the field. "Want to take a turn and play again?"

He plucked a blade of grass and tossed it away. *"Nay,"* he said. "I'd rather sit here with you for a while."

Caroline ducked her head to hide her uncontrollable smile. Sweeter words she was sure she had never heard. "Me too," she whispered so no one could hear. "Me too."

Caroline rocked against Andrew as he pulled the buggy into the parking space in front of the bakery. Emma lay sleeping in the seat next to her. Her toddler had her legs stretched out, her dark curls in Caroline's lap.

Andrew hopped down from the buggy, and despite the summer heat, Caroline immediately missed his warmth beside her. He tethered the horses, then came around to the other side.

"I'll take her in," he said. Caroline didn't protest.

She followed Andrew around to the back of the bakery and tried the door. Locked.

"I guess Esther went somewhere," she said, digging her key out of her bag. She opened the door for Andrew and followed him inside. She set her bag down as he carried Emma into the bedroom. He returned a few minutes later.

"I braced the pillows around her, but she was sleeping like a baby."

Caroline laughed. "Would you like some pie?"

"Lead the way."

Side by side, she started the coffee while Andrew cut the pie and served them each a slice.

Together they sat down and prayed, then started their afternoon snack.

"I wonder where Esther has gone."

Andrew shrugged and shoveled in another bite. Then he stopped chewing and swallowed hard. "You don't think she went out to see *Onkle*, do you?"

Caroline shook her head. "*Nay*. All she has is the three-wheeler. It would take a goodly while to get all the way out there on a bike."

"You're right." Andrew took another bite, but Caroline could tell that he wasn't convinced.

Pie forgotten, she pushed back from the table and started for the door of the apartment. She and Esther kept their bikes in the dry storage right next door.

She grabbed the key on the way out, half expecting Andrew to follow her. But he didn't. She unlocked the door to the storage room to find only one bike in the cool shadows.

With a gasp she closed the door, relocked it, then ran back into the apartment. "Andrew," she hissed under her breath as to not disturb Emma. "Her bike is gone."

He cut another piece of pie. "That's *gut, jah?*"

Caroline stopped. It was good. For sure and for certain. *"Jah."*

"Then why do you come in here like the world outside is ending?"

She collapsed back into her chair. "I . . . I'm just surprised is all. It has got to be at least five miles to your farm."

"She must have really wanted to go see him."

"If that is where she went." Esther could have easily taken her bike to go visit someone in town or even over to the grocery store. "Just because she's gone does not mean that she went to see Abe Fitch."

Andrew smiled around his last bite of pie. "I have a feeling that she did."

Caroline picked up her fork and started to eat her pie again. What would happen if Abe and Esther did become a couple? If that were to come to pass, she and Andrew wouldn't see each other quite as much. They would have no excuse to visit each other as they worked to get Esther and Abe together. The thought made her stomach drop.

"Are you *allrecht*?" Andrew reached out and touched her arm, then jerked away as if he'd been bit.

"*Jah.* Of course." She nodded toward his empty plate. "Would you like another piece of pie?"

"*Nay.*" He patted his trim stomach. "I'm sure I could not hold another bite."

"More *kaffi*?"

"I'll get it." Andrew stood and retrieved the coffeepot from the stove top. He poured them both a fresh cup, then returned to his seat across from her.

Being that close to him, having him carry Emma to bed, then partnering in the kitchen to slice the pie and pour coffee. The word "family" popped into her head, clear as day. This had to be what it was like to be married, to have a husband and helpmate. And suddenly she wanted that more than she had ever wanted anything in her life.

She pushed that desire away. Surely the Lord had a plan for her. But right now, she was unable to see what it could be. Was she destined to remain here in Wells Landing? Go back home to Tennessee? Get married? Or perhaps remain a widow here in Oklahoma?

"I guess I should be going." Andrew stood and made his way to the door. He grabbed his hat off the peg and plopped it on his head. "I need to go check on the puppies and feed the horses."

She stood, fighting the urge to call him back, ask him to

stay. Instead she followed him out the door and around to his waiting buggy.

He slid the door open, then turned to face her. "I had a *gut* time today, Caroline."

"Me too."

"When it comes my turn to host will you help me get everything together?"

"*Jah*. Of course." A burst of wind rushed through, fluttering the strings of her prayer *kapp* and pulling at the strands of her hair.

She reached up to tuck the strand behind her ear, but Andrew's hand was already there.

As natural as the sunrise, he captured her hand with his.

Blue eyes locked on hazel ones as he raised her hand to his lips and kissed the skin on the back of her fingers.

"Andrew, I—" Her words weren't really a protest, just something to fill the space between them.

Then he took care of that as well, tugging on her hand and pulling her completely into his arms.

Caroline was certain she had never been in a sweeter place than inside his embrace. His body was warm and solid and felt good under her touch as she braced her hands against his shoulders to steady herself.

He didn't give her time to protest, just lowered his head and captured her lips with his own.

Color and light exploded behind her lids as Andrew's mouth pressed to hers. Caroline was sure she had found a little piece of heaven on earth. On and on, he continued to kiss her. On and on she kissed him back, marveling at the miracle of it all. The kiss itself was like a wildfire, burning hot and threatening to take over.

It needed to stop, yet she wanted it never to end.

A car sped by, trailing a honking horn behind. Caroline jumped and pulled away from Andrew. This was wrong. He was her friend. They had promised that to each other. A terrible mistake. And the fact that they had been doing it on Main Street where just anybody could have witnessed the embrace . . .

Caroline pressed her palms to her hot cheeks, then ran her hands down the front of her apron.

The people in the car would be talking about it all night, the Amish couple kissing in the street. If luck was on her side, the car was full of tourists from out of town and not members of the Wells Landing *Englisch* community. Or even one of the Mennonites from Inola. Otherwise the bishop could possibly find out and—

"Caroline, I'm so sorry." Andrew sounded like he had a sore throat, his voice raspy and cracking. "I didn't mean—"

She shook her head. A million things ran through her mind. *Don't apologize. Where do we go from here? Did you like it as much as I did?* "Be safe driving home," she said. She refused to meet his gaze and turned on her heel and rushed back around the side of the bakery and into the apartment.

She shut the door behind her, leaned against it, and pressed her hand to her mouth.

All the harsh words her father had spoken to her came flooding back, ugly words he had used to describe her behavior. Not true, but hurtful all the same. Now the doubts came. If she could be with Trey, then come here and respond to Andrew's kisses that way, with willing abandon, did that make her as bad as her father implied?

Caroline stumbled to the couch, confused and tangled. Instead of sitting down, she fell to her knees, clasped her hands together, and braced her elbows on the cushion in front of her.

"Dear Lord," she prayed, closing her eyes tight. "I need help, Father God, help in understanding what just happened and what it means for me. Perhaps I am as unworthy as my *vatter* said." The thought made her stop.

One thing she had been taught since coming to live with the Beachys was that she was worthy of the Lord's love and good grace. Esther had taught her that. Temptations were all around. She had to fight them and be victorious. But was there anything wrong with her and Andrew sharing a kiss? Nothing more, just a kiss?

"Dear Lord, help me understand what had happened here. I want Andrew to be my friend, but now . . . now my feelings are starting to change. Please help me to figure it out and do what is right for all of us involved. *Aemen*."

Esther arrived home shortly before dark.

Caroline had put Emma in the high chair with cheese and crackers to snack on while she cooked their meal.

"Esther," she admonished, wiping her hands on a dish towel and meeting the woman halfway between the kitchen and the front door. "I've been worried sick. I checked the phone messages thinking you might be hurt or worse."

"Forgive me, Caroline."

"Of course."

"It was just so quiet without you and Emma in the house that I decided to take a ride."

"I noticed your bike was gone."

A flush of pink stole into her plump cheeks. "I rode out to see Abe."

So they had been right. Caroline hid her smile. "Come sit and tell me all about it."

Esther planted a kiss on the top of Emma's head, then settled into one of the kitchen chairs. "There's really not much to tell. He was working on a chest of drawers, so I made him stop. We went in the *haus* and ate, then walked down to the pond they have on the property. Next week he says he'll take me fishing."

Caroline slid into the seat opposite her good friend. "That's fantastic news." She took Esther's hand into her own, squeezing it encouragingly.

"How did your afternoon go?"

Caroline glanced away, hoping Esther couldn't see the confusion in her eyes. *"Gut, gut."*

"What aren't you telling me?"

A small laugh escaped her. "You sound just like my mother. She always knew when—"

"When what?"

"Andrew kissed me," she said quietly.

"Gut himmel," Esther exclaimed. "That is *wunderbaar gut* news."

"Good heavens" wasn't an adequate description for the sizzle of Andrew's kiss. "I don't know." Caroline sighed. "We're supposed to be friends."

"I take it this wasn't a friend-kiss."

Caroline shook her head and swallowed hard.

Emma banged on the high chair, demanding more food. "Mamamama," the toddler chanted.

Caroline rose to get her *boppli* something more to eat.

"You know my John was my friend. Always."

"It's not like that."

"Of course it is." Esther stood and opened the oven to check on the casserole. Green beans bubbled on a pot on the stove. Applesauce and peppers sat on the table, ready for them to start eating. Caroline had accomplished it all automatically. She hadn't thought about what she was doing, what she was preparing. All she could think about was Andrew and the sweet heat of his lips on hers.

"Tell me why you are so upset, *liebschen*."

Emma squealed and kicked her feet as Caroline gave her another cracker, then slid back into her seat.

Esther snagged a pot holder and removed the casserole dish from the oven. She set it on top of the stove, turned all the burners off, then spun to face Caroline.

Why am I so upset?

Because she liked it. Because they had agreed to only be friends. Because he had made it more than clear that he wasn't in the market for a new love. Because she hadn't wanted it to stop.

"Because he is my friend. I value that," Caroline said. "I don't want to stop being his friend, but now every time I see him I'm only going to be able to think of his k—this afternoon."

Esther pursed her lips. "That must have been a great kiss."

"It was." Caroline dropped her head into her hands. "Now what am I going to do?"

Esther shrugged, then took down three plates for the *nachtess*. "All I can say is talk to the boy. If your friendship means a lot to him as well, I'm sure the two of you can work something out."

Caroline pushed to her feet, fixed them glasses of iced tea, and gathered forks and the salt and pepper shakers before returning to the table. "Listen to me going on about Andrew. Tell me more about your afternoon with Abe."

Esther blushed. "We had a *gut* time," she said simply. "Though not as eventful as yours."

Whether that was a *gut* thing or a bad thing, Caroline wasn't sure.

"But I think we may be connecting. With the Lord on my side, he may even notice me yet."

Dear Andrew,

I was so froh to get your letter. And so very happy that you are settling into life among the Beachys. Who knows? You might even decide to make it your permanent home.

Danny has always been something of a busybody. But he means well. If you are not ready, don't worry about the plans of others. Until someone has walked in your shoes, they cannot know the heartache that you carry. It may not seem like it now, but the pain will fade. God takes care to heal those who are in need. Every day the pain lessens a bit more, maybe not enough to see from day to day but surely from week to week.

I've heard that Beth's elders are talking of moving away. They may go to Indiana or Pinecraft, but until they say as much before the church I won't believe it. It would be gut for them to start over, leave those memories behind. Some folks calling it running. I call it a clean slate to begin again. I wish . . . Well, I guess it doesn't matter what I wish. I decided to stay and that is that.

I'm so very pleased to hear that you are making friends. Caroline sounds like a gut maedel and you are lucky to be able to count her as a friend.

Before I forget, Mamm sends her love. Dat too. Be sure to write and keep us updated.

Ich liebe dich,
Lizzie

Chapter Twelve

Andrew pushed his hat back on his head and wiped the sweat from his brow. Today had turned out hotter than yesterday, and talk at the hardware store said it was only going to get worse.

The warmer weather was one thing he hadn't gotten used to yet. Perhaps it would take a couple of years . . . if he even decided to stay.

He settled his hat back in place and started the tractor for the return trip into town. He'd come out to the farm to pick up the special-order bench-and-table set his uncle had made for a couple in Tulsa. They were arriving this afternoon to pick it up, and his *onkle* only told him after lunch was over that it was needed at the showroom in town.

Not that Andrew had eaten much during mealtime. Food tasted like the sawdust that peppered the workroom floor. And his eyes felt like grit. He hadn't slept much last night. Every time he closed his eyes, all he could see was Caroline's sweet face, those hazel eyes looking like bottomless green pools as she stared up at him.

Why had he kissed her? Even more, why had he kissed her like *that*? He could have given her a friendly peck on the cheek. It was not normal for Amish to kiss one another in passing, but it would have been a sight better than the kiss they shared.

Nay, better wasn't the word. That kiss couldn't have gotten much better, but it would have been for sure more appropriate to kiss her cheek, shake her hand, or even just tip his hat, but no . . .

Instead, he had pulled her close and kissed her in a way that he had never kissed another. Not even his beloved Beth.

Andrew wiped his forehead again, checking the gauges on the tractor as he chugged along. Was it getting even hotter outside?

Oklahoma weather was unpredictable as it came, but his discomfort now had more to do with thoughts of last night than the actual atmosphere around him.

He pulled the tractor into the lot behind the shop to unload the furniture straight into the storeroom.

Danny came out, the sound of the tractor alerting him to the fact his cousin had returned.

Andrew swung himself to the ground and went around to the attached wagon to unhook the bungee cords and the padding he had wrapped around the two benches and matching table.

"Danki," he said to Danny as his cousin began to help him unwind all the wrappings. Together they carried the furniture through the back door of the shop.

"So what happened with Sarah yesterday? I saw you talking to her."

Andrew set down his end of the bench. "We talked about how I'm not ready to start courtin' and that I have a cousin who insists on interfering with my decisions."

"Anyone I know?"

"And that if he's not careful, he could wind up getting her hopes up for something that is never going to happen."

"Sarah told Julie that you told her that she would be the first to know when you are ready."

"That's not exactly what I said." He made his way back outside and waited for his cousin to come take up his end of the next piece.

"That seems to be what she heard."

Andrew sighed. He'd come to Oklahoma to get away from his troubles with women. It seemed that he had traded grief for two women he had no idea what to do with: one who wanted to spend time with him, and one whom he wanted to spend time with.

The thought brought him up short. He must have jerked, stilled, or jumped. Whatever he did, it brought Danny's attention around to him.

"You *allrecht*?"

Andrew nodded, unable to speak. *"Jah,"* he finally croaked, but the word was anything but convincing. He wanted to spend time with Caroline. More than time. He wanted to get to know her. Discover why she had come to Wells Landing from Tennessee. Find out all there was to know about Emma's father. Everything there was to know about Caroline.

Danny continued to talk as they carried the second bench and then the table into the storeroom.

"Okay, Andrew?"

"What?" Andrew looked from his cousin to his uncle.

When had *Onkle* come into the room?

"I asked if you wanted to come to eat with me tonight," Danny repeated.

"Nay."

"You didn't even let me say who I was eating with."

Andrew shook his head. "I don't want to know." But he did want to go see Caroline.

"You like her." Danny's words were filled with surprise.

Had he said that last part out loud?

"Jah." There. He'd admitted it. He liked Caroline Hostetler. Maybe even more than liked. He wanted to go see her. See Emma. Spend time with them. Drink lemonade. Play board games. Get to know each other better.

"Ach, that's *gut."* Abe wiped his hands on a rag, then stuffed it in his back pocket. "She's a good one, that Caroline."

Andrew smiled, getting used to the idea of liking someone even if it felt a little too soon since Beth had died. But maybe this was all part of God's plan.

Abe patted him on the back and hobbled toward the door of the shop. "Polish this up and wait on the *Englisch* to come by and pick it up, then you can take the rest of the day off."

He was going to need it. It was going to take some time to fully embrace the idea of liking Caroline Hostetler. He smiled to himself. But it was a challenge he was looking forward to conquering.

Caroline pulled a large pan of sourdough rolls from the oven and sat them on the cooling rack. Her eyes flickered to the wall and the large industrial clock that hung there.

Today had slowed to a crawl as she waited for . . . what? What exactly was she waiting for? Andrew to come down and apologize? Say he was glad he had kissed her? Or that he was remorseful because his heart still belonged to another?

She sighed. The last was the most logical. It hadn't been so very long since he had lost his love. It had been two years since she had last seen Trey. And she knew deep down that she would most probably never see him again. They had made their choices. No sense going back on it now.

"What's wrong, *liebschen*?"

"Nix."

Esther shook her head. "You and I both know that is not the truth."

Caroline sighed again. Checked the clock again. Shook her own head.

"Andrew?" Esther asked.

"Jah." He had been on her mind nonstop since the night before. She had hardly slept, hardly eaten, barely dragged herself to work. Not that lying about would be any more productive. She needed to talk to Andrew. Clear the air, figure out what had happened between them the night before.

Truth was she needed to hear him say it, that he was still in love with another and he had no right kissing her the way he did.

Once he said that, she could start pushing it from her mind, right where it belonged.

"Why don't you walk down to the furniture store and talk to him?"

The strings on her prayer *kapp* swayed as she shook her head. *"Nay."* It would never do for her to be so forward as to walk down there and demand he talk to her. The idea was as brazen as the English. Her Swartzentruber upbringing would not allow that.

Esther patted her arm. "I don't think he'd think less of you."

"Nay," Caroline repeated. She would have to wait until her opportunity to talk to Andrew.

Somehow she knew he would be down to talk to her. Eventually. She would just bide her time and bite her lip until he came to see her.

* * *

It was Thursday morning before Andrew got the courage to walk down to the bakery and talk to Caroline. Even then, she was in the park, no doubt having lunch with Lorie and Emily. But when he made his way across the street, he found her sitting at a table staring at a sandwich. She was alone.

"Mind if I sit down?"

Her head jerked up and her eyes widened. She swallowed hard and gave a nod.

He stepped over the picnic table bench and sat directly across from her. "I've been meaning to come down and see you." For the last four days he had been thinking about what he wanted to say to her. Mulling over what needed to be talked about. Now the words deserted him.

"Jah," she agreed, staring at some point above the crown of his hat.

"I . . . I guess I should say I'm sorry for kissing you, but that's not the truth."

Her gaze whipped to his.

"I know we had an agreement and all, but . . ." He held his hands out palms up.

"But what?" she asked on a whisper. Her hands nervously folded a paper napkin until it was no bigger than a quarter.

He took her trembling fingers into his own, stilling their busy motions. "But I think God brought me here for a reason."

She shook her head, a myriad of mixed emotions swimming in her hazel eyes. "I don't know what to say."

Andrew smiled. "*Jah* or *nay* would be a *gut* start."

"What about Beth?"

He still held her hands in his, and he gave them a reassuring squeeze. "I guess this goes to show that God's plan is in His time."

She dropped her gaze to their joined hands.

"We don't have to make any commitment or promises. I know you are dealing with the loss of Emma's father. We can just take it slow and see where it leads us. We could come out of this just friends or . . ."

"Or what?"

"Or more." He offered a small shrug. "I don't know what will happen."

"Are you asking to court me?"

A small smile trembled on his lips. "I guess I am."

It seemed hours before she answered. "*Allrecht* then," she finally said. "We'll take it slow."

Happy warmth burst in his chest. He squeezed her trembling fingers between his own. No firm plans, just a promise to get to know one another better. But in the beauty of her smile, he saw the future and it was *gut*.

The bell over the bakery chimed its warning. Esther looked up to see Caroline walk in.

"Did you have a *gut middawk*?" Esther asked.

"Um . . . *Jah*," Caroline answered. "Andrew met me out there."

"I know. He came by here looking for you. I sent him over there. Did you get a chance to talk?"

"Jah." She went to the sink and washed her hands, concentrating on the task with more attention than it truly warranted.

Something must have happened during Caroline's break that dazed her.

The thought had no sooner crossed Esther's mind than Andrew opened the bakery door, sticking his head inside. "I forgot. Would you like to come out to the farm tonight? I thought we could have supper and maybe let Emma play with the puppies for a while."

"That sounds *gut*."

"I'll come by in the buggy about seven, *jah*?"

"We'll be ready."

"You too, Esther."

Esther swung her attention back to Andrew. "Me?"

"*Jah*. I'm sure *Onkle* would love to have you over as well."

She certainly hoped so. They'd had a *gut* time together Sunday, but she couldn't say that he'd made any indication that they would ever be anything more than *freinden*.

"See you tonight." He gave them a wave and started back down the street toward the furniture store.

Esther turned to Caroline. "Would you like to tell me what that was about?"

Caroline shook her head. *"Nix,"* she said, drying her hands on a paper towel and throwing it into the trash. "Andrew wants us to get to know each other better."

Esther clapped her hands together in sheer glee. "Oh, that is *gut*! Like dating?"

"Like seeing if maybe we might want to court."

Esther propped her hands on her hips and studied her young friend. "That doesn't sound definite at all."

Caroline shrugged. "We're going to take it slow."

They might be saying that, but if two people ever belonged together, it was Andrew and Caroline. Little Emma needed a father in her life, and if Esther had even one thing to say about it, that father would be Andrew Fitch.

a fantastic mood for some time. Ever since Caroline had agreed to start a courting of sorts and see where things might progress for them. He knew it was soon for him to start dating after Beth, but he was sure that God had placed Caroline in his life for a very *gut* reason. He couldn't just let her go without giving a try to what could be.

He dropped off his letter to his sister at the post office and continued over to the park. One of the best parts of the last few weeks had been meeting Caroline in the park for lunch.

He smiled to himself. Her usual routine of meeting Emily and Lorie had changed into meeting him, and today he had an even bigger surprise for her.

He tugged on the leash he held in one hand. The once-runt of a puppy glanced up from the banana peel that he'd been smelling to once again trot behind him. He had the perfect gift for her and Emma: the pup they had enjoyed playing with during each visit to the farm. The rest of the puppies had been spoken for long ago, most of them going to farmers and ranchers. One had even gone to live with a boy who lived halfway across the state. The only one left was the runt.

Oh, the bundle of fur had eventually caught up with his *bruders* and sisters in spunk and energy, but he was still a small little fella. Anybody seeking a working dog had reservations about taking one that seemed like less than the rest of the litter. Andrew had hoped that once the others were gone, someone would take in the one he had dubbed Moxie. That was his first mistake: naming the dog. The other was allowing Emma to play with it so much. The silky black-and-white border collie had taken to the small girl. Andrew loved to watch the pair play together. Sometime yesterday afternoon watching them play in the grass, Andrew came up with the idea to surprise Caroline with the gift.

He couldn't wait to see her face when he brought the pup to her today.

His smile deepened as he entered the park. Caroline had been watching for him, for she stood and waved him over.

Emma squealed as he approached, clapping her hands at the sight of the dog trailing behind him.

Caroline looked from him to the puppy, then back again. "Did you decide to keep him?" she asked.

Andrew stepped over the bench across from her and hooked Moxie's leash around one of the legs of the table. "Something like that."

Caroline was nothing if not smart. Her eyes narrowed. "Why do I get the feeling that I'm not going to like what you are about to tell me?"

Andrew tried to look hurt. "I hoped you would like to have this sweet puppy."

"Have it? As in to keep?"

"Jah."

Caroline shook her head. "I don't know, Andrew. Esther might not want to have a dog in the house."

"I'm sure Esther wouldn't mind that much. Just look at him. And Emma loves him."

Emma climbed down from her seat next to her *mudder* and plopped herself next to the puppy. She giggled hysterically while Moxie licked her face, tail wagging like crazy.

"Andrew . . ."

"Moxie will be a terrific watchdog for the three of you."

"Moxie?" she asked.

"I saw it in a movie."

"Oh."

"It means spunky and brave."

Caroline looked to where Emma and the pup were playing. "I guess it wouldn't hurt to ask Esther."

Andrew smiled in triumph. Esther was worse than an

Englisch granny and could not deny Emma anything. Moxie had just found himself a new home.

"Esther," Caroline called. "Are you ready to go?"

It was Sunday morning, and if they didn't hurry they'd be late for church. It had just turned out to be one of those mornings. Emma had dumped her entire bowl of oatmeal on her head, the puppy had decided that he couldn't wait a moment later to go outside and had used the kitchen floor as a bathroom, and Caroline had cut her finger slicing cantaloupe to go with their biscuits. So after Emma had another bath and Caroline took Moxie outside to finish his business, after she had re-mopped the floor and bandaged her throbbing finger, they barely had enough time to pedal to the Kauffmans' for today's service. Thankfully they didn't live too far out of the town limits, but if Esther didn't *mach schnell* they'd be late for sure.

"Esther," Caroline called, her voice trailing off as Esther came out of her bedroom. "Are you ready?"

The older woman shook her head. "I can't find my shoe."

"Only one of them?" Caroline shifted Emma into a more comfortable position on her hip.

Esther shrugged. "It's strange, *jah*? I took them off last night in my room. I thought I left them by my bed."

Emma squealed and clapped her hands, a sure sign that Moxie had managed to wriggle around the baby gate Caroline had used to secure him in the kitchen while they were gone. "Maybe not so strange after all," Caroline said. She deposited Emma in the playpen and scooped the puppy into her arms. She put him back in the kitchen and refastened the gate, taking extra measures to make sure that he would stay where he belonged while they were gone.

"Have you checked under the couch?"

"Why would it be—?"

Moxie barked.

"Oh yeah."

Esther found her missing shoe under the couch as Caroline had suspected. Thankfully Moxie hadn't done any major damage to it, just chewed the laces and left a few small teeth marks on the rubber sole.

"He's a menace," Caroline said as Esther locked the door. She shook her head as she buckled Emma into her seat on the back of the bike and made sure she was strapped in nice and secure.

"Oh, he's just a pup," Esther protested once they were on their way. "John and I had one just like that right after we first married."

Caroline shook her head. "That's no reason to allow him to disrupt everything."

Esther cast her a speculative glance. "You sure are tense for a girl in love."

"Who said I was in love?"

Esther shrugged. "You're not in love with Andrew?"

Was she?

"I don't know." If she was in love, wasn't it time to tell him the truth about Emma? She didn't like to think about such things. They had promised to take it slow, and that was just what she planned to keep doing.

Until the day that slow was no longer enough, and Andrew asked her to marry him.

If he even would. What if she told him the truth now and he had already decided that it was too soon to marry again? Was it worth destroying his feelings for her if there was nothing for either of them to gain?

Caroline had prayed about it, long and hard. She would wait to see how this would work out between them before she said anything. How could she just spill something like that out? No, it was better to keep some things to herself. The decision still weighed heavy on her heart, but who would benefit from the truth? Certainly not Emma. Honestly, she couldn't see how any of them would benefit from her telling the truth.

Trey was gone. The matter was as simple as that. After many nights of prayer, Caroline realized that the truth would only hurt those involved. And it was something she'd best keep to herself.

The decision wasn't an easy one to make. She still doubted her decisions. Not a day went by that she didn't think about it, didn't wonder if she was doing the right thing. Not a day that she didn't bow her head in prayer and talk to God about all that was bothering her.

Add to that a hyper puppy, her job, her relationship with Andrew, and well, she was a little stressed.

"It just seems like there's a lot going on right now."

"It does at that."

Englisch wedding season only added to the workload. Of course, Caroline was grateful for the work. She could bake and decorate cakes with the best of them. The added orders gave her more to concentrate on besides her deceit.

But the thought of telling Andrew the truth and having him walk away from her forever nearly broke her heart in two. If that wasn't love, she wasn't sure what was.

Esther cast a sidelong glance at Caroline as they sat on the backless benches. The church service was about half over, and Esther couldn't remember how many times she had looked over at her young friend. There was something bothering Caroline, for sure and for certain. Esther felt like she was a patient person, but she was growing antsy to know what Caroline had on her mind.

If nothing else, she wanted Caroline to be happy. It was one thing the young widow deserved.

Esther allowed her gaze to wander up the men's side until she caught sight of Abe, his dark curly hair a bit *strubbly* this Sunday morn.

Esther ducked her head and stared at her hands to help hide her sudden smile.

A bit more *strubbly* than usual, she amended. That was just Abe. And one of the many reasons why she loved him. In their world of conformity and unification, he was himself, his own person. Yet that person still fit within their structure. She was still a little shocked that no woman had ever taken the time to see beyond his distraction to the man underneath. He was so incredibly smart, a *gut* businessman, and he needed someone to look after him. Esther was just that person.

Everyone stood and turned to kneel for the final prayer, and Esther was grateful. The minister Dan Troyer preached today's second sermon, and though his message was always beneficial, he felt it his duty to deliver the Lord's word with a matter-of-fact monotone and a dry demeanor. More often than not when he spoke, Esther found herself drifting off rather than benefiting.

In turn, that made her spend much more of her day in prayer asking for forgiveness for her inattentiveness.

The bishop ended the prayer with a resounding *"aemen,"* and the congregation stood.

"Esther, can I have a word, please?"

She turned as Maddie Kauffman approached. Despite the restaurant owner's permanent frown and stern disposition, Esther liked her. A body always knew where they stood with dour-faced Maddie. How the Lord ever brought her and the easygoing Henry Kauffman together was a mystery to be sure.

"Of course, Maddie." She smiled pleasantly, though she could tell from the stiff rod of Maddie's spine that she was not going to like where the conversation was going.

Esther took a deep breath and steeled herself against what was to come. Since Maddie was Lorie's stepmother and Lorie and Caroline were such *gut freinden*, Esther could only assume that Maddie wanted to speak to her *mudder* to *mudder*, as it were, about the relationship between Caroline and Andrew. She had already heard about the kiss they shared one night a few weeks ago. And right on Main Street, at that. But since they had walked a straight-and-narrow path since then, talk had died down, and they hadn't had a meeting with the deacon.

"If this is about Caroline and Andrew," Esther started as Maddie shook her head. She clasped Esther by the elbow and steered her out of the barn and into a private corner. That is, if a corner of fence next to the pasture out in the open and the bright afternoon sun was private.

"It's not about the young'uns." Maddie sucked in a deep breath, and her mouth took on an even more pinched look than usual. "It's about you and Abe Fitch."

Esther couldn't hold back her gasp of surprise.

"Jah." Maddie nodded. "There's been talk all around about the two of you. I've even heard that you spent the night out there at his farm."

Esther's eyes widened until they hurt. "But that's not true."

"I never said it was," Maddie said defensively, crossing her arms and looking down her sharp nose. "I'm merely informing you of what's going on. Don't be surprised if you get a visit from the deacon. The elders cannot let infractions like this go without notice."

Esther wasn't sure if Maddie was talking about the

content of the rumors or the rumors themselves. Surely the elders wouldn't allow such vicious gossip to be spread.

"I just thought I should tell you." Maddie's voice sounded like she had done Esther a favor, but Esther knew Maddie's heart wasn't always in the right place.

"*Danki*, Maddie, for telling me." It was always best to take the high road, her John always said. She had a fight on her hands, but it wasn't with Maddie Kauffman.

Esther brushed past the woman and went in search of Caroline.

Dear Caroline,

I have prayed long and hard about this matter. And though I have decided to tell you what happened, I'm still not sure that I am doing the right thing.

Let me back up a bit. I went into the store the other day to take in some jars of jelly to sell. While I was in there the strangest thing happened. This young Englisch man came up to me and asked my name. You know how your father feels about such familiarity, but I understand it is the way of the English. I told him my name, and he asked me if I knew a girl named Caroline. My heart stopped beating in my chest. I just looked at him and tried to keep breathing. I guess I waited too long, for he shook his head and walked out the door of the shop.

I'm somewhat used to the strange ways of the English, but it was more than that. He looked so familiar to me. At first I didn't recognize him and then I realized he has the same dark hair and gray eyes as your Emma.

I promised myself I wouldn't ask questions about Emma's father, but could that be him? You told me that he didn't want anything to do with you or the baby. I want to believe that you told me the truth, but this day caused me to think. If he is indeed Emma's father, why is he looking for you now?

Perhaps he regrets turning you away two years ago. Perhaps he wants to make amends.

I've always held the hope in my heart that one day you would return to us here, and we could be a family once more. Now I wonder if I'll ever see you again.

I don't know what you'll do with this information, my sweet Caroline, but I hope that it brings you some measure of happiness to know that Emma's father might have come around after all.

I love you always,
Mamm

Chapter Fifteen

Caroline folded her mother's letter back to rights and slipped it into the envelope. Her heart pounded and her mouth was dry. This was it. She had asked God for a sign to show her that she had taken the right path. This was as big as they came. Trey was looking for her.

She took a deep breath to keep the tears at bay. All these years she had consoled herself with the fact that she had made her choices. She had got on the bus that had brought her here. She had made the decision to take the money Trey's parents gave her and buy a bus ticket with it. Now it seemed as if the wind was shifting.

She closed her eyes and leaned her head back against the booth in the diner. Emma pounded the high-chair tray demanding her attention, but the images of the past swamped her.

She remembered it like it was yesterday, that rainy night in August when she had gone to their house. "House" seemed like such an inadequate word for the gigantic structure.

They told her that Trey didn't want to see her. He had even gone back to school a week earlier than planned. And he hadn't even told her. He'd just left. She had cried and pleaded, right there on their front porch. Distraught, she sank to her knees. What was she to do with the baby?

Trey's father had pulled out his wallet, handed her five hundred dollars in cash, and told her to "take care of it."

At the time she hadn't known what that meant, but she soon realized. Trey didn't want their baby. Her family no longer wanted her. So she packed a bag and headed for Colorado.

Emma pounded the tray once more. Caroline raised her head, blinking her eyes open and free of the tears that had gathered behind her lids. The time for crying was long since gone.

"Caroline, are you *allrecht*?" Millie Fisher stopped at her table to refresh her coffee.

She forced down the knot growing in her throat. "I think I'm coming down with something." She certainly sounded like it. True, she had just been put through an emotional wringer, and like the clothes her mother ran through the one on their back porch, Caroline felt twisted and out of sorts.

Millie gave her one last concerned look, then walked back to the waitress station.

Caroline tore off another piece of biscuit and gave it to Emma.

"*Danki*," her daughter said, and fresh tears arose in Caroline's eyes. What would she do without the sweet child? And what was she supposed to do now about the girl's father?

"*Ach*, Caroline, you look *baremlich*," Emily said as Caroline sat down at the picnic table next to her.

She placed Emma on the bench beside her and faced her friend. "How sweet of you to say so."

Lorie smacked Emily's hand. "You're not supposed to say that to a lady." Emily opened her mouth to protest, but

Lorie interjected first. "I don't care if she is your best friend. *Ach*, Emily, one would think that your father hasn't taught you any manners."

"*Jah?* Well, just because my father is bishop doesn't mean that I have to go around lying to everybody about how they look."

"Did your mother never teach you that if you don't have anything nice to say, then keep your mouth closed?"

Caroline smiled. These were her *freinden,* and she loved them.

"What's so funny?" Lorie asked.

She shook her head. "I'm just glad we are all friends."

"For certain," Lorie agreed. "Can you imagine how she would talk about you if we weren't?"

They all laughed.

Caroline took a deep breath and noisily let it out. "I need to talk to you two about something."

Emily nodded. "Talk away."

But ever-more-intuitive Lorie cocked her head to one side. "Andrew?"

"*Nay . . . Jah . . .* Sort of . . ."

Emily and Lorie exchanged a look.

"I seriously hate it when you do that."

Lorie grimaced. "Sorry. But I'm not surprised. It seems like the two of you have gotten pretty serious over the last few weeks."

"*Jah*, I suppose." Caroline picked at a place on the table. "It's just . . ."

"Just what?"

"I was hoping that maybe we could meet somewhere a little more . . ."

"Private?" Lorie supplied.

"*Jah.*"

"Sounds juicy."

Lorie elbowed Emily. "You should behave yourself. You are supposed to be a beacon for the young people of this community."

Emily made a face. "You sound like my *mamm*."

"Somebody needs to."

Emily elbowed her back. For all their bickering, they were the best of friends, bonding in a way that Caroline could only skim. They had accepted her into their relationship, but between Emma and the fact that she hadn't grown up in Wells Landing, she had a slight disadvantage. Not that they treated her any differently. It was just different was all. But two better friends she couldn't ask for.

"Let's meet tonight at the restaurant. No one's using the banquet room. We can go in there and talk."

"I appreciate that, Lorie."

Her friend nodded. "It looks like you need to get something off your mind."

"*Jah,*" Caroline said. For sure and for certain.

Esther agreed to watch Emma, and Caroline made her way down the sidewalk to the restaurant. She still wasn't exactly sure what she was going to say to her friends, but she needed advice in the worst way. She only felt a little guilty at not sharing this news of Trey with Esther. The woman had been a lifeline to her these past couple of years, but she wasn't sure that Esther could ever understand what led her into Trey's arms. Esther had fallen in love and married her childhood sweetheart. Emily and Lorie were younger. She just hoped they could understand what she was dealing with. Someone had to. She couldn't be the only Amish girl to ever succumb to the pleasures of the *Englisch* world.

She opened the glass doors and stepped into Kauffman's. As usual it was busy, though the dinner crowd was slowly dying down.

"Hi, Caroline." Millie waved as she wiped down a table. "I can seat you in just a second."

"I'm here to meet Lorie and Emily."

"They're in the banquet room. Go on back."

"Danki." Caroline made her way to the banquet room, her knees trembling. What if she told her friends her deepest secret and they shunned her? What would she do then?

"Caroline." Lorie motioned her into the room. "What are you doing out there?"

Only then did Caroline realize that she was hovering just outside the doorway. She shook her head and ran her hands down her sides. "Nothing, I . . . Just thinking."

Emily looked to Lorie. "Sounds serious. Come sit down." Emily patted the chair next to her.

It was time. Caroline inched into the room, perching on the edge of the seat, her back as stiff as an overstarched apron.

"I ordered you a water. Do you want anything else? Tea? Lemonade?"

"Nay." Caroline took a big gulp of water to ease the dryness in her throat. "Emma's father isn't dead."

There. She'd said it.

Emily slapped her hand on the table. Lorie's mouth fell open. Both of them gasped.

"I knew it," Emily said.

Lorie elbowed her into silence. "What do you mean, Caroline?"

She couldn't look her friends in their faces. Instead she kept her head down and concentrated on folding unnecessary pleats in her apron. "I mean he's still alive and living in Tennessee."

"So you've been lying to everybody?" Lorie asked. Her tone was strained and filled with hurt.

"Nay." Caroline jerked her gaze up to scan her friends' concerned faces. *"Jah.* But not intentionally," she quickly added. "Everyone just assumed I was a widow, and I never told anyone any different."

"Not even Esther?" Emily asked.

Caroline shook her head.

Lorie laid her hand over Caroline's trembling fingers. "Does this mean you are going back to live with him?"

"Maybe I should start at the beginning."

Both her friends nodded.

"His name is Trey Rycroft."

"That's not a very Plain-sounding name."

A small, rueful smile played at the corners of her mouth. "That's because he's English."

More gasps.

"I met him at a party and fell instantly in love with him. He was so handsome and confident. Anyway, it seemed like he felt the same way about me. We started spending a lot of time together . . . alone. His friends didn't understand his wanting to be with me, and I certainly couldn't let him spend time with my friends. One thing led to another and . . ." Caroline shrugged.

"When I realized that I was going to have a baby, I went to his house." She closed her eyes against the painful memories.

"You never told him that he has a daughter?" Lorie asked.

"Nay. Though I tried. I went to his house, but his father told me he had already left for school. He—he gave me some money, and I used it to buy a bus ticket."

"Gut himmel." Emily sat back in her seat and fanned herself with a stack of paper napkins. "That's some story."

"Caroline," Lorie started, "why didn't you tell us?"

She shook her head and swallowed the lump clogging her throat. Tears welled in her eyes. "I was afraid to lose your friendship."

Lorie slung one arm around her and pulled her in for a quick squeeze. "You could never do anything to ruin my love for you."

"Jah," Emily echoed the sentiment.

"Danki." Caroline wiped away her tears and sniffed. "I got a letter from my mother this week. It seems that Trey is looking for me."

"As he should be," Emily admonished. "He has a child he has never seen."

Caroline shook her head. "He doesn't even know she exists."

Lorie gasped. "What are you going to do?"

"I think—" Caroline sighed. "I think I need to go back to Tennessee and tell him. He deserves to know that he has a daughter."

"What about Andrew?" Emily asked.

"That's the hardest part. I think I might be falling in love with him. He's so *gut* and kind."

"He loves Emma so much," Lorie added.

"But if I have a chance to start a life with Trey . . . Well, I have to try now, don't I? For Emma's sake."

"What makes you think he wants you now if he ignored you two years ago when you needed him the most?" Emily crossed her arms and cocked her head to one side.

"Haven't you been listening?" Lorie asked. "Trey didn't see her that night. For all she knows, his father lied about him being gone."

"So you're just going to pick up and go to Tennessee?" Emily was shaking her head before Caroline even opened her mouth to reply.

"Jah."

"What happens if Trey doesn't want anything to do with Emma?" Emily continued despite Lorie's warning look of censure.

Just the thought of him turning away their child sent a stabbing pain through Caroline's heart. "Then I come back."

"What if he wants you to stay there and be the family you never got the chance to be?" Lorie asked quietly.

Maybe it was just her hopeful heart, but that sounded more like the Trey Caroline had met and fallen in love with. She should have realized at the time that Trey cared about her. But she had been too caught up in her whirling emotions, misery, and hormones to see through the cloud of pain his father's words caused.

What if Trey wanted them to be a family? She had loved him once. Loved him enough to go against everything she had been taught. She was older and wiser now. Could she give up her life in Wells Landing, her job at the bakery, Andrew, to go and live with Trey?

Caroline gave her two best friends a small smile that she hoped looked confident when she felt anything but. "We'll just have to see once I get there."

Dear Mamm,

I guess you know by now that the man you saw in the market was indeed Emma's father. His name is Trey Rycroft. He is a gut man and comes from a wealthy Englisch family.

I know I owe you a big explanation about what happened that summer, but it's too much to put in one letter. Rest assured that I will explain. Though I will do so in person. I have decided to come back to Ethridge and see if I can meet with Trey. Even as I write this my hands are shaking at the thought. I do not know how he will react to knowing that he has a daughter. See, I never got to tell him before I left. I know you've always thought that he was the one who gave me the money to leave town, but in fact it was his father. His family didn't approve of him seeing me, so I'm certain his father never even told Trey I'd been by to see him.

I guess I should have worked harder to find him and tell him the truth, but I was so racked with shame I only wanted to go someplace, any place, and start again.

I am making arrangements to come back to Ethridge. I'll let you know as soon as I can as to my day of arrival.

Until then . . .

Love,
Caroline

Chapter Sixteen

"Tell me again where you are going?" Esther folded her arms in that motherly fashion that had Caroline shaking her head over the fact the woman had never had children of her own. She was a natural.

Caroline folded another dress and placed it in her suitcase. "My *grossdaadi* fell and hit his head. He's in the hospital."

"I know what you told me. I'm just having trouble believing that there's not more to this story."

Caroline whirled around to face her. "I am telling the truth."

"I did not say that you were being dishonest."

The breath left Caroline in a huge rush, and she felt herself crumble under the weight of her deceit. She had kept so many secrets, lied to everyone she loved. She was tired of the dishonesty.

She eased down on the bed, trying to find the words to tell Esther the truth. It was the least she could do considering everything Esther had done for her since she had come to Wells Landing.

Tears welled in her eyes. "I haven't been totally honest

with you." Her fingers twisted in her apron as Esther drew near and sat down on the bed next to her.

"About your grandfather?" Esther asked.

"About everything." Caroline gulped down a sob and straightened her shoulders. She had made the decision to hide the truth from all these wonderful people in Wells Landing. But no longer.

Esther took Caroline's hand into her own and gave it a reassuring squeeze. "Tell me."

She took a moment to gather her thoughts. Ever patient, Esther waited for her to ready herself to begin.

"As you know, my home district in Tennessee is very conservative."

Esther nodded.

"The elders don't allow the young people to have a run-around time. Most of the young people know whether or not they can keep up the traditions of their parents. I was certain I could. So it was no big decision to bend my knee and join the church. Then I met him."

Esther held her hand throughout the entire story. How Caroline had met Trey, fallen in love with him, and then survived the utter heartbreak of hearing that he had gone back to school without even bothering to tell her good-bye.

"But it was all a lie." Caroline wiped the tears away with the back of one hand. "Trey never knew about Emma."

"A sadder tale I've never heard," Esther said, drying tears of her own.

"I'm sorry," Caroline said. "I never meant to deceive you. But—"

Esther shook her head. "We all believed what we wanted to believe about you."

"I'm not sure I understand."

Esther smiled. "You are a *gut* and kind person. That's all

we could see from you. So we made up a past that fit the person we see in you."

Even though her chest was constricted with heartbreak and trepidation, Caroline laughed. "Are you saying that I'm a *gut* girl, so that's what you saw in me?"

"Jah," Esther said. "That's exactly what I'm saying."

"I'm not sure my *vatter* would agree with you."

"I've been in this world for a while, Caroline Hostetler, and one thing is certain: You can't judge a person by the sum of one of their actions. You made a mistake," she said, brushing a hand over Caroline's shoulder. "God forgives and so should we."

Grateful tears welled in Caroline's eyes. "You mean that?"

"Of course I do." Then Esther drew her into her arms and gave her a bone-crushing hug.

Other than Andrew, Caroline would miss Esther the most. She squeezed her friend a little tighter and said a small prayer that when all of this was done, she could still count this woman as friend.

The trip back to Ethridge was no easier than when she left. Emma did not like riding. She did not like having to sit on her mother's lap for the trip, but it was so much cheaper to buy one ticket. Caroline had thought that Emma would sleep for most of the trip. Instead she was fussy. She had thought that she could sit Emma in the seat next to her in the event that the bus wasn't completely full, but that only happened a couple of times during the hours they were on the road.

But even worse, the trip meant hours and hours with her own thoughts. Caroline laid her head against the window, closing her eyes against the scenery passing by in a blur. She rubbed Emma's back as her *boppli* finally slept.

She, Caroline Hostetler, was a coward.

She had tried to tell herself that she hadn't had any time to talk to Andrew before she left. But the truth was she knew that averages were against her. She had heard someone talking in town once about a law of averages. She wasn't sure exactly what that meant until they explained. The more times something happens in a person's favor means a greater chance for it to turn and fail. Emily, Lorie, and Esther had all forgiven her for the transgressions in her past. The chances were against her for Andrew to do the same.

She hadn't realized just how much she cared about Andrew until she had to think about doubt, hurt, and distrust shining in his eyes. She couldn't stand there and pour her heart out to him only to have him turn her away.

So she had left. And left him a letter trying her best to explain what had happened and why she was gone.

Caroline sighed. She still wasn't entirely sure what this trip would mean for her and Trey. There were just so many possibilities. What if he wanted her to leave? What if he wanted her to stay? What if her family welcomed her back? What if they didn't?

Being back with her *mamm* and *dat* was the one thing she had wanted since the day she left. But could she walk away from the life she had built? And what of Andrew?

She sighed. There was no use going down that road. By the time he read her letter she would be halfway to Tennessee. He would probably never forgive her. After all, he had jumped into a relationship with her when he was still grieving for his Beth. They had known then that what they had was special. But now Caroline was certain her lies had ruined it for them both.

She kissed the top of Emma's head. At least Emma

wouldn't remember. But as for Caroline . . . She would never forget.

She stared out the window at the passing scenery, then closed her eyes again, as it made her dizzy. They were somewhere in Tennessee between Memphis and Nashville. She had breathed a sigh of relief as they crossed over the big Mississippi River and managed not to look as the driver swung through traffic like she had never seen. At the bus depot she had kept her head down and managed not to attract too much attention as she waited for the bus that would finally take her home.

Just another hour or two and she would be back in Ethridge.

She wasn't sure how she was going to get from the bus depot in Lawrenceburg to her parents' farm on the edge of Ethridge, but she would figure it out when the time came. She had written her mother and given her the specifics on her bus ticket, the time she would arrive, and the route number. She thought her mother should know when she was arriving. It was one thing to disappear in the middle of the night and quite another to just show up again with no warning.

She sighed. There was no guessing how her father was going to take her appearance. Yet another thing she would address when the time came.

She must have dozed off when they drove through Nashville, and it was dark when the driver pulled the bus to a stop. Everyone got off the coach to stretch their legs. Caroline couldn't imagine that they were all staying in the small town, though Ethridge did get its share of tourists.

Thankfully the last leg of their journey produced an opening beside her and Emma could sit in her own seat. Caroline had strapped the child into the big chair and prayed for the best. Emma had not liked the constriction, but had eventually settled down and gone to sleep.

Caroline undid the seat belt and scooped the stretching Emma into her arms. "We're home, wee one." The pet name brought back memories of Andrew and the sting of tears to her eyes. She blinked them back. She was just tired. It had been a long trip, and it wasn't over yet. Aside from the ride to her parents' *haus*, she still had to face her *vatter*.

She swung her bag over her shoulder and made her way toward the front of the bus.

The driver shot her a sympathetic look as she climbed down the stairs.

"Is there a phone inside?"

He pointed toward the left. "Just to this side in between the restrooms. Do you need some help?"

"*Nay* . . . no, I can manage." She had enough to call a cab to take her to neighboring Ethridge.

She made her way inside. The building smelled worse than the barn after a summer rain. But she would only be there long enough to collect their other bag and call for a ride.

"Caroline Hostetler?"

She blinked in surprise as a nicely dressed man approached. "*Jah?*"

"I'm Don Harper. Your mother called me."

"*Jah?*" She adjusted Emma on her hip and gathered her thoughts.

"She hired me to take you home."

Home.

Caroline's shoulders slumped with gratitude. At least she didn't have to think any more about how to get to the farm. "I need to get my bags."

Don Harper waited patiently for the porters to bring in the luggage and carried both bags to his car.

The last thing Caroline wanted to do was sit in a moving vehicle for another spell, but at least they weren't far from Ethridge.

Don Harper stashed her bags in the trunk and left Caroline to buckle Emma into the child seat in back.

Emma, exhausted and unused to such confinements, started to cry, but Caroline finished the task and slid into the front.

"Ready?" Don Harper asked.

Caroline buckled herself in. As ready as she could possibly be.

He started the car and put it in gear. "My wife runs the general store."

Caroline thought she had seen him before, otherwise she might not have gotten into the car that easily.

"Won't be long, and I'll have you home."

There was that word again.

Emma's wails made conversation impossible, not that Caroline had much to say. Don Harper must have sensed her reluctance. He kept whatever was on his mind to himself as they made the trip.

Soon the white lights of his car cut across her parents' house as he turned into the drive.

It was dark, but everything seemed the same. Such was the way of the Amish. Any changes had to be carefully examined for any repercussions. Whatever changes made it through were seldom and slow to come.

Her driver pulled the car to a stop and fiddled with something on the dashboard. He put it in park, and he got out without turning off the engine.

"I'll just get your bags," he said over Emma's cries.

Caroline stood and stretched, then opened the back door of the car to get the screaming baby.

Emma's cries slowed to teary hiccups as she unbuckled

her and cradled her close. Caroline steeled her heart against the tears. It was time to be strong.

She straightened and followed the driver to the porch.

"I'll just leave your bags here?"

Caroline nodded. Though it was customary for drivers to spend some time at the house with the people who hired them, Don Harper seemed to sense that there was more than joy to this homecoming.

"Let me get you some money," she said, reaching for her shoulder bag.

Don shook his head. "It's already been taken care of. Good night, Caroline. Welcome home."

He descended the wooden steps and made his way through the dark and back to his car. Caroline was still outside when he drove away.

She took a deep breath. Standing on the porch was not what she needed to be doing. It was time to face her family for the first time in nearly two years.

She raised her hand to knock, then changed her mind and turned the doorknob instead.

Everything looked just as it had the night she left. Same worn couch and wooden rocker. Same scarred table. Same kerosene-burning lamps.

Having heard the noise, her mother appeared at the doorway that led to the kitchen.

"Caroline?"

"*Mamm. Wie geht?* I'm home."

Dear Andrew,

By the time you get this I will be well on my way back to Tennessee. I'm sorry that I couldn't wait and talk to you before I left. My grossdaadi is in the hospital, and I am needed at home immediately.

I wish I had more time to explain. Please forgive me, but I don't know what I'm going to find when I get back home. How my family will react to my return. As for Wells Landing, I have enjoyed my time in Oklahoma, but my family is in Tennessee. I'm not sure when, if ever, I'll return to Wells Landing.

It's not fair of me to ask you to wait for me. You have proved to yourself that you are ready to start courting again. I hope that you will be happy in everything that you do, whether you stay in Wells Landing or return to Missouri. You are such a very special person and deserve a gut wife to take care of you and grow old with you. I hope you find all the happiness that you deserve.

> *Love,*
> *Caroline*

Chapter Seventeen

Andrew folded the letter and placed it back in the envelope even though he wanted to crumple it into a ball and pitch it across the dining area in Esther's bakery. He took a deep, calming breath and looked to Esther. "I don't know what it means."

The look in Esther's dark blue eyes was one of sadness and confusion. She gestured to the letter on the table. "May I?"

He nodded.

Esther slid into the booth opposite him and removed the single sheet of paper.

He drummed his fingers as she read the words.

"She's gone back to Tennessee," Esther finally said.

"*Jah*, I understood that part. Why?"

"Her *grossdaadi* is ill."

But Andrew had a sinking feeling around his heart that it was more than that. "Is she coming back?"

Esther stared out the bakery window.

"Esther?"

She sighed and turned to face him. "I don't know."

Hurt ran through him. How could she just leave? Was

she afraid? Did he push too hard, too fast? Did he expect too much too soon?

He hadn't realized he had closed his eyes against the heartbreak and whirling thoughts until Esther laid her hand on top of his. "She never meant to hurt you."

He swallowed hard. Somehow he did know that. And yet . . . "Is there more to it than what she told me?"

Esther pulled away and leaned back in her chair. "Why would there be more?"

Andrew shrugged, but he had his answer. Caroline would not be returning to Wells Landing. He just wasn't sure what he could do about it.

Esther waited until the door shut behind Andrew until she drew in a relieved breath.

She couldn't imagine why Caroline didn't want to tell Andrew the truth. But she understood all the same. Caroline was in love with the *bu*. Yet despite her talk otherwise, she wasn't planning on returning to Oklahoma. She hadn't come right out and said the words, but Esther knew the truth. She could see it in those expressive eyes.

For all the work that Caroline had put into learning to live among the Beachys in Wells Landing, her conservative upbringing had never been far under the surface. She was a *gut maedel*, despite the mistakes she had made. Telling the entire district her secrets was not something Caroline could do and then face those very same people the next day as they came into the bakery. It just wasn't in her.

Esther sighed and finished wiping down the table. Caroline and Emma had not even been gone for a full day. Yet Esther missed them so much it hurt.

One thing she learned a long time ago was the Good

Lord was a great healer. And with time all their pain would lessen.

Tonight she would say a prayer for Andrew, for Caroline and Emma. For the *Englisch bu* Trey and everyone involved.

She had hated not being able to tell Andrew about the promise she had made to Caroline, but she was a *gut* Amish woman, and she would keep her word.

Esther stopped putting the chairs on the tabletops, the thought stilling her motions with precision ease. She had promised Caroline that she wouldn't tell Andrew about Trey, but Caroline had never said a word about telling Abe Fitch.

It was sneaky, but what was that *Englisch* saying? All's fair in love and war? Well, as a peaceful woman, Esther didn't know the first thing about war. And she might not know a great deal about love. One thing she was certain about: 1 Corinthians 13:13. *And now these three remain: faith, hope and love. But the greatest of these is love.*

Smile on her face, she turned the *Open* sign to *Closed* after the last customer left. Then she brushed out her hair and carefully pinned it back into place. She changed into a clean apron and headed down Main Street to the Fitch Furniture Store.

It was perhaps the most forward thing she had done in regard to Abe Fitch, maybe in her entire life. But her friend needed her.

She entered the bright showroom with the gorgeous wood pieces all arranged and set up like a body would expect to see them. A jar of yellow flowers sat in the center of a long wooden table. A lamp on the dresser that matched the bed she had bought for Caroline. Signs were hung and the pieces dusted. All in all the place never looked better, a sure sign that Abe had help by way of his nephew Andrew Fitch.

No sooner had the bell over the door stopped ringing than Andrew came out of the back, wiping his hands on a rag. He spotted her, and his eyes grew wide with surprise. "Esther. I didn't expect to see you."

She took a steadying breath. "Is your uncle around?"

He glanced toward the back, then to Esther once again. "*Jah. Jah*. I'll get him for you."

"That would be *gut*."

She willed her heart rate to slow and schooled her features into a mask of patience when she wanted to jump up and down and holler for him to hurry. None of that would be beneficial for the cause she had. Patience was definitely in her favor.

A few moments later Andrew returned, his uncle right behind him.

Abe squinted at her through the thick lenses of his glasses. "*Ach*, Esther Lapp, what brings you in today?"

She folded her hands over her middle. "I've come to invite you to dinner tonight, Abe Fitch."

Her gaze was focused on Abe, but she thought she saw Andrew smile.

"*Jah?*" Abe asked, still squinting at her.

"*Jah*. I have some business with you and I think it best be discussed over a fine meal."

Abe scratched the side of his head, his hat tipping to one side with the motion. "*Allrecht*. Would you like to meet me at Kauffman's?"

Esther shook her head and tried to appear confident. If what Maddie Kauffman had said about Esther and Abe and the rumors that were flying around Wells Landing were true, this was not a smart move. But she had more important things to worry about than idle gossip. "*Nay*. You can just come by the *haus* after work. We can talk then."

If Abe was shocked by her request, he didn't let on. He gave her a little wave and shuffled back to the workroom.

Esther nodded in turn to Andrew and Danny, who had materialized from nowhere to see what was going on. She trusted Andrew, but Danny was a talker. Everyone from the bishop to the guy who ran the gas station across town would know that she had asked Abe Fitch to supper before they even sat down to eat the meal. It was a chance she was willing to take.

Andrew watched Esther leave with a mixture of awe and confusion.

"What was that all about?" Danny asked.

"I don't know." He walked to the door of the shop and opened it, staring down the street at Esther Lapp's departing form. She marched toward the bakery with the same determination that she had used when talking to *Onkle*.

Danny chuckled. "I've never seen her quite so . . ."

"Forceful?" Andrew supplied.

"*Jah*." Danny took a long drink from his water bottle, then pointed the mouth toward Andrew. "You don't think this has anything to do with Caroline leaving, do you?"

"Maybe." Andrew shrugged despite the pain hearing her name caused him. "Maybe she thinks that it's time to stop beating around the bush with *Onkle* and come out and say her feelings." Or maybe his and Caroline's matchmaking had finally paid off. As much as it would pain him, he would write her and let her know. Someday.

"Speaking of feelings," Danny started, "what about the

four of us going to Kauffman's tonight for supper?" It wasn't quite a request.

"Danny, I—"

His cousin held up a hand to stop his words before he even got good and started. "Sarah really likes you. The least you can do is give her a chance." The unspoken *since Caroline is gone* hung heavy in the air.

Andrew sighed. The last thing he wanted to do was give Sarah false hope, but if being with Caroline over the last few weeks had taught him anything, it was that he could live again, learn to love. Except now the one he wanted was somewhere else. He wasn't sure what was worse, knowing that Beth was gone forever not by her choice or that Caroline had chosen something else over him. Or perhaps it was a someone.

Now he was just being ridiculous.

"Come on, cousin. It'll help keep your mind off things."

Danny was right. He needed to keep his mind clear of the things he couldn't change.

"Allrecht." He gave a reluctant nod. "Dinner tonight." *Just the four of us.*

It was nearly seven-thirty when Moxie started barking, signaling to the fact that someone was at the door.

Esther had just finished taking the casserole from the oven and set it on the cooling rack when the puppy alarm went off.

She had been a little skeptical about having the dog in her house, but now that Caroline and Emma were gone, she was glad to have him for both his guarding capabilities and his companionship.

It was strange to her how she had only lived with the pair for two years, but their absence left a huge hole in her heart.

She patted the pooch on the head and slipped him a piece of fat off one of the pork chops she'd made.

She wanted tonight to be extra special and had even considered going down to the library and checking out an *Englisch* cookbook and making something the likes of which Abe Fitch had never seen, but instead opted to go with the proven route.

She wiped her hands down her sides and smoothed back her hair. "I'm coming," she hollered over Moxie's excited barks.

As expected when she opened the door, Abe Fitch stood on the other side. "Esther." He waited patiently for her to invite him in.

"Get in here, Abe Fitch. Do you want the entire town to start talking about us?" She pulled him inside and resisted the urge to see if anyone saw her let him in.

Abe's forehead puckered into a frown, an expression she wasn't used to seeing on him. Normally he went around with a sort of dreamy look on his face. But his confusion at least meant he was paying attention. "*Was iss letz*, Esther Lapp?"

Esther released his elbow and tried to act normal. No sense in going *ab im kopp*. "Maddie Kauffman's been talking around. Don't want her to get the wrong impression."

"*Ach*, and what might that be?"

"Never mind that, Abe Fitch," she said, hoping he didn't notice the blush she felt heating her cheeks. "Supper is ready and on the table."

Thankfully, Abe didn't protest. He swept off his hat and hung it by the door, then followed behind her to the table.

They sat down and bowed their heads in prayer.

Esther thanked the Lord for the beautiful day and the

wunderbaar-gut food they were about to eat. She asked for Caroline's safe return to Tennessee and the words to tell Abe what needed to be done.

"Aemen," he said.

She murmured a response, then offered him the platter stacked with pork chops. "Would you like one?"

"Jah." He used his fork to spear one and deposited it on his plate.

They passed the other dishes to one another and set about their meal. The truth of the matter was Esther wasn't sure how to tell Abe the truth about why Caroline had left.

"What's on your mind tonight, Esther?"

"Jah?" His words were so unexpected it took her a heartbeat to realize he was talking to her. Or maybe it was the fact that never once as he spoke did he stop eating or look up from his plate.

But he was looking at her now, calmly chewing his last bite and waiting for her to respond.

She laughed, a choked sound, then took a gulp of iced tea to ease the constriction in her throat. "Why do you think I've got something on my mind?" She tittered, then immediately wished she could call back the words. Or the tone.

"Because you're not normally this nervous around me. And you told me as much when you came down to the furniture shop this afternoon."

Ach, jah, so she had. Esther cleared her throat and gathered her wits and courage. "I need to talk to you about Caroline and Andrew."

"Jah? Seems to me there's not much to talk about anymore. She went home to see her *grossdaadi,* and it doesn't sound like she's coming back given the letter she wrote to Andrew."

"He let you read it?" Esther pushed her plate aside and folded her hands on the table.

"Jah." Abe continued to eat, grabbing another biscuit and adding a liberal dollop of butter. "And he hasn't seemed like himself since then."

"That's what I wanted to talk to you about." She took a deep breath and braced herself to continue. She had gone back and forth between telling him straight out or trying to bring it up in casual conversation. But somehow that seemed a bit deceptive. It was bad enough that she was telling Abe at all. She had promised Caroline that she wouldn't say anything to Andrew, but she never said anything about telling Abe. It was a conscious deceit, but one she would have to use to her advantage. "Caroline went home because Emma's father came back."

Abe stopped eating, his loaded fork suspended somewhere between his plate and his lips. He closed his mouth and swallowed hard, the bite redeposited on his plate as he set his fork down. "I thought he was dead."

Esther shook her head.

"Then she's still married."

Esther shook her head again.

"Ach, woman, would you tell me what in the world is going on?"

"Emma's father is English. He and Caroline were never married." She said the words slowly as if somehow they wouldn't sound so damaging that way. She watched his expression for signs of condemnation.

But Abe's expression was only one of surprise. He sat back in his seat. "You don't say."

"Listen . . . Abe . . . I think it's a shame that Caroline and Andrew were growing so close to each other and now it's all lost."

"Well, I can't do a thing about Andrew's mind on something like that. I'm not one for passing judgment, but this seems very unfortunate for all."

"I don't think you understand. Andrew doesn't know."

Abe's mouth twisted from side to side, pulling his beard this way and that. He reached up and stroked it back into place. "And you think if he did know that it would change things?"

"*Jah*, I do. I think they were so very close to falling completely in love."

"Andrew needs a second chance at love, and it sounds like Caroline needs a new start as well."

Esther tried to temper her smile. She had been so scared about telling Abe Caroline's secret. He could have come back with condemnation, censure, and disapproval; instead he leaned forward and braced his elbows on the table in front of him. "Do you think that if you told Andrew why Caroline has gone that he would . . . ?"

"First off, I promised Caroline that I wouldn't tell Andrew. That is something you'll have to do for them."

"I don't know, Esther." He shook his head and sat back. "Why did Caroline go back? Is she still in love with this *Englischer*?"

Esther pressed her lips together. "It seems the *Englisch* boy doesn't know that he's a *dat*."

"This changes things," Abe said.

"I don't see how."

"It seems to me that Caroline is headed toward putting her family together. And it sounds like it's a long time in coming. I do not think we should interfere with that."

"I'm not talking about interfering—" Esther started, but Abe was already shaking his head.

"Only a woman would consider that telling him something so dramatic would not be interfering." He cut a bite off his pork chop and fed it to Moxie under the table.

"Abe Fitch, I expected better from you."

"What?" he asked, squinting innocently through the thick lenses of his glasses. "I saw you feed him twice whilst we were eating."

"Not about the dog. About Andrew and Caroline. They deserve a chance."

He tilted his head in a thoughtful way. At least she had his full attention again. "And . . ."

"And it could be said that if we don't interfere and give them a chance to work through this that we are interfering as well."

A frown puckered his brow. "I'm not sure I understand any of what you just said."

"Never mind, Abe. The least we can do is pray about it, *jah*?"

"I agree that taking things to the Lord is a *gut* idea, but—"

It was her turn to cut him off before he could finish the thought. "You pray about it, Abe. You can do that much."

"Jah."

"Now," Esther said, pushing back from the table, "how about some coffee and pie?"

"Would you like some help?"

She shook her head. "You stay here and finish feeding Moxie your scraps."

He pushed his glasses a little higher up the bridge of his nose and smiled. Esther's heart melted a little bit more. Surely a man kindhearted enough to feed a puppy under the table would do everything in his power to support true love.

She smiled to herself as she got their desserts together and carried them back to the table.

Abe was still waiting on her, his plate scraped clean.

"I hope you like apple crisp and ice cream," she said, sliding a bowl in front of him.

"Jah," he said, scooping up his first bite before she had even sat back down.

That was a *gut* sign.

"So that's why you invited me here tonight? To ask me about Andrew and Caroline?"

"Jah. I mean why else?" Esther shrugged and concentrated on getting the right amount of apple crisp to ice cream on her spoon. It gave her something to focus on instead of those suddenly intense blue eyes of his.

"I thought it might have something to do with all the matchmaking Caroline and Andrew were doing."

Esther sat down her napkin, shock prickling her all the way to her fingertips. "Matchmaking?"

He nodded.

"Caroline and Andrew?"

"Jah. All those dinners after church . . ."

"And trips to the farm."

"You look surprised."

"I am." How did he notice all of Caroline and Andrew's attempts to get them together when she hadn't? "Why didn't you say anything?"

Abe finished off the last of his dessert and sat back in his chair. "Well, I figured that you weren't interested in me that way."

Esther blinked and opened her mouth, but she couldn't find the words to respond so she closed it again and blinked for a second time.

Abe raised an eyebrow. Evidently he expected some sort of response to his declaration.

"I . . ." Esther pressed a hand to her chest, right over her pounding heart. "Why would I not?"

He quirked his mouth to one side. "I know you loved John Lapp."

"I did."

"He was a *gut* man, that much is certain. And you've never remarried. I figured you were still pining after him. If you're still in love with your husband and you've never remarried, how could another man find a place in your heart?"

Esther was struck completely mute. She could only stare at Abe and mull his words over in her head.

But she took too long to decipher what he had said.

Abe pushed back from the table and stood. "I think I should be going now. *Danki* for *nachtess*."

His words set her in motion. Esther stood with such speed she nearly knocked her chair over backward. "Wait."

He stopped, hand on the doorknob and Moxie at his feet. "Are you saying that you haven't minded all this matchmaking the kids have been up to?"

"I haven't minded a'tall."

Her heart skipped a beat. "And what exactly does this mean?" She was surprised at herself. When had she gotten so brazen?

"I s'pose that depends."

"On what?" she all but whispered.

"You."

Esther felt her knees start to shake. *"Jah?"*

"John Lapp was my friend, Esther. I would never do anything to change your memories of him. So if you're not ready, if you're still in love with him, then we go on with our lives."

"And if I say I am ready?"

"Then we can start courtin' for real."

There went her heart doing that stuttery thing again. "Can I have a little bit of time to pray about it?" she asked.

"Jah, of course." He started out the door, but stopped half

in and half out of her apartment. "I'll be by tomorrow for the answer, say about three."

Esther smiled. "I'll make sure to have some coffee ready."

Andrew couldn't believe he let Danny talk him into going out with Sarah again. He had so much on his mind lately that his instincts were down. He hadn't thought it through. He'd just been too tired to argue.

"I know." Julie giggled and covered her mouth, her eyes flashing from Danny to him and back again.

They were seated in one of the back booths at Kauffman's. They had been taken to their table, served waters, and given menus, but so far, all Andrew had been able to concentrate on were the memories of the last time he had been there with Caroline.

"What do you think, Andrew?" Danny asked, stirring his lemon around with the end of his straw.

"What?"

"I told you he wasn't listening," Julie admonished.

Sarah blushed.

"We're planning on going out to the Millers' pond to go swimming tomorrow. You want to come?"

He opened his mouth to excuse himself from the excursion when Sarah said, "Please."

And Julie added, "Come on, Andrew. It'll be fun."

Why not? He deserved to have a little bit of happiness instead of pining away for something that could never be. Caroline had left without even telling him good-bye in person. She had only written him a letter.

How much could he mean to her if that was all she felt she needed to give him? Not much.

His thoughts were far from charitable, but his sadness had quickly turned to anger. He had thought that they meant something to each other. *Ach*, but was he wrong. "Sure," he said, tamping down his anger. "That sounds like a lot of fun."

Dear Caroline,

I just received your letter. I'm so froh that you made it safely back to Tennessee. I was so worried about you taking such a long trip alone with your boppli. It seemed very dangerous at best.

I understand why you felt you had to go. I hope your grandfather is doing better. Every night I pray that he finds his health again either here on earth or with our Heavenly Father.

You didn't mention Emma's father in your letter. I worry about you going to find him. I guess I'm afraid that he will want to take Emma away from you. Perhaps I have been reading too many of those Englisch magazines. It's just as feasible that he would want to marry you and sweep you and Emma away to live happily ever after, as they say.

Andrew hasn't taken the news of your departure very well. He came to talk to me and even brought the letter you left him so I could read it as well. I still do not understand why you wouldn't tell him the truth. I'm positive that boy is in love with you and was hurt deeply that you left the way you did. It seems only fair that you tell him what has happened. I hope someday you can. Maybe after you talk to Trey and clear things with him.

You'll never guess who came to supper with me

last night. Abe Fitch! He's coming by to talk to me this afternoon. We're going to discuss courting. Jah, you read that right. Abe Fitch and I just may be officially courting by this time tomorrow. I feel as giddy as I did the first time I ever saw John. I'll write more when I can to let you know what Abe and I decide.

I must close for now. The oven timer just went off. Must go see about the new cookies I baked. They are called Hawaiian Delight. I sure wish you were here to taste them with me.

Please give Emma a kiss from me and tell her that I love her so. I miss you both more than you will ever know.

Esther

Chapter Eighteen

At ten minutes till three, the bell over the bakery door rang and Abe Fitch shuffled in.

Esther tried to hide her panic but was sure it showed regardless. A bus had come in from Tulsa bringing a church group of quilters. All the ladies had to come into the bakery to grab a snack and a cup of coffee and settle down a little before the bus headed back to the city.

Normally buses weren't a problem, but with Caroline gone this one was. Esther ran herself near ragged trying to fill her regular orders as well as take care of all the walk-ins.

She appreciated the business, but she was frustrated all the same. How was she going to continue on without Caroline?

The only way was to hire someone else, but that seemed like she was admitting that Caroline wasn't ever coming back to Wells Landing.

The thought made her sad beyond belief.

Maybe she could get Jodie to increase her hours. Just for a while.

"*Ach*, Esther Lapp, it looks like a tornado blew through here."

Esther swiped a loose strand of hair and pushed it back

under her prayer *kapp*. "Worse," she said with a sigh. "Tour bus."

Abe laughed. "I left Danny and Andrew haggling with some ladies who wanted a deep discount on furniture."

"I'm sure they appreciate that very much."

Abe shrugged. "How else will they learn?"

Esther sighed and looked around the messy dining room floor. "Jodie will be here in a few minutes, but I think it's going to take longer than that to clean up this mess."

"I guess it's been hard without Caroline."

"Jah." Esther sighed again. "I don't want to hire anyone else." She grabbed the broom by the handle and started to sweep up the crazy mess of wax paper wrappers and tracked-in debris.

Abe took the broom from her. "I can sweep, you clear the tables."

Esther had never had anyone help her before Caroline had come to Wells Landing, and the gesture was almost more than she had hoped for.

Abe was sweeping up the last of the trash when Jodie arrived a bit late, pink-cheeked and breathless. "I'm so sorry, Esther. My *bruder* fell just as we were leaving. My *mamm* had to get him in the buggy and over to the doc's. She stayed there with him. I had to walk the rest of the way."

"No worries, child. Is he going to be *allrecht*?"

"Jah," Jodie said. "I think so. Just some stitches and a headache."

"Gut, gut," Esther said. "Get your apron and wash your hands. I'm going to take a little break with Abe Fitch, *jah*?"

Jodie blinked as if she had been struck deaf, then smiled from ear to ear. *"Jah,"* she said loud enough for Abe to hear. Then she lowered her voice and added, "Caroline would be so proud," for Esther's ears only.

Esther hid her own smile and turned back to Abe. "*Danki*

for the help, Abe Fitch. Just give me a moment, and we can talk."

He shot her a quick nod.

"I'll get you some snacks together," Jodie said, then snapped her fingers as inspiration struck. "I'll make it to go so you can take it to the park, *jah*?" Without waiting on their okay, she began to pack a paper sack for them.

Esther excused herself and made her way back to the apartment that she had shared with Caroline and Emma. Now only Moxie waited for her to return.

She scratched the pooch behind the ears. "Hey, pup, you want to go for a walk?"

Moxie barked out his response, and Esther laughed.

She gave him one last pat on the head, then made her way to find a clean apron.

She was not trying to impress him, she told herself as she donned the clean garment and washed her hands and face. She removed her prayer *kapp* and brushed her long brown hair out. *When had she gotten so gray?* She parted it down the middle and secured it at the nape of her neck. Definitely when she wasn't looking. She smiled at her own joke and repinned her prayer *kapp*.

There. She was serviceable, she told herself, turning this way and that as she looked into the tiny bathroom mirror. Then she reached up and pinched some color back into her cheeks.

"Foolish old woman," she muttered to her reflection, then she checked to make sure that she didn't have anything stuck in her teeth and went to fetch Moxie's leash.

When she arrived back at the front of the bakery, Abe was waiting on her with two coffees and a bulging paper sack in hand.

Though his hands were full, Abe offered her one of his

elbows to take as he guided her across the street and into the city park.

This was definitely something Esther had missed since John had passed away. Having a man to escort her, a companion at her side. She had proven to herself and to others that she could survive on her own, even in a culture that thrived on togetherness.

She could support herself, make her own way. She didn't have to lean on anybody in order to survive. It made the thought of walking side by side with Abe Fitch all the more sweet.

Let me talk, she said to herself as they made their way to one of the picnic tables.

"Did you say something?" Abe asked.

Esther shook her head, hoping that if she had, she would be forgiven her unintentional lie. She released his elbow and slid onto one side of the bench.

He set their snack on the table and took Moxie's leash from her. "You look like you could use a rest. Let me take this here fella for a walk, *jah*?"

She stretched her legs out in front of her. The energetic part of her wanted to walk beside him and find out what he had decided about telling Andrew the truth. But the tired part of her—and she was going to call it her tired part and not her cowardice—just watched him patiently wait for Moxie to finish his business before directing him back to where she waited.

Abe looped the puppy's leash around one of the table legs and stepped over the bench just across from her.

Esther pushed his coffee across to him and opened the so-full paper sack. "Cookies or coffee cake?"

He gave her a look.

"Right," she said, doling out both in front of him. If there was one thing she had learned about Abe Fitch in the last few weeks, it was that the man sure enjoyed his sweets.

He took an appreciative bite out of the coffee cake. Esther was a little too anxious to eat. She sat, hands folded, and resisted the urge to tap her fingers while Abe ate.

"You should have your snack," Abe said, starting on the stack of cookies in front of him.

Evidently, Abe wasn't going to talk until their snack was complete. Esther picked up a cookie and nibbled the edge. There was just too much at stake: the two of them, Caroline and Andrew. So much hinged on what he was about to say.

"We can't eat and talk?"

He shrugged, and she was sure that she saw a sparkle of mirth in those blue eyes. "What do you want to talk about first?"

"Caroline," she said. The young people, they were the most important. She and Abe had their chance at happiness in life. It was time for the young'uns to have theirs.

"You want me to tell Andrew all about Caroline's troubles."

"Jah."

"It seems to me that it's almost . . . gossiping."

"Abe Fitch, you are making more of this than needs to be. All you have to do is tell Andrew that Caroline wants him to follow her to Tennessee."

Abe stroked his beard. "If it's so easy, why don't you tell him?"

Esther felt the blush, hotter than the hot Oklahoma summer sun. "Because I promised I wouldn't tell him."

Abe squinted at her. "But it is okay to tell me?"

"I didn't promise to not tell you."

"You are a sneaky one, Esther Lapp." But he smiled, taking the sting from his words.

"So you'll do it."

He nodded. "These *kinner* deserve to be happy, *jah*?"

Esther smiled, exhaling her relief. *"Jah."*

"Now"—Abe cocked his head to one side and eyed her thoughtfully—"what are we going to do about the two of us?"

"What do you suppose we should do?" Not much of a response, but she was too nervous to be hopeful, too hopeful to be uneasy. He had said that he had admired her for years.

He looked away, staring off into the grassy expanse of the park. "Esther, I think you are a fine woman."

Her heart sank. That sounded like a brush-off if she had ever heard one. "But . . . ?"

He turned back to her, his eyes alight with a blue fire. "No but. You were the one who wanted to pray about it."

"And you didn't?"

He shook his head. "The good Lord told me long ago that you were the woman for me."

A small kernel of happiness burst in her chest. *"Jah?"* she whispered.

"I always thought you were a handsome woman. Even when you were married to John Lapp." He shook his head. "Then after he died, it seemed that you were determined to make a go of it single, so I left well enough alone."

Esther's breath caught in her throat. "Are you saying . . . ?"

"That I've had my eye on you for longer than I can remember? *Jah*." He reached across the table to where her trembling hand lay and took it into his own. "I'm willing to give it a try if you are."

Esther laughed. "What do you think I've been trying to do?"

Abe returned her laugh with a smile of his own. "I thought you were just trying to get the kids together."

"That too."

"Well, I guess it's time to see if we can make both of these relationships work."

She couldn't stop her wide smile, nor did she want to. Then she stopped. "Wait, if you have known for a long time that you wanted to court me, why didn't you tell me that last night? Why make me wait until today?"

Abe ducked his head, then looked back up at her with a grin. "I had to make you wait a little bit. No sense in letting you think you were already walking around with my heart."

"Am I?"

He took her trembling hand into his own. "For sure and for certain."

The day was a perfect one by most standards. The sun was shining in the pristine blue sky. There was a light breeze out of the north that swept in and kept everything cool despite the mid-nineties temperatures.

"This is going to be so much fun," Julie gushed as they parked the tractor at the edge of the cornfield. It was a short walk from there down to the pond that sat in the middle of the two fields, the trees surrounding it forming an oasis in the sea of corn.

"*Jah,*" Sarah agreed, looking around. "You don't suppose anyone else is here, do you? Or maybe coming?"

Danny shrugged and transferred the picnic basket he carried from one hand to the other. "Hard to say. Why?"

Andrew thought he saw a touch of pink rise into Sarah's cheeks before she turned away. "No reason."

Julie sighed and turned in a complete circle as she walked, arms out at her sides, a big smile on her face. "It's a *wunderbaar* day."

"Jah," Danny agreed, though his gaze was centered on the girl in front of him instead of their surroundings.

The temperature dropped several degrees as they ducked into the thatch of trees surrounding the pond. The mighty oaks and springy evergreens added both shade and seclusion to this favorite spot of the Amish kids.

On the banks, Julie and Sarah excused themselves to take off their dresses. Once they were out of sight, Andrew started to unlace his shoes and take off his socks.

"I really think Sarah likes you."

Andrew frowned. "I don't see why you think that. She's hardly looked at me all day."

Danny took off his hat and tossed it to the ground, then started unbuttoning his shirt. "Maybe if you acted like you like her."

"I do like her." *Just not like that.* Andrew swept his own hat from his head and stripped down to the shorts he wore under his pants.

"You miss Caroline."

He stopped, his shirt half-on and half-off. *"Jah,"* he said quietly. But what good did that do him? She had left him behind without a word since. "I miss Emma too." It was amazing how such a small creature could own such a big piece of his heart, but there it was. Emma and Caroline. His girls that were no longer his.

"Have you tried to contact her? Write her a letter, get her a message by phone? I'm sure Esther would let you use the bakery phone."

Andrew shook his head. "I wouldn't know who to call anyway."

"What about a letter?"

"And say what? I can't believe you left to go see your sick grandfather?"

Danny cocked his head to a thoughtful angle. "If that's all she's doing, then why did her letter make it seem like she was never coming back?"

It was the one question Andrew had never let himself ask. He was afraid of the answers. "I don't know."

"Did you miss me?" Julie sashayed out from between the trees where she and Sarah had gone to change. She wore a black swimsuit like the *Englisch* favored, though this one covered more skin than most. Her hair was still in its tidy roll at the nape of her neck, but her prayer *kapp* had been left behind with her *frack* and apron.

Danny stilled, his gaze soaking in the image of his girl-friend.

Jah, they'd most likely be married this fall if the look on Danny's face was any indication. Andrew was happy for his friend. He truly was. But if Beth had lived, they would probably be getting married this fall.

It was the first time she had come into his mind in weeks. The thought made him sad. Maybe that was why Caroline left. Maybe this was God's way of telling him to slow down, take things in the time they came, and not to worry about the unknown.

Julie gave a turn so that Danny could get a glimpse from every angle, then she ran to the fishing dock and jumped into the pond, Danny right behind her.

"They are such a sweet couple, *jah*?" Sarah asked from behind him.

Andrew turned back to her. Sarah stood at the edge of the trees wearing a black one-piece swimsuit of her own. She also had a pair of *Englisch* short pants on over the suit, and in place of her prayer *kapp* she wore a bandana.

"Jah." He had such conflicting emotions, and Danny's determination to set him up with Sarah was not helping matters in the least.

"Is someone coming?" She turned her head to the side as if listening for the crunch of footsteps through the trees.

Andrew shrugged. "I wouldn't be surprised if Jonah shows up. After all, it's his daddy's pond."

"You really think so?"

Julie squealed behind them as Danny pulled her under the water. She retaliated with a quick splash to the face. But it was the dreamy look in Sarah's eyes that had Andrew's attention.

"You like Jonah."

Sarah shook her head and ran her hands nervously down the sides of her shorts. "Oh, *nay*, I already told you that I have put in to teach this upcoming year."

Andrew squinted at her, studying the wide-eyed expression on her face. "Putting in to teach and liking Jonah Miller are not two things that cannot happen at once."

"Jonah goes with Lorie Kauffman," Sarah added. "Everybody knows that."

"Jah," Andrew said, though he was unconvinced. "You ready to swim?"

"Sure." She headed toward the dock as Andrew smiled. "Don't worry. Your secret's safe with me."

After the day of playing in Millers' pond and seeing Sarah's face light up like fireflies on a summer night every time someone mentioned Jonah's name, Andrew was exhausted and *hungerich*.

Her love for Jonah was destined for a terrible fate given that Jonah and Lorie had been going around together for as long as anyone cared to remember. But Sarah seemed happy to love him from a distance and hang her bonnet on teaching the young scholars of their community.

Danny took Julie and Sarah home first, then swung by the farm to let off Andrew.

Their picnic lunch was mighty tasty, but that had been hours ago. Hours of diving into the pond, splashing in the water, games of Marco Polo, and just hanging out.

Once he figured out that Sarah didn't have her heart pinned to him, Andrew could finally relax and have a little fun, though the furtive glances and stolen touches between Danny and Julie were enough to make him feel like they should have come by themselves. Or perhaps that was why they had invited him and Sarah along: to keep them on the righteous path.

"Andrew? Is that you?" Abe hollered as Andrew let himself into the back door of the house.

"Jah," he called, heading straight for the kitchen. He found some sandwich makings in the propane-powered refrigerator. He gathered up what he could, shut the door with his foot, and set his items on the kitchen table.

"Gut himmel, bu. Did you forget to eat today?"

Andrew took a bite of the apple he still held and smiled a little sheepishly at his uncle. "Swimming always makes me hungry."

Abe eyed the mess of food with a shake of his head. "Go ahead and eat, then there's something I need to talk to you about."

The words seemed innocent enough, but something in his *onkle*'s tone made the bottom drop out of Andrew's stomach. He swallowed the bite of apple around the lump forming in his throat. *"Jah?"*

"About Caroline."

Andrew's appetite was gone in an instant. "What about Caroline?"

Abe waved a hand toward the sandwich fixings littering the table. "You can eat first."

He shook his head. "It can wait."

Abe sighed. "I went to dinner at Esther Lapp's last night. It seems there are a few things about Caroline that we didn't know."

"Like?"

"Emma's father isn't dead."

Andrew felt as if his heart had been stabbed with a blade. If Emma's father wasn't dead, then . . .

"He's English," Abe continued, twisting the pain in his heart. "They were never married."

He let the words wash over him, trying to take them all in, but he felt like a sponge in too much water. There wasn't enough of him to absorb it all and it seemed as if the knowledge might choke him. "But—" he managed to stammer.

Abe leaned forward and clasped his hands between his knees. "I know this comes as a shock to you. It surprised us all. Caroline seemed like such a *gut maedel*."

"She is a good girl." The words burst from Andrew without thought or forewarning. There he was defending her when she had told him nothing but lies. Had everything that happened between them been a lie? That moment in the park, their kiss, all the *gut* and wonderful times they had shared? "Why didn't she tell me the truth?"

Abe laid a hand on Andrew's knee, but he was too sensitive, too raw, and the heat seemed to burn his skin. He wanted to get up and run, run as fast as the horses that they stabled for their owners, run until he couldn't run any longer, run until this pain was gone.

"I think we see what we want to see in people. We wanted her to be a certain kind of person, so we all saw her that way."

"So this is my fault." Andrew's very being bubbled with emotions: anger, hurt, longing, and love.

"It's no one's fault, son. It simply is."

Caroline hadn't wanted him to know the truth. He stood
up too fast, the chair sailing out behind him and landing on
the floor with a thud. "I'm going for a walk."

"What about your food?"

He shook his head. "I'm not hungry."

Abe's mouth pressed down in a firm line. "I'm sorry."

"*Jah, Onkle* Abe, me too."

"I'll clean up this mess. You go clear your head."

"*Danki,*" he said before swinging out the back door.

Normally watching the horses in the pasture calmed him
in a way that only prayer could beat, but the sight of the
beasts didn't give him the serenity they usually afforded
him, and he wasn't sure he could pray about this matter. Not
yet, anyway.

He started toward the stables. Might as well muck the
stalls. He didn't have anything better to do than wonder why
Caroline had thought it okay to deceive him.

Anger bubbled inside him as he rolled up his shirt
sleeves and got down to work. His *elders* would tell him that
the Amish way is to forgive, but how could he? He slid the
shovel under a messy pile and dumped it into the wheelbarrow. She had plenty of opportunities to tell him about
Emma's father, plenty of times when they were alone. He
was a fool.

He scooped up another load of soiled hay. She could
have said the truth on countless occasions, yet she had
decided to keep it to herself.

Another scoop went into the wheelbarrow. That could
only mean one thing, that she didn't trust him with the
knowledge of the truth. The thought hurt him more than he
could imagine.

Or maybe she didn't tell him because she was still in love
with this *Englischer*.

He stopped, resting his arm on the shovel's wooden

handle. His breath wheezed in and out of his lungs from the exertion and the thoughts whirling around in his head.

Caroline was still in love with another.

That explained it all.

Onkle was right. She was a *gut maedel*, but even *gut* girls made mistakes. Love. Why else would Caroline go against everything she had been taught? She had told him how conservative her district was. With a *gut* Amish woman like Caroline, only one thing would make her break her vows to family and church.

He stoked his anger, surely a move that would have his sister Lizzie protesting. But how else was he supposed to survive heartbreak on top of heartbreak?

If he stayed mad, maybe he'd be able to survive.

Dear Esther,

It seems so strange to be writing you from Tennessee. I hope this letter finds you well. The air here is strained, but I guess that is to be expected. They are saying Grossdaadi won't be with us much longer. I know this will make my mamm and dat sad, but they understand that he is no longer to be a part of this world. We go to visit him nearly every day, but he doesn't know that we are there. It's so bedauerlich. I wish that I had gotten to spend more time with him while he was not so grank.

Since he is in the hospital in Lawrenceburg, I have taken to staying in his haus. It is better that way. My vatter is still a bit reluctant to fully forgive, and he is dealing with all the problems with his father's medical bills and expenses. Having me and Emma underfoot is a stress that he doesn't need.

Mamm comes by every day and begs for us to move back into the main house, but I change the subject to avoid answering. Then I pray that the Lord forgives me. I do not want to hurt my parents any more than I already have, but every time she leaves I see heartbreak in her eyes. I'm so torn as to what I should do.

I have been unable to find Trey. I don't understand how someone can come looking for a

*body and then disappear. But he has. His family no
longer lives in the house they owned before, and the
people living there now do not know where they
moved. My only hope is to go into Nashville and see
if I can find him. Perhaps in the Englisch phone
book. I hear they have everyone listed by name and
address. If I can't find him this way, then I suppose
I'll have to wait to see if he comes around again.*

*Emma sends her love. We miss you and Moxie too
and pray every day that you are both doing well.*

Please write when you can.

Love,
Caroline

Chapter Nineteen

"Where do I find an *Englisch* phone book?" Caroline asked Don Harper the driver as he navigated the busy Nashville streets. It was beyond Caroline how anyone could live in such a large place and keep their head about themselves.

Don Harper shrugged. "What do you need one for?"

"I don't really know where I'm going." She picked at a place on her skirt, then swung her attention back to him. "I mean, I know where I want to go."

"Nashville."

"But I don't know where to look for him. I've heard that everyone is listed in an *Englisch* phone book. I suppose that's where I'll find him." She had explained everything to Don Harper. Well, as much as she dared. She had simply told him that she needed to find someone and asked if he would be willing to hire on to take her into Nashville.

"Not everyone," Don said. "If they only have a cell phone and no landline, then they won't be listed in the phone book."

"Oh." Caroline's hopes deflated like a leaky balloon. Her only hope now was to go to the apartment where Trey used to stay and see if by any chance he still lived there. "Can we check where he used to live?"

"I'm here for you. We can go wherever you want."

She remembered how to get to the apartments where Trey had lived while going to school. If her memory was correct, he should have graduated the year Emma was born. But she knew he had plans to attend law school after that. What were the chances that he still lived in the same place after two years?

She knocked on the door to apartment 6A to no answer. She could leave a note and tell him that she had been by, but she didn't even know for sure he still lived there. And she certainly didn't have a phone number where he could reach her.

Dejected, she trudged back to the car where Don and Emma waited.

"No answer?" he asked as she got back in his sedan.

She shook her head. She was trying to do the right thing. So why was it so hard? She bowed her head.

Dear Lord, I am doing my best to right past wrongs. Please help me in my search, guide me so that I might find Trey, and show me the way that I can do what is right for all involved. Aemen.

She could feel Don's gaze on her as she raised her head.

He backed the car out of the space and pulled onto the street. "If you will," he started, "I have an idea."

She gave her nod of confirmation.

A couple of blocks later he pulled into a corner coffee shop.

A wave of memories washed over her. How many times had she sat there with Trey drinking lattes and talking, just being together? This small shop had been their rendezvous destination. As much as she didn't want to set foot in the place again, she wanted to go in and visit twice that.

Don put the car in park and got out, coming around to open her door before opening Emma's as well.

"I've got my laptop in the trunk. We'll go in and have a cup of coffee and tap into their Wi-Fi. Maybe we can find out something about your Trey online."

Caroline unstrapped Emma from the car seat in the back.

But something must have shown on her face. Don Harper shut the lid to his trunk and asked with a concerned frown, "Is there something wrong?"

Caroline shook her head, simultaneously asking for forgiveness for the lie.

"Don't give up hope," he said, steering her toward the shop entrance.

Caroline stopped. "It's not that. We used to come here together."

"Really?" He reached around her and opened the door. "I think that's good luck, then."

"Jah," she said. "I'm just being *gegisch.* Silly."

Don Harper smiled and his blue eyes twinkled. "I know what it means."

"From driving the Amish?"

"From being ex-Amish myself."

Caroline was surprised. "You're Plain, but—is that why you agreed to help me?"

"Jah," he said. "That and the fact that you looked like you could use some help."

It had never been easy for her to accept assistance from others. But leaning on friends and depending on them was one of the lessons that Andrew had taught her.

Andrew.

How she missed him. How she wondered if she would ever see him again.

Don Harper ordered them each a coffee and a chocolate milk for Emma while Caroline found them a table and sat the *boppli* in a high chair.

She had to find Trey. She just *had* to.

What if his parents lied to her, what if he knew nothing about Emma or that Caroline had come looking for him that rainy night two years ago?

Trey deserved to know he had a daughter. What would happen after that was anybody's guess. But the potential outcomes were enough to tie her stomach in knots.

"Let's see here." Don took a silver-framed pair of reading glasses from the front pocket of his shirt and opened his computer case. In a few short minutes he had the computer up and running, humming with all the answers to finding Trey. She hoped.

"What's his name?" Don asked as he tapped several keys, then checked the screen again.

Caroline sat across the table from him, staring at the brand name of the computer and wondering what was happening on the other side. Not that she knew a thing about such matters. "Theodore Marston Rycroft the Third. But they call him Trey."

Don eyed her over the top of the glasses. "Any kin to Senator Rycroft?"

Caroline shrugged as Don typed in the name. "I didn't spend much time with his family. But I seem to remember Trey saying that his father had a nickname as well."

"Like Duke?"

Recognition sparked. "*Jah*, like Duke."

Don turned the screen around to face her, and Caroline gasped as she saw the face of the man who had sent her away. "He's in the government?"

"Newly elected last year."

"And their house?"

"Who's to say? Sometimes politicians keep their local houses, sometimes they move to Washington, DC. Since their son is older and in college, they might have made the move complete."

Caroline bit her lip and tried to contain her whirling thoughts. "Do you think Trey moved with them?"

"I don't know. Let me put in his name and see if I can come up with anything."

"Danki."

"Gern gschehne," he replied with a smile. He turned his concentration back to the computer screen.

Don tapped a few more keys and waited as the computer did its job.

The waiting, that was the hardest part for Caroline. She had been holding her breath for years waiting on something she hadn't realized. Now she knew. She had been waiting on Trey to find her, Trey to change his mind, Trey to know that they had a daughter. And now that the waiting was soon to be over, Caroline was anxious, nervous, and antsy at the delay that was left.

"Caroline?"

The voice that sounded behind her was as familiar as her own even though it had been almost two years since she had heard it.

Slowly she turned and looked into those familiar gray eyes, eyes that she had seen nowhere else but in the face of the daughter they created so long ago.

A wave of heat washed over her. After all this time the wait was over. "Trey."

Andrew pushed the broom around the workroom floor with more force than necessary. In fact, everything he had done in the last week had been accomplished with unnecessary effort. But everything seemed to take longer, more energy, and was harder than it had been before.

He guessed that was the reason the bishop preached a lot on letting go of one's anger. His anger with Caroline ate at his energy and kept his mind on constant edge. He hadn't slept more than two hours at a time even with all the extra physical work he'd put in. The stalls in the stables had never been cleaner. The workroom was practically sawdust free. All of the furniture in the showroom gleamed with a fresh coat of polish.

"Andrew." His uncle's voice gave him pause.

Andrew rested the broom at his side and turned to face him.

"I need you to go down and ask Esther if she still wants the dresser that matches the bed she bought."

The bed she bought Caroline.

"Why don't you go down there?" He hated the surly note in his voice, but once the words were out there he couldn't take them back. "I mean, you two are something of an item these days."

Abe seemed not to notice his tone or had grown so used to it over the last few days that he no longer noticed it. "I am not so smitten that I cannot wait until tonight to see her again."

Smitten. The exact same word he had used to describe his uncle's feelings to Caroline just a few short weeks ago.

Why did everything around him remind him of Caroline?

"Let me sweep this up."

But his *onkle* shook his head. "I'll finish the floor. You just get down to the bakery."

Andrew handed over the broom and dusted his hands. What was the use in arguing?

With barely a glance at his uncle, he left the shop and made his way toward Esther's.

The sun shone brightly on the beautiful day. The weather mocked his anger and his sadness, tried to coax him out of himself, but Andrew would have none of it. He had to remain angry lest he fall completely apart.

The bell over the door jangled as he made his way inside.

Esther turned, her eyes lighting up when she saw him. Not from surprise, though. His *onkle* must have called to tell her he was on his way. If that was the case, why didn't Abe call and ask her himself?

"Abe sent me down to check on the dresser. Are you still interested in it?"

"Jah," she said. "Come sit down and let's talk about it."

What was there to talk about? She either wanted it or she didn't. But he bit his tongue and kept his hateful words to himself. If he kept going in this direction he'd be a surly old man before this time next year.

Andrew slid into the booth she indicated while Esther poured them each a cup of coffee.

"Would you like a cupcake or a cookie?"

"Do you have any of those cowboy cookies?" He could have kicked himself in the pants for bringing up the cookies. But it seemed as if his heart was in tune with all things Caroline even if his brain didn't want to admit it.

"Jah," she said, plucking a couple from the case and setting them on a small paper plate. "Course'n I made these."

Of course.

Esther placed the cookies and coffee onto a tray and carried them over to where he waited.

She deposited the food on the table and slid into the seat opposite him. "I was wondering if you had heard anything from Caroline."

He should have smelled this set up a mile away. *"Nay."*

"But you talked to your uncle, *jah?*"

He gave a small nod. He couldn't meet Esther's dark blue gaze. He had hardened his heart against all things Caroline. It would see him through into the coming years. He didn't know what that might be, but he was certain it would be without Caroline.

"Have you . . . have you thought about going to see her?"

His gaze jerked to hers. "Why would I think about something like that?"

"Andrew Fitch," Esther exclaimed. "I wouldn't have thought you would let such a small problem sway you so."

He sat back in his seat and eyed her steadily. Anger and hurt boiled inside him, each threatening to take over. "I would not call this a small problem."

"As I see it, it's only as big as you let it be."

"And what about Caroline?"

"That girl loves you, Andrew, and I believe that you love her as well."

"And Emma?"

"Of course you love Emma."

He shook his head again. "A child deserves her father."

"A child deserves to be raised by parents who care for one another, who love their children, provide for them, and serve God."

"Caroline can have all that and more in Tennessee. Plus her family close." Family was so very important. He had been thinking about going back home. Wells Landing now held as many bad memories as Missouri.

Sad, he amended. The memories weren't bad, only sad.

Esther reached out and touched his hand where it lay on the table.

He pushed the thoughts aside and met her concerned gaze once again.

"Caroline never meant to hurt you."

"I know," he replied.

"Promise me," she said. "Promise me you'll pray about it."

How he wanted to tell her no. Praying was one step down from hope, and that was something he couldn't afford right then. But to tell her he wouldn't even lay the problem at God's feet was cowardice at its best. "*Jah*," he finally said. "I promise."

Esther smiled. "*Gut*. I can't ask for more than that."

Caroline started to tremble.

"Oh my God, it is you. Sorry." He made the same face he'd always made when he thought he had done something to offend her sensibilities. They had never been on the same step spiritually.

He pulled her out of her seat and into his arms. His embrace was warm and sweet and felt like home.

"You're shaking." He pulled away from her and ran his hands down her arms as if it had only been hours, not years, since they had seen each other last. "I wasn't sure I'd ever see you again after the way you just disappeared."

Caroline shook her head. "I did nothing of the sort." Then she stopped. Now was not the time to argue. "I have someone you need to meet."

A confused frown puckered his brow as Trey turned his attention to Don Harper. He held out his hand to shake. "Trey Rycroft," he said.

"Nice to meet you. I'm Don Harper. I've been helping Caroline look for you."

"Like an investigator?"

"Just as a friend."

She was glad the two men introduced themselves. She had completely forgotten her manners. But the person he truly needed to meet had yet to be presented. "Trey, this is Emma."

He glanced down at their daughter. She shoved a piece of bread in her mouth and blinked back at him with identical eyes.

At first Trey looked confused, then realization dawned. He crumpled into the chair across from Emma, staring at her, then Caroline in turn. "I don't know what to say . . . I—"

"Perhaps the two of you should take care of this someplace more private."

At least Don Harper still had his wits about him.

"Jah," Caroline said.

Trey agreed. "We can go to my apartment. It's close."

Her heart started thumping double time in her chest. This was what she had been waiting for; this was what she had come home for. And now that it was really happening, she was more nervous than she had ever been in her life.

She said a small prayer of thanks and another for understanding and wisdom. When she was done she realized that the two men had been discussing plans.

"Is that okay with you, Caroline?" Don Harper asked.

"What?" She blinked several times, trying to get her bearings back.

"Trey has offered to take you home this evening. I want to make sure that you agree before I leave."

Take her home. *Jah*, they had a lot to talk about. Perhaps it was best that he did take her home. To her *grossdaadi's haus* or her *elders'*? Maybe it was time for him to meet her parents, though she had no idea what their talk would render for the future. "*Jah*, that will be fine."

Don seemed reluctant, but then his shoulders relaxed a bit and he stood. "You have my number if you need me."

Caroline dipped her chin, unable to do more by way of response. So many emotions clogged her throat: remorse, regret, anxiety, hope.

"I'll get Emma's car seat so you can put it in your car."

She hadn't even thought about that. Trey looked stricken as well and paled a bit beneath his tan.

Caroline gathered Emma as Don Harper packed up his computer and Trey said a hasty good-bye to his friends. Caroline tried not to stare and see if he was with another girl. As far as she could tell they were just a group of friends out to get a cup of coffee and relax a little. At least Trey had gotten his coffee.

Don was more practiced at installing the car seat. He had it in Trey's backseat in no time while Trey and Caroline watched. She could feel Trey's gaze flick to her and Emma. Then she knew the exact second when he looked away.

"Danki." She ducked into the back of Trey's fast-looking car and buckled Emma inside. The car smelled like him, like his clothes and his aftershave. It was a scent she would forever associate with him. She resisted the urge to close her eyes and simply breathe in the memories. Instead, she dug around in her purse for the money to pay Don.

Trey beat her to it, handing Don a folded up one-hundred-dollar bill.

Don started to protest, but Trey would hear none of it. "Thank you for helping Caroline find me."

Don Harper turned to Caroline one last time. "Are you sure you'll be okay?"

She nodded, the strings of her prayer *kapp* brushing across her neck. She shivered, all her senses heightened since she'd spotted Trey.

Don hesitated for a moment more, then turned to go back to his car.

Caroline was left alone with Trey.

Trey's hands were shaking when he started the car. How fortunate that his father had gotten him the sporty sedan instead of the two-seater coupe that he had originally wanted. Where would he have put his daughter?

My daughter.

A chill ran over him. His daughter. He had a daughter, and he didn't even know her name. He was sure Caroline had mentioned it in the coffee shop, but for the life of him, he couldn't remember now.

He cleared his throat and cut his gaze toward the woman seated to his right. "Does she have a name?" What a stupid question. But how was he supposed to know how to act? It wasn't every day a man was told he had a daughter he never knew about.

"Her name is Emma."

Emma.

There was no question as to whether she was his. She had his coloring, his dark hair, his gray eyes, his dimple in her tiny little chin.

How strange to look into his own eyes set in the face of another.

A hundred questions swirled around inside his head, intertwining and rendering him speechless. There were so many things he wanted to ask, so many things he needed to know. The very first being why she had never told him. But given the shaking in his hands and the heavy flow of Nashville traffic, it was best to wait until they got back to his apartment before they started this long-overdue conversation.

"He seems very protective of you," he said instead. Trey wasn't sure how he felt about the way the other man hovered over Caroline and Emma. Something in the way Don Harper catered to them made him feel as if he was an intruder in what should have been his own life.

"He's a *gut* man."

"And he's just a friend?" He chanced a look in her direction. She was watching the road with a mixture of nervousness and fear.

He realized he was driving a little too fast on the busy streets. Caroline wasn't used to riding in a car or being in such a large city. At least he didn't think she was. He had no idea where she had been for the past two years.

She was still dressed as Amish, the same way she had been dressed when they had forged their forbidden relationship.

He tamped down the questions and suspicions and left those for when they got to his apartment. He needed to give this his entire attention. They both did.

A few minutes later, he pulled his Mercedes sedan into the gated complex that he had called home for the last year. Ever since his father had won the election and moved to the nation's capital.

He eased into his designated parking place and cut the engine. They were there. All of his questions were about to be answered. He got out of the car as a sudden wave of anger washed over him. His hands started shaking anew, and he shoved them into his pockets to hide their tremble.

He should help Caroline get the child from the back of the car, but he was nearly humming with the anger that coursed through him.

The child. *His* child. Their child.

He had missed nearly two years of her life. How could

Caroline have been so selfish as to keep his daughter from him for so long?

Caroline hefted the baby from the backseat and settled her on one hip. She slung her diaper bag over the other shoulder and nudged the car door shut.

Help her, his inner voice urged, but he pushed it down. She had been taking care of the child for nearly two years without his help. Had made the choice to exclude him from their life. What was the sense in starting now?

He hit the button on his key fob to lock the car and motioned for her to follow him.

Somehow he managed to keep himself together until they were completely inside his apartment. He shut the door behind them and tossed his keys onto the table by the entrance.

Caroline hovered just inside, unsure of her next move.

"I think you have some explaining to do." When had his father hijacked his body? The words were something straight out of Duke Rycroft's vernacular.

"I have some explaining to do?" She whirled on him, those beautiful hazel eyes flashing with an anger of her own.

"You kept my daughter from me for almost two years. I believe that deserves an explanation, yes." As much as he tried to keep it down, his voice raised with every word. Yelling was not the answer, and yet he couldn't seem to help himself.

She opened her mouth to retort, then closed it again. She shook her head and the strings of her little cap swayed with the movement. The child reached up, grabbed hold of one, and twisted it between her chubby little fingers. "I did not come here to yell at you. Nor did I come to allow myself to be yelled at in return. If we can't talk about this in a Godly tone, then maybe we should postpone this until another day."

He shook his head. "No, I . . . I'm sorry, I just . . ." He pushed past her into the apartment and stalked to the liquor cabinet. It was too early in the day for a shot of Tennessee's finest, but whoever made up that rule certainly hadn't just found out that he was a dad.

He poured himself two fingers of whiskey and raised the glass to his lips, when Caroline softly spoke. "Please don't."

He stilled.

"We can't talk about this without drinking liquor or fighting? We used to be able to be with each other and not worry about the differences."

She was right.

He lowered his glass and turned back to face her. "Why didn't you tell me?"

"I tried, but—can I sit down, please? She's getting heavy."

His manners had obviously fled with his good sense. "I'm sorry. Of course. Sit. Is she sleepy?" He motioned toward the child. She had laid her head on Caroline's shoulder, the hand still clutching the strings now fisted around them, thumb sticking out and popped into her tiny bow of a mouth.

"*Jah*. It's past her naptime."

He knew nothing of naptimes or any of the other baby-related activities that Caroline had been engaged in these past few months.

"This chair rocks," he said, motioning toward the recliner.

She shook her head. "I normally just lay her down. I can't rock her when I'm at work, so I put her on my bed and let her sleep."

She worked. His Caroline had a job.

"She can sleep in here." He led the way down the hall and into the master suite.

The bed was unmade, the gray sheets rumpled. He'd

slept well last night, but tonight might be a different story altogether.

"What do you need me to do?" he asked, for the first time offering to help.

"Hand me those pillows." She laid the child on the bed and braced the pillows around her. Then she brushed back those dark curls and placed a sweet kiss on her forehead. "Sleep tight, wee one," she whispered before leading him out of the room.

Shell shocked was the only way to describe how he felt. Numbly he followed behind Caroline.

"I don't want to fight," she said the minute they were back in the living room. "There's a lot that needs to be said, but fighting is not going to help."

"I don't want to fight either." He motioned toward the black leather sofa. "Sit down and get comfortable. We have a lot to talk about."

Caroline perched on the edge of the shiny black couch and waited while Trey went into the kitchen. He returned a few minutes later with two glasses of water.

"This is all I have." He shrugged. "Except for some wine."

She shook her head and pushed down the memories of her and Trey drinking wine out of paper cups as they hid out from the world. "Water's fine. *Danki*."

He handed her the glass and took the seat opposite her. Like her, he sat on the edge of his seat even though he had said they would get comfortable. Yet nothing about this situation was comfortable.

"How long will she sleep?"

"A couple of hours usually."

"So, you want to begin?"

"I guess." She sat her glass on the short table in front of

the couch and twisted her hands together in her lap. "I never meant to keep Emma from you."

"I'm not sure how you can say that. You disappeared." The words stung though he didn't raise his voice, didn't shout like she had the feeling he wanted to.

"I had to."

"You had to." It wasn't quite a question. "I'm trying to understand here, Caroline. I loved you, and you just left. Didn't say a word. Didn't tell me you were leaving or that you were pregnant." This time his voice did raise in volume. He shoved up from the chair, pacing in front of her and glaring at his glass as if the liquid in it wasn't nearly strong enough for what needed to be said.

"I came to tell you. I went to your house. Your father answered the door and said that you had already gone back to school. I told them about the baby." Her fingers twisted tighter in the folds of her skirt until the skin showed white. She didn't know why she couldn't tell Trey about the money his father offered her. But she couldn't. What good would it do to add more insult to the injury this situation had caused all of them?

"And then you just left?"

"Jah." She wiped her tears away with the back of her hand. She swore to herself that she wasn't going to cry. The time for tears had passed. But they just kept coming, pent-up emotions from trying to be strong. She took a deep, steadying breath. "My father wouldn't speak to me, couldn't look at me. He still won't say my name."

Trey collapsed back onto his chair, his renewed agitation deflated. "But you are staying there . . . at home with them, right?"

"I've been staying in my *grossdaadi*'s house, which is next door, but once he's out of the hospital I'll have to move in with *Mamm* and *Dat*." She took a drink of water. She didn't want to add that once he left, it would be so they could bury him. Who knew what would happen to his house then?

"Where have you been all of this time?"

"I bought a bus ticket to Colorado," she started. "But I got sick and got off in Oklahoma. By the time it passed, I guess I was sort of settled. So I stayed there."

"In Oklahoma?"

"*Jah*. There's a Beachy settlement in Wells Landing."

"Beachy?"

She shook her head. "It's a different kind of Amish. They aren't as conservative as the Amish here."

"And they don't care that you had a baby?"

The heat of a blush flooded into her cheeks. "They think I'm a widow."

He nodded with a sort of understanding, but didn't admonish her the way she expected. "Why did you come back?"

"My *mamm* told me you were looking for me."

"That was her in the store."

"*Jah*. She wrote me and told me that you had talked to her."

"But she didn't know who I was."

"She did. It's your eyes, you see. They are just like Emma's. I had sent her a picture a couple of months ago."

"Like a photo? Isn't that against the rules?"

She raised one eyebrow in his direction.

"Oh," he said, taking in her implied meaning. She had violated so many parts of the *Ordnung*, what was taking a picture?

"She wrote me and told me about you," Caroline continued.

"So you decided to come see me. Now. After all this time."

"You aren't being fair."

He took a sip of water, then blew out a heavy breath. "No, I'm not. And I'm sorry." He took another drink, then grimaced. "What do we do now?"

Caroline shrugged even as her heart started to pound. What did they do now? "I don't know."

Emma started crying in the other room. Normally she slept longer than this and woke up in the best mood a *mamm* could ask for.

Caroline rose and went into the bedroom, only then realizing that it was the room where Trey slept. The intimacy sent shivers skidding down her spine.

Emma sat on the bed, rubbing her eyes and hiccupping.

"Shhh . . ." Caroline cooed as she lifted the child.

Trey stood behind her watching her every move. "Is she okay?"

"She must have had a bad dream."

She turned as Trey shoved his hands in his pockets. "All this is a lot to hear about in one afternoon."

She agreed as she rocked Emma from side to side.

"I'll take you home," he said.

"And then what?"

"We can talk more tomorrow."

Andrew slipped into his nightshirt and padded over to the bed.

A part of him wanted to just fold back the covers and climb inside, but he had never gone to bed without praying before. As much as he wanted to forget his promise to Esther, he couldn't do that either.

He eased down onto his knees and braced his elbows on

the cool sheets of the bed. With his fingers laced together, he bowed his head.

"Dear Lord in heaven, I cannot say that I am not confused by the choices You have presented to me. I came to Oklahoma to spare myself the grief of living around all the places I was accustomed to seeing Beth. I had no idea when I got here that I would meet someone like Caroline. And then to have her taken away, just when I started to think that I would have a forever happiness . . . Lord, I do not know what to make of this. Are we meant to be together? Or was I just seeing a relationship and an opportunity where there was none? I'm confused, Lord, and I need Your help in understanding Your will. Please, Lord, allow me a sign to know what it is that You want from me. I've been told my entire life that if I needed anything I need only turn my eyes to God. Here I am, waiting for a sign, turning my eyes to You trusting You to lead the way. Thank You, Lord, for all the blessings I have received today and the ones that will surely follow tomorrow. *Aemen*."

Andrew climbed into bed and promptly fell asleep.

The next morning, Andrew awoke with a renewed sense of spirit. He had to trust in the Lord. That was the one constant he had been taught his entire life.

He had to rely on the Lord to lead him, show him God's will for his life. He had to let go and let God be in charge. And that could only come with a letter to Caroline.

Dear Caroline,

*I truly hope that this letter finds you well. And
Emma too. I won't lie; these last couple of weeks
have been hard on me. I have prayed and prayed
and wondered about you and why you left. I
understand that it was something that you thought
you had to do. But I don't understand why you felt
the need to not tell me the truth.*

*Onkle Abe told me about your Englischer.
Honestly, I don't know how I feel about it. I know
that we all make mistakes. It is a short fall from
grace. But that you felt you had to hide that from
me speaks to what's in your heart. I can only assume
that you care for this Englischer very much. What
am I saying? You must care for him very much. I
understand. And I'll be all right. I had hoped that
you and I could have more than the strong
friendship we had built, but it seems that it was not
part of God's plan.*

*I am writing to let you know that I care for you
deeply, but I understand the choices that have to be
made. Choices that have the best interests of
everyone in mind. Especially wee Emma.*

*I wish you nothing but the best, Caroline, in all
things. May God be with you the rest of your days.*

*Always,
Andrew*

Chapter Twenty

Caroline stood at the dented mailbox and read Andrew's letter, her heart dropping with each word. She blinked away the tears as she folded the letter and placed it back into the envelope. There was no time left for crying. Oh, the mistakes she had made.

She glanced back toward the house where Emma was napping peacefully in her bed, then in the direction of the barn where her father was working. He had yet to speak her name, to say even the smallest word to her. She had been there nearly three weeks.

If anyone was going to change the relationship, it had to be her. The time had come to make amends.

With a heavy sigh, she tucked the letter into the waistband of her apron and started for the barn.

The interior was cool, dark, and so familiar. She breathed in the scent of the air tinted with the smell of hay and horses, fresh earth and leather.

"Dat?" she called, treading cautiously over the hay-strewn floor.

No answer.

She could hear him, though, or rather what he was doing.

She could decipher the raspy sound of a horse brush against hide.

She found him in the last stall brushing down Daisy, his favorite mare.

He hardly looked up as she approached, just kept his head down and his hands on his task.

"I was hoping that we might talk today."

He gave a grunt that was neither a yes or a no.

"I know that you are disappointed in me. And I can't say as I blame you."

There was a hitch in his brush stroke as she spoke, then he recovered and kept about his chore.

"I never meant to hurt you or *Mamm*. I know I've said this before, but it's true."

He brushed.

"But if I had it to do over again, I can't say that I would change anything. Because if I did, I wouldn't have that little *maedel* in there, and I could never take that back."

"The Lord forgives. I just hope that someday you can find it in your heart to forgive me too."

She waited for him to stop brushing, to turn to her, say he could forgive her, ask if they could start over, but he didn't. She sighed. Surely God would help his heart thaw where she was concerned.

He kept on brushing Daisy as Caroline turned on her heel and made her way back to the house.

Trey had said they would talk more today, though she didn't see how. He had dropped her off last night, then driven away as if the devil himself was on his heels. They hadn't made any plans on when and where. That lack of communication only fueled her surprise when she saw his shiny black car pull into the driveway shortly after *middawk*.

She and *Mamm* had been baking bread. In her true fashion, she was wearing more flour than she had used in the recipe. Aside from her *strubbly* state, she simply wasn't ready to talk to Trey again. After their meeting yesterday, the letter from Andrew, and her stalled run-in with her father this morning, she was feeling a bit bruised. She needed a little time to recover, get her mind back right.

The hardest part of all was Andrew. He didn't want her anymore. Oh, he said he knew that people made mistakes, but she could read what he didn't say as clearly as the things he wrote outright. He was setting her free, sending her on her way. How could he love her now that he knew the truth?

She supposed Abe or Emily, maybe even Lorie, had told Andrew the truth. It was bound to happen eventually. Though it hurt all the same.

She pushed the thoughts away lest her tears start anew. She had cried enough in the last couple of weeks to last for the rest of the year.

Instead, she wiped her hands on a dish towel and brushed the loose flour from her apron.

"Who could that be?" her mother asked, looking out the window. Caroline followed her gaze just as Trey got out of the car. "Oh." The sound was unreadable.

"He said he wanted to talk more today." Caroline hated the tremble in her voice, but it was there all the same.

"Do you think that's a *gut* idea?"

"I don't know." But the thought of her father and Trey in the same room was not a peaceful one. "*Mamm* . . . can you watch Emma for me?"

"*Jah*. When do you think you'll be back?"

"I'm not sure. Maybe a couple of hours."

"Jah," she said again. "That'd be *gut*."

Her *mamm* didn't have to say the words. It was a bad idea to have Trey inside. Not now . . . maybe not ever.

"I'll be home as soon as I can," she said and flew out the door lest her father come out of the barn to investigate.

Stupid plan. Of course he would come see who pulled up in an *Englischer* car. Their house was too far off the beaten path for them to be included on the wagon tour, and hardly anyone drove by without a destination in mind.

"Hi, Car—"

"Hi, Trey. Let's go." She hopped into the car as Trey watched, his mouth hanging open.

But then he caught sight of her *vatter* standing in the door of the barn, that deep frown marring what was the normally straight line of his forehead.

Trey backed up a couple of steps, then turned and made his way quickly back to the car. He slid inside and started the engine. "I don't think your father approves."

Caroline burst out laughing. Maybe it was the tension of the day, or finally finding Trey, or maybe laughing was better than crying after the letter she had gotten from Andrew. Whatever it was, she couldn't stop the giggles as they spilled out.

Trey let out a chuckle or two of his own as he backed the car from the drive and set it toward town.

He allowed her to have her hysterics, then wipe the mixed tears of joy and sadness from her cheeks before he spoke. "We have a lot to discuss."

"Jah. Where are we going?"

Trey gave a small shrug. "I thought we'd stop somewhere and get a cup of coffee."

Going into town with him was not the best idea, even in Lawrenceburg. It would surely get back to the church elders. That was all she needed, the bishop beating on the door demanding explanations she couldn't give. "Do you mind if we stay in the car?"

He shot her a small frown.

"It's just better if we aren't seen together."

His frown deepened. "That's something we need to talk about as well."

But he didn't protest further. He wound around the drive-through at the coffee shop and picked them up a couple of lattes. It warmed her a little inside that he remembered how she preferred her coffee and that she liked banana nut bread better than blueberry muffins.

Then he drove out of town to the state park where the chances of them running into someone either of them knew would be slim to none.

He found a shaded place to park and pulled to the side. He turned toward her, and the interior of the car seemed to shrink by half.

Being this close to him when they were all alone was unnerving. "It's a beautiful day. Can we sit outside?" She fumbled with the door handle as she spoke. Why was she suddenly so uncomfortable?

"Sure," he said, but she was already out of the car. She wrapped her arms around herself despite the day's rising temperatures.

Trey went around to the back of his car and opened the trunk to remove two collapsible chairs. He brought one over to her with a small lift of his shoulders. "The university has a lot of outdoor concerts in the park."

She nodded, though she had no idea what he was talking about.

Trey sat down beside her, looking off into the distance at the trees below. They had climbed a small hill as they drove and now sat at the edge of a small ledge overlooking the forest below. It was a wondrous sight, though completely wasted on her today. She had too many pressing issues on her mind to truly appreciate the beauty that God had made.

"I guess we have a lot of decisions to make."

"Decisions?"

Trey took a drink of his coffee. "We have a child together."

"Jah."

"My fath—what I mean to say is, this is something I can't just sweep under the rug."

She didn't understand him at all, but pulled her expression into one of openness and prepared to hear him out.

"I think we should get married," he continued.

"What?" Caroline jumped to her feet, flinging her coffee to the ground in the process.

"We should get married."

She stood over him, staring down and biting her lip. Married?

"Sit down, Caroline." He wrapped one hand around her elbow and tugged.

She allowed him to pull her back into her seat. It wasn't hard. Her legs felt like they were made of her *grossmammi's* jelly. "That's a big step," she finally wheezed. How many times had she wanted to hear him say that in those early months when she lay awake at night and worried about the child she carried? But like the *gut* people of Wells Landing, she had buried Trey and those dreams together. To have them resurface now . . .

"It is a big step, but a necessary one. We have a child together."

"I know this, Trey. I've been living it for the past two years while you were out at concerts in the park." She sprang to her feet and wrapped her arms around herself once again.

"Don't get mad at me. I had no idea."

He was right. Caroline's anger deflated in an instant. "I'm sorry," she said and returned to her seat. "It's just . . ."

"Hard. I know." Trey took her hand into his own, rubbing each finger the way he used to. "But we have to do what's right."

They may not have always had the same measure of spiritual conscience, but that didn't mean he didn't believe in God or doing the right thing.

But marriage?

"That's a big step. I'll have to think about it."

His eyes grew stormy. "What's there to think about?"

She tugged her hand from his grasp. "A lot. If I marry you, I'll be shunned."

"And they don't treat you differently already?"

"That's not the point," she said, staring down at her hands, her nervous fingers making pleats in the fabric of her apron. She had missed a smudge of flour on the side on her leg. She brushed it off and sighed. "I won't be able to sit with my family. I won't be able to take food from my *mamm*'s hand. And my father . . ." The lump in her throat blocked the rest of what she was about to say.

"I'm not saying it won't be difficult, but it will be worth it."

"Can I think about it?"

Trey's mouth pulled down at the corners, but he didn't deny her. "Fine."

"For now I think you should take me home."

Even as she said the words she thought about Oklahoma, about Esther and the bakery that had been her home for the last two years. About Andrew and cowboy cookies. Her eyes filled with hot tears, but she dashed them away with the backs of her fingers. She got back into the car as Trey stowed away the chairs.

Marriage to Trey. Was it a step worth taking?

A sign. That was all that he wanted. A sign from God that he was doing the right thing in letting Caroline go. Just why did it have to hurt so bad?

Everywhere he turned he saw her face. Or Emma. He had finally stopped fighting the memories and spent his days eating lunch in the park. But he couldn't keep this up forever.

Maybe it was time to go back to Missouri.

"Andrew?" He glanced up from his sandwich as Emily Ebersol approached. "Can we sit down?"

He hadn't noticed Lorie Kauffman standing behind her at first. He gave them both a nod and continued to eat as they sat across from him and got out their own food.

"Have you heard from Caroline?" Emily asked the question, but Lorie was the one looking expectant.

"I wrote her, but she hasn't responded."

"I wonder when she's planning on coming home," Emily said, to no one in particular.

Andrew sat his sandwich down on the brown paper sack he had been using as a plate. His appetite had vanished. "I don't suspect that she will."

"Why ever not?" Lorie asked.

Andrew didn't know how much Caroline had told her *freinden* before she left so he shrugged. "I just get the feeling she won't is all."

"You did write her and tell her that you wanted her to come back," Emily said.

He said nothing. What was there to say?

"Andrew?"

He looked up and met Lorie's deep brown eyes. *"Jah?"*

"Did you tell her that you wanted her to come back?" Lorie asked.

He shook his head. *"Nay."* The word was barely more than a whisper.

"Why not?" Emily put in.

"You do want her to come back, don't you?"

"Of course." But did he? His emotions seemed all jumbled up, twisted and knotted like his mother's yarn the time his sister Lizzie's kitten had started playing in the basket.

"Did you tell her that in her letter?" Emily asked.

"Nay," he whispered into the wind.

"Why not?" both girls exclaimed at the same time.

Because he was waiting, waiting on a sign from God. Nursing his pride. Wondering how he had let his heart get broken again.

"Andrew?"

He looked up into Emily's questioning blue eyes. "What do you want from me?"

Emily glanced away, exchanging a look with Lorie before she turned back.

Yet it was Lorie who spoke. "Caroline may be about to make the biggest mistake of her life."

His heart gave a hard thump, but he stilled his breathing and calmed himself. "How so?"

"Do you know?" Emily asked. "Do you know about Emma's *dat*?"

"Jah," Andrew said.

"If she stays in Tennessee and stays with him, then she will be shunned."

He hadn't thought of that.

"Even if she doesn't leave the church to marry him, how do you think the Swartzentruber will handle her having a baby and no husband?"

He shook his head. "They are very conservative." And

would shun her for sure. "But her family is there, her *mudder* and *vatter*."

"What about little Emma? How do you think they will treat her?" Lorie asked.

Andrew's heart gave a lurch.

"It's the best way, Andrew," Emily added. "No one here knows her secret."

"You know, and I know." And his *onkle* and Esther. But none of those people were willing to hold the mistake against Caroline.

"*Jah*, but we all love Caroline."

"And Emma," Lorie added. "I don't care what Caroline did in her past. I only care about now. She's been a *gut freinden* to me these past couple of years. I don't want to see her shunned."

"We all make mistakes," Emily said quietly.

"You love her, don't you?" Lorie asked.

He opened his mouth to reply, but Emily interjected, "Don't you lie, Andrew Fitch. I've seen the way you look at her when you think no one's looking."

"And everyone has heard about the kiss on Main Street." A tinge of pink stained Lorie's cheeks.

"*Jah*," he said. "I love her."

"Then what are you waiting for?" Lorie asked.

"A sign." That was all he needed, something to tell him that he should go after her and do everything in his power to bring her back to Wells Landing.

"Andrew Fitch, I thought you were smarter than that," Emily exclaimed. "Go after her."

He couldn't stop his frown of confusion.

Lorie reached into her shoulder bag and pulled out a red, white, and blue envelope. "Consider this your sign," she said, pushing it across the table to him.

Inside was a round-trip ticket to Tennessee. He looked back to the two women across the table from him.

"We all pitched in," Emily said.

Lorie tossed him a smile. "Even Jonah."

"Now go get her back."

Dear Esther,

I must admit that I am more confused now than I have ever been. I hear you daily whispering in my ear to pray about it, but right now I don't feel like God is listening. Or maybe He is. Maybe He is telling me what to do but I can't hear the words over the others around me.

Trey asked me to marry him last night. How I would have loved for him to have asked me that two years ago. I would have married him in an instant. So why do things seem so different now?

Last night I lay awake in bed, wondering and praying, hoping God would give me the answer. But all I could hear was my own jumbled thoughts.

I need to do what's best for Emma, and having her father in her life is certainly the best. Yet all I can think about is how she will be growing up. Of course Trey doesn't want to join the Amish. And his is a political family. They care so much about what the world thinks of them that I don't believe he'd be happy on a small farm. That only leaves us one choice.

It saddens my heart beyond belief to think that I will be shunned. I have missed my mother so much these past couple of years. To know now that she won't be able to write me letters or eat with me makes my heart and stomach hurt. It seems that I have made so many bad choices in my life. Why is making the best one hurting so much?

I must close for now. Trey will come by tomorrow. I'm very nervous about it. He will be meeting my family for the first time. I'm not sure how my father will act, but I can only pray for understanding and hope God is listening.

Give Abe my best. I am glad that the two of you are finally starting to court. You both deserve the world full of happiness.

You didn't mention Andrew in your last letter. I hope he is doing well. I miss him more than I can say. And probably more than I should. I'm sure he's forgotten all about me by now.

Emma sends kisses.

> *Love,*
> *Caroline*

Chapter Twenty-One

Esther placed the platter of chicken in the center of the table, then slid into her seat opposite Abe.

They bowed their heads and said their prayer.

"Well," she said, the minute they had given their thanks.

"Well, what?" he asked, spearing a chicken leg with his fork.

"Is he going?"

Abe dropped the chicken onto his plate and shrugged as he reached for the potatoes. "I do not know."

"Surely he's said something."

"Nay." He dumped a load of the potatoes onto his plate and reached for the corn on the cob.

"Abe Fitch, is food all you care about?"

"Nay, but there's no sense in starving just so we can talk."

Esther shook her head, but started filling her own plate. "What is it going to take to get that boy to go?"

"I think he's worried."

"About what?" Esther asked.

"Sometimes it's better to wonder about the answers rather than know them for certain and be hurt by the truth."

"Would you stop talking in riddles and tell me what you mean?"

He swallowed his bite and wiped his mouth on the napkin. "What I mean is, sometimes the wondering is better than the hurting."

She thought about that a second. "You're saying that Andrew is afraid that Caroline will turn him down."

"Jah."

She scooted back from the table with such force that she knocked her chair over backward. Moxie let out a large "woof." The pooch was quickly growing into his bark.

"Where are you going?" Abe asked.

Esther righted her chair and straightened her prayer *kapp*. "I'm going to go kick that boy in the pants."

"Aren't you going to finish your *nachtess*?"

She shook her head. "There'll be time for eating after I get these two together."

Andrew looked up as Esther barged into the furniture store.

"Sorry, Esther, I was just about to close up. And *Onkle's* with . . . well, I thought he was with you."

"Jah," Esther said with a curt nod. "He's at my supper table right now."

Andrew frowned. "Then why are you here?"

"I've come to give you your sign." She handed him the letter she had received from Caroline that very afternoon. "If you don't go after her, that girl is going to make the biggest mistake of her life."

Andrew's fingers trembled as he took the envelope from Esther. Was this what he truly wanted?

That answer was easy. It was. He loved Caroline with

all his heart. Emma too. Their leaving had taken all the sunshine from his world. "But—"

"There is no room for buts. She thinks you don't want her. Unless you go after her—and soon—all will be lost."

He shook his head and started to hand the letter back to Esther. "Emma needs her father."

She refused his offering and instead crossed her arms around her ample girth. "I won't tell you that Emma doesn't need a father. *Jah*, that much is true. But Emma needs *a* father. A *gut* Amish *vatter*. Not some smooth-talking *Englischer*. If Caroline marries Trey, then she'll be shunned by her folks and be forced to live among the *Englisch*. How long do you think such a marriage would last?"

The words were like a punch in the stomach. If Caroline were to become estranged from her English husband, she would not be welcomed back into the Amish church. She would forever be an outcast. "But—"

"Caroline misses you," Esther interjected. "Go to her and see what God has in store for the both of you."

Andrew looked down at the letter, then back up into Esther's serious blue eyes. *Was* this the sign he had been waiting on all along?

"Would you mind repeating that, son?"

Trey stared at the bottom of the empty tumbler, then set the glass on the coffee table in front of him. This phone call was long overdue, but even in the days that he had been putting it off, he still hadn't come up with the right words to tell his father about Caroline . . . and Emma.

"I have a daughter." Repeating the words didn't take away their strangeness on his tongue. He had a daughter.

His father sighed on the other end of the line. "I was

afraid this would happen. As soon as I got elected, I knew something like this would crop up."

He had?

"You've got to be careful, son. There are people out there who will take advantage. I never thought I'd be saying this. You need to get an appointment with a doctor. You'll have to be as discreet as possible. If we can keep this away from the press, all the better. Especially until we can prove the child's not yours."

The image of large gray eyes set in the cherub face flashed through his mind's eye. "She's mine."

His father grew so quiet on the other end of the line that Trey thought they had been disconnected.

"Dad?"

"Why are you so sure?"

That was Duke, always pushing the boundaries of what was accepted. "Because she looks just like me." Trey wanted to shout the words, but he managed to keep his tone even. Yelling wasn't going to make the situation any better.

"This won't look good."

"There's more."

"More?"

"She's Amish."

His father swore under his breath. "This looks real bad, son."

Trey shook his head. He had known Duke Rycroft would react this way. His first concern had always been and would always be what the public thought.

And he knew that it would look like he had taken advantage of an innocent.

How did a man explain to the media that he had fallen for Caroline right from the start? The differences in their home lives and the way that they had been raised were nothing compared to the pull he'd felt toward her.

He was pretty sure she felt the same. He hadn't coerced her into something she hadn't wanted. Theirs was a pure love, strong and true. Or at least it had been. But the media would turn it inside out and make it something dirty and wrong.

Maybe they should have married, or maybe they should have held off showing their love. But there wasn't a person out there who hadn't made a mistake at least once in their life. Not that the press would understand.

Just the thought of Caroline fighting off the media and their endless hounding sent shivers down his spine. She wasn't prepared for that. But it was coming, like it or not.

"What are you going to do about this?"

Trey sat forward on the couch and braced his elbows on his knees. He wanted to bury his face in his hands, scrub his knuckles over his stinging eyes, but he held on to the receiver. "I'm going to marry her."

His father grew quiet once again. Trey could almost hear him chewing over the words. "Do you really think that's the best idea?"

He didn't know what to think anymore. He had been searching for Caroline, hoping to see her again, get the infatuation he held for her put to rest. One day they had been happily hiding out from their parents not worried about one thing their complicated future would bring, and the next she was gone.

He thought he would find her, see if what they had was as real as it had been all those months ago. But instead he found he had a child, a thought that wiped all else from his brain. He was a father.

"What would you have me do, Dad? Just ignore her?"

"Of course not, but marriage?"

What was he saying? It would be scandal enough when the press found out that he had fathered a child out of wedlock. Then to not marry her? Did his father realize what he was saying?

"Just hear me out," Duke said. "Maybe if we give her a little more money and—"

"Please tell me you're joking." If he wasn't, then Trey was likely to be sick to his stomach. He and Caroline had created a life. He couldn't just walk away from Emma and pretend she didn't exist. "Do you know what her church would do to her if I don't marry her?"

"I don't. But she's not my concern."

Red flashed behind Trey's eyes. "I'm going to let you go now, and hopefully I can forget you even said that."

"You should listen to me, boy. She's not one of us, and she never will be. Marrying her would be the biggest mistake of your life."

"That may be. But since I can't take it back, I'm sure going to make it right."

With that, he hung up the phone, his father's sputtering echoing in his ears long into the night.

Caroline's heart gave a hard pound when she heard the roar of the engine and the crunch of the tires against the gravel road. Trey had arrived.

She brushed her hands over her apron, then ran them over the sides of her hair. Her prayer *kapp* was in place. Emma was dressed in her first ever *schlupp schotzli* and looked cute as a button even if Caroline said so herself. Everything was in place for Trey's visit.

It was a simple plan really; they were going to have pie

with her parents, then Caroline had planned a buggy ride around Ethridge. He hadn't gotten to spend very much time with Emma. That was something they needed rectify immediately. Though Caroline wasn't keen on answering too many questions from the good citizens of their community, it was only a matter of time before someone started adding up the time that Caroline had been gone and Emma's age and came up with the truth.

"I see your *Englisch bu* is here."

Caroline let out a nervous sigh. "*Jah*. Do you think *Dat* will come out of the barn?"

Grace Hostetler's mouth pulled down at the corners. "Don't expect too much from your father, Caroline." She used a dishcloth to wipe the table down one last time before their company came into the house. "This has been very hard on him."

"I s'pose." But not talking to her surely wasn't helping any.

Caroline knew that the situation couldn't be easy for him. She had left the community, but he had stayed. He'd had to explain why his daughter, his only child, had suddenly vanished.

She pushed away the thought and went to let Trey inside.

"Trey." She greeted him with a forced smile. He looked as handsome as always in his fancy *Englisch* clothes, and Caroline wondered again at the waste of it all. Was it necessary to have so much? She shook her head at her own thoughts and motioned for him to enter.

He entered the house as if he were stepping into a pit of snakes. She knew the feeling. She had felt that exact same way as she had stood on his father's front porch all those many months ago.

Her *elders' haus* was a far cry from Trey's sleek black-and-gray apartment with its carpeted floor and artwork on the walls. She wasn't embarrassed, but she knew it couldn't compare in his eyes.

"Trey, this is my *mudder* Grace."

He reached a hand out for her to shake. "It's a pleasure," he said, but his voice cracked on the last word.

"Come sit down, Trey, I've made us some coffee," her *mamm* said.

"And we've got pie," Caroline added. "So we can talk."

He gave a stiff nod and followed them into the kitchen. "Is your father here?"

"*Jah*," Caroline said. "But he's working in the barn."

Her mother let out a discreet cough, then indicated some point behind them both.

Caroline turned as her *vatter* entered the room. He held a giggling Emma high in his arms.

It was one thing she could say about her *dat*. He might have trouble forgiving Caroline for her transgressions, but he didn't hold a single one against this *grossdochder*.

Without a word, Grace poured him a cup of coffee and set it in front of his place at the table.

Dat murmured his thanks, sliding into the chair at the head of the table and setting Emma on her feet.

Everyone took their seats, staring around at the others while no one was ready to make the first move.

Unable to take it any longer, Caroline spoke. "We have a great deal to talk about."

Trey cleared his throat. "I've asked your daughter to marry me. It's the only solution."

Caroline shook her head. "It is not."

"It is."

"*Halt!*" Her father rarely raised his voice, and the fact that he did so now alarmed Caroline.

Trey nervously drummed his fingers on the table but managed to hold his words.

"I'm not sure marriage is the answer," her mother said quietly.

"There has been a dishonor," her father protested.

Trey had the good grace to flush at the accusation, but still he said nothing.

"A wedding now would be like shuttin' the barn door after all the horses have escaped," her mother added.

"I want to do what's right," Trey finally said. "My family will not accept scandal lightly."

Not words of love, but shame. "Is that all this means to you?" Caroline asked. "Disgrace?"

He took her hand into his own and squeezed her fingers. "Caroline, I love you. I always have." But she saw him swallow hard as he said the words.

He might have loved her once, but she wasn't convinced his feelings were true if it took him two years to wonder what happened to her, why she had disappeared, and where she had been.

He just had found more than he had expected.

Men like Trey were used to women falling at their feet. She was a novelty. Intriguing and unique.

And then there was Andrew.

"There is more here at stake than talk of love." Her mother lifted her coffee cup and took a delicate sip, an action Caroline realized was meant to hide her own misgivings.

"Jah," her *dat* said. "There's the *meidung*."

Trey looked to her.

"A shunning," she supplied. Her heart dropped at the thought. If she married Trey, it would be worse than a shunning. There would be no going back.

"And they will shun you if you marry me?"

"Worse," Caroline managed to whisper. "I would never be able to come here again."

A frown creased Trey's forehead even as her *mamm's*

eyes filled with tears. "I'm afraid I don't understand. If we get married, then it fixes everything."

Caroline shook her head. "*Nay*. Because you are English, and I am Plain . . ."

"We have to get married." Trey all but pounded his fist on the table.

"If'n you don't get married," her father started.

"Then Caroline could stay here and be with us," her mother finished.

Trey shook his head in apparent disbelief. "And what then? Be shunned or whatever by everyone in town?"

"It would only be for a short time. Perhaps a few months. Being turned away by the members of the community is better than having to be cut off from my family completely." Caroline cast a glance over to where Emma played with a set of plastic blocks and a wooden pull toy that her father had made. "Bittersweet" was the word that popped into mind. Being here with her *mamm*, even if her *dat* was having trouble speaking her name, meant the world to her. If she were to lose all that now . . .

No one mentioned going back to Wells Landing.

"No." Trey shook his head, his voice gaining strength. "We need to get married. We have to do the right thing."

"I think this is something we need to talk about," Caroline said, trying to gather her courage to say the right thing . . . *do* the right thing. Trey had already stated that his family would want them to marry for appearance's sake, but what about Emma?

"I'll not have my *grosskinner* growing up *Englisch*," her father said. He looked to her *mamm*. Grace in turn cut her eyes to Caroline.

"That's not the only question we have to consider," Caroline said.

"I find this remarkable." Trey stood, his agitation finally

getting the better of him. "I'm discussing the merits of an unwed mother remaining unwed with some of the most conservative people in America. It's as if you want her to be shunned."

Her father stood, his eyes flashing with anger and something Caroline could not identify. "I will talk of this no more tonight." He stalked off, tipping his chair over as he left the room.

"*Dat*," Caroline called, but he continued on, slamming out of the house and no doubt heading for his precious barn. She jumped to her feet mumbling an excuse before hustling out the door behind him.

Trey couldn't pinpoint exactly where the conversation had turned so wrong. His legs felt like rubber, and his heart burned in his chest. He only wanted to do what was right. Marry Caroline. Be a father to their child. How could that be wrong? And how could her family be opposed?

Grace stood and righted the chair, her calm remarkable in the wake of the storm he had just witnessed.

"Trey, would you mind?" She gestured toward the living room.

He hadn't noticed it before but the child sat on the floor crying loudly, most likely from the ruckus of their argument. "Uh . . ." He almost said no. But if he and Caroline were going to be married and be a family, then consoling the child would be a part of his duties. "Of course."

He scooped her into his arms, her warm weight strangely soothing. Her wails subsided to small hiccups as he bounced her the way he had seen some mothers do. And she smelled good. Like Caroline and . . . and baby. That was the only way he could describe it: sweet, sweet baby.

He rubbed her back as she took a shuddering breath. The motion itself seemed like a new beginning. And that was when Trey fell in love. Deeply in love with his own daughter.

Something fierce and proud rose inside him. He would do anything to protect her. Anything. He wanted to secure her future and let her know how much he loved her.

Which started with marrying her mother. Not because his father demanded it, but because that was the only way they could be a family.

"I don't understand," he told Grace. It was really remarkable how much she looked like Caroline. He had noticed the resemblance in the country store and even more so now. Same hazel eyes and honey-blond hair. Grace's was a bit lighter and shot through with gray. They both wore the same pained expressions, at least they had as Caroline raced after her father.

"Don't understand what, Trey Rycroft?"

"I only want to do the right thing."

Her lips pressed into a small frown. "Taking Caroline and Emma away from us once again is the right thing to do?"

She had missed the point entirely. He instinctively snuggled Emma closer. If Caroline didn't marry him, he wouldn't be able to come visit her here. It would be a sure tip-off to the church leaders and the press. With their distinctive gray eyes it wouldn't be long before someone put two and two together and came up with an unplanned pregnancy. His father's career would be rocked. Caroline's life would be hard. No doubt she would be punished for her lapse, and the media would be on her in a flash hounding her for details and sordid facts.

And what of Emma? It was a tragic tale, one worthy of every tabloid in America. What a field day they would have: Amish girl, senator's son, and a love child.

But if he married her, would her life be any different? Surely, word would get to the press. It was a short dig to Caroline's conservative roots. Would a hasty wedding stop the papers from printing every last detail?

No.

And Caroline would be thrust into his world. It was a good world, filled with everything she could ever want: nice house, expensive cars, good schools, and more than an eighth-grade education for Emma. Opportunities galore.

And completely cut off from her family.

Still the question remained: Was marrying her the right thing to do?

He just didn't know. What he wanted and what they needed tumbled around in his head along with all the limitations and opportunities.

He kissed the top of Emma's head and silently wondered if now would be a good time to start praying.

Dear Esther,

I felt the strong need to write you this letter. I know we have never met but we have very precious common ground—Caroline and Emma.

Caroline tells me that your district is more liberal than we are here in Tennessee, and I worry that you might think the worst of us. But that's not the reason for my letter. I'm writing you to give my thanks. You took care of my dochder and took her in when she had no one else.

I know this letter is long overdue. I have no reason a'tall for my delay, but I do thank you and appreciate all that you did for Caroline and Emma. You will never know how much it means to me to know that Caroline had someone to care for her in her greatest time of need.

The decisions that she has to make now are difficult ones, perhaps the most difficult of her life. Please add her to your nightly prayers. She needs wisdom, understanding, and peace during this turbulent time. Above all, please pray that God's will be done.

Ever grateful,
Grace Hostetler

Chapter Twenty-Two

"Dat?" Caroline once again entered the barn looking for her father.

Too many emotions charged the atmosphere around the table, and the cool, earthy interior of the barn was a welcome relief. No wonder her father came out here to think. Barns were about as peaceful a place as one could find.

"Here," he said.

Caroline followed the sound of his voice until she found him sitting on a bale of hay, a leather harness in one hand and a rag in the other.

The smell of saddle soap was a balm to her nerves, bringing to mind all the wonderful memories of her and him in this very barn, working with the horses while her friends learned to sew and cook.

She had always been what the *Englisch* called a "Daddy's girl." It wasn't that she was her father's favorite, but his only.

She could only image how much her leaving hurt him. How embarrassed he was that he couldn't even raise one child to follow a righteous path.

Was there a best answer to their problems? Marrying Trey or staying here? And what of Wells Landing? She pushed those thoughts away. Andrew had made his feelings perfectly clear. He had cut her loose. Returning to Oklahoma was no longer an option, if it had ever been. She wasn't sure she could live there in the same town with him knowing that he would never love her as much as she loved him.

"*Dat*," she said, easing down onto the stack of hay beside him. "I'm sorry." It was all she could think of to say. She was very aware that the words were not enough to erase the past two years of hurt and distrust, but it had to be said. It was a start at least. "I never meant to cause you pain or dishonor."

"Why?"

She took a shuddering breath. She had always known that she would have to answer that question eventually. But all the preparation in the world couldn't have readied her for the actual time. "I'm not sure. There was just a connection between us, something bigger than the both of us. Maybe God's will?"

"You think it was God's will for you to sin outside of marriage, run away, and then have a baby?" His tone clearly implied his disagreement.

"I just know that every step we take leads us to who we are right now. If I hadn't done those things, then we wouldn't have Emma." She sighed. "I won't tell you that it's been easy, but I wouldn't trade that *maedel* for anything in the world. I can't go back on that, nor do I want to. Like it or not, Trey is Emma's father. He only wants to do right by us."

"In *Englisch* standards. What about here?"

She wasn't sure that she wanted to marry Trey, but perhaps that was her will battling God's own. She knew who would win that one.

"It's like I'm losing you all over again." Her father's voice was choked.

"What would you have me do? Stay here and bring more dishonor onto your house? Every time I hear a buggy go by, my heart starts to pound and I wonder if this time it's the bishop to tell me about my sins and what I must do to make them right with the Lord."

"People are kinder than you think."

"Nay." Caroline shook her head. "They will say that they forgive, and they may even actually forgive, but no one will forget. Emma will suffer."

Her words struck home. Hollis Hostetler bowed his head. Whether he was praying or simply resigned, Caroline didn't know.

"Is this what you want, to marry this *Englischer*?"

"I don't know," she answered truthfully. Her greatest concern was for Emma. What would the marriage mean to her? Did she want her *dochder* growing up *Englisch* in a family that had never wanted her from the start? To be separated from her Amish grandparents?

If Caroline stayed in Ethridge, she would be shunned for a time. Most probably a long time. If she married Trey, the consequences would be even worse. "I don't know what I should do."

"All you can do, my girl, is take it to the Lord."

Take it to the Lord.

These words stayed with Caroline long after she left the barn and made her way back up to the house.

Trey was still waiting for her, looking wholly uncomfortable on her family's wooden-framed couch. Emma was sitting next to him, playing with blocks and babbling away in the language only she understood. Mostly it was a mixture of English and *Deutsch* with a few random sounds thrown in for good measure.

"Caroline." Trey's eyes lit with relief as she entered the

house. He stood. "I didn't want to leave without saying good-bye."

"You're leaving?"

He watched as she went to the couch and scooped Emma into her arms. "This isn't something we can solve in an afternoon," he said. "I thought maybe we should let everything settle again and take it up in a day or two."

"*Jah*, okay."

"Walk me to my car?"

She gave a quick nod and followed him out of the house.

Her thoughts were still in turmoil trying to take it all in, make sense where there was none.

She held Emma on one hip as she followed Trey to his shiny black car.

He opened the door, then turned to face her, making no move to actually get in the car and drive away. "I only want what's best for us—you and Emma."

"I know. The problem is figuring out what is best."

His gray eyes searched her face as if the answer was written there. "What we had was good." He took a step toward her, clasping her elbow and urging her closer. He lowered his head, his intent clear.

Caroline turned away before his lips could make their mark. The kiss on her cheek was sweet and warm. She closed her eyes against the maelstrom of memories and shook her head. "Don't confuse me. Please."

He released her arm and took a step back. "Okay," he said, though hurt flashed in his eyes. "I'll see you tomorrow?"

She shook her head. "I don't think so."

"The next day."

"*Jah*, okay." Though she knew it would take more than a day to sort through all the choices that had to be made.

But a choice was imminent, she thought as Trey backed

his car out of the drive and onto the road. It wouldn't be long before the bishop came calling to talk about the mistakes she had made. She needed her answer before that happened.

She pressed a kiss to the top of Emma's curls.

She had a lot of praying to do.

Trey unlocked his apartment door, something his father said niggling in the back of his mind. Something about money.

He sighed as he sat his keys on the table and resisted the urge to pour himself a stiff drink. Alcohol was not the answer.

It had been a long drive home, a trip filled with memories new and old. Even worse, the smell of her clung to him. Not Caroline's, but Emma's. A strange mixture of lavender and baby. It was nothing like he had ever smelled in his life. It made his heart thump painfully in longing for something . . . he just didn't know what.

When he had looked into those sweet gray eyes and seen himself staring back, the future and the past . . . everything at once, he knew he'd do anything to protect his baby girl.

Caroline was right; there were tough decisions to be made. But his logic could only find one: marriage.

He sank down onto the couch, phone in hand, and dialed his parents' number.

"Hello?" His mother answered on the third ring.

"Hi. Mom."

"Trey." His name was a rush of air, as if she was relieved that he had called.

He supposed that after he hung up on his father the other day, her fears were somewhat justified.

"How are you?" she asked.

"I'm . . . you know."

"Yes, dear, your father told me."

He could almost hear her shake her head, and relief flooded him. This was his mom, his understanding rock throughout his entire life. If anyone could make sense of the mess he found himself in, it was April Rycroft.

"I went to see her today."

"Your father says the baby looks like you."

"Identical. It's a little weird to look into my eyes in someone else's face."

"Tell me about it."

He laughed. He'd inherited those distinctive gray eyes from his mother.

"How did it go?"

He shrugged even though she couldn't see him. "I don't know. Her parents don't want us to get married. Something about shunning and the church. It's complicated."

"What is it that the two of you want?"

"I want to do what's right." Emma's face flashed through his mind's eye. "She's just a baby, you know?"

"I know. What about the mother?"

"I'm really not sure what Caroline wants. I thought marrying her was the best option, but she doesn't seem to think so."

"Has she said as much?" his mother asked.

"Not really, but she seems reserved." He thought about his rebuffed attempt to kiss her this afternoon. "I know it would be a big change for everyone, but I can give her everything she and Emma need: house, car, education."

"What about love?"

"Of course." He said the words, but his stomach fell. Did he love Caroline? Did she love him? Would the feelings that had survived between them be enough to keep them together through all the changes that were about to take place? "I know it's a big step, but it's what's best for everyone." Especially his father.

And Emma. She needed both parents. That was the one thing he was certain of.

"Just keep an open mind and don't be so hard on your father. He means well."

"I know." Trey sighed and rubbed his eyes. He was definitely in for another sleepless night.

"When she came by the house . . . well, I didn't approve of what your father did. He only wanted what was best for you."

Trey's stomach sank. "What are you talking about?"

His mother grew so quiet that Trey thought they might have lost the connection. "Maybe you should talk to your father about this."

"I'm talking to you."

"I thought you knew."

"Knew what, Mom?" He tried to keep his voice at a normal volume, but it rose with each syllable.

"Your father offered her money."

"Money? When? For what?"

"Really, Trey." Her voice grew agitated. "This is something you should discuss with him."

"When?" he asked through clenched teeth.

"A couple of years ago."

He took a deep breath hoping to calm his rising anger. "How come I never knew she came to visit?"

She paused, no doubt shaping her answer into the best form before speaking. "Your father thought it best that we not tell you. School was about to start and . . . and we didn't think you needed the distraction."

Distraction? "And what was the money for?"

"Trey . . ."

"Did he know that she was pregnant?"

"Trey, I—"

"Did he?" He hated browbeating his own mother, but his anger and frustrations were rising by the second.

"Yes."

He felt sick. His father had offered Caroline money to . . . He couldn't even think the word. It was too vile.

No wonder she fled. No wonder she didn't want to marry him. Who could blame her?

"She's a fine woman," he said, his jaw so tight he was afraid he'd crack some molars. "I'm going to marry her and give our baby my name. You can count on it."

Trey waited the two days that she had asked him to, but Caroline still wasn't ready to face him. She had dreamt about Andrew the night before. He seemed to be calling to her across the sparse grass of her family's yard. He was holding Emma in his arms and waving to her. A big smile graced his face and reflected in the aqua color of his eyes.

She wasn't sure what it meant, but it kept her up from the wee hours of the morning until dawn when she heard her father stirring around.

Now she was tired. Her hands trembled, and she wasn't sure how she was going to make it through the day.

But she had promised Trey that they would talk again today, and she would keep that promise.

She rose from the couch the minute she heard his car in the drive, anxious to get the ordeal over and done.

Trey smiled as she opened the door, and she realized that when he smiled like that she remembered why she had fallen in love with him to begin with. But was it too late?

"Come in," she said, holding the door open for him.

Trey stepped inside, rubbing his hands together in apparent excitement. "I thought we'd take Emma to the zoo today."

All the way into Nashville? She wasn't up for it. But she couldn't say no. Trey looked so pleased with himself that she simply couldn't. Besides, it might be a *gut* idea to get away from Ethridge and all of the confusion. Maybe among strangers and animals they would be able to talk more freely and make whatever plans they needed for the future.

"Let me get Emma's bag."

It wasn't long before they had Emma's car seat installed in the back of Trey's car and Emma strapped inside. Then they were speeding down the highway toward Nashville.

"You look tired," he said.

"I didn't get much sleep last night."

He gave her a quick glance, then turned his attention back to the road ahead. "Me either."

She thought he might be about to say something else, but he hesitated. "I don't know how to begin."

"At the beginning?"

He smiled at her poor attempt of a joke, then his expression sobered. "Why didn't you tell me that my father paid you to . . . go away?"

"Would it have made any difference?"

"I guess not."

"*Jah*, then. There was no reason to tell you about the money he offered me."

His lips pressed together in a look of grim understanding, and Caroline had the feeling that the matter was far from over.

They rode in silence for a few miles before he cast his gaze in her direction once again. "Wouldn't you be more comfortable if you took off your head thingie?"

Her hands flew to her prayer *kapp*. "*Nay* . . . no . . . why?"

He shrugged, his hands loose and confident on the wheel. "I just thought it'd be a good idea for you to start dressing more English."

Whatever for? Thankfully she managed to keep the question to herself. She knew why Trey wanted her to dress like the English. Because he wanted her to marry him, give up all things Amish. Including her family. The thought made her stomach pitch.

"I don't know," she murmured, the idea making her squirm in her seat. She had never dressed *Englisch* before. Not even when she and Trey had been sneaking around. She might have gone against a lot of what she had been raised to believe, but giving up her prayer *kapp* and *frack* would be like stripping away her identity. Part of her being.

He shot her that sweet smile that had melted her insides from the very first time she had ever seen him. Maybe it was the time that had passed, but now she recognized it as what it really was: coercion. He wanted something from her, and he was willing to pull out all the stops to get it.

"Are you embarrassed to be seen with a Plain girl?"

He laughed, his smile lingering on his lips. "Caroline Hostetler, you are far from plain."

"You know what I mean."

"I do. But don't you think you would be more comfortable if you were to take your hair down?"

Would she be more comfortable? Or would the action just show her how much she didn't belong in Trey's world?

Only one way to find out.

She reached for the pins holding her *kapp* in place.

Trey swerved a bit as he took his eyes from the road to watch her. He seemed almost mesmerized by her actions.

"If you don't watch where you are driving, then I'm not going to do this."

"Right." He turned his attention back to the front, but turned to look at her every few seconds.

"Strange" was not the word to describe how it felt to have her hair down during the middle of the day. She put it up first thing in the morning and took it down the last thing before going to bed.

But strange seemed to be the direction her life was taking these days. And there was nothing she could do to stop it.

She had left Oklahoma to find Trey, reconciled with her parents only to have the man at her side want her to walk away from it all once again.

"We could run by the mall and get you some different clothes if you like."

"It's not necessary," she said, head down as she tried to get used to the feeling of her unbound hair and traveling faster than she thought man was intended.

You better get used to it, a small voice taunted. If she married Trey, all this would be a part of her life.

"I know it's not necessary, but I think it'll be good." He glanced to the backseat where Emma was peacefully playing with a colorful plastic car toy Trey had brought for her. It had its own miniature steering wheel and toot-toot horn. "We can get some things for Emma too."

Caroline shook her head. "You don't have to do that."

"Of course I do," Trey said. "That's my job. And once we are married, I'll buy you things every day. No time like now for you to start getting used to the idea." He exited the highway as they neared the city limits.

Caroline didn't comment as he drove them to the mall. All she could think about was the confident way he spoke about the two of them binding themselves to each other for a lifetime.

Was that really what she wanted?

* * *

"Oh, *nay*." Caroline shook her head as Trey steered his shiny car into her parents' driveway. They'd had a fun time in Nashville, but she was tired and the sight before her was more than she wanted to deal with right now.

"What's wrong?" he asked.

Caroline swallowed back the lump of worry in her throat and pointed toward the buggy parked off to one side. "That's the bishop's buggy."

Her hands flew to her head. But her prayer *kapp* was at the bottom of the shopping bag that Trey had stored in the trunk of the car. "Oh, *nay, nay, nay*."

How was she going to explain the way she was dressed and her lack of a head covering to the bishop?

She had only done it because it was the only way to know if she could. She felt exposed and promiscuous in the tight-fitting jeans. And the clingy shirt had no modesty at all.

The bishop's horse had been unhitched from his buggy and was grazing in the pasture with the rest of the Hostetler animals. He had most likely come for supper and planned to stay long enough to talk to her.

"Calm down," Trey said, turning off the car engine and turning to face her.

"I can't be calm. This is bad, really bad." She started to bundle her hair at the nape of her neck. She had nothing to secure it there and it immediately tumbled back down. "The bishop would only be here for one reason, and that is to call me to task about . . . everything."

Trey laid a warm hand on her leg, and Caroline jumped at the soft touch. "What difference does it make?"

"It makes a lot."

"Not if you marry me." His narrowed eyes grew stormy. "You aren't going to, are you? You're not going to marry me."

"I don't know," Caroline cried. "I don't know what to do."

"I only want to help."

She sucked in a deep breath just as her *mamm* came out onto the porch. Even with yards separating them, Caroline could see the pain and apprehension in her mother's eyes.

She had done that. She had brought this shame and dishonor onto her family. Maybe Trey was right. Maybe there was only one way to solve it.

If she stayed here, no one would ever forget. Emma would pay the price in never having a father. No man would want Caroline after they found out the truth. Just look at Andrew.

The mere thought of his name sent a stabbing pain through her heart.

That time in her life was over.

The Bible said there was a time for everything: a time to reap and a time to sow. Now was her time to grow up. She had put her family through too much already. She couldn't continue to do this to them.

Lord, please tell me I'm doing the right thing. She prayed. Then she turned to Trey.

"Okay, *jah*," she finally said. "You're right."

He shook his head. "About what?"

"About everything."

"Yeah?"

"Jah," she said again. "I'll marry you."

Dear Lizzie,

I hope this letter finds you well and healing from your own heartbreak. I'm not sure how I found myself in this predicament. I came to Oklahoma to find peace and solace in a time without Beth and to heal from the pain of losing her. Instead I found love, deceit, and heartbreak.

I have been praying diligently to understand why Caroline would hide such secrets from me. And then to have her leave without even saying good-bye or telling her reasons was almost more than I could bear. I know now that she only wanted to protect herself and me from the truth, but there is no place for secrets in matters of the heart. And such matters make a man do things he never thought he might.

Tomorrow I will embark on what might be the stupidest thing I have ever done. I have a bus ticket that will take me to Tennessee to find Caroline and hopefully bring her back with me. I miss her and need her with me.

I never expected to fall in love again, never mind so soon after losing Beth, but it seems God has other plans in mind for me. At least I hope He does. Caroline has gone to Tennessee to find the father of wee Emma (a long story that I will relay later when I have more time). And though I love her more than

*I can say, I know that I have to compete for her
hand with an Englischer who once held her heart.*

*Please pray for me as I travel and pray that
somehow I can find a way back into Caroline's
arms. I want nothing more than to be with her. Be a
husband to her and a vatter to Emma.*

I'll write again as soon as I can.

*Love always,
Andrew*

Chapter Twenty-Three

A rush of relief washed over Trey. Caroline was going to marry him. They would be a family, and to the devil and back with his father's offers and worries about appearances.

One sure thing about the media circus, it always died down. As soon as fresh news hit, the press forgot the transgressions of the day before.

"That's wonderful," he said, reaching across the console to pull her close.

She shook her head and held up a hand to stay his approach. "My *mamm* is watching."

He pulled away. "Shall we go in and tell them the good news?"

She hesitated. "Maybe we should save that for another day." She shot a pointed look toward the bishop's buggy.

Trey didn't know a great deal about the ways of the Amish, but he knew that Caroline would have a lot of explaining to do. "You want me to come in?"

"Nay."

"I will, you know. You didn't get into this situation all by yourself."

She gave him a trembling smile. "It's okay. This is something I need to do myself. Then in a couple of days, when the dust settles, we can make our plans for the . . . wedding."

He didn't miss the slight hesitation before the word. She might be having misgivings, but he would make certain that they were taken care of and gone before she walked down the aisle. And he would do everything in his power to make that happen as soon as possible.

But for now . . .

"I'll come by in a couple of days?"

She swallowed hard.

Despite her doubts, the love he had for her grew a bit more. She was worried now, but not for long. He would show her how great life was going to be as they became a family. And he would put that smile back on her sweet lips.

Caroline watched Trey drive away with a rock in the pit of her stomach. Thankfully her mother had gone back into the house before Caroline had gotten out of the car, leaving her a few minutes alone to gather herself.

At least her mother hadn't seen her in the *Englisch* clothes that Trey had bought her.

She held Emma on one hip and plucked at the front of the orange-colored T-shirt she now wore instead of her modest blue dress. She had been terribly uncomfortable in the clinging outfit, but she would have to get used to it. Marrying Trey and living among the *Englisch*, she would be expected to dress like other *Englischers*. It was just the way it was.

She supposed she would get used to it eventually.

Lord, I pray that I'm doing the right thing. Emma needs a father. And Trey wants to marry. So why does it feel like I might be making the biggest mistake of my life?

Mistake or not, she had promised Trey that they would get married. She would keep that promise to him and give Emma hope for the future.

"*Allrecht*, Emma, my girl, let's get this over with." She kissed the top of her *dochder*'s head and started toward the house.

She wasn't sure whose gasp was louder, her mother's or her father's.

Bishop Glick was strangely calm, as if he had heard so many bad rumors about her that nothing as mundane as *Englisch* clothes could surprise him.

"Caroline, what have you done?" Her mother rose, moisture in her eyes, and Caroline had to blink back tears of her own.

"Trey asked me to marry him, and I said yes." She let Emma slide to the floor. The child immediately toddled over and climbed into her *grossdaadi*'s lap.

Caroline swallowed back the lump of regrets and turned toward the bishop. "I'm sure you are here for me."

"*Jah,*" he said.

She lowered herself into the seat opposite him and folded her hands on the table in front of her.

"I take it Trey is the baby's *vatter*?" Bishop Glick asked. "*Jah.*"

"And he is *Englisch*, as the rumors tell me?"

"He is." Caroline dipped her chin with more confidence than she felt.

The bishop stroked his beard, the round lenses of his glasses glinting in the late-afternoon light. "As a member of the Amish church, you understand what it means to marry an *Englischer*."

Caroline took a steadying breath and kept her gaze trained on David Glick. "It means a *meidung*."

She heard her mother's breath catch, the sound at direct odds with Emma's sweet babbling.

"Are you prepared for that?" the bishop asked.

"Jah." Her voice was barely above a whisper.

"You will join your life with his until death."

To her credit, Grace Hostetler managed to keep her sobs to herself.

Caroline hated that everything had to come out this way. The entire situation was unfortunate, trying, and downright painful for all involved.

But soon, very soon, she would be Trey's wife. Soon after, life would settle into a new normal for her. Her heart thumped at the thought. She had no idea what that normal might be.

"I understand," she managed to say. It was necessary. By marrying Trey, she would save Emma from a stigma she would carry with her for life. She couldn't allow her daughter to be punished for her sins.

The bishop studied her with knowing green eyes. The clock on the wall clicked off three full seconds. Everyone seemed to hold their breath. Even Emma grew quiet as if she knew something important was about to happen.

Finally he spoke. "If'n you change your mind, you know what must be done."

"Jah, danki," she said and stood to escort him to the door.

He'd won that round, Trey thought to himself as he pulled his car onto the highway and headed for home. Yet the victory seemed hollow and heavy at the same time.

Hollow because despite Caroline agreeing to marry him, he had the feeling that the choice was not one she wanted to make. And heavy for the circumstances he now faced.

In September he would start his final year of law school.

He'd have a wife who was basically from another time and a child he barely knew. That wasn't all. They would surely be thrown into a media circus once the hounds got wind of their wedding.

He sighed. They hadn't even talked about the wedding. His mother would surely want to put together something a little more elegant than a trip to the courthouse, but Trey felt an urgency to make this right like he never had before. Maybe by the end of this week, first of next at the latest.

There was no time for a reception with hundreds of people, hors d'oeuvres, and an open bar. This needed to be done and filed so they could get on to the business of living.

Trey ran through a Chinese takeout and took his solitary dinner back to his apartment. He let himself in, not really wanting to be alone, but not wanting company either. Except for Caroline. He would love to have her sitting across from him. Soon . . . very soon.

He sat down at the table and started to eat. A little wave of guilt washed over him when he realized that he hadn't said grace.

Never once while he and Caroline had been going around together had she not prayed. In fact, she prayed before *and* after she ate.

How were they going to address the question of faith? He had grown up in church, but didn't see himself as particularly spiritual. Attending Sunday morning services had been more of a show for the public than anything to do with God.

He couldn't ask Caroline to walk away from God after she had just abandoned her family. It seemed like they both had a lot of adjustments to make.

He finished eating and took the paper containers to the

trash. His mind was still going ninety-to-nothing with all of the decisions and choices still to be made.

On top of it all, he needed to call and talk to his parents. His father would need to call his campaign manager. A lot of people would need to know about the wedding, and soon. He sighed and grabbed his phone. He didn't really have a date, but it was time to get the party started.

"Trey?" His father answered the phone as if he had been sitting there just waiting for it to ring.

"Hi, Dad."

"I take it you have something to tell me."

Trey cleared his throat. He wished he had planned for this moment better. "I'm getting married."

His father cursed under his breath, but the tone was unmistakable. "Son, you need to think this through."

Trey rubbed his eyes. "I have thought it through, and this is best for everyone."

"I don't know how you can say that."

"Can I talk to Mom?"

"Trey, this is serious."

"I am being serious. I'm serious, and I am marrying Caroline. I'm going to be a father to Emma."

His father swore again. "None of this would be necessary if she had done what she was supposed to."

Trey really didn't want to go through all of this right now. Besides, what good would it do? His father was as stubborn as they came. There was no changing Duke Rycroft's mind about anything.

"Let me talk to my mother," he said through gritted teeth. "We have plans to make."

The day after the bishop's visit, Caroline's family got the sad news that her grandfather had passed. Even though his death had been expected, Caroline was not prepared when the call came to their *Englisch* neighbor's house.

How many more blows could her family take?

Trey hadn't been happy that they would have to wait a few more days to be married, but Caroline needed to be there for her father at least this one last time.

They buried her *grossdaadi* on Friday. In true Amish form, Hollis Hostetler had pushed his grief down and not spoken his father's name since they found out about his death.

Caroline had moved back into the main house. Now that her *grossdaadi*'s house was empty, her cousin and his wife were moving in. It was *gut* timing for the young couple. Their year of living with family had almost drawn to an end. They hadn't started a house of their own knowing that the eldest Hostetler was not long for this world. Just like everywhere else, land in Ethridge was getting hard to come by. More often than not, houses were handed down rather than new ones built.

"Are you sure you're going to be *allrecht*?" Sue Miller touched Caroline's arm as she made her way down the porch steps.

"Jah." Her grandfather had been put in the ground, condolences had been given, and the other mourners had headed for their own homes. The Millers were the last to leave. Already the house seemed too quiet.

Sue gave her arm one last squeeze and walked quickly toward her buggy and her husband, who waited in the driver's seat.

Caroline watched until they pulled onto the road and out of sight. Then she looked toward the barn, wondering if her father was in there thinking about his father. Or if his grief was so deep that he wouldn't let the memories in at all.

"Poor *Dat*," she whispered to herself. Her father had

been through so much, having to deal with her sins and now losing his father. She could do nothing to help him with the pain of death, but she could keep patching the holes in the bridge between them and continue to pray that they could meet somewhere in the middle.

The sound of a car engine gave her pause. She wasn't sure why, but she stopped and waited as the car crept along the road, then stopped just in front of their driveway.

Her first thought was that it was Trey coming to talk as they had decided, but the car was blue, not black, and bigger than the one Trey drove.

They must be looking for someone. Caroline raised a hand to shade her eyes for a better look at who was driving. But the glare of the afternoon sun was too great. Perhaps she should walk over and see if she could be of any help to the poor lost *Englischer*.

Before she could take even one step in their direction, the car turned into the driveway and inched closer.

As it neared, she could see that the driver wasn't English, but Plain. Perhaps a Mennonite who had known her grandfather once upon a time. Yet there was something familiar about the man behind the wheel.

"Andrew," she breathed, hardly able to believe her eyes as he cautiously parked the car and got out.

She stumbled over her own feet as she made her way to him, still not certain if he was real. She drew herself up mere feet from him, now able to look into those sea-colored eyes and smell the detergent used to clean his shirt and the essence that was part of him. He was real.

But why was he there?

Andrew accepted the cup of *kaffi* from Caroline's mother. *"Danki."*

She gave a small smile and slid into the chair opposite him. Caroline sat to his right, and he wanted nothing more to grasp one of her hands in his and absorb some of the pain and disbelief from her eyes. She looked like she had been hit by the bus that brought him all the way to Tennessee.

"I'm sorry that I came on such a sad day." They had buried her grandfather that morning. He could see the exhaustion and strain in their eyes. But he'd had no way of knowing. He only wished that he had come sooner so he could have been there for them.

All he wanted now was a chance to see Caroline, talk to her in private, tell her all his feelings for her. Make sure she didn't do something stupid like marry the *Englischer*. But all that would have to wait.

"It's *allrecht*," Grace Hostetler said. But he could see the strain of the day in the downward curve of her mouth.

He'd finish his cup of coffee, then find a hotel somewhere and come back tomorrow. Or the next day. The family needed a little time to grieve. He could afford them that—a little time. But he could hardly wait to tell Caroline how much he loved her and how he wanted her to marry him. But he would have to wait. He didn't want the day he proposed to be the day of her *grossdaadi*'s funeral.

"How did you get here?" Caroline asked.

"I took a bus from Wells Landing, then once I got here I rented a car."

"A car?" Grace asked.

Andrew shrugged as if it were no big thing. "It's no different than driving a tractor." Well, not *a lot* different.

"*Ach*, that's right," Grace said. "I had forgotten the Amish in Oklahoma used tractors. Caroline wrote me and told me that once."

"But you need a driver's license to drive a car, *jah*?" Caroline asked.

Andrew ducked his head. "I got one in the last years of my *rumspringa*. It is still valid." He felt the heat fill his ears and knew they had to be as red as his *mamm*'s canned beets. He had come here to ask Caroline to marry him. He hoped this measure of liberalism didn't ruin his chances with her family.

They made small talk about the bus trip and the weather. Andrew told Caroline the latest stories about Moxie while he devoured the sight of her.

All too soon his cup was empty, though he still had so much he wanted to say.

He stood. "I should go now."

Grace followed suit, wiping her hands down the sides of her black dress. "You are welcome to stay."

Andrew shook his head. *"Nay, danki."*

"I'll see you to the door." Caroline rose from her seat.

Together they walked out onto the porch.

"Can I come visit tomorrow?" Andrew asked. "I have some things to talk to you about."

She gave a small nod. "*Jah*. There are things that need to be discussed."

Before he could question the seriousness of her tone, the sound of tires crunching against gravel floated to them on the summer breeze.

Andrew looked to the street as a shiny black car turned into the drive.

But it wasn't someone looking for a place to turn around, for it kept coming like it had a reason to be there.

The car stopped and a handsome *Englischer* got out, his gaze shifting from Caroline to Andrew and back again.

He pocketed his keys and approached. As he got nearer, it became apparent that he was accustomed to being on an Amish farm. Or maybe it was *this* Amish farm.

"Caroline," the stranger said in greeting.

He might be a stranger to Andrew but not to the woman at his side. There was something familiar about him. It was his eyes. They were gray, a remarkable gray, and just like Emma's. This *Englischer* had to be her father.

The man bounded up the stairs and took Caroline's hands into his own. He stared deeply into her eyes and looked as if he wanted to kiss her right then and there.

Caroline took a step back and away from the man, and Andrew wanted to believe the action was a good sign. But he couldn't let his hopes get too high. At least not until he got his chance to talk to Caroline alone.

"Trey, this is Andrew Fitch. He's from Oklahoma. Well, Missouri, but he's living in Wells Landing now with his uncle."

Andrew extended one hand to shake, and Trey was forced to mirror the gesture. Though he was certain the last thing the *Englischer* wanted to do was shake hands with him. There was a wariness about Trey that belied the confident way he'd strode to the porch.

"Andrew, this is Trey Rycroft."

"Her fiancé," Trey added.

Andrew's heart sank to the soles of his shoes. "Your what?"

Trey smiled, and as much as he hated to admit it, Andrew could see why Caroline had fallen for the *Englischer* so long ago. The man was handsome to a fault and confident beyond measure. Andrew hated him on sight.

"Caroline has agreed to marry me."

"But"—Andrew turned toward her—"you'll be put under the *bann*."

She swallowed hard. *"Jah."*

He couldn't let this happen. He couldn't let her marry this

man . . . ruin her life. "Caroline, can I speak with you . . . alone?"

Trey opened his mouth, no doubt to protest, but closed it again as Caroline said, *"Jah."*

Andrew wanted to grab her by the elbow and drag her to the middle of the yard where they wouldn't be overheard, but allowed her to lead him to the end of the porch. They were far enough away from the *Englischer* that every word wouldn't be overheard as long as he kept his voice at a strong whisper.

"Caroline, what are you doing?" he asked as soon as they had gone as far as they could. He leaned against the porch railing, trying to appear as if this wasn't the most important conversation of his life.

"I'm building a family," she said, but her eyes were focused on a spot to the left of his ear.

"With an *Englischer*?"

She looked down at her fingers, tightly fisted in the fabric of her apron. "He's Emma's *vatter*."

"I know that."

Her gaze jerked to his. "You do?"

"*Jah*. It's obvious, isn't it? With those stormy eyes?"

Caroline's gaze fell to the planks beneath their feet.

"Why are you marrying him, Caroline?" Andrew asked quietly.

"I don't have many more options."

"You do."

"Like what?" she asked, her voice small.

"You could marry me."

Dear Esther,

    I surely hope this letter finds you well. It has been a grueling few weeks. Grossdaadi passed on, and we laid him to rest. I cannot understand why it's not easier to see someone you love go even though you know their time is near. The hardest has been for my dat. He has become sullen and will hardly talk. This is certainly a blow for me since we had finally patched up our relationship. I won't say that it's perfect, but the forgiveness has started for us both. He loves Emma and would do almost anything to make that child happy. I guess that is the way of grandparents.

    I have another big decision to make. Trey (Emma's father) has asked me to marry him. I think my parents are against it because they know I will be put under the bann. But I feel the most important thing is for Emma to be taken care of. She needs to have the best life possible. I feel that if I stay with the Amish here, then no one will ever forget the circumstances of her birth. Bann or not, she will be forever treated differently.

    I had no more made the decision to marry Trey when Andrew showed up at the house. Now my decision is even more complex as he too has asked me to marry him. Oh, how I wish I could talk to you. Perhaps I will try to sneak away and telephone you. There's a pay phone near one of the stores in town. How I would love to hear your voice and your wisdom. My mamm is trying to help, but I fear she is too emotionally involved to be a fair judge in the matter. And God seems to have stopped giving me guidance. Or perhaps He is trying to tell me that this is a decision I must make on my own. One thing is for certain: It won't be easy. It seems there are many hearts on the line here. Whatever decision I make, someone will end up hurt. I just have to make sure that someone isn't wee Emma.

Tell Abe I said hello and Lorie and Emily that I thank them for sending Andrew to me. Even though his appearance has made my decision a harder one to make, it was gut to see his face.

Take care, dear Esther, and write when you are able.

Love,
Caroline

Chapter Twenty-Four

Caroline started to tremble. Was he serious? "What?" was all she could manage to ask.

"Marry me," Andrew said again.

He made it sound so simple. "Marry me." And all their problems would be solved.

But what of Trey?

She chewed her lip and glanced back to where he stood watching them with hooded eyes. Caroline had the feeling that he wished Andrew would disappear in a puff of smoke.

"Andrew," she said, turning back to him. "I've already told Trey I would marry him." Her heart broke in two as she said the words. Was it possible to love two men? Did she love Trey as much as she had before? As much as she did Andrew now?

His grasp was warm and gentle as he wrapped his fingers around her arms just above her elbows. She had to fight the urge to lean into him and absorb some of his steady strength. "You don't have to marry him. You can marry me. You can come with me back to Wells Landing. We can be a family—you, me, and Emma."

"He's her father," Caroline whispered.

"I know he's her *vatter*, but no one will ever love her as much as I do . . . and no one will ever love you as much as I do now."

"I—" What was she supposed to say? She had made her promise to marry Trey. To not back out of the arrangement. Trey was taking a lot of resistance from his family. He wanted nothing more than to do the right thing. Do what was best for them all.

Emma needed steady and true. She needed a life without upheaval and chaos. Would she find that with her father . . . her *real* father? With grandparents who wanted nothing to do with her and a father who didn't understand her mother's way of life?

And what of God?

"Please think about it."

How could she do anything but think about it? The problem would be knowing the right thing to do.

Caroline stared at the dark ceiling above her bed, her mind whirling like a windmill in a storm. That was a good way to describe what she felt. Andrew coming here only intensified the raging that continued inside her.

How was she supposed to know what was best for them? She had prayed and prayed, but God had been strangely quiet. It was as if He was saying this decision was all hers. He couldn't direct her through this.

Across the room she heard Emma let out a soft snore, and a smile fluttered to her lips. She loved the child more than anything on the earth. And she only wanted what was best for her.

If only she could figure out what that was.

With a small groan of frustration, she threw back the

covers and padded into the kitchen. Maybe a glass of milk and a piece of pie. She opened her mother's icebox and retrieved the jar of milk, placing it and the remainder of the apple pie they'd had with supper on the counter.

What a day, she sighed to herself as she cut a wedge of the sweet pie and placed it on a saucer.

"Will you cut me a slice, or is this a private party?"

Caroline looked up to see her mother framed in the kitchen doorway. "*Nay*, not private." She scooped a second piece of pie onto a saucer, then took them both to the table. "I'm sorry I woke you."

Mamm shook her head and eased down into one of the chairs. "I wasn't really sleeping."

Caroline sat down next to her. "How's *Dat*?"

Her mother shrugged. "You know Amish men. He'll pretend that he doesn't miss his *vatter* until he almost believes it himself."

Amish men were like that, hiding their feelings until they had everyone convinced that they didn't have those emotions. But not Andrew. He had been open with her from the start, telling her about Beth, how he was mourning her death and only wanted to be friends. But then something happened. Friendship turned into love. And now this . . .

"What's keeping you awake, Caroline Grace?"

She sighed and picked up her fork, cutting a piece of the pie and praying for the right words. "Andrew asked me to marry him today."

Her mother sat back in her chair, surprise lighting her features. "Andrew did?"

Caroline nodded.

"And what of Trey and his proposal?"

"I don't know," Caroline whispered.

"But you told Trey yes, *jah*?"

"Jah."

Was it the right thing to do?

"That's something you'll have to decide for yourself."

Caroline didn't realize she had spoken aloud until her mother answered.

Her mother gave her a small shrug and scraped up her last bite of pie. "Right has a lot of different faces, *liebschdi*."

"How can I go back on my promise to Trey? He has sacrificed so much since he found me again. His family is against our marriage. Did you know his father gave me money so I could . . . ?" She searched for the words. "So I didn't have to be pregnant any longer."

Mamm gasped. "You never told me that."

"At the time I didn't understand it myself."

"That's the money you used to go to Oklahoma?"

Caroline nodded.

"Perhaps that is your answer."

But Caroline was more confused now than ever.

Her mother rose from the table and gathered up their plates. She deposited them in the sink, then made her way back to Caroline's side. *Mamm* laid one hand on top of hers. "Try to sleep, my sweet Caroline. Maybe everything will look different tomorrow."

Caroline hoped so, but she wasn't convinced that anything would be more apparent after the sun came up in the morning. Not without God there to guide her.

Andrew pulled the rental to a stop in front of Caroline's parents' house and cut the engine. He took a deep breath, eased out, and stood. He didn't think he would get used to driving around in a car. Thankfully he wouldn't have to.

He had thought that he would come here, and Caroline

would be so grateful he had come after her that she would fall into his arms and that would be that.

Instead, she was already engaged to marry the *Englischer*. Emma's father. How was he supposed to compete with that?

He had to. It was that simple. If he didn't at least try, then he couldn't succeed and grasp the happiness that he so desperately needed. That they both deserved.

He bounded up the stairs and knocked on the door. Today was the day. He had to convince Caroline to not marry the *Englischer* Trey. Instead, she needed to agree to marry him and return with him to Wells Landing.

He smiled as Caroline opened the door. *"Guder mariye."* Andrew couldn't read her expression. Was she happy to see him? One thing was certain, she looked tired, like she hadn't slept much the night before. "Will you and Emma come for a walk with me? That is . . . if you want to . . . walk, I mean . . ." What was wrong with him? He had practiced all last night and most of the morning. He had one shot at getting this right, and so far he was wasting it.

"Emma is off with my *dat* somewhere."

"I hope she'll be back soon. I've missed her."

Caroline's hazel eyes intently studied him.

"Then will you walk with me? I'd offer to take you for a drive, but . . . well, my driving skills are not up to *Englisch* standards."

Perhaps it was the sheer truth in the sentence, but his words seemed to break through the barrier between them.

Caroline smiled for the first time since Trey had shown up the afternoon before. That smile was just one of the many things that Andrew had missed since she'd been gone. "A walk would be *gut*."

She stepped out onto the porch and together they started toward the big field of corn.

"It's coming along nicely," Andrew said, inspecting the large green stalks.

But Caroline was having none of his small talk. "Andrew Fitch, you did not come here to talk about *mei vatter*'s corn."

"Nay," he said. "I didn't."

They walked for a few moments in silence. Then Andrew spoke. "I came here to ask you to marry me."

"Didn't you already do that?"

He cut his gaze over to Caroline, but her expression was unreadable. "I did, but you never answered."

Caroline stopped so suddenly that Andrew continued to walk several more feet before he realized that she was no longer at his side. "Andrew, I've already told Trey I would marry him."

He backtracked to her side. He wanted to take her hands into his, move in close, let her know how much she meant to him. He couldn't lose her and Emma both. He had come all this way. "Caroline, I love you."

She bit her lip and turned her face away as tears started to fall down her cheeks. "Don't say that."

"Why not? It's the truth."

"Truth or not, it doesn't matter."

This time he did take a step closer and grasped her hands into his own. Despite the warm sun of the Tennessee summer, her fingers were cold as ice. "Caroline, look at me." He gently squeezed her fingers when she kept her gaze averted. Finally, she turned those hazel eyes, still swimming in tears, to his. "Tell me you don't love me."

Her teeth sank a little deeper into her bottom lip, and

the strings on her prayer *kapp* swung wildly as she shook her head.

"Tell me you don't love me, and I'll get in that car and drive away. You'll never see me again."

"Nay."

"Then why are you going to marry him?"

"Andrew, please understand me. He's Emma's father. Don't you think he deserves a chance to be in her life?"

When she put it like that . . . He exhaled and all of his arguments blew away like the seeds of a dandelion. "What about you?" he finally asked. "What about me? Your *mamm* and *dat*?" When she didn't answer, he continued. "You'll be placed under the *bann*. By giving Emma an *Englischer vatter*, you're cutting her off from the rest of her family."

But she only shook her head. "He's her *vatter*," she said again.

"Does he love you?"

"I think so, *jah*."

But that wasn't what Andrew wanted to hear. "He can't love you like I do."

"Andrew, don't. I have already made my promise."

There was this part of him that couldn't walk away, couldn't let it be. It wasn't part of the Amish nature to fight, but he couldn't just stand by and let love slip through his fingers a second time.

"What would you have me do, Caroline? Come back tomorrow or the next day? How long before you believe my love is real?"

"I don't doubt your feelings, Andrew."

"But you're still going to marry him?"

"Jah," she said quietly.

"Then I guess there's nothing else to say." He turned and started back toward the corn, pushing aside the chin-high stalks and trying to be gentle when all he wanted to do was shove them out of his way.

"Andrew."

He could hear her rustling behind him, but he didn't stop. If he did, he didn't know what he'd do.

She caught up with him at the edge of the field nearest the house. "Andrew."

He stopped and turned, unable to stop himself from facing her, looking into her beautiful eyes one last time.

"This is not how I thought this would turn out," she said, tears sliding down her cheeks.

Andrew swallowed hard. "Me either."

"I never meant to hurt you. Do you believe me?"

"Jah," he said. Then he took her hand because he couldn't help himself and pulled her close. She came toward him willingly. He wanted just one last look at her. One last touch. He cupped her face in his hands, ran his thumbs along her cheekbones, memorizing each curve and freckle.

Then he pulled her to him and kissed her.

Trey pulled into the driveway at the Hostetler farm without immediately noticing the two people at the edge of the cornfield. At first he didn't recognize the couple, but after a few moments, when the kiss ended, he realized it was Caroline and the Amish man from Oklahoma.

He tried to bring up jealousy, but the embrace looked so much like good-bye that he couldn't muster up even a twinge.

Trey waited in the car until the man got in the blue rental and eased down the street. Then he got out and approached Caroline.

"Trey," she said, wiping tears from her cheeks. "What are you doing here today?"

"I thought we could make some plans for the wedding."

She sniffed and managed a watery smile. "*Jah*. Come inside. *Mamm* just made pie."

He allowed her to direct him toward the house.

There was something wrong with the whole situation, but he just couldn't put his finger on what it was.

"Why aren't you wearing the clothes that I bought for you?"

She looked down at herself with a shake of her head. "I'm still Plain, you know."

"I do, but I thought you would want to get used to wearing them."

"There's plenty of time for that."

She led the way into the house and seated him at the table before pouring them both a cup of coffee and slicing the pie.

"Where's your mother?"

"Probably down in the barn with *Dat*. She loves to take Emma down there."

He wanted to see his daughter, but he couldn't bring himself to demand that she go and get the child. Soon Caroline's parents would have to give up the child for good if what they were telling him was correct and by marrying him Caroline would be placed under a *bann*.

The thought came with a searing pain in his stomach.

Maybe there was a way around it. Maybe since Emma wasn't part of the church, she would be able to visit with her grandparents.

He didn't know all the ins and outs of the religion, so he asked.

Caroline thought about it for a minute. "Technically, I suppose, the bishop would not be able to find a reason for my *elders* not to see Emma, but . . ."

"But what?"

"He could still make their lives hard if he is against it."

"Why would he be against it?"

She shrugged. "It's hard to explain, but the church does not take well to members leaving. It shows bad for the ones who stay if others come and go as they please."

Trey shifted his weight, shoved his hands in his pockets, and tried to understand. "If you leave the church, they will *bann* you."

"It's like being excommunicated."

"And your parents will not be able to see Emma because of what you've done?"

She swallowed hard. "*Jah*, that's right."

Trey stared at her for a moment, then finally asked, "Why are you doing it then?"

Her mouth pulled into a shape that wasn't quite a smile or a grimace, but somewhere in between. "Because it is the right thing to do. She is your daughter, and you deserve to share in her life."

He took her hand into his and squeezed her fingers gently. "Thank you," was all he could say.

Caroline's words haunted Trey all through the evening and on the drive home. They echoed through his dark, empty apartment and seemed to mock him as he wandered from room to room. Even as they planned their vows for the following week. Just a quick trip to the courthouse. Hasty vows and the rest of their lives stretching out in front of them.

She would marry him and give up everything so he could raise Emma.

He flipped on the lamp beside his big leather couch and sat down. His gaze flickered around the room. He couldn't imagine Caroline here in this apartment, dressed in jeans and a T-shirt, hair cut like the girl down the hall. He couldn't see Emma playing on the big gray rug, toys scattered across the floor.

He picked up his phone and dialed.

"Mom," he greeted her, thankful that she had answered and not his father. He needed her gentle ways tonight.

"Hello, dear."

"We're all set for next week."

Even as he said the words, doubts and disbelief filled him.

"Do you want me to come home?" *Me, not us.* Trey wondered if his father would ever accept Caroline into the family. Would Duke Rycroft eventually come to adore Emma the way Hollis Hostetler did?

Trey pushed away the thought that his father had given Caroline money to "take care of" the pregnancy. That was old news and could be forgotten, but could there be a healing?

"No," he finally said. "Don't come. It'll be small and—"

"Average" almost slipped out of his mouth. But was any marriage average? "I'd rather you visit when you can spend time with Emma and get to know her."

His mother sighed. He knew she thought she was too young to be a grandmother, but once she saw Emma, any reservations she had would disappear. How could anyone *not* love Emma?

"I've got to go now, Mom." He didn't really, but what should have been an encouraging phone call had turned downright morose. "I'll call you after the ceremony."

"You can call if you need me."

He needed her tonight. "Okay."

"I love you, Trey."

"Love you too." He hung up the phone and leaned his head back against the couch. He closed his eyes, but the image of the kiss he'd witnessed was there to greet him. Caroline had gently rebuffed his touch since they had met back up with each other, and yet it seemed to him that her kiss to another was filled with longing and love.

He hadn't bothered to ask her what she had been doing for the last two years. If she had met someone or fallen in love. He'd been so busy with school that he hadn't had time for romance. But Caroline wasn't in school. She had been working, living, raising their daughter as a widow.

Did she love this Amish man who had come hundreds of miles to see her? Did she want to marry him? Why else would a man travel that far other than love?

Were Trey and his proposal standing in the way of Caroline and her happiness?

So many questions and not enough answers.

Dear Lizzie,

    I have a heavy heart as I write you today. It seems I am too late in making Caroline my wife. She has promised herself to another, an Englishman. I am afraid that after tomorrow I will never see her again.

    My heart should be breaking in two, but I feel numb. I never thought I would say this, but losing Caroline has been harder than losing Beth. Maybe because I knew Beth would never truly be mine. She lived at the grace of the Lord every day. Each day we had was a gift from above and we treated it as such. Now I wish I had done the same with Caroline. Did I squander my opportunities in confidence? Did I push her away as I came to Oklahoma buried in my own grief? I thought she would understand me since she had lost so much. Little did I know I would find my true love. Little did I know that she was not destined to be mine.

    Tomorrow I am going back out to her elders' farm one last time. I asked if I could visit with Emma. I have come to care so much for the wee maedel, as if she were my own flesh and blood. I had imagined that Caroline and I would raise her together, become a family, have more children, and grow old together. Now I know that just wasn't what God had planned for me. Perhaps I will be like

*Onkle and make myself a bachelor for the rest of
my days.*

*I'm sorry this letter is so melancholy. I am afraid
I will be this way for many more days to come.
Please add me to your prayers that I may see the
sun again.*

> *Love always,*
> *Andrew*

Chapter Twenty-Five

Caroline took a deep breath and stepped out onto the porch as Trey got out of his car and came toward the house.

"Hi," he said, giving her a tiny wave and an even smaller smile.

"Guder mariye," she replied. "Good morning." Why did she feel so awkward around him these days? There was a time when she had caught sight of him and launched herself into his arms like a regular *Englisch* girlfriend. But it seemed these days the sight of him only represented the sadness that was to come.

She said a small prayer. She shouldn't be so negative. It wasn't fair to Trey. She had made the choice to be with him all those months ago. She had known what he was when she lay with him. Sin wasn't without price.

She had loved Trey once upon a time, but that was before she met Andrew. Trey represented the taboo, and she wondered if she truly loved him or the freedom he'd offered.

"Can we go for a walk?"

She agreed, though his request surprised her. Trey was more apt to ask to go for a drive instead of a walk. Perhaps this was a *gut* sign that their marriage would be a compromise of worlds. She could only hope.

Together they headed off around the house and toward
the pasture.

Trey reached for her hand, and Caroline had to resist the
urge to pull back from him. They were about to be married.
And for sure, holding hands was an accepted form of pub-
licly shown affection.

"You don't want to hold my hand?"

She looked at him then. His gray eyes were studying her
as if he could peel back the layers to the truth beneath her
skin. "Amish don't usually hold hands."

He gave a nod of understanding, though his jaw muscles
seemed bunched and strained. "A few more days and you
won't be Amish."

"Jah," she said, her voice tinged with more sadness than
she had intended. "I know." She tried to relax her fingers in
his grip, but it seemed as if every nerve in her body was on
alert.

"Where are we going?" he asked.

She indicated the crop of trees about a hundred yards
away. "There's a pond just on the other side of the trees. My
dat used to bring me down here to fish."

He didn't say anything, just kept walking until they
cleared the trees and came upon the idyllic pond.

She was going to miss this place. "Just to the other side
there is the bishop's *haus.*"

An old plastic chair sat off to one side, dirty and ne-
glected, just another reminder that her life had changed and
was about to again. But the old fallen tree trunk looked
sturdy enough to hold them both.

Trey sat down, and Caroline sat next to him, trying to
seem at ease when she was anything but.

"Do you love him?"

"What?" It was perhaps the last thing she had expected Trey to ask her. They were to be married in a matter of days.

"Do you love Andrew?"

Her heart gave a painful lurch at the sound of his name. "Does it matter?" She stared at her hands in her lap. She had twisted her fingers into the folds of her apron. Why would he ask her this now?

"I think it does."

She turned to him, her eyes surprisingly dry. There had been so many lies told over the years she could not bring herself to say another. "I'm sorry, Trey. I don't want to hurt you, but *jah*, I do love Andrew Fitch."

Trey sighed and bowed his head. Then he turned her hand loose to rub his eyes as if his head was beginning to hurt. "Knowing the truth now hurts a lot less than marrying you and not knowing the truth until after."

It was Caroline's turn to sigh. She had messed up this time, messed up bad. "I care for you, you know."

"Yeah."

"I loved you once."

"Yeah."

"Love isn't the only reason two people get married." Even by *Englisch* standards this was the truth. "Just because . . ." She swallowed hard and started again. "Just because we don't love each other doesn't mean that we can't have a *wunderbaar* life together."

"What would happen if you were to marry Andrew?"

"Marry . . . Andrew?"

"I saw him kiss you yesterday. He's crazy about you. And he's Amish. What would happen if the two of you were to get married?"

Caroline bit her lip, her thoughts going in circles. "I suppose we would go back to Oklahoma."

"And Emma? Would she be able to see your parents?"

"Once the *meidung* has been lifted. The shunning."

"They'll still shun you?"

"*Jah*. I sinned against the church. The bishop here is obligated to tell the bishop in Wells Landing that I have not asked for forgiveness. I would have to serve my shunning there."

"And after that?"

Caroline shrugged. "I suppose we would just live."

He grew quiet, the only sounds around them were the ones of the farm. The lowing of the milk cows, the tweeting from the birds. Every so often she could hear the purr of a faraway engine.

Then Trey's mouth pulled into a thin line. "If Andrew wants to marry you, he can."

"What?" she asked, sure the wind was playing tricks on her hearing. "What did you say?"

"If Andrew wants to marry you, adopt Emma, make a family, then I won't stand in your way."

As she studied his face, twin tears fell from his eyes and slid down his cheeks to drip off the edge of his jaw.

She had never seen a man cry before. Never seen Trey display so much raw emotion. She brushed away a new tear before it could fall.

Trey clasped her hand into his own and pressed a chaste kiss to her palm.

"I'm not sure if what we had together was really love or merely the allure of the forbidden. But Emma . . . I would do anything in my power to give her the best life possible. I can see now, that life isn't with me."

Caroline's heart pounded loudly, painfully, in her chest. Her mouth was too dry to speak, not that she would have been able to get words past the lump in her throat.

"If I . . . step aside, then Emma can have everything. A

mother and a father who love her, grandparents who adore her. A good life. That's all I could ever want for her."

Andrew's hands shook as he put the car into park and got out. One more day and he could pack up his cursed driver's license. He hated driving. Or maybe he just hated the nerve-wracking situation he found himself in.

He wasn't sure what to expect, whether Caroline would be there or not. But seeing as how he parked behind the shiny black car he knew belonged to Trey, she most probably was. Not that it mattered. This visit was for him to see Emma one last time. He retrieved the doll from the backseat of the car and shut the door.

Normally an Amish girl got her first doll on her first birthday and her second, bigger doll when she turned three. Emma still had well over a year before she turned three, but Andrew wanted to give her something to remember him by. Even if the faceless doll would get lost among the *Englisch* treasures that Trey's family could bestow upon her.

Coming here was a stupid idea.

He fisted his hand around the doll, suddenly not caring if he wrinkled the dress. He was a sentimental fool, buying a present, insisting that he see Emma one last time.

He should get back in his car and drive straight to the bus station. Forget Emma and Caroline, forget he ever had his heart broken in Tennessee.

"Andrew?"

And there she was. Caroline came around the house, Trey at her side. They held hands, each one looking a bit teary-eyed through their trembling smiles.

Beyond stupid. Coming here was beyond stupid.

"I'm sorry," he said, unable to meet her gaze, unable to

look at either one of them. "I shouldn't have come here. I brought this for Emma." He thrust the doll toward Caroline. "Give it to her, and tell her that I love her."

But Caroline didn't reach for the doll.

He shook it at her, but still she remained where she was. Trey cleared his throat. "I'm not sure how to say this—"

"It's *allrecht*," Andrew interrupted. "I'm leaving."

"Please don't leave," Caroline said.

"I'm stepping aside," Trey added.

Andrew wasn't sure if he could trust his ears. They had started to hum. "What?"

"Caroline and I have talked, and we feel that it's best for everyone involved if I step aside." Trey's voice was thick with some unnamed emotion.

"I don't understand," Andrew managed to say. Hope rose in him like the swells of the ocean, but he couldn't get lost in the sensation.

"We're not getting married," Caroline said.

"What about Emma?" It wasn't the most intelligent thing to ask, but now that it was out there he wanted to know. "I thought this was to give her a family."

Trey and Caroline both nodded, but he said, "That's where you come in."

"Me?"

"Emma is still going to need a father. An Amish father. I was hoping that would be you."

"I don't understand." Technically, he supposed that he did, but Andrew was too leery to take the words at face value.

"Perhaps we should go inside and talk," Caroline said.

Andrew shook his head. "Are you telling me that I am free to marry Caroline?"

"That's exactly what I'm saying."

"I thought she was marrying you."

A concerned frown puckered Caroline's brow. "Do you not want to get married? I mean, yesterday you said you did."

Forgetting all the unanswered questions asked and all those still unspoken, Andrew took a step toward her and dropped to his knees. He wrapped his arms around Caroline and pulled her close, knocking his hat to the ground as he pressed his cheek into her apron.

He felt her fingers in his hair as he continued to hold her, unwilling to let her go in case this was all some horrible joke. Or a dream.

"It's not a dream," Caroline murmured.

He must have said those words aloud. He pulled away to stare at her through his tears.

She brushed back his hair, tears of her own sliding silently down her cheeks. "Come on in the house. We have a lot to talk about."

It was hours later when Trey finally left. There were so many decisions to be made. Since Trey had never been listed on the birth certificate, Andrew was free to adopt Emma. Against their protests, Trey insisted that he would give financial support. In the event that Emma ever asked, they agreed to tell her the truth about her birth father and would allow her to contact him at that time. Trey was stepping aside because he loved her that much. It was the least Caroline could do to support him in that decision.

Sometime after several cups of coffee and a piece of her mother's buttermilk pie, Trey said good-bye. It was a teary farewell for them both. He would never know what his decision meant to her. He had given her Emma, and now he'd provided her with the family she'd always hoped for. He brushed aside her tears with his thumb and kissed her cheek. Then with a small wave, he drove away.

And the planning continued. Caroline and Andrew would be married once they returned to Wells Landing. It would be so much easier to bring her parents out to Oklahoma than all of their family and friends to Tennessee.

But still one problem remained.

"I know the bishop here will have to write Bishop Ebersol and tell him what he knows." Caroline kissed the top of Emma's head. She was perched in Caroline's lap as the three of them—Caroline, Emma, and Andrew—watched the sun go down from the front porch.

He would call them "her sins," but Caroline could only see Emma as the blessing she was.

"*Jah.* Then what?" Andrew asked.

Caroline shrugged. "I suppose I will have to serve a shunning period." Most likely lasting at least six weeks, perhaps longer. But it would be worth it to have the burden of her secret lifted from her shoulders.

"And then we get married."

Caroline smiled. Andrew as her husband. It was a dream come true. "Where will we live?" She had been so caught up in the idea of marrying the man she loved that she hadn't given a second thought to where they would live. Until now.

"On the farm, of course."

She tilted her head to the side to study his handsome features. She couldn't wait until he started to grow his beard. How good-looking he would be. "You don't want to go back to Missouri?" She didn't care where they lived as long as they were together.

"*Nay.* I like living in Oklahoma, don't you?"

"*Jah.*" She loved everything about Oklahoma. After all, it was where she had met Andrew. Where they would raise their children together.

"I was thinking about buying a few horses of my own. Maybe farming a bit."

"Really?"

He took her hand into his as the sun eased down the horizon. "How do you feel about being married to a farmer?"

"That sounds *wunderbaar*, as long as that farmer is you."

It was without a doubt the hardest thing he had ever done.

Trey sat back on his couch and laid his head back. He closed his eyes and said a quick prayer that he had done the right thing. But the peace that had settled in his heart was enough to let him know this was the best decision for them all.

It still hurt, the pain bittersweet. He knew it would be with him for his entire life.

There would be days when he would have doubts. But in those times he vowed to take a page from Caroline's book and say a prayer. Perhaps God was truly the answer he needed when times got tough.

Caroline would be proud, he thought, and reached for the phone to call his parents.

The Mennonite driver met them in Tulsa and drove them to Wells Landing. They arrived just before lunch, having traveled through the dark hours of the night.

It was hard going riding all night, but with Andrew there to help her, Caroline made it just fine. So strange how another set of hands provided so much, or maybe it was the knowing that she had a partner, someone who cared about Emma as much as she did, that made her burden seem lighter.

"Do you think they will be surprised to see us together?" Caroline asked as Andrew paid the driver.

He shrugged, but smiled. "I don't think so. I think this is what they had planned from the start."

"That we would come back together?"

"*Jah.*"

Caroline shook her head in disbelief. "That was very confident of them."

"I suppose." Andrew took her bag and slung his own over his shoulder as she perched the sleepy Emma on her hip.

"Did you believe this is how everything would turn out?"

He stopped, tilting his head to the side. "This is how I prayed everything would turn out."

She smiled and started toward the bakery door. "It's *gut* thing that God answers prayer, *jah*?"

He flashed her a grin of his own. "It is at that."

The following Wednesday afternoon, the bishop called Caroline to let her know that he would be stopping by to talk to her that evening.

Her heart thumped painfully in her chest as she hung up the bakery phone.

"Caroline, whatever is the matter? You look pale as a sheet."

"That was the bishop. He's coming by tonight to talk to me."

Esther gave a stern nod, then turned back to the bread that she had been kneading when the phone rang. "I guess from the look on your face it's safe to say that this is not about the wedding?"

"Who said anything about a wedding?"

Jah, Andrew had asked her to marry him while they were in Tennessee, but he hadn't mentioned a word about it in the two days since their return.

"You know that boy is crazy about you."

"Jah."

"Boy plus girl plus love equals wedding."

And normally that was the truth. "I have a *meidung* coming. We really can't make any wedding plans until after that is over. And . . . well, it's a big sin I'm up against. It may be months before the *bann* is lifted and Andrew and I will be free to start our life together."

Esther shook her head, the strings on her prayer *kapp* dancing around her shoulders. "You might be surprised. Bishop Ebersol is a fair-minded man, for sure."

Emily's father was a fair man, even if he seemed a little hard when it came to matters of her friend. Still, she wouldn't allow herself to be overly confident. She could only imagine the letter Bishop Glick had sent to Cephas Ebersol. David Glick was as conservative a bishop as there was. She had no doubt he didn't spare a word in telling her sins in every detail that he could uncover.

She knew he meant well. Explaining her shortcomings and outlining them for Bishop Ebersol, David Glick was, in his mind, doing her a favor. He was allowing her the chance to confess all and receive a clean slate for her efforts. She should be thankful. Instead she was apprehensive.

"What about you and Abe Fitch?" It was better to change the subject than to dwell on matters she couldn't change.

Esther blushed and covered the dough with a cloth. "We're taking it slow. He's been coming for dinner, and afterward we've been taking a walk."

"He didn't come by last night."

Esther braced her hands on her ample hips. "We wanted to give you a little time to get settled in. Now, with the bishop coming by . . ."

"You could go there."

Esther shook her head. "And leave you to face the bishop by yourself?"

Caroline wished the words didn't make her stomach pitch. "I thought you said he was a fair man."

"*Jah*, that I did, but I'm not leaving you to face him alone. Your mother wouldn't be very happy if I'm not here to support you."

Caroline wrapped one arm around Esther and pulled her close. "*Danki,* Esther."

Esther patted her hand reassuringly. "It'll be *allrecht, liebschdi*."

And she knew it for the truth. She just wasn't sure how long it would take.

Dear Lizzie,

I can only say that God is gut. We made it back to Oklahoma safe and sound. I tell you, though, I can hardly believe what happened. Trey (Emma's father) stepped aside so that Caroline and I can be married. I can't tell you how froh this makes me. When I got to Tennessee, she was all set to marry Trey. I'm still not quite sure how all this happened. How hard it must have been for him to walk away from his daughter, but we all agree that it would be best for Caroline and Emma. Now she will be able to stay in the church. (Did I tell you Trey was English?)

I'll let you know when we decide on a date to get married. We still have a lot to go through with the church. Caroline will have to confess and go through a shunning time. But once we meet with the bishop we'll have a better idea as to when we might be able to join our family.

Please say a prayer that the bishop will go easy on Caroline. She understands the consequences of her actions. She knows that what she did goes against what we've been taught . . . what the Bible says. An extended shunning will not change what she has done. I can only pray that the bishop will see past mere actions and take Caroline and Emma into account when he passes his judgment.

I'll let you know as soon as we do . . . on all accounts.

Love always,
Andrew

Chapter Twenty-Six

Caroline about jumped out of her skin when the knock sounded at the door. She looked to Esther, who sent a sharp look back. Then the plump baker rose from her seat at the table and went to let the bishop in.

He wasn't a very tall man, but something about the way Cephas Ebersol carried himself made him seem much bigger. The gray streaks in his chest-length beard gave him the air of wisdom, and the sharp light in his dark blue eyes saw through any façade and straight to the bones.

Caroline swallowed hard as he stepped into their apartment. He and Esther exchanged their niceties, and he hung his hat on the peg inside the wall where their black bonnets were also kept.

"Caroline." The bishop greeted her.

"Bishop." She stood. "Would you like a cup of coffee?"

The words had no sooner left her mouth than another knock sounded.

Caroline and Esther exchanged another look.

"That must be Andrew," the bishop said.

"Andrew is coming?" Caroline asked as Esther made her way back to the door.

"*Jah*. This concerns him, too."

Caroline felt a warmth in her heart as Andrew came in. His eyes sought her out immediately, and just knowing that they were together helped to calm Caroline's nerves.

Esther went into the kitchen to get them all coffee and cookies. And all too soon they were seated around the table.

"I suppose you know why I am here."

"*Jah.*" She also knew that since the bishop was there and not the deacon, it was serious.

"I received a letter from the bishop of your district in Tennessee." He pulled the letter from a pocket inside his jacket and laid it on the table between them.

Andrew's hand found hers under the table and gave it a reassuring squeeze.

"He has made some pretty serious accusations."

"I understand." She nodded, strengthened by Andrew's support.

"In light of these allegations, a shunning would be in order," Bishop Ebersol continued.

Caroline swallowed back her fear and remorse. "I am prepared to accept that. I have done wrong in the eyes of the Lord and the church. I understand that a kneeling confession and a *meidung* are necessary."

The bishop sat back in his seat and thoughtfully stroked his beard. "I'm not sure that is the resolution we are looking for."

This was her biggest concern, her greatest fear: that the bishop would think a mere confession and shunning would not be enough to absolve her of her sins.

"What would you suggest, then?" She tried to make her voice sound confident and sure. She didn't quite succeed.

The bishop leaned forward and lowered his voice. "Caroline, there are some secrets that don't need to be repeated."

Her heart gave a pound of expectation. Was he saying what she thought he was?

"I've given this a great deal of thought, Caroline Hostetler. You came here alone and everyone assumed you were a widow. We took you in and didn't ask any questions. I've watched you live a Godly life. You've raised your daughter on your own, attended church, worked for Esther here. You've become a *gut freind* to Emily and others, and in general, you have been an integral part of our district."

Caroline held her breath as she waited for him to continue. Andrew squeezed her fingers once again, but kept his gaze on Cephas Ebersol.

"In the past two years you have been separated from your family in Tennessee. Living here and working here, and doing right by yourself. As far as I can see, you have served a shunning of your own design."

Dare she hope? "I don't understand."

The bishop cleared his throat then gave them all a small smile. "There are some secrets, Caroline, that just are better left as secrets."

"Are you saying there will be no shunning?" This from Andrew.

"Jah," Bishop Ebersol said. "I cannot see a purpose that would be served in having you stand in front of the congregation and confess sins they know nothing about. That would only hurt your standing in the community, and that of young Emma."

Hope and something more rose inside Caroline. She had found her home. God had truly led her here for a reason. *"Danki*, Bishop."

"I do not expect to talk about this matter again."

Caroline shook her head, unable to believe the astounding way that God had answered her prayers.

The bishop drained the last of his coffee and stood. "I'll see you all in church on Sunday?"

"Jah," they said together.

But as the bishop made his way to the door, Andrew stood. "There is one other thing."

The bishop turned. *"Jah?"*

"I have asked Caroline to be my wife. I am needing your blessing."

The bishop smiled. "I can't think of anything I'd like to see more. I'll come by the shop tomorrow, and we can discuss dates." He made his way to the door, but turned before his exit. "And that little sideboard in the window. Helen has had her eye on it since Abe put it up for sale."

"I'm sure we can work something out," Andrew said.

The bishop donned his hat, and with a nod to each of them, let himself out.

"Would anyone like some more coffee?" Esther stood to get the pot. Emma, who had up until then been playing quietly in her playpen, chose that moment to pull herself to her feet and demand attention.

Caroline rose to fetch her daughter, still a little numb from the shock she'd just received.

"Let me." Andrew stood and lifted Emma high into his arms, laughing at her squeal of joy as he blew a raspberry in the crook of her neck.

"I can hardly believe this is happening," Caroline said, loving the two of them together. Her heart ached for Trey and the sacrifices that he had made. But hopefully one day in the future she would be able to reunite them, even only for a time.

"It is a little unbelievable."

"Not just the shunning," Caroline explained. "But that we are going to be married."

Andrew smiled. He let Emma slide down to the floor where she toddled to her toy cart and started to play. Then he pulled Caroline into his arms and showed her just how real it was.

At just after three the following afternoon, Abe walked into the bakery.

Esther tempered her smile and wiped her hands on a dish towel before coming around the counter to greet him.

"*Goedemiddag*, Abe Fitch. Did you come down for some more of those cowboy cookies?"

Abe took off his hat, holding it against his chest as his eyes studied hers through the thick lenses of his glasses. "*Nay*, Esther Lapp. I came for something else."

"Lemon bars? Pumpkin bread?"

He shook his head. "Did you know the bishop came by to talk to Andrew about marrying your Caroline?"

"*Jah*, I'd heard some mention of it."

Abe ran the back of one sleeve across his brow. She had never seen him so nervous before. "Andrew asked that the bishop allow him and Caroline to say their vows this coming September."

"That soon? Though I'm not surprised. That boy is smitten with her for sure." Esther was happy for her young friends. They had both been through so much, and each deserved this second chance at happiness. "What did the bishop say?"

"He agreed."

Esther was not surprised. After their talk the night before, she'd had a feeling that Bishop Ebersol thought it best that the kids start their new lives as soon as possible. "*Gut, gut.*" It was good, so why was Abe so jumpy?

"I talked to the bishop as well."

"*Jah?*"

He swallowed hard. "I asked him if it would be possible to have a double wedding."

"A double . . ." Esther felt the normal color drain from her face to be replaced by a warm heat.

"What say you, Esther Lapp? Will you marry me alongside our young'uns?"

Happiness froze her in place. She couldn't believe it was happening. After all this time, after the years that she had loved Abe from afar, he had proposed marriage.

"Esther?" A concerned frown wrinkled his brow.

"*Jah?* I mean *jah*! Of course I will."

"*Gut,*" he said, donning his hat and tipping the brim in her direction. "I'll be by after work, and we can all have dinner at the farm and discuss our plans."

"*Jah,*" Esther murmured again, unable to stop her wide smile as the bell over the bakery door jingled, and Abe let himself out.

"You have to tell us everything," Lorie said as Caroline slid onto the park bench next to Emily. "Everything."

Caroline smiled. What a wondrous two days it had been. Today was starting out to be just as promising. The sky was blue, the sun was shining, and she was surrounded by *gut freinden* who loved her. "Well," Caroline started, making a mental note to bring Emma back out to the park after her nap. It was too gorgeous a day to spend it entirely indoors. "Last night, we all went out to the farm to make wedding plans."

Lorie and Emily clapped their hands together and nudged each other.

"I told you," Emily said.

"You only knew because your *dat* is the bishop," Lorie protested.

"Still, I was right." She gave them a small smirk, then took a drink from the to-go cup in front of her.

"Andrew and I aren't the only ones getting married." The words left Caroline on a rush of air. She'd been about to bust with excitement from holding them in.

"What? Who?" the girls asked over each other.

Caroline smiled. "It seems that Abe Fitch has made his intentions known to Esther Lapp. They shall be getting married in September as well."

"September?" Lorie exclaimed. "That's just a couple of months away."

"We had talked about a December wedding, but we asked the bishop if we could get married a little before the wedding season. My folks have to come all the way from Tennessee, and I would hate for them to get caught out here in an Oklahoma snowstorm."

They all nodded in agreement. There was one constant when it came to the weather in the Sooner State, and that was its unpredictability. It could be sixty-five degrees on Christmas Day, or there could be a foot of snow on the ground. A body just never knew.

But secretly Caroline was glad. She was more than ready to start her life with Andrew.

"September doesn't give us a lot of time to plan a wedding," Emily said.

"It doesn't have to be anything big—" Caroline started, but Emily and Lorie immediately shook their heads.

"This is your wedding," Lorie said, a romantic gleam lighting her deep brown eyes.

Her wedding. Just the word sent excited chills racing up her arms.

Emily nudged her. "Who knows? We may have another wedding coming soon." She looked pointedly at Lorie.

But the blonde shook her head. "Jonah and I broke up again."

"Again?" Caroline asked. What was wrong with the couple that they bickered constantly? It was as if they were inexplicably drawn to each other even though they had nothing in common.

She shook her head. "He wants to get married, and before we do that, I have to join the church."

Of the three of them, Lorie was the only one who hadn't knelt before the congregation and pledged her life to God. Caroline didn't fully understand Lorie's reluctance but knew that it had something to do with the paintings she had secreted away in the room above her family's restaurant.

Lorie had taken her there and shown them to her once, though Caroline didn't think Emily had any idea of their existence.

"What is with you two?" Emily asked.

"Us?" Lorie exclaimed. "What about you and Luke?"

A dim light filled Emily's dark blue eyes. "You didn't hear?"

Caroline shook her head. She had been so wrapped up in her own problems that she hadn't given much thought to the talk around town.

"He finally did it."

"He did?" Lorie asked.

"He left?" Caroline added.

Tears welled up in Emily's eyes and she dashed them away with the back of her hand. *"Jah."*

"To drive a car around in circles." Caroline hated her incredulous tone, but she could hardly believe what she was hearing.

"It's called racing," Lorie said.

"It's called stupidity," Caroline accused. "He gave up everything to drive a car in circles."

She was normally not one to cast stones. She had been through her share of troubles and knew better than to accept rumors at face value. But in leaving Wells Landing, Luke Lambright had hurt Emily. Caroline was as fiercely protective of her friends as they were of her.

"Well, it's not like he'll be shunned. I mean, he hasn't joined the church. He could come back someday," Lorie said.

Emily shook her head. "I have, though."

Caroline caught the underlying meaning. Emily's father was the bishop, hard though fair. But Cephas Ebersol was as no-nonsense as they came when he dealt with his daughters. With Emily being the eldest of his five daughters, he expected her to set the example. Hanging around with the likes of Luke Lambright was not behavior he condoned.

Emily shook her head and replaced her melancholy with a sweet smile. It didn't reach her eyes, but Caroline allowed her to change the subject and silently prayed that Lorie would do the same. "Enough about that. We have a wedding to plan."

And with those words, Caroline allowed herself to be swept along as her best friends planned a wedding like Wells Landing had never seen.

The Oklahoma wind gusted lightly and cooled the heat as the sun set on the farm. Andrew couldn't imagine a better place to walk and talk and plan his new life with Caroline. The farm offered him peace and relaxation, enough solitude for reflection. Now all he had to do was start his new plans, but a lot of that had to do with the woman at his side.

"Caroline." He held her hand in one of his as they walked, Moxie running around their feet. In his other he held the handle to the wagon in which Emma rode. "September will be here soon." Not soon enough, though.

"Jah."

"After we are married, I do plan on farming a bit and raising horses. I can run *Onkle*'s business here and perhaps show more profit for that side of our endeavors while he continues to build furniture." Woodworking was definitely Abe Fitch's second love . . . right after Esther. But Andrew enjoyed working the land too much to spend his days cooped up in a shed drilling holes for door handles.

Caroline smiled. "That's a *gut* idea, Andrew."

"And . . . well, *Onkle* and I have been talking, and he's going to bring this up to Esther tonight, but . . . I want you to go to part-time at the bakery."

She opened her mouth, he was sure to protest, but he held up a hand to stay her protests.

"Just hear me out," he asked. "You go to part-time in the bakery. Abe can move into the apartment with Esther, and you and I will move out here to the farm. What do you think?"

"Are you joshing me, Andrew Fitch?"

He couldn't read her expression, couldn't tell if she was happy about the idea or thought he had lost his mind. *"Nay.* I think the farm is a wonderful place to live. It'll be the best place to raise Emma and . . . and any other children we might have." He hated the heat rising in his neck, but he wasn't used to discussing such matters with women. He and Beth had never gotten to that stage in their relationship.

Caroline stopped so suddenly he had to backtrack to her side. "You really mean it? We'll live here?" she asked.

"Jah, if that's *allrecht* with you."

"*Allrecht?* It's *brechdich*."

Magnificent. He couldn't have said it better himself.

He pulled her close, wrapped her in his arms, and kissed her right there. In the middle of the farm with green pastures around them and blue skies above. Emma and Moxie playing around them. Andrew had found his everything with Caroline.

Brechdich, indeed. It was perfect.

Dear Lizzie,

I am writing with such wunderbaar news! Caroline and I are to be married the first weekend in September. The wedding will be on that Saturday, and I am counting on everyone to be there. I know it's unusual to have a wedding on Saturday, but we are hoping that it will allow everyone we love to be in attendance. It seems that weekend weddings aren't all that uncommon here since a great many of the people in Wells Landing live and work in town.

I cannot tell you how happy I am that God led me here so that I could meet Caroline. I will miss living in Missouri, but I am gaining so much here. We are going to move into Onkle's house, where I can farm and breed horses. It seems the Englischers here like to race horses. Thoroughbreds bring in a lot of income, so with any luck and the good Lord's grace we should be able to make a fine living. I hope so, since we have a little one to raise. And hope to have many more.

I can't wait for you to come to Oklahoma and meet Caroline and Emma. You are going to love them. Can't wait to see you in September.

Andrew

Epilogue

Weddings were always a big deal in Wells Landing, but nearly half the town and part of Missouri seemed to be crammed into the living room at the farm.

Caroline did her best not to look scared silly as she and Emma took their place in the chairs across from Andrew and his side sitters, his brother Saul and his cousin Danny.

But she was.

She sat down next to Emily and Lorie and pulled Emma into her lap.

She inhaled the fragrance of sweet baby and laundry soap, hoping the familiar smell would soothe her.

She had been waiting for this day all summer long. And now that it was really here, she felt a little nervous, a little nauseous, and a whole lot terrified.

It was a little unorthodox to have Emma stand in front of the bishop with them, but Andrew had insisted. Their marriage was more than the union of two people. They were creating a family, and all family members should be present for that.

A smile trembled on Caroline's lips at the thought.

"Are you *allrecht*?" Andrew asked as they sat across

from each other and waited for the church elders to enter the room.

They hadn't spoken to each other during the meeting with the church leaders from both of their districts. They had listened intently to their words of wisdom and encouragement in the matters of matrimony. It had been decided that Cephas Ebersol, Emily's father, would preside over their wedding.

Caroline nodded. How could Andrew look so confident and sure when she was as *naerfich* as a sheep among wolves?

The thought drew her up. These people gathered around were her friends and family, Andrew's friends and family. They had taken her in when she had no one. They had stood by her when she needed help. She was more than blessed to be a part of such a great community.

She took a deep breath to calm herself. As if God had laid a hand on her shoulders, her breath slowed and a peace descended upon her.

The elders entered from the back of the living room. There were six in all, the four from Wells Landing and two from Andrew's district, as not all were able to travel so far at the same time. Caroline was secretly glad that none of the elders from Ethridge came. She was well and truly leaving that part of her life behind as she started anew with Andrew. She no longer thought about it as keeping secrets, but more of a fresh slate to start again. Not many received the gift of a second chance, and she intended to make the most of it. Every minute of every day.

Dan Troyer, the minister in Wells Landing, walked to the front of the room and began to read from the Bible. "Wives, submit yourselves unto your own husbands, as unto the Lord. For the husband is the head of the wife, even as Christ is the head of the church: and He is the savior of the body. Therefore as the church is subject unto Christ, so let the wives be to their own husbands in everything. Husbands, love your wives, even as Christ also loved the church, and gave Himself for it; That He might sanctify and cleanse it with the washing of water by the word, That He might present it to Himself a glorious church, not having spot, or wrinkle, or any such thing; but that it should be holy and without blemish. So ought men to love their wives as their own bodies. He that loveth his wife loveth himself."

Caroline looked into Andrew's eyes and saw love shining there, a love as deep as the ocean. And she knew that she had finally found her home.

The minister continued to read from the book of 1 Corinthians detailing the proper conduct of a husband and wife and onto the Old Testament book of Tobit and his advice to his son, Tobias, "Take a wife of the seed of thy fathers, and take not a strange woman to wife, which is not of thy father's tribe."

They were coming from different tribes, so to speak. Her from the Swartzentruber Amish and him from a less-conservative Old Order district. But somehow they had found common ground in the Beachy community of Wells Landing.

Bishop Ebersol stood and took Dan Troyer's place in front of the congregation. "We have before us two people who have agreed to enter into marriage together, Andrew Fitch and Caroline Hostetler. If anyone here has objection to the union, he now has the opportunity to make it known." He paused to allow anyone time to speak, and Caroline held her breath. It was *gegisch*, she knew, but love could make a person as silly as they came.

"Since no one spoke, we can assume there are no objections." He looked to each of them. "If you are still of the same mind, you may come forward now in the name of the Lord."

Caroline handed Emma to Emily, then stood. She accepted Andrew's hand and together they walked forward to stand in front of the bishop.

Cephas Ebersol turned to Andrew first. "Can you confess, brother Andrew, that you accept our sister, Caroline, as your wife and that you will remain by her side until death separates you?"

"Jah," Andrew answered.

"And do you further confess that this is from the Lord and that you have come thus far due to your faith and prayers?"

"Jah," Andrew repeated.

Caroline's heart swelled with love for him.

Then the bishop turned to her. "Sister Caroline, do you confess to accept our brother Andrew as your husband and that you will remain by his side until death separates you?"

"Jah," Caroline whispered, then she cleared her throat. *"Jah,"* she said a little louder.

"And do you further confess that this is from the Lord and that you have come thus far due to your faith and prayers?"

"Jah," she said again, this time with all the confidence and love she held in her heart.

The bishop turned back to Andrew. "Brother Andrew, because you have confessed that you want to take our sister Caroline as your wife, do you promise to be faithful to her and care for her always, even if she is faced with adversity, sickness, weakness, or faintheartedness, as is appropriate for a God-fearing, Christian husband?"

"Jah," Andrew said with a smile. They had already been through so much together.

"And do you, sister Caroline, because you have confessed that you want to take our brother Andrew as your husband, promise to be faithful to him and care for him always, even if he is faced with adversity, sickness, weakness, or faintheartedness, as is appropriate for a God-fearing, Christian wife?"

"*Jah,*" she replied.

Bishop Ebersol once again quoted passages from the book of Tobit. "And he takes the hand of the daughter and puts it in the hand of Tobias," he said as he clasped Caroline's hand in his own. He took Andrew's hand as well and stacked their hands together before continuing with the blessing. "The God of Abraham, Isaac, and Jacob be with you and give His rich blessings upon you. May He be merciful unto you. I wish for you all of the blessings from God for a good beginning, a steadfast middle, and may you continue on through until the blessed end. All of this in and through the name of Jesus Christ. *Aemen.*"

They bowed their knees at the name of the savior out of love and respect.

Bishop Ebersol smiled. "Go ye forth in the name of our Lord, for you are now man and wife."

Caroline's entire body felt warm, and she wondered briefly if she might pass out. But Andrew squeezed her hand reassuringly. They were married now, forever and always.

The bishop invited one of the ministers from Andrew's district in Missouri to stand up and speak.

As he rose and made his way to the front of the crowd of people, Caroline gave Andrew a small smile. She squeezed his hand in return, and they went back to their seats. Whatever God had in store for them, they would meet it together. He had brought them this far.

Minister Troy King talked about the sanctity of marriage and wished Caroline and Andrew the best. He was followed by the deacon in Wells Landing.

Then her father stood and came to the front. Caroline's eyes filled with unexpected tears. She had known deep down that her father would most likely say a few words, but she hadn't thought about how that would affect her until now. They had come so far in the last few weeks.

Emma spied her *grossdaadi* and squealed. Everyone chuckled as he smiled at her. She squirmed down from her perch in Emily's lap and ran to him. Hollis Hostetler swung her into his arms and propped her on one hip. His own eyes filled with tears as he started to speak.

"The Lord has been *gut* to me," he started, his voice as rough as sandpaper. "And He saw fit to bless me with a daughter." He took a deep breath, and Caroline felt the bitter sting of tears in her own eyes. "Grace and I were never able to have another, and we have always been thankful for what we had. We love our Caroline.

"That's not to say that every road we have traveled has been easy," he continued. "We've had our share of heart-break and sadness. It's times like those when a person's faith is tested and stretched to its limits. This is when most people, some even the most devout of Christians, begin to lose faith in the Lord." He smiled. "But not my Caroline.

"Through all of her trials and tribulations, she has kept her faith. When she needed a chance to start over, this community here took her in and made her one of you. For that I will be eternally grateful. I am so glad that she found love here within this district and with a *gut* man like Andrew Fitch. A *vatter* cannot ask for more than his daughter to find a spouse who will love her and cherish her as he once did.

"Without a doubt in my mind, I know that God intended Andrew and Caroline to be together. Though why He wants her six hundred miles away from the rest of her family I have not yet ciphered. But I can pray about it. And I have. Caroline's mother and I have both prayed. We've talked to our church elders and come to a decision. We are moving to Wells Landing so that we can be closer to our daughter."

Caroline slapped a hand over her mouth to hide her gasp of surprise. She looked to Andrew, but he was staring straight ahead, a small smile tugging at his lips.

"We hope that you will welcome us as much as you have her, and we look forward to getting to know the *wunderbaar* Christian people here."

Caroline couldn't hold in her overflowing emotions any longer. She rose, tears streaming down her smiling cheeks, and went to her father. He wrapped her in a tight hug, the one she remembered from her childhood. She breathed in the familiar smell of him, the sandalwood-scented soap her mother used and the faint odor of tobacco smoke from the pipe he swore he never lit.

There were cheers and applause as he held her, and Caroline knew that whatever had been between them in the past, all was forgiven now.

The Lord had truly blessed her. She had Emma and Andrew, great friends like Emily and Lorie, Esther and Abe, and her family, since she had her mother and father back. It was more than she had ever dreamed possible.

Andrew came up and stood next to them.

From seemingly nowhere, her mother materialized, tears shining in her hazel eyes. Caroline's heart nearly burst with the joy and blessings.

She bowed her head and sent up a small prayer. *Lord, please watch over Trey and fill his heart with love and understanding. Give him everything he needs, and may he find his one true love someday. Someone to share his life with. Someone who will love him even more than I once did. And, Lord, please ease his mind in knowing that Emma will be well cared for and well loved. And when the time comes, may she forgive us all and know that everything we did, we did with her in mind. In Jesus's name . . . Aemen.*

Andrew touched her back, and she turned to smile up at him. She had everything she could want and more, she thought as she looked up into his eyes. God was good.

Dear Reader,

Any story is a series of what-ifs. *Caroline's Secret* came from "What if a young Amish mother is mistaken for a young Amish widow?" What if she is accepted by the community and what if she finds love there among people who don't know the truth? What if her baby's father comes back? What if he is English?

And the story goes from there.

I am a romantic at heart and require a happy ending. Always. Yet when dealing with two different men who love the same woman, with two lifestyles that are near opposite, and with the fate and future of an innocent child in the balance, someone is going to get hurt. Sacrifices will be made, and true love will outshine obligation.

I hope you enjoyed *Caroline's Secret*. It's a little different kind of story for me, but yet a romance through and through. As an author, it caused me tears. I have never before cried while writing a book. I hope that's a good sign.

The next book in the series is *Courting Emily*. You may remember Emily Ebersol, the bishop's daughter and good friend to Caroline Hostetler. Emily is caught between what she thinks she wants and the father who expects too much. She is torn between the flighty Luke Lambright and the steady Elam Riehl. Emily has the tough task of finding love and making her family happy . . . if both are possible at the same time.

Many blessings and happy reading!
Amy

AMISH WORDS

ach	oh
aemen	amen
allrecht	all right
baremlich	terrible
bedauerlich	sad
boppli	baby
brechdich	magnificent
bu	boy
danki	thank you
dat	dad
Deutsch	refers to Pennsylvania Dutch, a dialect of German spoken by the Plain people
dochder	daughter
elder	parents
English, Englisch	non-Amish person
foahvitzich	bossy
fraa	wife
frack	dress
freind/freinden	friend/friends
froh	happy
geb acht uff dich	take care of yourself
gegisch	silly
gern gschehne	you're welcome
goedemiddag	good afternoon
grank	sick
grossdaadi	grandfather
grossdochder	granddaughter
grosskinner	grandchildren
grossmammi	grandmother
guder mariye	good morning
gut	good
gut himmel	good heavens
halt	stop

haus	house
hungerich	hungry
ich liebe dich	I love you
jah	yes
kaffi	coffee
kapp	prayer covering, cap
kinner	children
liebschdi	dear child
mach schnell	hurry up (make quickly)
maedel	girl
mamm	mom
meidung	shunning
middawk	noon meal
mudder	mother
nachtess	supper
naerfich	nervous
narrisch	crazy
nay	no
nix	nothing
onkle	uncle
Ordnung	set of rules both written and understood
rumspringa	running-around time (at sixteen)
schee	pretty
schlupp schotzli	pinafore worn over the dresses of small girls up until age eight
schpass	fun
schtupp	family room
shveshtah	sister
strubbly hair	messy hair
vatter	father
Was iss letz?	What's wrong?
Wie geht?	How are things?
wunderbaar	wonderful

RECIPES

Amish Buttermilk Cookies

2 cups brown sugar
1 cup lard
1 tsp vanilla
2 eggs
1 cup buttermilk
4 cups self-rising flour
1 cup walnuts

Cream together brown sugar and lard. Add vanilla and eggs. Mix thoroughly.

Alternately add flour and buttermilk until all is mixed. Add nuts.

Chill overnight or several hours. Drop by teaspoonful onto greased cookie sheet.

Bake at 400° for 8–10 minutes. Enjoy! Makes about 4 dozen.

Hawaiian Delight Cookies

1 cup softened butter
8 oz. package cream cheese
2½ cups flour
2 tablespoons flour
½ cup chopped macadamia nuts
½ cup chopped pecans
3 eggs, beaten
1½ cups firmly packed brown sugar
½ cup shredded coconut
1 tsp baking powder

Preheat oven at 350°.

Grease muffin tin.

Cream together butter and cream cheese.

Gradually add 2½ cups of flour until well blended.

Shape dough into 1-inch balls.

Pat balls into prepared muffin tins, shaping into shells. Sprinkle ½ cup of nuts evenly into the shells.

In a medium mixing bowl, combine eggs and brown sugar. Mix well.

Stir in remaining nuts, coconut, 2 tablespoons of flour, and baking powder. Pour mixture evenly into shells, filling them half full.

Bake at 350° for 15–18 minutes.

Reduce to 250° and bake for another 10 minutes.

Makes about 3 dozen.

Cowboy Cookies

1½ cup all-purpose flour
1 tsp salt
1 tsp baking soda
1 cup shortening
½ cup sugar
1 cup firmly packed brown sugar
1 tsp vanilla
2 eggs
2 cups old-fashioned oats
12 oz. package chocolate chips
1 cup walnuts or pecans

Preheat oven to 350°.

Combine flour, salt, and baking soda in a medium-sized bowl and put aside.

In a large bowl, beat together shortening, sugars, and

vanilla until creamy. Add eggs, continuing to beat until light and fluffy. Gradually stir in flour mixture and oats. Next add chocolate chips and nuts.

Drop by well-rounded teaspoonfuls onto cookie sheet.

Bake 8–10 minutes.

Cool cookies on cookie sheets for two minutes before moving to a wire rack for further cooling.

Makes about 7 dozen.

Please turn the page for an exciting sneak peek at
Amy Lillard's next Wells Landing Amish romance,

COURTING EMILY,

coming in January 2015 from Kensington Publishing!

Prologue

"Come with me." Luke Lambright took her hands into his, warm and callused. Emily's skin tingled where he touched her. Oh, how she wanted to tell him yes.

Bright sunlight spilled all around them. How could she tell him *nay*? She had loved him as long as she could remember. She loved everything about him from his dancing blue eyes to his unruly hair that was as dark as a raven's wing. He was the handsomest boy she had ever seen. Since they were no more than ten or twelve they had talked about getting married, the children they would have, their house, their farm.

But now he was leaving. In broad daylight. Boldly walking away from the Plain life they had always known. Walking away from their shared dreams of a simple life in Wells Landing.

Luke wanted to experience the *Englisch* world, go to see movies, dance, and drive a race car for money. Even as much as she loved him, she couldn't understand what spurred his dreams in such a different direction.

"Luke, I—" She stopped short of giving him an answer. Her heart wanted to tell him one thing, but every other part

of her knew that she had to stay. Tears sprang into her eyes.
She blinked them back. "I—"

As if he knew she was about to tell him no, he pulled her
into the circle of his arms. He held her close. Pressed
against his warmth, she felt like she was home. His heart
pounded under her ear, his breathing steady and true.

"How can I leave?" She managed to keep her voice from
cracking, the building sob from escaping.

"How can I stay?"

She pulled away to look into his blue eyes. Normally
they sparkled with a mischief to rival any *Englisch* trou-
blemaker, but today they were cloudy with longing and hurt.

"You can't ask me to choose, Emily. I can't."

"I know," she whispered. "Nor can I."

Leaving with Luke, leaving Wells Landing would mean
saying good-bye to her family, her *mudder* and *vatter* and
all of her *shveshtah.* And because she had already joined the
church, a *meidung* for sure. A shunning.

"Ich liebe dich," he said, cupping her face in his hands
and pressing a kiss to her forehead.

"I love you too."

How could she leave? How could she ask him to stay?
Why, oh why did love have to hurt so bad?

He trailed his fingers down the snowy-white linen of her
prayer *kapp*, tracing an errant tear that had somehow managed to escape.

"I'll call you, you know."

She nodded.

"And I'll come back for visits. I'm not a member of the
church. They won't shun me."

She tried to smile at his hopeful words. But would her
father let her visit with the wayward son of the community?
She knew he wouldn't. *Dat* would barely let her see Luke
a'tall now as it was. They had been sneaking around so

much, they didn't even ask for courting visits any longer. And once he left the community—

"Are you afraid I'm going to forget you?"

Emily swallowed hard and gave a small nod. It was her worst fear of all: He would forget her and find some *Englisch* girl who understood things like race car driving.

"I could never forget you, Em. You're my best girl."

She closed her eyes as he traced the outline of her brow, the curve of her jaw. *Lord, please protect him; let him see the error of his ways. Let him come back to me.*

A car horn honked. Emily started at the noise, her nerves and emotions raw from the pain.

"I've got to go." He gave her a small kiss, just a brief touch of his lips against hers, and then he was gone.

Emily watched, tears running unheeded down her face as he hoisted his suitcase and placed it in the trunk of the car. He still wore his Amish clothes, though his shirt was untucked and his hat had been shucked long ago. Already he looked different. Already he was apart from her.

He looked back at her once as the *Englisch* driver revved the engine. Luke smiled and waved, then opened the door and disappeared inside.

She pressed the back of one hand to her mouth to stifle her sobs as the blue car pulled away, taking with it the only boy she had ever loved.

How was she ever going to live the rest of her days and be happy without Luke?

Chapter One

"Emily? What are you doing out here all by yourself?"

Emily Ebersol jumped as the voice sounded behind her. She whirled away from the sight of the beautiful Thoroughbred horses that Abe Fitch and his nephew kept and turned to face Becky Riehl. "W-what? I mean, *jah*. I'm fine."

Becky's gaze followed the line of sight and watched as the horses frolicked and played. Twin dimples dented her cheeks as she turned her attention back to Emily. "I didn't ask how you were. I asked what you were doing out here alone. There is a wedding celebration going on at the house." She gestured behind her toward the rambling farmhouse Andrew Fitch shared with his *onkle* Abe.

"*Jah*. Right." Had she been that deep in thought that she hadn't even heard the teen's words correctly? "I just—" Needed a break? Had to get away? Wanted some time alone? She tipped her head toward the pasture. "You know."

Becky stepped up to the fence and folded her arms across the top wooden slat. "They are *schee*."

Emily allowed her gaze to wander back to the beautiful horses dotting the lush green field. The scene was pastoral and peaceful, yet it brought her no comfort. "Why aren't you with the others at the singing?"

Caroline and Andrew's wedding was over, but the celebration had just gotten started. There would be a singing in the afternoon and another in the evening with more food and cake in between.

Becky made a face, somewhere between a smile and a grimace. "They're still getting everything ready, but I don't think I'm staying."

"Is Billy Beiler sitting with someone else?"

The young girl sighed. She'd had a crush on Billy since as long as Emily could remember, even when they were both in the schoolhouse and Emily was their teacher.

"You know tradition," Emily said. "He'll sit with a different girl at each singing. All the *buwe* will."

Becky sighed again. "That still doesn't mean he'll sit with me."

As true as the statement was, Emily could offer no rebuttal. What sort of advice could she give? The one man she wanted had left the Amish entirely. She hadn't heard from Luke in months, even with all of his promises to call. And she worried that by now he had forgotten all about her. She pushed the thought away and concentrated on the girl before her. "He surely can't sit with you if you are out here with me."

"Will you go in with me?"

"Of course." Despite the differences in their ages, Emily had always gotten along well with Becky. She supposed it was the other things they had in common that bonded them together. Like the fact that both of their families relied on dairy animals for their primary living, and the number of girls in each house. Both Emily and Becky had four other sisters to share the burdens of cooking and cleaning.

Emily linked her arm with Becky's and turned them back toward the house where the wedding celebration was in a small lull. The first round of dinner had been served and the next wave was waiting.

The last thing Emily wanted was to go back into the house and watch her friend Caroline with all her wedding-day happiness. It was petty of her, she knew, but seeing her friends and their pleasure together was almost more than she could take in such a large quantity. She'd have to pray about it tonight. Maybe again in the morning.

If only Luke hadn't left.

"The twins were sad when you didn't return to teaching this year," Becky said as they made their way up the drive toward the house. "Little Norma too."

"*Jah*. I miss teaching them and seeing them each day." She was sad as well, but that decision had been taken from her by no choice of her own.

Normally the singing would be held in the barn, but it was a beautiful early fall day and the benches had been set up around back. The weather in Oklahoma was typical, the sun shone bright and the wind ruffled the leaves in the trees. It was far too nice a day to sit indoors.

"*Dat* thought it would be best for me to help with the girls and with *Mamm*'s business."

Becky nodded as if she understood, but the young girl would never truly know how Emily felt. Teaching had been the one thing that had been hers and hers alone. To have to give that up mere weeks after Luke had left . . . Well, she had prayed and prayed. Maybe she would understand one day herself.

They had just rounded the corner when Elam Riehl, Becky's older brother, approached, the brim of his hat pulled low over his eyes. "There you are, Becky. It's time to go."

Becky bit her lip and cast her glance to where the young people were starting to settle themselves in their seats.

"Can't we stay just a little while longer? The singings are just about to begin."

Elam shook his head. "*Ach*, no. The cows have to be milked whether there are singings or not." Then he added, "*Goedemiddag*, Emily," as if he had only then realized his sister wasn't alone. He tipped his hat toward her, settling it a little higher up on his forehead.

"*Goedemiddag,*" she returned.

Why had she never noticed before how big Elam was? Maybe she only noticed now because his bulk seemed to block the sun. Or perhaps that was the fault of his serious green eyes and stern mouth.

His demeanor brooked no argument, and something in Emily hated the disappointment on Becky's sweet face. It wasn't her fault the cows needed to be milked. "If it's okay with your *bruder*, I can take you home if you want to stay for the singing."

"You will?" Becky gushed, then she sobered slightly as she turned back to Elam. "Is that *allrecht*?"

He seemed to weigh her words, against what Emily didn't know. Had he always been this serious? "*Jah*, fine. I suppose I can do without your help for a spell. But you can only stay for the first singing. After that *Mamm* will need help gathering eggs and such."

"*Danki*, Elam." Becky flashed her dimples in her brother's general direction, then looped her arm with Emily's once more. "Let's go, Em. Maybe we can still get a *gut* seat."

Emily allowed herself to be dragged across the yard. And she only looked back once to see Elam staring after them, hands on his hips and a saddened look tainting his features.

Elam was careful not to let the screen door slam behind him as he entered the house. He kept his hat on as he made his way across the living room and into the kitchen. Just a quick glass of water, then it was on to milking. He stood at the sink and poured himself a drink, staring out the window at the backyard as he took a sip.

"Elam, is that you?"

"Jah, Mamm."

He heard the bedroom door close behind her, then her soft footsteps as she came down the hall.

"Is he sleeping?" he asked as she appeared at the kitchen door. Her eyes were heavy and tired and deep lines bracketed her mouth.

"Jah." She shot him an encouraging smile as if to say everything was fine, but they both knew that wasn't the truth. Things hadn't been all right in a long time.

"Where's Becky?" she asked.

"I let her stay at the wedding. They were about to have a singing."

Mamm nodded. They both wanted Becky to have as normal a *rumspringa* as possible. *Jah*, she was needed at home, but there were other important things in life as well. Yet the attempt at normalcy was beginning to take its toll.

"Emily Ebersol offered to bring her home. Are the twins here to help?"

Mamm smiled, and this one almost reached her tired blue eyes. "They took the girls down to the pond to fish. I thought that would be *gut* for *nachtess, jah*? Fresh *katfisch*?"

"Jah."

"I can call them back if'n you need their help."

Elam shook his head. "I'll go fetch them." He needed them to sweep the floors, help with the milking machines, and tote the milk to the cooler. Even with them, there was still so much to do.

"Joy?"

At the sound of *Dat*'s call, *Mamm* turned. "I was so

hoping he would sleep until supper." She sighed, the sound resigned and heavy.

Guilt stabbed at Elam. "I should hire you some help. Or at the very least make the girls help more." But neither choice set well with him.

How much longer could they go on this way? How much longer before one of them broke?

Mamm turned back, patted him on the cheek, and attempted her smile once again. "I'm all right, Elam. If any help gets hired, it'd be for you. Now go get your milking done. There's nothing to worry about here."

She made her way down the hall, but Elam knew there was plenty to worry about. Plenty more and then some.

Emily bumped shoulders with Becky as the horse cantered along. The singing had gone almost according to plan. Billy Beiler hadn't sat with Becky, but he had talked to her a bit afterward.

Yet Emily had to cut their chat short, haunted by the somber look in Elam's eyes as he told his sister to come home right after the singing. It wasn't just his eyes, though. His whole demeanor was chock-full of seriousness and woe, as if he carried a burden too big for even his broad shoulders to manage and too precious to share with others.

"Is Elam always that . . . stern?" She tried to pick a word that didn't sound so negative.

"I prefer to think of it as thoughtful," Becky chirped. It was amazing to Emily that Becky was so bubbly while Elam was not.

"Thoughtful, then," Emily amended.

Becky shook her head. "Only since the accident."

How had she forgotten the terrible accident that had rendered James Riehl practically helpless? Or maybe she had thought in the year since he had been kicked in the head by a cantankerous milk cow that he had somehow become whole again.

"How is your *dat*?"

"The same." Becky shrugged, though her dancing blue eyes dimmed just a bit. Was her perpetual joy just a front to hide the stresses at home?

Regret swamped Emily. She'd been so caught up in her own problems that she hadn't given the trials of others a second thought. Her father would be so disappointed if he knew. Just one more thing she needed to pray about. The Amish always cared for their neighbors, always looked after the community. That philosophy went double for a bishop's daughter. She had fallen down on both accounts.

Emily bit back a sigh as she turned the buggy into the packed-dirt drive that led to the Riehls' dairy farm. She didn't know how many cows they kept, but she knew their property stretched almost into the next county. Was Elam taking care of business by himself? There were no other Riehl sons, but surely a cousin or two came around to help from time to time.

She pulled the horse to a stop. Surely . . .

"*Danki* for the ride, Emily. That was sure *gut* of you."

"*Gern gschehne,*" she replied, though her attention was centered on the rambling farmhouse and its peeling paint.

She hadn't realized the Riehls had fallen onto such hard times. Did anyone in the district know? She'd have to ask her father about it the minute she got home.

"Becky," she started. "Can I stay and help you gather the eggs?" She wasn't sure where the words came from, but once they were said she was thankful for them. She had been wallowing in her own problems for far too long.

"You'd do that?" Becky's eyes sparkled, then her smile

faded. She shook her head. "*Danki*, Emily. That is a kind offer to be sure, but the chickens are my responsibility."

As if they had tarried too long, Elam emerged from the milking barn, a scowl marring his handsome features.

The thought drew Emily back. Elam was a handsome man, or at least he would be if he didn't look like he'd taken a big bite from a green persimmon.

"Becky, time to work."

The young girl gave a quick nod, then turned her gaze back to Emily. "Thank you again."

"Becky." Elam propped his hands onto his hips, his impatience evident. "*Mamm* needs you inside."

"*Jah, bruder.*" She turned as if to go into the house, but not before Emily saw the shine of tears in her blue eyes.

"Some potatoes for you?"

"Huh?" Emily turned as her sister Mary nudged her shoulder to get her attention. "Oh, *jah. Danki.*" She took the bowl from her sister though her thoughts were still on Elam's stern frown and the glitter of tears in Becky's eyes.

"Have you heard from Luke?" Mary leaned close as she handed off the bowl full of mashed potatoes, her voice so soft that only Emily could hear. "Jonah Miller said he called his uncle yesterday."

At the mention of his name, thoughts of all others fled from her mind. "He did?" It was hard to temper her response to a whisper when she really wanted to shout with glee. Luke had called!

"*Jah.*"

Her heart thumped hard in her chest. "Who told you that?"

"Girls." Their father glared at them from the head of the table.

"*Jah, Dat,*" Emily murmured, passing the potatoes on to

her sister Susannah. She'd have to talk with Mary later, after supper, maybe during chore time.

As the oldest, Emily was expected to oversee her sisters in the evening milking. It tended to go a bit faster since all five of the Ebersol girls were available to help. In the morning, their chore time was split between milking their herd of dairy goats and taking care of the rest of the family's livestock. With more hands to help, surely she and Mary could sneak a minute or two to talk.

Excitement filled her as she thought of news from Luke. It had been months since he'd left, nearly four to be exact, but this was the first she had heard from him.

He had promised to call, but she knew how difficult that would be. It wasn't like he could call the shanty out in front of their house. Her father was as sure to get that message as any one of the Ebersol family. Nor was Luke big on writing letters. He was more into action, living, breathing, having fun.

But he had called. Emily ducked her head and smiled down at her plate lest her father see the joy she could not contain. Luke had called. He had gotten a message to Jonah Miller. He hadn't forgotten about her after all.

More from Bestselling Author

JANET DAILEY

Calder Storm	0-8217-7543-X	$7.99US/$10.99CAN
Close to You	1-4201-1714-9	$5.99US/$6.99CAN
Crazy in Love	1-4201-0303-2	$4.99US/$5.99CAN
Dance With Me	1-4201-2213-4	$5.99US/$6.99CAN
Everything	1-4201-2214-2	$5.99US/$6.99CAN
Forever	1-4201-2215-0	$5.99US/$6.99CAN
Green Calder Grass	0-8217-7222-8	$7.99US/$10.99CAN
Heiress	1-4201-0002-5	$6.99US/$7.99CAN
Lone Calder Star	0-8217-7542-1	$7.99US/$10.99CAN
Lover Man	1-4201-0666-X	$4.99US/$5.99CAN
Masquerade	1-4201-0005-X	$6.99US/$8.99CAN
Mistletoe and Molly	1-4201-0041-6	$6.99US/$9.99CAN
Rivals	1-4201-0003-3	$6.99US/$7.99CAN
Santa in a Stetson	1-4201-0664-3	$6.99US/$9.99CAN
Santa in Montana	1-4201-1474-3	$7.99US/$9.99CAN
Searching for Santa	1-4201-0306-7	$6.99US/$9.99CAN
Something More	0-8217-7544-8	$7.99US/$9.99CAN
Stealing Kisses	1-4201-0304-0	$4.99US/$5.99CAN
Tangled Vines	1-4201-0004-1	$6.99US/$8.99CAN
Texas Kiss	1-4201-0665-1	$4.99US/$5.99CAN
That Loving Feeling	1-4201-1713-0	$5.99US/$6.99CAN
To Santa With Love	1-4201-2073-5	$6.99US/$7.99CAN
When You Kiss Me	1-4201-0667-8	$4.99US/$5.99CAN
Yes, I Do	1-4201-0305-9	$4.99US/$5.99CAN

Available Wherever Books Are Sold!

Check out our website at www.kensingtonbooks.com.